Last Train to Stratton

Stephen Terrell

ISBN: 9781704390840

To Gracie and Phoebe

ACKNOWLEDGEMENTS

Thanks to my many friends and colleagues who have offered encouragement over the years, and particularly those who took time to review and comment on earlier drafts. Special thanks to Jackie and Mike Cesnic, Mike King and Ted Waggoner for their friendship, and offering their time and critiques of early drafts of this novel. A big thank you to Barbara Shoup, a fantastic writer and Executive Director of the Indiana Writers Center, writer Holly Miller and all those associated with the Midwest Writers Workshop for their feedback and encouragement. Also, thanks to all the members of the Speed City Chapter of Sisters in Crime for friendship and patience with the author.

I want to single out my good friend Janis Thornton. A wonderful author in her own right, she not only offered invaluable suggestions and a sharp eye for errors, but had faith in this project even when that of the author sometimes waned.

Lives with no meaning go straight past you, like trains that don't stop at your station.

-- *Carlos Ruiz Zafón, The Shadow of the Wind*

Railroad trains are such magnificent objects we commonly mistake them for Destiny.

— *E.B. White, One Man's Meat*

PROLOGUE

The times when our lives change, when everything before is altered and everything after is different, are seldom recognized as they happen, rarely understood for the ripples that extend beyond the horizon to places we cannot see. Life does not come with highway signposts that warn "Danger Ahead" or "Go Slow," or perhaps more importantly "Do Not Enter."

Robert Frost wrote of two roads diverging in a wood, but most watershed junctures are not so obvious, so visible, so tangible. Instead, significance is concealed among daily comings and goings. The import of decisions and events may not appear for years – decades – a lifetime later, when in quiet reflection, we glimpse the ghosts in our memories, discerning faint shadows of people and happenings that, knowingly or unknowingly, shaped not just the path of our lives, but the way we perceive the human experience.

While the tumultuous 1960s shook the foundations of society, I cruised through those years on a steady, seemingly well-planned course. I was a budding star in the newsroom, my career progress measured in headlines and bylines. My personal life flourished in an isolated singularity of booze, cigarettes, baseball and uncommitted sex.

But beginning in the fall of 1972, my life transformed like shifting tectonic plates that cause the ground to fall away and reveal an unfamiliar world around me. Looking back on a brief window between Nixon's zenith and the Nation's Bicentennial, I can see those transformative moments stacking up in my life one upon another like so much cordwood. Some jarred me instantly like a stray hand on high voltage. Others were part of the mundane daily routine, their significance overlooked until long after the concrete had set.

Such was the case in June 1975. My life shattered, I sat in a cluttered office in a western suburb of Chicago, interviewing for a new job for the first time in more than a decade. It was a small-town job, and in its dullness I expected to find a numbing balm for the pain that scorched my life.

I was wrong.

ONE – *Starting Over*

Aug. 1, 1975, DETROIT, MICH. (WIRE SERVICES): Notorious former Teamsters Union President Jimmy Hoffa is missing. Long associated with organized crime figures, Hoffa was last seen Friday morning on his way to a business meeting, according to his family.

Hoffa's abandoned car was found outside a Bloomfield, Mich. restaurant. Police are investigating the matter as a suspected homicide.

The dime-sized spot on my khaki trousers caught my attention, the remnant of a drop of mustard from lunch a few days, or maybe a few weeks ago. As I fidgeted in an uncomfortable wooden chair for my first job interview in more than a decade, the spot stared back at me like an angry wart. Would someone notice? I should have looked closer before leaving my apartment. But I didn't look closely at much anymore.

"Quite a resume you've got there," Ed Gordon said, peering at me over rimless glasses. In his hand was the one-page summary of my life – at least my professional life. Degrees, employers, job titles, a smattering of ego-wall awards that journalists give to each other.

Ed sat behind an expansive well-worn desk covered with ledger books, stuffed manila folders and stacks upon stacks of yellowing newspapers. In his early 60s, he was rotund with a broad face dominated by an oversized walrus mustache. Ed was in charge of day-to-day operations of Barrett Community News, a company that started with a single weekly newspaper and now owned more than thirty suburban and small-town newspapers throughout the Midwest.

"I've never seen someone with ten years at a major daily apply here. Not unless they got fired."

I forced a smile. "I still have my job. No one's asked me to leave."

Ed gave a small grunt. "Most of our applicants don't have talent or experience. We get a few hacks who washed out at daily papers and local housewives who do the church bulletin and think they can run a newspaper. And ever since that damned Watergate mess, colleges have been churning out hordes of journalism grads who picture themselves as the next Woodward or Bernstein. They're full of dreams about confidential sources and Pulitzer Prizes when all we do is report that Johnny won the pine wood derby and Suzy won the spelling bee."

"I've read a few issues of your papers. I know what they're like."

Ed grabbed a pack of cigarettes from the corner of his desk and offered me one.

"Quit last year," I said.

Ed busied himself trying to find a lighter among the stacks of paper on his desk.

He was right. Journalism was white hot. Reporters brought down a president, and the entire country was asking who the hell was Deep Throat?

My experience was more mundane – a decade working the Chicago crime beat. I was a card-carrying member of the Saturday Night Knife and Gun Club. My life was a collection of low-lifes and cops, headlines and deadlines. If it bleeds, it leads. More blood, more ink. It was a game, and the first with the story won.

But that past August the foundation of my world shattered. Nearly a year later, I only knew one thing for certain. I could no longer stomach a daily routine of blood, death, violence and grief written in 40-word leads of who, what, when, and where.

Ed got his cigarette lit, took a deep drag, then continued. "These community newspapers are all about school sports and church socials. The police beat is fender benders, barking dogs and people complaining about a neighbor going to the mailbox in his underwear. It's nothing that will get you a national award."

"I'm not looking for a Pulitzer. But I think I can handle it."

"No doubt you can. You're ten times better than most of the people we have working on our papers," Ed said. "You know we don't pay shit compared to what you're used to?"

I smiled. "I'm fine with the money."

Ed took another quick glance at my resume then looked straight at me. "I have two questions. Why would you want to, and how long will you stay?"

I had anticipated those would be the questions. I'd prepared my answer in advance. "As to why, I need a change of pace. A small-town paper certainly is that. As for how long, I will give you a commitment for two years. Realistically, I expect that two years is about as much as you expect from anyone you hire."

The answer sounded as hollow and rehearsed as it was. I took a sip of coffee from a chipped white mug. "Of course, you can hire the housewife who puts together the church bulletin."

Ed leaned back in his chair. He spoke without removing the cigarette from the corner of his mouth. "I talked to Charlie. He had a lot of good things to say. Hates to lose you."

Charlie Kelso was my city editor at The Examiner. I nodded but remained silent.

"He says you're a helluva reporter. He wouldn't give me any details, but said you weren't being forced out. No misconduct. No drugs. No boozing. No dipping your quill in the company ink well. Nothing like that. But if I wanted more details, I'd have to ask you."

I took another sip of coffee while Ed kept his gaze fixed on me. I put the cup down.

"You asking?"

A small close-mouthed grin formed under the mustache bristle. "You're pretty cool. I like that in my editors."

A prolonged silence followed. Clearly, Ed expected me to say something. I cleared my throat and concentrated on keeping my voice steady. "The reasons are personal. I need a break from what I'm doing. Let's leave it at that."

Ed leaned forward. "I've known Charlie for more than twenty years. He said you're a great reporter. He said if you change your mind, there's always a job waiting at the Examiner. That's good enough for me. If you don't want to tell me your reasons, I can live with that. I'm offering you the job anyway."

Ed stood and held out his hand. "Welcome on board. You're the new editor of the Stratton Gazette, if you want it."

I stood and shook his hand.

Three weeks later I drove my six-year-old Chevy Impala on a pock-marked two lane that cut through an unfamiliar stretch of rural northwestern Indiana. I towed the smallest U-Haul trailer I could rent. It bucked and swerved as I hit a pothole. I counter-steered. The trailer straightened, saving my few possessions from scattering across a field of head-high detasseled corn. I was less than a hundred miles from The Loop, but it could have been a thousand – a million miles.

Without an air conditioner, the heat inside my car was oppressive. At 60 miles per hour, the wind through the open windows offered little relief, more like a blast furnace than a cooling breeze. The blacktop seemed liquid, distorting amid the rising heat waves. I drove on through the unchanging blankness of fields and fence lines.

The nation was in the middle of what news magazines termed the National Malaise. Only a year before, a president had resigned. Nixon the Crook was gone. Five months later, Vietnam fell to the Communists. Unemployment climbed; inflation skyrocketed. It was a soul-sucking national gut punch. America's sense of invincibility and superiority vanished. In its place, anger, uncertainty, doubt and self-loathing permeated the country, ripping a gaping hole through the collective national psyche.

I barely noticed. My injuries from the previous year were personal. They were bone deep. Soul deep. To the few friends who stayed in contact, my recovery, however slow, was in process. I was healing.

But I knew the truth. There was no healing. I was gashed open. I was bleeding out.

I nearly missed the small road sign that pointed toward my destination: "STRATTON – 8 MILES." Ten minutes later, I crested a small rise and got my first sight of Stratton. Scattered among modest ranch houses with immense vegetable gardens were several small businesses -- an auto repair shop housed in an old filling station; a farm implement business; a neatly kept mom-and-pop roadside motel; a dingy convenience store with a handwritten sign advertising "Weekly Special: Baloney – 3 lbs / $1." A handful of churches proclaimed on roadside signs that "Jesus Saves" and "Visitors Welcome."

I came to a flashing red light. No green. No yellow. Just a single flashing red light. I checked the handwritten directions on a sheet torn from my reporter's notebook. The Dairy Point drive-in faced me, a volunteer fire station on my right and the town cemetery on my left. I turned left onto Main Street. Two blocks later I pulled to the curb across the street from a dreary single-story gray stone turn-of-the-century building. Gold lettering on the two storefront windows announced "Stratton Gazette."

TWO – *Brats and Spilled Beer*

Three years earlier: October, 1972

Oct. 8, 1972, WASHINGTON, D.C. (WIRE SERVICES): Latest national polls show President Richard M. Nixon is headed to a landslide of record proportions in November against Democratic candidate Sen. George McGovern. President Nixon has a 26-point lead, 61-35, among likely voters.

Ernest "the Hammer" Arrigo had more blood on his hands than any man I ever interviewed. He ran an empire of prostitution, gambling, loan sharking and drugs from a small neighborhood bar on the Southside of Chicago. He was a childhood friend of Richard Daly, the powerful czar-mayor of Chicago. Despite denials from both men, rumors persisted that they remained close. I interviewed Arrigo two weeks before his trial on federal racketeering charges under a new law the feds called RICO. Arrigo laughed off the charges. Six weeks later a jury found him guilty, and he faced twenty to thirty years in federal prison. Even for someone as connected as Arrigo, that got his attention.

Eight months after the verdict, on a blustery late October morning, I found myself in the Dirksen Federal Building, the black glass and steel tower at the corner of Jackson and Dearborn in the Loop. Arrigo's appeal was being heard by the Seventh Circuit Court of Appeals. Since I served as the trial reporter, Charlie Kelso assigned me to cover the appellate hearing. Slick Sammy Reuben, known as the lawyer to the Chicago Mob, represented The Hammer. The three-judge panel seemed intrigued by Slick Sammy's argument that the new RICO law was too vague and unenforceable. A middle-aged U.S. Attorney defended the statute, but the judge's questions leaned toward Slick Sammy's position. When the hearing concluded shortly before noon, I was surprised that I had a decent story. It wouldn't make page one, but it would be worth a byline in the city section.

The benefit of covering a federal appeals hearing was the Dirksen Building's proximity to the Berghoff, Chicago's iconic German restaurant. The restaurant was upscale, but for working stiffs on their lunch hour, the lure was the standup bar. No stools, just dark wood, brass foot rails, oversized black and white photos from the early 1900s, and the hubbub of a hungry lunchtime crowd. A couple of brats and a dark beer, consumed with an elbow on the bar and one foot on the brass foot rail, was unquestionably the best lunch in Chicago.

Thirty minutes after the oral argument concluded, I stood at the bar with a mug of dark beer in hand. I took the last bite of my second bratwurst smothered in sauerkraut and brown mustard. The world was good, or if not good at least tasty.

That's when I met Kate.

A noisy group of four or five businessmen in dark suits tried to slide into a spot next to me with only enough room for two people. They nudged up against me, a subtle territorial war not unusual among the lunchtime crush. It surprised me to see a woman in a dark suit slide next to me. She had her back to me, carrying a black leather purse only slightly smaller than the luggage I took on my last vacation. Focused on the men with her, she didn't bother looking as she shifted her luggage-sized bag.

I don't know what got her attention first, feeling her purse hit my beer mug or if me yelling, "Shit! Watch what you're doing!" By the time she turned around, half my beer was soaking into my dress shirt and my only suit.

"Oh my God," she said, her hand going to her mouth. "Oh my God. I'm so sorry." She surveyed the extent to which I wore my beer. "Oh my God," she repeated

The men around her looked on, smirks painted across their faces. A short rotund guy with wire-rimmed glasses and a squeaky voice shouted, "Nice move, Kate."

She turned her head, emerald green eyes shooting daggers at the speaker. She turned back to me. The bartender handed me several clean bar towels. I sopped up the beer from my clothes.

"I'm so sorry," she said. "It's all my fault. I . . . I . . ."

I held up my hand. "It's okay." My voice betrayed more than a trace of irritation. "I'm sure my editor will love me coming back to the office smelling like a brewery."

She signaled for the bartender. "Bring him another beer." She turned back to me. "Your lunch is on me."

"No," I said, looking down at my clothes. "Just my beer." I gave her a small smile and shook off the bartender from bringing another.

Her face flashed with what I thought might be anger, but the look disappeared before I could be sure. "I'm so sorry," she said again, reaching into her purse. She pulled out a business card and handed it to me. "Send me the cleaning bill."

I read the card. Katherine M. Billings, Analytical Specialist, Beinart and Telesky Investment Banking.

"Impressive," I said, still holding the card. "What's an analytical specialist do? I mean, other than spilling drinks on hapless strangers?"

She shook her head. "It's a fancy title for somebody who studies financial reports."

I continued to dab at my clothes with the bar towels. "So, what's a young woman with a fancy title doing in a standup bar for lunch?"

"Besides spilling beer?" She gave a small mischievous smile that came as much from her eyes as her mouth.

I gave a short laugh, and her smile broadened. "Yeah," I said. "Besides that."

She nodded toward the four men behind her, now lost in their own conversation. "We closed a billion dollar deal this morning. Actually, they closed it. I did some background work, so they invited me along to have a celebratory beer."

"One of the boys?"

"It's their game," she said, her smile disappearing. "At least for now. If I want to play, I have to play by their rules."

"You go by Kate, right? I heard one of those guys call you that."

She nodded.

"Zack Carlson," I said. I held out my hand. She shook it, her grip firm. I slipped a business card out of my jacket pocket and handed it to her.

"Reporter, huh?"

I nodded. "Working on a big story. Seems there's some woman is terrorizing downtown bars, dumping beer all over patrons. But I think I've got a good lead."

Kate's emerald eyes fixed on me. I was uncertain if they revealed anger or amusement.

"Look, I'm sorry about the beer. I've got to hang out with these clowns, but make sure you send me the bill for the cleaning."

"It's just beer. It will dry."

"Send me the bill and I'll take care of it," she said. She turned back to her group. I threw some money on the bar not giving her the opportunity to pick up my tab. I left to find a taxi back to my office, but I made sure I had her card in my wallet.

THREE – *Peanut Butter Pie*

August 16, 1975, SALT LAKE CITY, UTAH (NEWS SERVICE) A Salt Lake City man has been arrested for fleeing police and possession of burglary tools.

Theodore "Ted" Bundy, 28, was arrested when he ran a stop sign and failed to stop for police. The front passenger seat of Bundy's car had been removed. In the car, police found a crowbar, an ice pick, a pair of handcuffs and a ski mask.

The Stratton Gazette was housed in a musty smelling building from another time: cracked, yellowed floor tile, slap-dash brown wood paneled interior, stained pine trim from the seconds rack at the local lumberyard.

A dour, stout woman sat behind a steel desk covered with scattered papers. She was something over 30 and less than 50, her mid-length black hair showing the first streaks of gray. The new state-of-the-art IBM Selectric typewriter in the center of the desk seemed out of place among business furniture from a half-century before.

"Can I help you?" she asked, her voice firm and without warmth.

"I'm Zach Carlson, the new editor. I'm here to meet Roy Shoemaker."

Before the woman could answer, a voice boomed from behind the closed door. "Zach?"

There was a shuffling noise of someone moving behind the thin wall. The door opened and a short stout man walked out. He wore a starched white shirt with the collar open and the sleeves rolled to his elbows. He looked out through a thick pair of heavy black-framed eyeglasses.

Roy introduced himself with a forceful handshake. "I was hoping you'd make it before lunch," he said. "Today's peanut butter pie day."

"What's that?"

"Special pie they make on Tuesdays at Shelby's. That's a local restaurant. Best thing you'll ever put in your mouth. But let me give you the nickel tour."

The floor plan was rudimentary. Roy introduced the receptionist as Shirley Wilmes. She sat in an area adjoining the entrance. Roy's office — what would now be my office — was small, furnished with a scarred oak desk, a high-back cracked maroon leather chair and a gunmetal book shelf. The office looked out on Main Street through a large plate-glass window.

"You have to watch yourself," Roy said, nodding toward the window. "People look in that window as they pass by. If you're picking your nose or scratching your ass, everybody in town will know inside of thirty minutes."

"I'll keep that in mind," I said.

The rest of the office was a single large room furnished only with two battered metal tables, a few folding chairs and shelving stacked with old newspapers. Off to one side were two doors, one marked "Restroom" and the other "Dark Room."

"You any good with a camera?" Roy asked.

"A little rusty, but I can get by."

"That's all you'll need. Get lots of people in your photos. Especially kids. Lots of kids. People in town like to see their kids in the paper. Now let's get lunch."

#

Shelby's Place was a rustic-looking restaurant and bar at the east edge of town. Six booths lined each of the side walls with a row of four-top tables arranged in the middle. Through an open doorway I saw the adjoining bar with a pool table, a neon-lighted jukebox and a small area for a band.

A matronly woman greeted Roy by name and showed us to the only empty booth. "Emma will be with you in a minute," she said, handing us single-sheet coffee-stained menus. The menu reminded me of the roadside greasy spoons I'd become accustomed to while making summer drives from Chicago to Wisconsin – sandwiches, soups, chef salad and a daily special.

A busty waitress wearing a blue denim shirt with the restaurant name stretched tight across her breast came up to the table. It was the first time I met Emma Musgrave.

"How y'all doin', Roy?" she said. "Who's your friend?"

"This is Zach Carlson, new editor of the paper."

"You leaving already, Roy? You just got here."

"I was just filling in until we got the real deal," Roy said, nodding in my direction.

She turned toward me and gave a small wink. "Glad to have you in town, Mr. Real Deal. Special is chicken and dumplings. Whatcha drinkin'?"

After drinks came, Roy warned me about the limited choices for meals in Stratton.

"I've been surviving on burgers, pot pies and frozen dinners," I said. "I guess I'll survive here."

Emma brought our sandwiches and fries. She flirted with Roy about how the town wouldn't be the same without him, then left us alone.

"In a small town – any town, really – there are always a few places to find out what's really going on. This is one. It's where you go to hear stuff. Make sure you eat here three or four times a week."

"So where are the other places?"

"The coffee shop. It's in the pharmacy right next to the office. That's where the farmers and businessmen come for their morning coffee. You'll learn more about what's happening by just sitting and listening than you will in a week of interviewing people."

"What if I don't drink coffee?"

"Start."

As we ate, Roy detailed the weekly schedule of deadlines for the newspaper. I was used to short deadlines and breaking news. A story written on Monday would be forgotten by Thursday. A weekly was different. Distribution was Wednesday afternoon. About a third of the newspapers went into news racks at stores around town. The rest were delivered by mail on Thursday. Lead times were days, not hours, long.

"The woman you met at the office is Shirley Wilmes. She's a bit of an odd duck, but she's fantastic at what she does. She's very conservative, so don't swear or make off-color jokes around her. Hell, don't even compliment her. She seems to take offense. But she shows up on time, answers the phone, handles the classifieds, types up the local gossip columns or anything else you need. Most important, she grew up here and knows the town and everyone in it."

I nodded.

"You got a place to stay?" Roy said.

"Checked in at the Crestwood Motel. Figured I could stay there a few weeks."

Roy gave a signal to the waitress I took for a "bring pie" sign.

"That's where I stayed," Roy said. "Doris and Harry run the place. Retired couple. Nice folks. Not fancy but clean. I'm checking out and heading home as soon as we're done talking."

"I'm on my own after this?"

"It's all yours," Roy said. "I'm your regional editor. If you run into any problems, call me. But keep in mind, this isn't big-city journalism. Don't piss anybody off for a while."

Emma brought two oversized pieces of deep golden pie topped with clouds of meringue. It looked damn good.

"Emma must like you," Roy said with a smile. "You got the bigger piece."

As I speared my first bite, Roy watched me with a glee that bordered on creepy. It was exquisite. Cool, light, velvety; the taste of peanut butter but not the texture. Pie crust worthy of the Palmer House pastry chef flaked into my mouth.

Roy forked up a half-fist size first bite. He paused with his fork only inches from his face. "Paper's all yours," he said. Then Roy put the enormous chunk of pie in his mouth and his face glowed in ecstasy.

FOUR – *This Ain't Mayberry*

September 6, 1975, SACRAMENTO, CAL. (WIRE SERVICES). Lynette "Squeaky" Fromme, a disciple of the Charles Manson Family, attempted to assassinate President Gerald Ford today. Miss Fromme pointed a loaded gun directly at President Ford, but the gun did not fire.

Miss Fromme was a member of the Manson Family which was responsible for the gruesome 1969 murders of actress Sharon Tate and 6 others. She was not charged in those crimes.

In Chicago, my sleep was accompanied by the rhythmic sounds of traffic punctuated by the wail of sirens. Not so in Stratton. Even with the thin walls at the Crestwood Motel, there were few sounds after dark except for an occasional vehicle in need of a new muffler and the procession of nightly trains passing through on three rail lines.

In the silence, I stared aimlessly at spots on the white walls, hoping sleep would come. My mind spun like a motor with stripped gears, revving at high speed, but never with a purpose. I kept the motel television tuned to late-night shows out of Chicago, hoping for distraction that would lead to sleep. It was a habit I picked up during the past year. When sleep did come, it was fitful and unrewarding.

Each morning, I dragged myself into the office, stopping for a cup of coffee at the next-door pharmacy coffee shop, where I was greeted by suspicious glances. It was during my second week that a silver-haired man in his mid-50s wandered over to the Formica table where I was taking the first sips of my coffee.

Bill Olsen was slim, his sport shirt and slacks crisply pressed and his hair immaculately groomed. He introduced himself as a local businessman and member of the town board.

"The September meeting of the Chamber of Commerce is always set aside to welcome the new teachers in town. Be a good idea if you showed up, too. You can meet some town folks."

"Thanks," I said. "I'll bring my camera and do a story on the meeting."

Bill beamed like I had just agreed to be his prom date.

So, on the second Thursday of September I found myself in the local VFW hall with a group of well-fed businessmen and their wives, most in their 50s and 60s, several school administrators, and eight fresh scrubbed faces of the new teachers in town. The women wore bright print dresses, thick makeup and heavy doses of floral perfume. The men smelled of Bay Rum and Vitalis hair tonic. They wore starched white shirts, narrow ties, and ill-fitting sport coats purchased twenty or thirty pounds earlier.

I found a seat next to a young couple who introduced themselves as Gary and Libby Middleton. We ate tasteless chicken with sticky mashed potatoes covered in white gravy. Dessert was a brownie served on a plastic covered paper plate.

Gary was starting his first job out of college as the new high school physical education teacher and swim coach. Libby was teaching English at a neighboring school district. Halfway through the meal, Gary asked if I played chess.

"A little. I know how the pieces move."

"We have a chess group that gets together twice a month. Why don't you join us?"

"I'm not very good."

"It's not about being good. It's about having something to do. Gotta be better than sitting in that motel."

He had a point.

As the meeting was breaking up, a well-dressed man in his mid-40s walked up to me. His features were sharp, and he carried the aura of someone in command. "I'm Garrett Deiter, principal at the high school."

I shook his outstretched hand.

"The schools are at the center of this town," he said. "Sports mostly, but other things too. We've got a new high school. Just opened last year. When you get some time, stop by. I'll give you a tour and introduce you around."

"Sounds good," I said. "Do you have any time next week?"

"I try to keep my afternoons free. Just stop by any day between 1:00 and 3:30."

A week after the Chamber of Commerce meeting, I found myself driving by the new high school. I decided it was a good time to take up Principal Deiter on his offer to give me a tour.

The new school was much larger and more modern than I expected. I parked and quickly found the main office. A plump woman with a well-rehearsed smile greeted me from behind a counter. I introduced myself and told her why I was there. She disappeared down a small hallway, returning after less than a minute.

"Mr. Deiter's office is the one at the end. Just go on back."

Garrett Deiter stood behind his desk, meticulously dressed in a pin-striped navy suit and starched white shirt. He greeted me with a firm handshake and pointed to an uncomfortable looking straight-back wooden chair next to his desk. "Good to see you Zach. Sorry about the chair. It's one I use for students. When a teacher sends them here, I never want them to be comfortable."

"I don't know about them, but I was never comfortable in the principal's office."

"What can I do for you?"

"I was driving by, and thought I'd stop in and take you up on your offer to show me around. I've got to say, from the outside, the school seems pretty impressive."

A polite smile crossed Garrett's face, then was gone. "I'm dealing with a bit of an emergency today. Maybe we could reschedule next week?"

"No problem," I said. "Nothing too serious, I hope."

Garrett was quiet for a moment, as if deciding how much he should say. "It will be all over the gossip mill in town by the end of the day. I might as well give you the actual facts. Someone vandalized my car last night."

"Some kid key your car?"

Garrett shook his head. "Wish it was that simple. Nearly totaled my car."

"Damn. What happened?"

"It was sometime during the middle of the night. They gouged the paint. Probably used a screwdriver. Slashed all four tires, broke out the driver's side window and threw paint inside the car. The dealer where I had it towed found sand in the gas tank. If I started the car, it could have destroyed the engine."

"Police find who did it?"

"Local police? They can't find their own ass with both hands." Garrett paused, then added, "Sorry, I don't use that language in school."

"No apologies needed. You have any idea who did it?"

Garrett studied me. "On the record or off?"

"Just for my background. I won't use names unless it comes from the police."

Garrett turned in his chair and stared out his window. He didn't turn back when he started talking.

"We have a rough element in this school, in this community. They come mostly from eastern Kentucky. Coal mining and moonshine is about all they got back home. They come up here following a relative, looking for work. Fighting seems to be a way of life for them. They fight the coal companies, the revenuers, each other. They bring that attitude with them."

"Anyone in particular?"

"Last week I suspended two boys for fighting. They jumped this kid who was dating one of their sisters. One of the boys had a knife. He was lucky I didn't have him arrested."

"You suspect those boys vandalized your car?"

Garrett turned in his chair and faced me. "Them or their kin. When you deal with these folks, you have to watch your back. Obviously, I wasn't watching close enough."

I nodded, then stood. "I'm going to have to do a story on this. I'll keep it pretty basic. Principal's car vandalized. Police investigating. That's about it unless the police make an arrest."

Garrett gave a short laugh. "You haven't met the local cops yet, have you?" Garrett stood to see me out. "If you write something about these folks, watch yourself."

With a single phone call to the County Sheriff, I tracked down the incident report on the vandalism. After a few minutes of flattery and flirting, I convinced the young woman who answered the phone to read the report to me, saving me a thirty-minute drive to the county seat in Amelia.

I wrote a four-paragraph article with the unimaginative headline "Principal's Car Vandalized."

The following Thursday, just after Shirley left for lunch, I sat at my desk with a sandwich reviewing the latest issue that was delivered to new stands and the post office the previous afternoon. I found only two small typos – not great but nothing to cause me to lose sleep. The front page was dominated by a new fund-raising project by the local Lutheran Church. The article on vandals attacking the principal's car was below the fold on page two, next to the list of local police runs from the prior week.

As I took the last bite of my sandwich, the phone rang. I answered with a standard, "Stratton Gazette. May I help you?"

"You the guy that wrote that story 'bout the principal's car?" The voice on the phone was raspy, the words slow and drawn out.

"I'm the editor. I wrote that story. Can I help you?"

"I think ya'll better keep your nose out of other people's bid'ness, if you know what's good for you."

"That's what newspapers do. We report on other people's bid'ness." I instantly regretted mocking his words.

"You just keep it up, smartass, and see where it gets you."

I gave a sharp laugh. "I thought small towns were supposed to be friendly."

"This ain't Mayberry and you ain't Aunt Bea. I'm giving you fair warning. You won't get another."

"Look, asshole, I covered the Chicago crime beat for ten years. I wrote about mobsters and rapists and murderers. I've been threatened by people a lot scarier than you, and it hasn't worked yet."

"Ya'll livin' out at that motel, ain't you? You better just watch what you put in that paper, less'n you want the same thing happen to you that happened to ol' Deiter. Maybe worse." The phone went dead.

A chill pricked at the back of my neck. Over my years at the Examiner, I received more threats than I could count. Most were by guys wearing handcuffs and jailhouse jump suits. But there was something more personal about this. It took a moment for it to sink in. He mentioned where I lived.

No, this wasn't Mayberry.

FIVE -- *Blues, Booze and a Cigarette*

November 1972

NOV. 21, 1972, PEORIA, ILL. (WIRE SERVICES): Mass murderer Richard Speck was re-sentenced to eight consecutive 50 to 150-year sentences for the 1966 torture, rape and murders of eight student nurses in their Chicago Southside dormitory.

Resentencing was required when Speck's death penalty was overturned as a result of the United States Supreme Court decisions holding the nation's death penalty statutes unconstitutional.

A couple of weeks after my first encounter with Kate Billings, I sat at my desk feeling a bit smug. Charlie Kelso informed me that my story would lead on the front page. A drug deal on the Westside had gone bad. The resulting shootout claimed three lives, including a nine-year-old girl jumping rope. The copydesk slugged the headline: "Double Dutch; Triple Death."

It was my second page-one story of the week.

I pulled Kate's business card from my wallet. Ever since our first meeting at the Berghoff, I looked for a reason to call. Congratulating myself for a good week seemed reason enough.

I called with the expectation of first talking to a receptionist, but Kate answered on the second ring. I called many important people in the course of my career: prosecutors, government officials, business moguls and mob kingpins. Never once did I hesitate or falter. But when Kate answered the phone, I stammered.

She remembered me, a good start. But the good start fell apart when she turned down my offer of dinner Friday night. "My byline is on the front page – twice. I'm on a roll. Besides, you spilled a drink on me. You can't turn me down." That's what I wanted to say.

I didn't.

Instead, I said, "Oh." A professional with words and all I said was, "Oh."

She saved me. It was the first of many times. She developed a knack for pulling me out of my insecurities, my despair, my failings – and my own hubris. But this was the first time.

"Some friends and I are meeting up at Kingston Mines," she said. "It's a blues club up on Halsted. You know it?"

"Sure."

"Why don't you join us? Little Willie Anderson is playing."

"I've heard him play. He plays a mean harp."

"We'll get there about eight. I'll grab an extra chair. Once the music starts, I can't guarantee we can keep somebody from snagging it."

"Sounds great. I'll be early."

With a short "goodbye," the call ended.

#

Kingston Mines was located near Lincoln Park, north of the Magnificent Mile and south of Wrigleyville. I knew it well. It had the look of a dive bar, but catered to an upscale customer base that was mostly white, mostly college educated and mostly employed in Loop high-rises.

I arrived to a thick haze of smoke, the smell of stale beer and the din from a roomful of conversations conducted at maximum volume. I spotted Kate seated with six other people at a long table across from the bar. She looked up, and I gave a small wave. Her face broke into a full smile, and even through the smoke I could see her emerald eyes shining like twin lighthouse beacons.

By the time I reached the table, Kate was on her feet. She gave me a one-armed hug and a quick air kiss. "Everybody, here's the reporter I threw a beer on at the Berghoff."

Kate introduced me around the table. They were college friends and neighbors. No one was from her work. I took that as a positive.

A dozen or more longneck Old Style bottles scattered around the table let me know the night's drink of choice. I ordered the same.

The group peppered me with questions. What paper did I work for? Was covering crime exciting? Did I ever help solve a crime? Did I really cover Richard Speck's murders? Did I ever talk to him?

Soon the excitement of blood, death and headlines waned. The conversation turned to a current photography exhibit at the Chicago Museum of Art, and whether Cabaret, Godfather or Deliverance was the best movie of the past year. I was thankful for the change from talking shop with other reporters, competing for the most gruesome war story about multiple murders, dismembered bodies and shotgun-painted walls.

Kate pulled a lighter and a pack of cigarettes from her small bag. As she put the cigarette in her mouth, I took the lighter from her hand and lit the cigarette. She inhaled deeply and blew a long stream of smoke toward the ceiling. "I only smoke when I'm drinking," she said with a small smile. "Or after sex. But I'm thinking about giving it up." After a pause, she added, "Smoking, that is." Kate gave a short laugh. "Did I get your attention?"

"Yep," I said. "You did that."

"Don't get any ideas, big boy. I don't fuck on the first date." She added, "And this isn't even a date."

I took out my own pack of cigarettes and lit one. "You going for the shock effect? Not sure it works on someone from a newsroom."

"Maybe," she said with a mischievous grin.

The crowd became a crush. People with beers in hand filled the edges of the room and pushed against the back of our chairs. It became difficult to carry on any type of conversation without shouting, but Kate and I tried.

We talked mostly about her, not because she was boasting, but because I kept asking. It was in my nature.

She grew up in a little town in Wisconsin just north of the Illinois line. I figured her for a Joni Mitchell / Judy Collins type, but she was a big fan of Led Zeppelin, Black Sabbath and The Kinks. She loved the cinema as she called it. Her favorite movies were the Five Easy Pieces and Carnal Knowledge, both starring Jack Nicholson. I told her that Five Easy Pieces resonated with me.

She warned me about her highly competitive nature. That was how she ended up working at Beinart and Telesky. Math always came easy. She started as a math major at Northwestern University, but soon developed a keen interest in how numbers projected into successful businesses. Three years running she finished in the top three of the university's mock investment competition. After a summer internship, Beinart and Telesky offered her a financial analyst position. She started a week after graduation. That was three years ago.

Our conversation ended when Little Willie Anderson took the stage. We listened to two sets, the music loud and full of energy. When the band took a second break, we stepped outside for some air. We both lit up. As we smoked, the conversation came easily. The final set was about to start, but I didn't want to go back in.

"Want to go someplace quieter?" I asked as I crushed out my cigarette with my shoe.

She took a deep drag and let the smoke ease out in a long stream. "There's a little place not far from here. Let me get my coat."

Twenty minutes later we found ourselves in a neighborhood bar two blocks off Halsted. We sat across from each other in a well-worn booth, me sipping Johnny Walker Black while she nursed a B&B up.

"So, Zach," she said, pulling another cigarette from her purse. "What about you? I've told you about me, but all I know about you is that you're a reporter and you like the blues."

"Nothing much to tell. Grew up in Evanston. My dad was a mid-level executive at Sears. My mom sold real estate and Avon. They got divorced when my dad got transferred to Los Angeles. I was eight. Majored in journalism at Illinois, then got a job on the crime beat at the Examiner. Been there ever since." I took a sip of my scotch. "Like I said, there isn't much."

Kate brushed her mid-length black hair out of her face and smiled. "You tell about yourself like Jack Webb questions suspects. 'Just the facts, ma'am.' No embellishment."

"That's who I am."

"Any siblings?"

"No. I had one, but she died."

"That's terrible."

"I was young. She was younger."

"What happened?"

"She was born with spina bifida. Couldn't walk or talk or anything. Someone had to look after her 24/7, so Mom quit work."

"That must have been tough on you."

I shrugged. "It wasn't like we played together or anything like that. She only lived until she was five. Not long after that my dad got transferred to L.A. My mom stayed behind, and they got divorced. That's about it."

Kate reached out and took my hand and a chill crawled up my arm. Her eyes seemed electrified, staring straight into me. "There's more to you than you want to tell, Zach. But you don't have to tell me everything at once."

She kept holding my hand across the table. "I have to go into the office tomorrow, so I better call it a night. If you're still interested, I'd like to take you up on that dinner you asked about."

I nodded. "Absolutely."

SIX – *The Three Sisters*

September 22, 1975, SAN FRANCISCO, CAL. (WIRE SERVICES): President Gerald Ford escaped a second assassination attempt in 17 days today when a woman fired one shot at the President as he exited the St. Francis Hotel. The President was unharmed.

Sara Jane Moore, 45, was tackled by a bystander as she attempted to fire a second shot. Secret Service agents took Ms. Moore in custody. Just 17 days ago, President Ford was the target of an assassination attempt by Manson Family member Lynette "Squeaky" Fromme.

Roy called them the Three Sisters. Three women wrote what everyone in town called the visiting news. Esther Bickel and Ruth McKinney, were actually sisters. The third woman, Louise Frost, was a cousin.

Every Tuesday morning, an envelope was delivered to the office containing three stacks of papers: "News from Stratton," "News from Dunham," and "News from Swingley Corner." The columns were for publication in the following week's newspaper. Each article was single spaced, typed on ancient typewriters with worn keys and faded ribbons. The circles in the e's, a's and o's looked as if they were filled in by pencil.

I had never read anything written so poorly.

For several weeks, I spent my Tuesday mornings swilling cup after cup of coffee and trying to revise the columns into something resembling the English language.

Swingley Corner News By Mrs. Louise Frost

Mrs. Velma (Talmedge) Stoner received a surprise visit last Saturday night from her niece Mrs. Enola (Eugene) Braddock, formerly Enola Stoner, who visited with her two years old baby girl Amanda. Enola and her husband Charlie live in Lafayette and decided that they would stop by for a visit on their way to visit other relatives in South Bend. Velma whipped up a dinner of her special chicken pot pies and green beans out of her garden, which was much to the delight of all.

On Sunday morning Rev. Harold Sampson of the Swingley Corner Christian Church delivered an excellent sermon about the story of the Good Samaritan, which was enjoyed by all. Special prayers were made for Susie Pruitt, who is finally going to have surgery on her hemorrhoids.

On and on they went, page after page. It took three weeks for me to reach my breaking point. I walked to Shirley's desk with a handful of typed sheets where I had bled red with my editing marker.

"I need something stronger than coffee if I'm going to read this crap anymore," I said, more to myself than to Shirley.

Shirley glared through her thick-rimmed glasses. "Alcohol never improves anyone's ability to do work," she said.

"Do people really care what Homer and Bertha served to her cousin Sam, or whether Mary Strongbow is having bowel trouble?"

Shirley stopped typing and looked up, her expression stern. "That's why a lot of people read the paper. You may think the news you write about the town board or police is more important, but people around here want to see names in the paper – their own, their kids, neighbors, friends, even names of people they don't know. About half the circulation for this paper is outside the county. Some is even outside the state. It's the way people stay in touch with where they grew up."

The answer was more thoughtful than I expected. "Sounds like you're familiar with that."

"I haven't always lived here," she said.

I put the papers down on Shirley's desk. "I'm finally done editing this shit. It's yours to retype. "

I knew my mistake before the words had completely cleared my lips.

"I don't appreciate that language," Shirley said, her voice icy.

"Sorry." I tried to feign regret although I had no remorse about my choice of words. "I'm used to Chicago newsrooms. Believe me, that's mild for what passes for conversation in the Examiner news room."

Shirley's gaze did not warm. She pulled a glass jar up from her desk. A dozen quarters tinkled on the bottom. "Swear jar," she said. "This isn't Chicago. Costs you a quarter every time you swear."

"Really?"

"Most businesses in town have one. End of the year, the money gets donated to a Christmas fund at one of the churches."

It dawned on me that I was expected to pay a tribute. I pulled out a quarter and let it drop into the jar. As the quarter bounced against the glass bottom, I tried to lighten the mood. "So, in your dozen years here, how much have you put in the jar?"

"None." Shirley's voice was flat. She was serious.

In the back of my mind I suspected this year might be a record contribution.

Looking at the stack of papers on Shirley's desk, I had one of those moments of inspiration – the kind that you later learn wasn't so inspired. "Can you call the Three Sisters and get them into the office tomorrow afternoon? I'm tired of spending a full day editing their columns."

"You sure you want to do that? I don't think they will take kindly to a stranger telling them to change what they've been doing all this time."

"I'm sure," I said.

Shirley gave me a dubious look but picked up the phone and dialed.

Behind me, the door opened. I turned and found a vaguely familiar man and a stout woman that I assumed was his wife. It took me a second to place the man as Bill Olsen, the businessman who invited me to the Chamber of Commerce meeting. Each of them held a huge white paper bag prominently displaying the logo of Olsen Pizza and Chicken.

“This is my wife Claudia,” Bill said. Claudia was broad-shouldered woman with fair skin and blonde hair that looked styled by a bowl and a dull knife.

"Thought you might be hungry," Bill said, holding up the bag in his hand. "We got you a dozen pieces of our roasted chicken plus some side dishes of potato wedges, baked beans and slaw. It's on the house."

Bill and Claudia held out the bags to me, giving me no choice but to take them. "This is the best chicken you ever tasted. I guarantee it."

I nodded, looking for a place to put the bags.

"When you get a chance, come over and I'll show you through our new Christmas Shop. We just got in a shipment of these beautiful hand-blown glass ornaments. It would make a great story for the paper."

"I noticed your shop last week," I said. “When does it open for the season?"

"It's open now," Bill said. "It's open year-round."

"All year?"

Bill nudged his wife. "Claudia, tell him about how we got the idea."

Claudia gave an energetic nod. "We visited Frankenmuth last year. That's in Michigan." She spoke with a hint of a Scandinavian accent. "They got all sorts of Christmas shops up there that are open all year. While we drove back, I told Bill that we should open a shop here." Claudia was almost giddy. "We thought other stores could decorate for Christmas all year. Lots of people would come to see that. Can you imagine the whole town decked out for Christmas all year? It would be beautiful."

Bill leaned toward me and lowered his voice, like drawing me into a conspiracy. "Now we get to deduct all our travel. With the restaurant, we can't deduct crap. But now we can go to Las Vegas, New York. Heck, next year we're taking a trip to Europe. We can take it all off our taxes. But that's not for publication."

“Of course not,” I said.

“Well, we gotta get back for the lunch rush. Stop by any time."

Without me saying a word, they left. I stood with two bags of chicken and side dishes.

"It's actually pretty good chicken," Shirley said.

I walked around the corner and put the bags on her desk.

"Would you like this?" I said. "I can't take bribes to do stories. Not even food bribes. But I don't want it to go to waste."

A look of genuine surprise formed on Shirley's face. "Thank you, Zach," she said. "We'll eat it for dinner tonight. There will be leftovers for tomorrow, too."

Shirley lived with her mother and eleven-year-old son in a small house a few blocks away. It didn't take particular insight to know that between Shirley's slightly above minimum wage job and her mother's social security, having a free meal or two would stretch the monthly budget.

"By the way, does Bill Olsen run any ads for that restaurant of his?"

Shirley gave a short loud laugh. "That man has the first nickel he made. After people leave, I've seen him walk up to tables and pick up the leftover napkins and put them back in the dispenser. He runs a two-inch coupon ad for homecoming and another for graduation. That's it."

"Has he run an ad for his new Christmas Shop?"

Shirley laughed again. "No. I heard he ran an ad in the South Bend newspaper, but I didn't see it."

"If he wants a story on that Christmas shop, he's going to need to run an ad."

#

The next afternoon, Shirley came in to my office to announce that Mrs. Bickel, Mrs. McKinney and Mrs. Frost had arrived. When I looked at her askance, she lowered her voice. "The Three Sisters. I put them around the big table."

"I'll be with them in a minute. Do you have the originals from their columns?"

Shirley nodded. "I got them retyped, but the originals are still on my desk."

Shirley impressed me with her ability to read my copyediting marks and promptly get the columns retyped. She was quirky, but her skills were beyond question.

"Put the originals on the table. I'll be with them in a minute." I pulled a dollar from my wallet. "Could you go next door and get a large coffee for me? I think I'll need it."

Shirley shook her head. Her look said "how can you be so stupid," but she said nothing.

"What?"

"It's Wednesday," she said. "Everything's closed on Wednesday afternoon, including the drug store coffee shop."

I stared blankly, trying to comprehend. After a moment I said, "What happens if someone gets sick and needs a prescription?"

"If it's good weather, you call out to the Elks Golf Course. That's where all the businessmen in town are on Wednesday afternoon, playing golf or more likely just drinking. If it's bad weather, you can call Mr. Perry's house. He's the pharmacist. Or you drive over to Amelia. It's a Thursday close town."

I finished the final paragraph on the story I was writing, then got up to meet The Sisters.

Three women sat around the table, their ages between late 50s and late 60s. All three wore shapeless floral dresses. Their hair was piled high, their faces layered with heavy makeup. As I greeted them, old lady smells of lilac, violets and denture breath swept over me.

I took a seat across from them, plastered a forced smile on my face, and began. "I've read your columns," I said softly.

Each woman smiled and puffed up in their chairs. My mind filled with cartoon images of chickens sitting on their nests, puffed with pride at their latest eggs. The realization hit me that each of these women, dressed in their church-going Sunday best, expected praise for their works of literary perfection. I didn't need coffee; I needed a double shot of Wild Turkey. There was nothing to do but begin.

"I know you've been writing these columns for a long time. But the paper is no longer owned locally. It's now owned by Barrett Newspapers. They've made an investment in the newspaper and in this community."

The smiles were still there although the one worn by Esther Bickel was fading. From the time I exchanged greetings with the women, I sensed that Esther was the leader. Her dress was a bit more stylish, her perfume a tad less intense, her gaze more mistrusting.

"Barrett Newspapers has certain, uh, standards. They expect the writing in their newspapers to be, uh, a certain quality."

The faces looking back no longer smiled. None except for Shirley, who stood against the wall observing with bemusement.

"Let's start with the format. That's the easiest thing to correct," I said. I immediately knew that my word choice was wrong. Correcting implied mistakes. I should have phrased it as a new policy. "You need to double space your columns. Single space is just too difficult to edit."

The three exchanged horrified glances as if I had just let loose a juicy fart right in front of them and asked them to rate the fragrance. Under her breath Louise said, "Well, I never."

I kept smiling, but the realization was sinking in. This was not going well.

Esther spoke up. "We've always done it that way. Nobody had any problems."

I tried to smile even more. My jaws ached. "I know you want the paper to be better."

"I don't see anything wrong with the way it's always been," Ruth said, her voice icy.

I turned to suggestions about their writing. Their glares became daggers. I gave a basic lecture about writing in active tense, using short sentences and eliminating adjectives and adverbs. Full rebellion was not yet upon me. But it was close.

"I need you to cut down on some of the names you put in your columns. There are just too many."

It was as if I jumped on the table, dropped my pants and took a dump in front of them. No, that wasn't quite right. Had I done that, they would not have looked at me with such outright loathing.

"It's like this sentence." I picked up a sheet and read from one of their columns.

Billy and Sharon (Henshaw) Rodzinski's daughter Pamela Frances Rodzinski has been admitted into the Daughters of Rachel. Catherine Marie Pendergast, daughter of Carl and Mary (Briskie) Pendergast, was the presiding officer at the meeting in the place of Joan Anne Dobbins, who was visiting her Aunt Dalphinia (Dobbins) Brewer in Chicago. She was accompanied by her parents Doris (Jones) and Frank Dobbins.

I looked up, giving the most sympathetic expression I could muster. "We could get the same information across by simply saying 'Pamela Rodzinski, daughter of Bill and Sharon Rodzinski, joined the Daughters of Rachel,' whatever that is."

For an instant, I thought they were going to attack. I swore Esther and Louise positioned themselves for a flanking maneuver while Ruth prepared to launch herself right over the table in a frontal assault. But they just sat in silence, faces turning red.

Finally, Louise spoke, seething with barely contained outrage. "People want to read names. Unlike you, we don't go looking for news. People call us. They tell us who is visiting, or who is sick, or what's happening with their kids. That's what people care about."

"I understand," I said, even though I didn't. Why would people care about who was visiting whom, who was sick or what people were eating? "I still want you to write your columns and put in names. But I really don't think we need the lineage of everyone."

"This is ridiculous," Ruth said out loud.

I stood, signaling an end to the meeting, partly out of self-preservation. "Just try it my way next week," I said. "I don't expect you to change overnight, but just try some of my suggestions. I think you'll find that people will like reading your columns much more."

The Sisters stood. Without saying a word to me, they walked out.

"Remember, double space," I shouted as the door banged shut.

I watched as they quick stepped across the street and gathered in a conspiratorial circle. I surmised that the discussion related to my arrogance, stupidity, and perhaps my parentage.

"I think that went well," I said, my words full of sarcasm.

Shirley shook her head at my utter ignorance. "Do you know how they get paid?" Shirley asked.

I shook my head. "No. Corporate handles all of that. I just get the paper out."

"They get paid by the column inch," Shirley said. "They include all those names because people want to see their names in the paper. But it makes their columns longer, and they get paid more. It's not much, a dime an inch, but it matters to them."

"And that stuff about double spacing," Shirley continued. "They pay for their own paper. They single space because they only use half the paper that way."

I stood silent, suddenly feeling very stupid.

Shirley was not done educating me.

"These women have been writing this stuff for years. Everyone knows them. People call with news about a grandson graduating or a cousin who is sick, and the next week it's in the newspaper. It makes them important. You may be right. They don't write very well. But you've only been here a couple of weeks. They've been here all their lives. It's their community, not yours. Your advice attacked not just them, but their place in the community."

I stood there just looking at the floor for several minutes, rolling Shirley's words around in my head. Finally, I looked up. "Think they're going to quit?"

"No," Shirley said. "But there are going to be a lot of people around town who will be told about your high-minded big-city ways. And they won't like it."

I shook my head and went back to my office. I promised Ed I would stay for two years. I wondered if I could keep the promise.

#

The following Tuesday afternoon, I stood next to Shirley at her desk when a short pot-bellied man in wrinkled Sansabelt slacks came in. He handed an oversized envelope to Shirley, not saying a word. After he left, Shirley handed me the envelope.

"This week's columns," Shirley said.

"Who was that?"

"Louise's husband."

"He ever drop off the columns before?"

"Nope."

I went to Perry's Drugs and got the largest cup of coffee they sold. When I returned, I picked up the envelope from Shirley and went to my desk. I could immediately tell that it contained a thicker stack of papers. With a sense of dread, I opened it.

Each page was double spaced. Hallelujah and praise the Lord. A small victory. They actually listened.

But then I started reading.

Nothing changed. The sentences ran on in stilted language that, if anything, was worse. And there were more names than ever.

I started revising the pages, converting passive into active voice, striking out the most distantly connected names. After forty minutes I completed three pages and needed another cup of coffee.

"Screw this shit." I wasn't sure if I said the words out loud.

I walked out to Shirley's desk carrying the stack of papers in my hand. "Ignore my editing marks," I said with a forced smile. "Just correct the spelling and type them up the way they are."

Shirley gave a grin that was closer to a smirk. In Chicago, I would have called it a shit-eating grin, but I was learning.

I started back to my office but turned back. "Call them," I said. "Tell each of them to come in and pick up a ream of paper to type their columns. When they need more paper, we'll give it to them."

Shirley held up the swear jar. "I heard you," she said.

I took a five-dollar bill out of my wallet and threw it in. "That should get me through the rest of the week," I said.

#

That night back in my motel room I lay on the too soft mattress watching the Cubs game on television. I had no idea who they were playing or the score. It was just a soundtrack to my isolation.

I stripped out of my clothes and turned to a news broadcast out of Chicago. The anchor read about a double homicide on the city's west side, the latest statistic in a climbing murder rate. After a few minutes, it too slid into background noise. I looked at the whitewashed walls decorated with cheap mass-produced landscapes, furnishings with peeling faux walnut veneer, and the pile of thin over-bleached towels stacked on a tarnished chrome rack outside the bathroom.

It was time to find someplace else.

I let the television drone.

Nothing from my past belonged to me. Nothing in my present life fit. I didn't see a future. In the recesses of my brain, I played with what at one time was unthinkable to me -- that non-existence seemed preferable to existence.

I was too much of a coward to take any action on my darkest thoughts. I had witnessed too much death. It was never painless, even for those who left by way of a cocktail of alcohol and pills. Anguish always filled the faces of the dead.

There was no dignity in death. I was present too many times when investigating officers and meat wagon drivers made fun of victims who shit and pissed themselves in their last moments. I saw the daily routine of detectives and reporters who shared gruesome photos like trading baseball cards. I had been in the morgue where bodies were stored in trays. I saw medical examiners eating ham sandwiches as they carved open bodies. I didn't have the courage for that.

At three a.m. With the television still droning on, I drifted into my ritual nightmare-filled sleep.

SEVEN – *The Landlord*

October 3, 1975, NEW YORK, NY (FINANCIAL WIRE SERVICES): W. T. Grant department store chain, with over 1,000 stores, filed bankruptcy today. With over $1 billion in debts, it is the largest retail bankruptcy in American history.

The bankruptcy is second only to the massive $3.3 billion Penn Central Railroad bankruptcy which threatens rail traffic throughout the East and Midwest.

Three weeks living at the Crestwood Motel was more than enough. I asked Shirley if any promising ads for apartments or houses for rent were scheduled to run in the upcoming issue.

She skimmed the classified ads she had typed for the coming week. "These two are trashy," she said, pointing to the listings under "Real Estate - Rental."

Shirley continued to guide her finger down the column of ads. "Here's one for a three-bedroom house at the edge of town. Donny Wright is renting it."

I shook my head. "Bigger than what I'm looking for. Anything else?"

Shirley pointed to a small ad. "This came in yesterday. It's a one-bedroom upstairs apartment on Elm Street."

"Know anything about it?"

"I know the house. Walter Bradford and his wife live there. He's retired from the railroad. They both pretty much keep to themselves. When their daughters moved away, they converted the upstairs into an apartment."

"Sounds like it might work."

"The house sits close to a couple of railroad tracks. Don't know if that bothers you or not."

"I need to get out of that motel. Give me their number."

The house on Elm Street was a 1920s era two-story affair with weathered pale green clapboard siding. Exterior stairs along one side led to the second-floor converted apartment.

Walter Bradford answered the door. He was tall, nearly six feet four inches, and lanky. His hands were gnarled. Two fingers were missing above the first knuckle of his left hand.

"I'm Zach Carlson. I called you about the apartment."

Walter grunted and led me in to a cluttered living room that smelled of cigarettes, dust and stale furniture polish. It was silent except for the slow tick-tock of a grandfather clock. Across the room a frail gray-haired woman sat in a rocking chair, a colorful quilt spread across her lap and an issue of Ladies Home Journal in her hands.

"This is my wife Mae," Walter said. The woman nodded once but said nothing.

Walter told me the rent for the apartment. I thought it was the weekly rate until he said, "Make sure we get paid by the first. I don't tolerate no late payers." There was no lease, no damage deposit and utilities were included.

Walter took me up the outdoor stairs to see the converted apartment. "Used to be my daughters' rooms. When they got married, I turned it into an apartment."

It was one bedroom, with a large living room and a kitchen-dining area. The appliances were old but clean. The furnished living room included a gaudy floral couch and matching overstuffed chair, worn but useable. The bedroom included a simple white framed full bed and a matching dresser with a mirror. They seemed a bit feminine, but I didn't care.

"You married?"

"No," I said.

"Well, we don't want to see no parade of women in and out of here. And no parties."

I nodded my head.

"And don't tromp around. My missus ain't doing too well these days. We don't want to hear no footsteps on the first floor from you stomping around."

"I pretty much keep to myself," I said.

I took one last look around. There was enough room for my books and clothes. The rent was cheap and with no lease. If I didn't like it after a couple of weeks, I could move out.

"I'll take it," I said. We sat at the kitchen table and I made out a check for the first month's rent and handed it to Walter. He studied it carefully.

"This ain't a local bank."

"No. It's in Chicago. I opened a local account last week, but I don't have any checks yet."

"You sure it's good?"

"It's good," I said with a smile.

"Well if it ain't, I'm moving you out. I don't tolerate no bounced checks."

Walter pulled a key ring from a pocket in his overalls and handed it to me. "Lose that one and you have to pay for a new one," he said.

#

Poet Carl Sandburg called Chicago "Player with Railroads and the Nation's Freight Handler." When I moved to the upstairs apartment on Elm Street, I thought Sandburg got it wrong. The description fit Stratton. Three main railroad lines dissected the town, two were less than a football field away from my apartment. So too was an abandoned train station and water tower and a network of seldom-used industrial sidetracks.

Each night, at least once every hour, a mile-long freight train rumbled through on the Erie-Lackawanna, the closest of the railroad lines. Others rolled through on the Penn Central, what locals called the "Pennsy" from before the Pennsylvania and New York Central merged. Most times, I had not found sleep when the approaching blasts from the horn would signal the approaching train. Vibrations reverberated as multiple diesel engines pulled a mile or more of freight cars traveling to and from Chicago. In many ways, it was a relief to have an excuse for not sleeping other than the thoughts that endlessly danced through my head.

After the first month, the rumble of the trains seemed a comfort, like the persistent sound of waves on a deserted beach. I slept better, sometimes sleeping through some passing trains. Within two months, the trains blended with the night sounds of crickets, frogs and the hum of my melancholy.

My apartment was little more than a place to sleep. I went to the coffeeshop by 7:30, ate lunch and dinner at Shelby's Place or the VFW, and frequently spent evenings covering local board meetings or high school sports. My contact with Walter was minimal. I had no contact with Mae. When I paid my second month's rent, I asked Walter how Mae was doing.

"Passable, I reckon," he said, taking the check and closing the door. I didn't ask again.

As summer moved into autumn, I sometimes saw Walter through a yellowed window in the shed at the back of the property. He always wore coveralls and a long sleeve work shirt, his thick glasses perched at the end of his beak-like nose. He hunched over a workbench, tinkering on some unseen project. After six o'clock, the shed went dark. The only sign of life in the house was a dim light in the living room.

I was always looking for a good feature story. The early morning crowd at the drug store coffee shop and the lunchtime regulars at Shelby's Place let me know they appreciated the feature stories I wrote about local residents. When someone suggested I do a story about the history of railroads in Stratton, Walter Bradford popped into my head. He was an old railroad man. Somewhere beneath that exterior of leather-skin and gnarled hands, there might be a good story.

When I delivered my next rent check, I held it out to him, but didn't let go. "Mr. Bradford, I was wondering if you'd be willing to sit down and talk with me about working on the railroad. I thought it might make a good story for the paper."

A puzzled look came over Walter's face, as if he couldn't quite figure out how I was scamming him. With a snap, he pulled the check from my hand. But unlike before, he didn't disappear inside the house.

"Whatcha wanna do that for?" suspicion in his gravelly voice.

"If it wasn't for railroads, this town wouldn't exist. I thought people might enjoy reading about someone who worked on the railroads in their heyday."

Walter gave an unintelligible grumble. "You just wanna talk?"

"That's it."

He stepped inside the door. I thought our discussion was over, but he turned back toward me. "Don't just stand there. Come on."

Mae sat in the same rocker near the window. She looked even more frail than before, her skin yellow and drawn. I said "hello." She gave me a small smile, but said nothing.

Walter took a seat in a large worn leather recliner, which I took to be his regular chair. He motioned me to the couch across from him.

I started with the question that had been bothering me since my first night in Stratton when I heard the nighttime symphony of train whistles and rumbling locomotives .

"How many trains come through here every day?"

"It's down to about forty now. All the railroads is going bankrupt these days so that's all they run."

" Down to forty? How many used to come through here?"

"Back in the 40s, 50s, it was a hunnert trains a day, I reckon. Maybe more."

I did some quick math in my head. "That's more than four trains every hour, twenty-four hours a day. They really have that many?"

"Sure," Walter said. "They kept a daily count over at the Erie tower right over there." He pointed a craggy finger out the window toward the nearest tracks where an abandoned forty-foot tower stood next to the tracks.

For the next two hours, Walter told me about his life, and trains and an era that was all but gone. He grew up on a subsistence farm about fifty miles south of Stratton in Carrollton County, learning he did not want to be a farmer. At age 16 he left home. He got a job with the Monon Railroad cleaning workshops. After a few years, he moved up to yard worker. He met Mae when she was visiting a cousin, and three months later they married.

"I was a married man, so I needed to make more money. I hired on to the Erie as a fireman. That meant I was on the road, but the pay was good."

"You ride the trains in case they caught fire?

Walter gave a hearty laugh at my ignorance. "Them was steam engines. A fireman shoveled the coal to keep the fire burning in the boilers." It was the only time I heard him laugh.

"The Erie ran all along the Great Lakes – Chicago, South Bend, Toledo, Cleveland, Buffalo. All along there. Lots of mills and factories. Refineries, too. I'd leave on a Sunday night. Catch a local right out there." Walter again pointed a long crooked finger over my shoulder toward the Erie Lackawanna tracks. "Mostly worked on the runs from Chicago to Cleveland, but sometimes I'd get to Buffalo. I'd get back home Friday night."

The deep grooves in Walter's weather-beaten face deepened. "Lost my fingers helping a brakeman attach some cars on a siding outside Cleveland. That was 'long about '42 or '43, after the war started. Got my hand caught between the couplers. Snapped those fingers right off."

I felt queasy. "That must have been awful."

"Weren't nothing for them days," Walter said. "Everybody worked for the railroad lost fingers. Just wrapped my handkerchief around the stubs, then finished connecting the cars. Weren't nothing else to do."

"Must have been hard on your family with you gone so much."

Walter looked at me as if he didn't understand the question. "Mae raised the girls. I was earning the money. That's the way it worked."

He had nothing more to say.

"How is working for railroads different now?"

Walter gave a grunt and shook his head. "In the '50s, all them trains switched over from steam to diesel. It wasn't the same after that. When they was steam trains, they all stopped here in Stratton. Passenger trains, too. They was about a dozen passenger trains stopping here every day. Had too. Needed to fill up with water and coal. When the diesels came in, they didn't have to stop no more.

Walter hacked up something from deep in his throat. He pulled a blue pattern handkerchief from a hip pocket in his overalls, and spit it into it. "Now they ain't no passenger trains at all."

"When did you retire?"

"Company rules was you turned 70, you had to retire. Hell, I'm 84 now, but I could still be out there if they let me."

"So, what was it about the railroad? What did you like about it so much that you'd still be out there if they let you?"

Walter's head tilted up. Through his thick lenses, his haze-covered brown eyes looked past me as if he was seeing himself stoking the fires of some long-ago steam engine. He was silent, staring unfocused into some place no one else could see.

"It wasn't about liking," Walter finally said. "It was about working. You'd stand there in front of that open firebox, shoveling coal to keep the fire going. It was hotter than hell. The power of that engine run right into you, sometimes near a hunnert miles an hour, pulling five thousand tons of freight. You slapped the firebox door shut and lean out the window, letting the wind sweep across you. You finished the day exhausted and sweaty, covered in soot. But there was all that freight — steel and iron ore, coal, corn and beans, cars and refrigerators, tanker cars with God knows what – all of it 600 miles from where you started."

Walter's eyes dropped. "You were doing something worthwhile. That's what a man's supposed to feel like."

Walter stood up. "I got stuff to do," he said. He walked out of the room without saying another word. In the corner, Mae was asleep. I let myself out and immediately went to the office to write the story.

My feature story on Walter ran on the front page in the next week's paper. Walter did not cooperate for a photo, so I included a photo of the abandoned passenger station. I thought it might be my best feature story.

I wasn't sure if Walter got the newspaper, so when the paper came out, I grabbed four copies for him. When he answered the door that evening I held out the newspapers. "The article on you came out today," I said. "I thought you might want some extra copies for your family and friends."

Walter stared at me. "I saw it," he said.

He shut the door leaving me on the doorstep with a handful of newsprint.

#

Less than a month later, Mae Bradford died. The funeral home called in the obituary, and Shirley brought it to my attention.

Shirley wrote up weekly obituaries from information the funeral home provided. I didn't know Mae Bradford, but I thought writing her obituary myself was the least I could do.

Two days later, I stopped to pay my respects at the funeral home. A dozen people milled around. Seated in the front by the casket, Walter looked uncomfortable in a black suit, stiff white shirt and navy tie. When someone approached, he stood, shook hands saying nothing, and resumed his seat. As far as I could tell, he said nothing during the twenty minutes I was there.

A tall thin woman who looked to be in her early 60s approached me. "I'm Rose Babbidge, one of Walter and Mae's daughters. Thank you for coming," she said. "And thank you for your story on daddy. That was real nice. Momma liked it."

"It was my pleasure," I said.

"Daddy's a little hard to get along with, but he's not a bad man."

I nodded. Rose walked away to greet someone else. I left, never having spoken to Walter.

Mae Bradshaw was the first person I knew in Stratton to die. She would not be the last.

#

Several weeks later, I saw Walter in his workshop. I gave a brief wave. Rather than returning my greeting, he put down the drill he was holding. With a fixed glare on his face, he stomped out of the shed.

"I want you out," he said, his voice raised.

I wasn't sure I heard him correctly. "What?"

"I'm tired of hearing you tromp around 'till all hours. Sounds like a herd of horses up there. You find a new place and get your stuff out of here."

I stood there dumbfounded. It seemed like a joke, but Walter Bradford didn't joke.

"Mr. Bradford, I always take off my shoes when I get home. I don't play the television or my music loud. And I've never had a party."

"Out," Walter said. "Just get out." He turned and walked back to the shed.

I was angry. I did not understand what set him off. As the next few days passed, I became even more upset with his tirade.

I asked Shirley to screen the new classifieds for apartments. But there were few rentals available in Stratton. Those advertised were too large or places Shirley warned were not fit to step foot in.

I dropped off the next month's rent in an envelope tucked into Walter's front door. He cashed the check and did not say anything to me. He did not approach me again about moving.

In the evenings, I sometimes caught glimpses of Walter in his workshop, but I never signaled a greeting. He never looked in my direction.

When I would come home after dark, I would often see Walter's figure, the image diffused through the living room curtains, sitting in his recliner, a reading lamp the only light. He would have a book in his hand, but I never saw him turn a page.

More than once I took a step or two toward the door. I thought perhaps I should ask him if he was all right, if he wanted company, if he needed something. But I didn't. I left him alone with whatever memories floated through his head.

Walter became little more than an apparition.

EIGHT – *Dinner and Guy Lombardo*

New Year's Eve 1972

December 31, 1972, SAN JUAN, P.R. (SPORTS WIRE SERVICES): All-Star baseball player Roberto Clemente, 38, was killed today when a cargo plane in which he was riding crashed while flying relief supplies purchased by Clemente to earthquake victims in Managua, Nicaragua.

A native of Puerto Rico, Clemente spent his entire career with the Pittsburgh Pirates. He was a 12-time all-star, 1961 National League MVP and 1971 World Series MVP. He reached the 3,000 hit milestone in his final at bat last October.

A week after meeting Kate at Kingston Mines, we had our first proper date. We dined at The Pump Room where Bogie and Bacall famously ate in Booth No. 1 on their wedding night. It seemed a good omen. We saw each other the following week for a mid-week lunch, then after-work drinks. It quickly evolved into a pattern of seeing each other two or three times a week. We never talked about dating exclusively. It didn't seem like something we needed to say.

Not long before Thanksgiving, during dinner at a noisy place in Greek Town, Kate surprised me.

"My work schedule between now and the end of the year is going to be ridiculous," Kate said. "We've got all these closings lined up before year end. It's going to be very hard for us to get together."

My face must have betrayed my disappointment. I had not been in a relationship for three years, and that was only a relationship of convenient sex while waiting until something better came along. When something better did come along, it was for my girlfriend.

I looked forward to sharing the Christmas season with Kate, but now it seemed I was being dumped.

Kate took my hand. "It's not that I don't want to. I enjoy being with you. It really is my job. December at my firm is like April for accountants. Everyone wants to close by the end of the year. I'll be putting in eighteen-hour days, including weekends. I'm taking two days off for Christmas to go to Wisconsin and be with my family. That's it. The rest of the time, I'll be in the office."

I recovered into a forced smile. "There's nothing wrong with us?"

"Absolutely not. But it's just like you running out at midnight to cover somebody getting shot. It's what my job requires."

By the end of the evening, my confidence in our growing relationship returned. I gave Kate a long kiss at the end of the evening, certain it would not be the last.

Kate was right about her schedule. I never worked less than fifty hours in any week at the newspaper, and often more. But the hours she worked in December were beyond anything in my experience except when I covered the mass murder of eight student nurses by Richard Speck. We talked by phone most days. Occasionally we grabbed a quick thirty-minute lunch at a sandwich shop near her office. She ate most of her meals – breakfast, lunch and dinner – at her desk. Several nights, she didn't bother going home, just catching an hour or two of sleep at her desk.

My mother invited me to spend the holidays with her and Frank, her second husband, in Sarasota. She married Frank when I was in college. A few years later, he sold his accounting business and they retired to Sarasota. They had a nice home, financial security, and warm weather.

Frank seemed a good enough guy, but once we got past the futility of Chicago's sports teams, we had nothing to talk about. I didn't care about the stock market, his investments, his blood pressure or the comfort level of his new Cadillac; Frank didn't care about anything else.

I feigned a heavy workload and turned down my mother's invitation. I really hoped that Kate and I would find time together over the holidays, no matter how fleeting.

Kate visited her parents over Christmas. We talked by phone, but I limited myself to a single call per day so I didn't interfere with her family visit. During one of those conversations I asked Kate about New Year's Eve. Like me, she wasn't fond of New Year's Eve parties.

"Getting obnoxiously drunk, wearing silly hats, and listening to insipid music is not my idea of a good time," she said.

"How about me fixing dinner? I'm a decent cook."

"Really?" her voice laced with disbelief. "What will you prepare, mon chef?"

"Nothing elaborate, but it will be edible. If it's not, I have Gino's delivery number memorized."

On New Year's Eve, I showed up at Kate's apartment just after six, toting a bag of groceries, a bottle of champagne and a bottle of a far nicer pinot noir than I would ever buy for myself. Kate lived in a three-story brownstone four blocks from Wrigley Field. She had a two-bedroom apartment furnished with gently-used furniture that had once been expensive showpieces in someone's upscale home. It gave the apartment a homey, comfortable atmosphere.

She converted one bedroom into a home office, furnished with a leather chair on rollers, a polished rosewood desk and a matching bookcase. Several well-ordered stacks were on the desk. The bookcase was filled with portfolios, corporate annual reports, books on math, economics and business, and an assortment of business magazines I never heard of. Kate's bedroom was hidden behind a closed door.

Kate put a Dave Brubeck album on her stereo and poured two generous glasses of wine. I worked in her small kitchen, making chocolate mousse with fresh raspberries. While it chilled, I prepared hearts of palm salad, rib eye steaks with sautéed mushrooms, baby redskin potatoes and asparagus wrapped in prosciutto.

We ate by candlelight at the small table in her kitchen. Our conversation was light, catching up on the past few weeks and Kate's trip to her parents' home in Wisconsin. As we talked, I could see exhaustion creep across Kate's face. After we finished, I took the plates to the sink while Kate refilled the wine glasses. We moved into the living room. She turned off the music and turned on the television. "I always watch the ball drop," she said. "I know it's silly since it's in New York and an hour early, but . . ." Kate shrugged.

I sat next to Kate, wrapping my arm around her shoulders and pulling her close. We kissed gently and watched television.

"Dinner was wonderful," she said.

"We still have dessert."

Kate shook her head. "I can't eat any more." She took a sip of wine and smiled. "I hope you don't think I'm a party pooper, but I don't think I can make it until the ball drops. I'm exhausted and this wine is hitting me."

"You've been working your ass off," I said. "You have to be tired. If you want to call it a night, I understand."

"No," she said, putting her index finger to my lips. "I don't want you to go."

We sat there watching party-goers in tuxedos and long gowns blow into noisemakers and dance to Guy Lombardo's long-outdated orchestra. Ten minutes later, Kate was asleep. Her breathing was deep and rhythmic, her mouth slightly open. I brushed her raven hair from her face and delicately kissed her forehead. I watched the television, allowing myself a glimpse of what it might be like to share my life with someone -- with this someone.

It was way too early to have these thoughts. I had not been in a serious romantic entanglement since college. It was unfamiliar territory for me. Too soon, I thought. Way too soon.

The ball dropped in New York, and Kate slept on. I had envisioned this as the night we would have sex for the first time. But seeing Kate sound asleep in the crook of my arm, I realized this wasn't the right time. A month of eighteen-hour days had taken its toll. She needed the rest. It was time for me to go.

I clicked off the television. Carefully I slipped my arm from behind Kate, shifting my weight to get up.

"No," she said. Her eyes still closed, she took my arm. "Stay." Her eyes opened into narrow sleepy slits. "Stay with me."

Kate got up on unsteady legs. She took my hand and led me to her bedroom. With no display of modesty, she pulled her blouse over her head and stepped out of her skirt, then unsnapped her bra and let it fall. She slipped off her panties, pulled back the covers and slid into bed, patting the place next to her.

I undressed and eased next to her.

"Thank you," she said, her voice still full of sleep. She turned away from me, pushing her body against mine. My arm fell over her, taking her breast in my hand. In another moment, she slept.

I felt the delicate touch of her skin, smelled her body scent under the lingering trace of her perfume, heard her pulse through my hand until our hearts beat in tandem. More than an hour passed before I, too, drifted into sleep.

We awoke during the night and made love for the first time. Our lovemaking was slow and gentle, somewhere in the twilight between sleep and consciousness. Afterward we slipped back into sleep, our arms and legs intertangled.

In the morning, with early sunlight filtering through the bedroom blinds, we made love again. Rested, we gave in to our hunger. When she came for a third time, we climaxed together then fell into an exhausted tangle of arms, legs and sweat.

Our breakfast was leftover chocolate mousse and raspberries with cups of strong coffee. We lounged in each other's arms, sharing mimosas and cat naps. Then we made love again.

I needed a shave and a change of clothes, but Kate insisted I stay. We caught an afternoon movie and ate Chinese takeout for dinner. I spent the night again.

In the morning, as we snuggled in the bedsheets, I leaned close to her. "I love you," I whispered. It was the first time I said those words in longer than I could remember.

Kate turned and kissed me. She didn't repeat the words.

"Let's see if you change your mind when we have our clothes on," she said.

NINE – *Along for the Ride*

October 10, 1975, WASHINGTON, D.C. (WIRE SERVICES): The Wholesale Price Index for September showed continuing high inflation across all economic fronts. Federal Reserve Chairman Arthur Burns warned that continuing inflation is a serious threat to recovery from the current recession.

Gus Kopetsky was a mean-spirited bully, a blowhard, a pompous ass kisser, and a coward. He also was the Stratton Town Marshal.

I met Gus on a Monday afternoon not long after I arrived in town. I needed to pick up the police reports – accidents, public intoxication, theft, domestics, lost dogs – whatever prompted people to call the police in a small town. The police station was located two blocks from the newspaper in half of a plain red-brick building. The Town Board meeting room occupied the other half.

I walked to the station about eleven o'clock on a Monday morning. When I pulled on the glass door, it was locked. The police department was closed. I was stunned. It never occurred to me that a police department could be closed. I stepped back and looked at a sign taped to the window. It gave a number to call if the office was closed.

Trying to absorb the concept of a police department being closed, I walked by a to my office and called the number. A woman answered, "Sheriff's Dispatch." I explained the reason for the call, and she put me to hold. In the background I heard a radio squelch. "SPD, who's on duty right now?"

There was a static-filled reply: "This is Kopetsky. I've got the calls right now."

"Marshal, this is Evelyn at the Sheriff's Department. What's your twenty?"

"I'm at the store dealing with a sumbitch salesman to get some credit. Bought some meat from him last week, and it spoiled on me."

"The new guy at the newspaper is on the phone. Wants to pick up the police runs from last week. Can you meet him at the station?"

"10-4. But it won't be for a while. This sumbitch is gonna give me some credit or get a ticket every time he drives through town."

"Marshal, this is an open frequency."

"Tell that reporter to meet me at the station in an hour."

That was my introduction to Gus. An hour later I met him in person.

I was at the town hall in exactly an hour, but waited another fifteen minutes before a Stratton police car pulled up. The man who got out wore khaki pants several sizes too small and a floral shirt pulled tight across his gut. He looked like a football lineman who had not aged well.

I introduced myself and said I wanted to pick up the weekend police calls.

Gus unlocked the door, continuing to swear about "that sumbitch meat man." He showed me where the reports were located. I started flipping through oversized index cards. Mrs. Liederbeck complained that her neighbor's dog was barking. Bobbi Sue at The Mouse needing help removing a drunk who refused to leave at closing. Another call from The Mouse that "Hank and Casey are fighting again in the parking lot."

"How long have you been town marshal?" I asked as I wrote notes summarizing each card.

"Almost four years. I retired after almost thirty years on Chicago P.D."

"How'd you end up in Stratton?"

"Wife and I wanted to move to a small town and find a little business we could run. The convenience store here in town was for sale at a pretty good price. We came down, looked it over. My wife liked the town, so we bought the store. Once we got down here, town board found out I was a retired cop. They asked me to be marshal. You been to my store, yet?"

"Not yet," I said. " Still trying to find my way around."

"It's the only store in town open after six. We sell beer. Come in sometime and I'll give you a six pack on the house."

I didn't say anything and just kept writing.

The door opened and a uniformed officer walked in. He looked in his late 20s, trim with light brown hair was just long enough to be combed with a part. "Hi ya, Chief," he said with more than a hint of a southern Indiana twang.

"Hey Clint," Gus said. He pointed toward me. "This is Zach, uh, what's your last name, Zach?"

"Carlson," I said, reaching my hand out to Clint. "I'm the new editor at the paper."

Clint gave me a firm handshake. "Clint Avery. I'm a town deputy."

"How many deputies are there?"

"Two," Gus said. "Clint here and Kenny Wyman. He's off at some training, but he'll be back next week."

I finished the last of my jottings and closed my notebook. "Is there any way I can ride along with one of your deputies some night? I used to do that occasionally when I was up in Chicago. Helped me get a feel for what the police go through."

"Sure," Gus said. "Arrange it with Clint anytime you want. Don't even have to ask me. You can ride with Kenny, too, but one time with Kenny will probably be enough." Gus laughed at his own joke. Clint joined in. I didn't understand what they found funny. But I would.

#

Clint worked the late shift from 6 p.m. until shortly after the last bar closed at 2 a.m. After that, police runs were handled by the two overnight county sheriff's deputies. Riding in a cruiser was better than staring at walls through my long sleepless nights, so riding with Clint became a regular activity. It was a better way to pass time than sitting drinking beer with aging veterans at the VFW.

Nights in the police cruiser were low key. Weekdays, the incidents were largely inconsequential: running a stop sign, a loud muffler or teenagers loitering after school-night curfews. On weekends, there were always runs to The Mouse for a couple of drunks ending up in a fight. Clint handled the situation by flashing his badge and barking a threat about telling someone's mother or wife, and if that didn't work, about going to jail. The only time he put a hand on anyone was to help the loser of the fight off the floor. Clint resolved the disputes by pointing the combatants in different directions with a command to "Go home and sober up."

Clint was decent company -- quiet, friendly with a quirky sense of humor. He asked a few questions about being a reporter in Chicago. I kept my answers short and evasive. He took the hint and didn't press the matter.

Clint was slightly more open about his background. He grew up in southern Indiana near a crossroads called Birdseye. "It's just a place where two highways cross and somebody decided to build a house and a store."

Clint was a Vietnam vet. He enlisted out of high school. "They trained me as a fueler. When I got to Vietnam, I was stationed at Lo Binh. Just drove my fuel tank from one end of the base to the other, filling up vehicles and equipment. Never saw any combat, really. I mean the gooks would loft some mortars into the base two or three times a month, but they never really hit anything. And I never went out on patrols." Then his voice turned serious. "But I saw enough of what killing does to people. When my hitch was up, I got out."

"How'd you get to be a cop?"

Clint laughed, and took a long drink of coffee from the Thermos he always carried. "I thought I wanted to be a preacher. When I got out of the Army, I went to this small Bible college in Missouri. I did one semester and knew that was wrong for me."

"Too many rules?"

"Too judgmental. And I guess I just didn't have enough faith." Clint looked over at me. "I just didn't feel like saying 'praise Jesus' every time I took a shit."

We both laughed.

"So why Stratton?"

"I looked into the State Police. The guy I interviewed with said I needed some experience and he knew that Stratton was looking for someone. So here I am."

"Seems like a pretty dull place for a guy with no attachments to the town."

Clint gave me a sideways glance. "You're the one from the big city. You'd know better than me," he said.

"What do you do for fun? There's not much around here. You date anyone?"

"My mom and a sister still live in Birdseye. I go home pretty regular. And I got a few friends up in South Bend. I'll go up there and stay with them. Sometimes we go into Chicago."

"I guess there's more to do up there."

Clint turned toward me. After a pause, he said, "I find people I have more in common with up there."

We let the conversation lapse and rode in silence. I had a feeling that Clint was letting me know something about another part of his life, but one that he kept closed. I wondered if Clint was queer, if that was why he found his friends elsewhere. Maybe he was. Maybe not. But I wasn't going to ask. Clint had a right to keep the personal parts of his life private, just as I did. He was a good guy, knew how to do his job without making situations worse, and was better company than the blank walls of my apartment. That was all I needed to know.

I rode one night with the other officer, Kenny Wyman. "Kenny the Cop" as he was called behind his back. In his mid-20s, he was no more than five feet seven inches, with a wiry porno mustache that drooped over the corners of his mouth.

Kenny talked about nothing but himself and how he wanted to bone any woman we saw between the ages of fifteen and fifty – maybe sixty. His braggadocio carried over to his dealing with people. It took little time to understand that he used his badge and gun to demand respect he otherwise could not earn. After my first ride with Kenny, I limited my ride-alongs to nights when Clint was on duty.

#

It was about 10:30 on a crisp fall night when the radio in Clint's squad car crackled. It was Gus Kopetsky's gravelly voice. "Stratton Unit 1 to Stratton Unit 2. Come in, Clint."

Clint picked up the microphone. "This is Unit 2. Whatcha got, Gus?"

"Just made a stop for theft from my store. Got the guy pulled over just east of my store. Meet me there. I need you to arrest him and cart his ass to jail."

"Open mic, Chief," Clint said.

"Screw that," Gus shouted. "Just get here."

Clint turned the car around. Five minutes later we pulled up next to the town marshal's car, its lights flashing. There was a dark late model Oldsmobile parked in front of Gus' car. Both vehicles were empty. Clint and I stepped out of the car, and Clint called for Gus.

"Down here," he shouted.

We found Gus on the far side of the car, sitting on top of a plump middle-aged man in a disheveled shirt and tie. The man's face was being pressed into weeds along the side of the road. His hands were cuffed tightly behind his back.

"This sumbitch stole some candy out my store." Gus' face glowed bright red. "Take him to the county jail and lock him up."

"What's the charge?" Clint asked.

"Theft. Shoplifting. Resisting. I don't care. I just want his ass in jail."

The man in the grass tried to turn his head toward Clint, his eyes pleading. "I don't know what he's talking about. I didn't do anything. I just bought a drink. I paid for it. The receipt's in the car."

"Bullshit," Gus screamed. "No one steals from me. Not cigarettes. Not candy. Not a goddamn stick of gum. You understand? You're lucky if I don't just bash your head in right here, you fat fuck."

The more I looked at the man on the ground, the more I became concerned. The light was dim, but he was turning ashen, the same shade I had seen on bodies at crime scenes.

"I didn't take anything," he said, on the verge of tears. "I picked up a couple of candy bars, but I put them back. I'm diabetic. I'm not supposed to eat candy anymore. So, I put them back." He started to cry. "I put them back."

Clint eased Gus toward his cruiser. "I'll handle this, Gus." Gus protested, but stayed by the car while Clint walked back to the man on the ground. Clint extended a hand, helped him into a sitting position, then kneeled close to him.

"What's your name, sir?"

"Scott Travers."

"Well Mr. Travers, just relax. Take a few deep breaths. I'll see if we can get this thing straightened out."

Clint removed the handcuffs and helped the man to his feet. The color began returning to his face. Clint pulled a handkerchief from his pocket and handed it to Travers.

"Wipe your face off. I'll try to find out what's going on."

I walked with Clint back to his patrol car. He picked up the radio. "Stratton Unit 2 to Base. Are you there, Karla?"

"Base here," said a female voice.

"Hey Karla, do you know anything about this guy Gus said stole some candy?"

Base was a police radio kept behind the counter at Kopetsky's Convenience Store. Karla was the store manager who handled police calls when she was working. Her exasperated tone resonated through the crackling radio.

"I tried to stop Gus. I yelled at him, but he just took off like a bat out of hell. That guy didn't steal nothing. He picked up a couple of candy bars, but he put them back on the rack. Said something about being diabetic. He bought a Tab and some Dentine, but he didn't steal anything."

"Thanks Karla. Out."

"I didn't see him put it back." It was Gus. He walked up next to Clint's car during the radio conversation. "But I had probable cause. I had probable cause."

Clint nodded. "Understand, Gus. You go back to the store. I'll take care of this."

Gus nodded and walked back toward his car. Just as he reached it, he kicked the ground hard sending pebbles scattering across the pavement. He got in his car, squealing his tires as he made a U-turn and drove off in the direction of the convenience store.

Clint watched the car go, then walked to where Travers stood.

"Everything's okay," Clint said. "You can go on your way now."

The man pulled his tie up and tucked in his shirt. Now that the threat of jail was gone, his anger blossomed. "Someone is going to pay for this. I didn't do anything. Somebody is going to wish this never happened."

Clint nodded. "I understand how you feel. I'm sorry, sir." Clint kept his voice level but with more authority in his tone than earlier. "We did have a witness who reported that you picked up the candy and he didn't see you pay for it. In that situation, the law gives the shopkeeper the right to detain you. It's called probable cause. That's what happened."

"But . . ."

"Mr. Travers, I suggest that you get in your car and go on down the road to wherever you are headed. If you persist, I will make out a report and we'll do an investigation. Of course, nobody is around to take your statement until morning. I'll have to hold you overnight. And if we do that, I'll probably have to write you up for your broken taillight. If I did that, you'd have to come back for court in three or four weeks." Clint paused and gave a knowing smile. "I suggest it's best that everyone just go on their way."

Travers grumbled under his breath, but got in his car. Clint hustled me into his patrol car. He followed Travers' car to the town limits and a bit beyond, keeping the patrol car close enough that Travers would be aware he was being followed. A mile outside of Stratton, Clint made a U-turn and headed back toward town.

"His taillight isn't broken," I said.

Clint gave a winsome smile. "I know. But he's not going to stop and check until he's in the next county, if then. Did you see the plate? That number means he's from Indianapolis. He won't ever want to come through here again."

I stared at Clint.

He shrugged. "Everybody just goes on their way and nothing ever happened."

After leaving Clint, I stopped in the VFW for a beer. Four men in their 50s sat at a table playing euchre. Two older men sat at the bar chain smoking cigarettes and watching a late Cubs game from the west coast. I sat at the bar and ordered an Old Style longneck. The icy beer soothed like a healing poultice.

I didn't concentrate on the game. I thought through the events of the evening, and whether there was a story that needed reported. Cops bullying and even beating people didn't shock me. I saw Chicago cops do much worse: a night stick to the mouth for asking a question, splattering kid's nose with a mag light because of his long hair, tripping a handcuffed suspect face first into pavement because he made the cop run to catch him. I witnessed the police riot at the 1968 Democratic National Convention and felt the burn of tear gas. It was how things were done.

But there was something about the way Gus went after that shirt and tie businessman. If Gus was right, the worst thing the guy did was pocket a couple of candy bars. But Gus wasn't right. The guy didn't do anything but buy a soft drink and gum.

I was impressed with how Clint handled the situation. He protected Gus from himself, and the business man from Gus. He let the guy go, but gave him a threatening hint of possible ramifications if he filed a complaint. The guy would cuss about his treatment in Stratton all the way home. But that was all. No one would hear about the incident again.

Not unless I wrote about it in the newspaper.

I finished my beer with a long gulp. It wasn't really news. No one was arrested. No arms were broken or faces smashed. What would a story accomplish except making an enemy of the town marshal and ending my night rides with Clint?

I flipped two ones on the bar for the dollar beer and left.

TEN – *Pieces of Life*

September 14, 1975, MILAN, ITALY (WIRE SERVICES). Soviet Union chess champion Anatoly Karpov won the Milan International Chess Tournament with a draw in his final match, laying claim to the World Championship title.

Karpov finished with 3.5 points to 2.5 for his opponent, Hungary's Lajos Portisch. American former World Champion Bobby Fischer, who last year resigned his world championship title, did not participate in the tournament.

By late September I was getting stir crazy. I remembered the invitation to the local chess club. So, on a chilly Thursday night, I found myself knocking on the door of Gary and Libby Middleton's apartment. The Middleton's lived in the downstairs section of a two-story faded white clapboard house owned by the town Clerk/Treasurer Orville Vehorn. It was walking distance from where I lived, but then everything in Stratton was walking distance.

Gary met me at the door. "Old Milwaukee okay?" he said, handing me the brown longneck bottle. I followed him into the living room where four chessboards were already set up and several men were standing around the room.

Libby walked in from the kitchen wearing a Little 500 tee shirt and well-worn jeans. "Glad you could make it, Zach. Welcome to the world of Bobby Fischer wannabes."

Gary rolled his eyes a bit, then introduced me to the others: Danny Stoddard, a scraggly hippie inventor, two other teachers and Mike Short, who owned the local HVAC business.

"Who wins?" I asked.

Mike looked toward Gary with a bit of a smirk. "Who wins, Gary?"

Gary raised his middle finger. I took that as an answer.

"Danny's the best," Mike said. "Gary is good, but he hasn't beaten Danny yet. The rest of us just piddle around."

I lost all three games I played. But the companionship was a welcome change from my exile. As I left the Middletons, I felt that most Thursday nights in Stratton would find me playing chess.

#

Gary and Libby invited me to dinner on the following Saturday. I took them up on the offer. It was my first social dinner since moving to Stratton.

Leroy Clemens, one of the teachers in the chess group, and his wife Jan, also a teacher, joined us. I was the only non-teacher at the table. They asked about my experience of being a reporter in Chicago and how I ended up in Stratton. I kept my answers short, providing little about my life before. It didn't take long until the conversation turned to the schools: bureaucratic red tape, administrators who forgot how to teach, and students who disrespected teachers and themselves. Leroy complained about the rule requiring men teachers to be clean shaven and keep their hair cut above their collar. "No wonder the students can't relate to us," he said. "We're all walking around looking like Ward Cleaver."

"Gee, Ward, don't you think you were a little hard on the Beaver last night?" Libby said, with a straight face.

After the laughter subsided, Libby took a more serious tone.

"I had another girl drop out of school today because she got pregnant. That's the third one and we're not even half way through the first semester."

"I had one last week," Leroy said.

Libby shook her head. "You know at my school only four kids from last year's graduating class attended college. That's four of seventy-two. At least half the girls who graduated last May are already married, most because they got pregnant."

I gave a short laugh that drew disapproving looks around the table. "Sorry," I said. "I don't mean to make light of this, but I thought rural America was supposed to be the last bastion of virginity. Schools in Chicago don't have those pregnancy rates."

"You have no idea what it's like." Libby said. "There's nothing around here for kids to do except to drink and sneak out to some deserted lane and have sex. People around here want to get their daughters married off. If they get pregnant a little early, it's almost expected. As long as they get married, nobody really cares."

"Haven't they heard of the pill?"

Libby shook her head. "It's harder for kids to get birth control than pot. The drug store keeps rubbers behind the counter. A boy has to ask for them. Same thing with birth control pills. A girl goes in to the drug store to pick up birth control pills, and ten minutes later everybody in town knows she's sleeping around."

The conversation meandered into less serious topics. We played cards and polished off the better part of a case of beer and two bottles of wine. But I kept thinking about high school girls and pregnancy. I started mulling around how to write story about teen sex in a small town.

ELEVEN – *How Will You Know?*

March 1973

March 29, 1973, SAIGON, VIETNAM (WIRE SERVICES): With no fanfare or celebration, the last American combat soldiers left Vietnam today, ending America's longest undeclared war.

A source in the American military warned that this is not the end of the war. "There's going to be a full-blown war starting up after we leave," the source said.

Few crimes shock Chicago. Among the city's points of historical reference were the St. Valentine's Day Massacre, Leopold and Loeb's thrill killing of a Boy Scout, and Richard Speck's 1966 rape, torture and murder of eight nursing students in their dormitory. Al Capone was as much a part of the city as the Chicago World's Fair, Richard Daly and Ernie Banks.

In 1972, the body count totaled 700 murders, up from 500 only two years earlier. By March 1973, the murder rate was on pace to shatter that record. No, nothing much shook Chicago. But no matter how common violence and death became, some crimes stopped the city in its tracks.

Charlie Kelso's phone call woke me a little after 4 a.m. Charlie's calls came at all hours. I never figured out when he ever slept. I searched my brain for any problems with the last story, one I turned in shortly after one a.m. Two punks gunned down a liquor store clerk for forty dollars and a bottle of cheap whiskey. Did I screw up rushing through the story, knowing Kate waited at my apartment? Did I misspell a name or get a wrong address? Worse, did I mix up the name of the victim with a shooter?

"The police radio is popping," Charlie said, his voice filled with an early-morning rasp. "I'm not sure what's going on, but it sounds like a multiple homicide. Three or four. I need you there."

I fumbled for the pad and pen I kept on my night stand.

Kate stirred in bed next to me. "What is it?"

"Work," I said, adrenaline already overcoming my drowsiness.

Charlie gave me the address. "Meyers will meet you at the scene. He's on his way."

Hurley Meyers was an historical relic and a friend. He was the first black staff photographer at the Examiner, and as far as anyone could recall, at any mainstream Chicago daily newspaper. As a teenager, he convinced a pawnshop owner to give him a battered Speed Graphic camera instead of wages for six months of shoveling coal and cleaning toilets. He used that Speed Graphic to take pictures at crime scenes in the waning days of Prohibition, selling them to the city's black-owned newspapers for a dollar each. Some weeks he ate. Some weeks he didn't. The camera still sat on Hurley's desk at the Examiner.

In his mid-60s, he was tall and lean with short wiry hair that long ago turned gray. His sharp eyes reflected a lingering sadness from the pain and tragedy he witnessed through his camera lens for more than four decades. Hurley possessed the rare ability to capture the essence of a scene and tell a story in a single black and white image.

After decades, he was a fixture at crime scenes. Cops respected him, even those for whom "damned nigger" was a common part of speech. When my press badge failed to get me past a police line, Hurley talked us through. If given a choice, I asked Charlie to assign Hurley to my stories. Besides, I liked his company.

I dressed, pulling on yesterday's khakis, shirt and sweater. Kate slipped out of bed, her bare skin luminescent in the ambient light that filtered through the window.

"You have to go?"

"Multiple homicide," I said. "I'm sorry, but I'm probably going to be working this all day."

Kate rubbed her body against me. "So, no brunch and a movie?"

"Sorry." I gave her a kiss, then headed out.

Using the battered city map I kept in my glove box, I found the crime scene. Without traffic and ignoring stop lights and speed limits, I arrived at the scene in less than twenty minutes.

It was an ordinary house on an ordinary street in a working-class neighborhood not far from Midway Airport. A dozen police cars were parked haphazardly in the street. Closer to the house were four ambulances and a coroner's wagon. I pulled up next to a car marked Cook County Children's Services.

I showed my press badge to get past the first line securing the scene. The young patrolman who checked my press card tried to hide his swollen eyes and the streaks from tears on his cheeks.

It wouldn't be long until the television vans would show up with their big lights and cameras. My experience was that once they showed up, the detectives shut up. I had no more than fifteen minutes to find out what happened.

I covered more homicides in a week than some TV reporters would cover in a year. That was an advantage. The detectives knew me. In nearly a decade of covering murders in Chicago, I never released a victim's identification before police notification, never revealed information told me in confidence, always respected information given on background, and never made a detective look bad.

I got my story. Detectives got positive publicity on which they could build their careers. It was how the crime beat worked.

I found Lee Phillips standing on the front porch of the house. He was a twenty-year veteran detective I knew well. A cordon of patrolmen blocked me from accessing the house, but I shouted out to Lee and got his attention.

He stepped off the porch and motioned a patrolman to let me through the line. Through weary deep-set eyes, he looked past me and into the darkness punctuated by an array of emergency lights. He said nothing, but nodded his head toward the side of the house. We walked without talking until we were out of earshot.

I took a pack of Camel unfiltered from my shirt pocket and offered Lee one. He took it, and I took one for myself. I lit them both off the same match. After taking a long draw, Lee let the smoke out slowly. Sleet began pelting us. We crowded under the roof overhang for refuge.

"I'm getting too damn old for this," he said, talking more to himself than to me. "I'm waiting for the crime scene guys and a photographer," he said. "When they get here, I gotta go."

"What's going on?"

Lee's eyes darted back toward the house. "I . . . It's bad, Zach. Really bad."

I waited. Lee gathered his thoughts. He took another long draw on the cigarette and tossed it onto the ground. "We've got four dead. Well, five if you count the guy that did this."

I gave a low whistle.

"We're still putting the pieces together, but from what we can tell, the husband and wife were asleep in their bedroom. Their daughter was having a slumber party. Four girls, all about twelve, thirteen years old. Just girls."

I had long ago learned that sometimes reporters could discover more by listening than asking questions. This was one of those times. I waited.

"This guy broke in. We haven't confirmed it, but we think he worked at a neighborhood store. One of those places kids go after school to buy pop and candy and stuff. That's what one of the surviving girls told us. She saw him there several times. At least she thinks she did. She's pretty shook up. I'm surprised she can talk at all."

"One of the surviving girls?" I asked.

"Two survived. We can be thankful for that."

I stayed silent. If I asked questions now, we would be cop and reporter rather than two guys talking. I waited.

When Lee continued, I could see he was playing the scene in his mind as he spoke.

"The guy got in through the back door. Put masking tape over a glass pane and punched it out, then reached in and unlock the door. He killed the parents in their bed while they were asleep. Slit their throats with a hunting knife. Nearly cut their heads off. Then he went after the girls."

Lee signaled for another cigarette. I fished two out and lit them.

"He raped at least two of the girls, maybe all of them. We have to wait for the medical tests to be certain. He raped this one girl and choked her until she blacked out. While he was attacking her friends, she regained consciousness and slipped out of the house. She ran to a neighbor. They called the police."

Lee took a long draw on his cigarette. "Damn, these unfiltered things are strong. This what you always smoke?"

I nodded. "You get used to it. What happened when the cops got here?"

"First officer on scene didn't hesitate. He ran in to the house with his gun drawn. Found the guy leaning over one of the girls. Blood was gushing from her throat. The officer blew him away. He tried to save the girl. Did everything he could, but it was too late. She lost too much blood. She was gone before the ambulance got here."

"Can you give me his name?"

"Patrolman William Harshbarger." Lee spelled it for me.

"How's he doing?"

"Pretty damned upset," Lee said, his focus fixed on the cigarette burning down between his fingers. "He was soaked in blood from trying to stop the bleeding. We got him out of here before the TV people showed up. Didn't want him all over the news covered in blood."

"You said two girls survived?"

"Yeah. The one that ran off and another one. If Harshbarger hadn't got there when he did, she'd be dead, too. No question he saved that second girl. Hope he realizes that."

Lee took a deep draw on his cigarette, taking it down to his fingertips. He flicked it out into the rain and darkness.

"Got any names of the victims?"

Lee pulled a notebook from his inside jacket pocket and flipped it open. "Not for release yet."

I nodded. The names wouldn't be used until notification of next of kin.

"Richard Hobart and his wife Rene. They're the parents that died. Best we can tell, he was a truck driver, she was a housewife. Their daughter's name is Rachel."

"Did she survive?"

Lee shook his head. "No. The other girl that died is Linda Rimstead. We've got a team notifying her parents right now."

We stood silent. The sleet pelted us even harder.

"It's a hard rain," Lee finally said. He wiped at his cheeks. I couldn't distinguish rain from tears.

#

My lead story ran on page one under a banner 48-point headline: "HORROR ON HOLMES AVENUE." Hurley Meyers's photo ran with the story, capturing the hollow haunting look on a veteran cop's face as the coroner's office removed a covered small body from the house. Sidebar stories written by other reporters covered every aspect of the crime: the horror of neighbors, the murderer's background, the city's soaring murder rate.

I wrote another story, too. It centered on the impact working a crime scene like this had on police and emergency workers. I thought it was the best thing I had written in several months.

Charlie didn't like it. "It's a fluff piece. Stick to hard news."

The story never ran.

#

It was two days after the story before Kate and I saw each other again. We met for a late lunch at Manny's, a coffee shop and delicatessen a few blocks south of the Loop.

We filled our lunches with conversation, sometimes about work but usually other things. This day was different. Kate stirred at her matzo ball soup. It was her favorite dish at Manny's, but she seemed uninterested.

"You not feeling well?" I asked.

"I'm fine," she said, not looking up.

"Something wrong? You barely touched your food."

Kate shook her head.

"What's going on?" I asked.

"How do you do it?" she said, her voice thin and full of hesitation.

"Do what?"

"How . . . how do you write those stories? How do you go to those places where people are killed and then write those stories?"

I put down my corned beef sandwich. "It's like the cops, I guess. It's my job, and I just do it."

"Do you . . . do you like it?"

This wasn't just an idle discussion. She wasn't just asking about whether I was happy in my job. She was asking about me, about who I was inside, and if I was the person with whom she wanted a long-term relationship. I thought for a long moment, rolling my response around before saying anything. After more than four months together, I loved Kate more than any woman who had been in my life. I was being asked to reveal something about myself. I didn't want to damage our relationship with the wrong answer, but I didn't want to lie to Kate either.

"That's difficult to answer," I said. "If I wasn't a reporter, I have no idea what I'd be doing. There is excitement in being at the center of action, walking past police lines that keep others out. I like digging into stories, finding out stuff other people don't know. Truth be told, I like seeing my byline in the paper and the respect I get when people recognize me from seeing my articles."

Kate looked straight into my eyes. "But all those deaths. This latest one. A whole family. And those girls. Doesn't it . . ." There was a pause. "Doesn't it bother you?"

I reached across the table and took Kate's hands between mine. She did not pull back. I took that as a good sign.

"Yes, it bothers me. It always bothers me." What I didn't say was the realization that the blood and death did not bother me as it once had. "I go to these scenes, and I see reporters who keep asking more and more details about how people died, how long they struggled, how much they suffered. They seem energized by it all. I don't think I'm like that. At least I hope not. If I ever see myself becoming like them, it will be time to move on, to do something else."

"Do you think you'll know? Do you think you'll recognize that you're becoming like them?"

I dropped my chin into my hands. "I think so," I said. But I wasn't so sure of my answer.

Kate got up and walked around the table. She put her arms around me, leaned over and kissed my cheek. "Just don't become one of them," she said, her voice just above a whisper. "I'm not sure I could handle that."

TWELVE – *Date Night*

November 11, 1975, SAULT STE. MARIE, MICH. (WIRE SERVICES): The 729-foot iron ore freighter Edmund Fitzgerald, largest vessel on the Great Lakes, sank last night in Lake Superior during a violet storm. The entire crew of 29 is presumed dead.

The Coast Guard reports finding lifeboats and other debris off the coast of Whitefish Point, Mich. No bodies have been recovered. With water temperatures below 50 degrees, a Coast Guard spokesman stated it would be unlikely for a person to survive more than three hours.

Over the first two months in Stratton, groceries consisted mostly of frozen dinners, frozen pizzas and a couple of six-packs. I skipped breakfast and ate most of my meals at Shelby's Place.

The food was better than what was in my freezer, and the atmosphere was better than the pervasive aloneness of sitting in my silent apartment. Customers scattered around the restaurant in twos and fours talking about family, friends, church, and town gossip. A constant clatter of dishes and clinking glasses played across the dining room. Country music played from the jukebox. And there was Emma.

Emma Musgrave waited on my table the first day that Roy took me to Shelby's for lunch, and she was my waitress nearly every time I returned, whether for lunch or dinner. Three other women worked as waitresses, but Emma usually ended up at my table. She greeted me with "What's new, newsman?" followed by a short laugh and a wink.

Emma stood only five feet two inches, carrying a few extra pounds in her hips and thighs. Her straw-colored hair pulled back, she greeted everyone with an expansive smile that made no effort to hide teeth that were chipped and not quite aligned.

On a cold night in late October, I found myself at Shelby's eating a bowl of passable Midwestern chili, the kind with hamburger, kidney beans and a sprinkling of chili powder. It was bland but comforting.

Emma walked to my table, her hips swinging a bit. "Need another beer, Zach?"

I nodded. "Do you ever go home?" I asked.

"Nope," she said. "I just live here in the storeroom."

I gave a small laugh, but her face remained serious. I became uneasy, coming to the realization that perhaps she did live in the storeroom. After an uncomfortable pause, she burst out laughing. Not a polite titter, but a full belly laugh.

"You are so damn gullible," she said. "How in the world can you be a newspaperman if you fall for shit like that?"

I rolled my eyes and broke into an embarrassed grin. I was exposed. No way to deny it.

"I pick up as many shifts as I can," she said. "Have to earn enough to take care of my daughter. But I do have a home."

"Lot of long days."

She shrugged. "It keeps a roof over my head. Not much of a roof, but better than living in a tent."

She brought back the long neck beer, put it down on the table, then took a seat on the chair next to me. "So, Mr. Zach Carlson, what brought you to the thriving metropolis of Stratton?

With my bottle in hand, I made a made a broad sweeping motion around the room. "This," I said. "The elegant cuisine and cold beer."

Emma furrowed her brow. "Nobody just comes to this town. You're either born here, got relatives here, or you're a school teacher. Why'd you end up here?"

I rolled the bottom edge of the bottle around the table while I rolled around my thoughts. I calculated how much, and how little, I wanted to say.

"I decided to leave Chicago," I said. "Barrett Newspapers just bought the Stratton Gazette. They were looking for someone. I applied and they hired me."

Emma gave a disbelieving smile. "I don't think that's all, Mr. Zach Carlson. There's a story you ain't telling."

I shrugged and pushed away my bowl.

"Sounds to me like there's a reason, and usually that means trouble with a job or a girl. So, which is it?"

"That's your expert opinion?" My tone was sharper than I intended, but I was not ready to share more about myself.

"I may be a small-town waitress," Emma said, her voice equally sharp. "But I'm not stupid. Don't treat me like I'm stupid."

I realized how condescending I had sounded. "I . . . I didn't mean . . . I don't think you're stupid."

A smile snapped back on Emma's face. "Damn skippy, you better not. Now, you want to go to a movie and get a pizza Saturday night?"

The conversation changed direction so fast that I wasn't sure that I heard her correctly. "What?"

"It's not hard, Zach. Do you want to go to a movie and get a pizza? The Royale over in Amelia is playing this movie, Dog Day Afternoon. It's got Al Pacino in it. I got the hots for him, and I heard the movie is pretty good. Would you like to go? I'll drive and pay for my own ticket. Yours too. It's a simple yes or no."

It was a simple question, but my emotional reaction wasn't. I had not gone out with anyone, not even for beer or coffee, since Kate. I never even considered it.

Emma smacked me on top of my head with a menu. "I'm asking you on a date," she said. "I've been waiting for you to ask, but hell, I'm not going to pine away sitting at home until you call. So, you gonna stand me up even when I'm the one asking?"

"Okay," I said, without thinking. I didn't want to embarrass Emma. It was easier to say yes.

"You can come over about six and I'll drive us to Amelia." She grabbed a napkin and scrawled an address on it and handed it to me. "Here's where I live. I'll see you then."

She got up and without even a look back, walked away.

#

I had not been to a movie theater in more than a year. Dog Day Afternoon was not a good choice for my return. I found myself gripping the arm of my seat so tightly that my hand began to cramp. I closed my eyes during the most intense scenes. At one point Emma turned to me. "Are you okay? Do we need to leave?"

"I'm fine," I said, patting her hand for reassurance. I noticed that my hands were trembling and my palms were damp. I took Emma's hand to steady the shaking.

After the movie we walked two blocks to a storefront restaurant with the awkward name Catt Pizza and Pasta. "I hope that's the owners name and not what's in it," I said.

"They used to call it Pussy Pizza, but the local ministers complained." Emma said, her expression unchanged. I reminded myself to never play poker with her.

We split a pitcher of draft beer and a pepperoni pizza made with canned sauce and frozen dough. It wasn't Chicago pizza, but it was better than the tasteless frozen discs I had been eating in my small kitchen. A jukebox in the corner played a constant stream of Dolly Parton, Charlie Pride and Loretta Lynn.

"Thanks for coming," Emma said after the pizza arrived. "Between work and my daughter, I don't get a chance to get out much."

"You mentioned her the other day. What's her name?"

Emma reached into her handbag and brought up a wallet. She flipped it opened to a half dozen plastic sleeves filled with school photos of a cute sandy-haired girl as she grew from year to year.

"That's Molly. She's twelve now."

"She's very pretty. All this time I didn't know you had a daughter."

"I'm pretty protective of her. I got pregnant in high school. He was a senior and captain of the football team, of course. He got into my pants my junior year after the homecoming dance."

Emma took a long drink to finish her beer. I refilled it from the pitcher.

"We got married. That's what you did if you got pregnant. I guess that's still what happens." She shook her head vigorously and gave a short laugh. "Oh my God, was that a big mistake. He joined the Army right out of school and was gone at basic when Molly was born. Soon as he finished training, he got sent off to Vietnam. And that was it."

"I'm so sorry," I said, my voice sympathetic.

"No," Emma said, with an easy laugh. "The sonofabitch wasn't killed. He was some type of desk jockey. Only fighting he ever saw was in some mamma-san's whorehouse." Emma took a sip from her beer. "He just sent me a letter from over there saying he didn't want to be married anymore."

"Just like that?"

Emma gave an emphatic nod. "He discovered -- and I'll quote you his exact words – 'a lot better pussy than me' -- pardon my language. He didn't want to be tied down anymore."

"That's awful. That must have been heartbreaking."

"Funny thing, I was just as glad to get rid of him. I knew he resented me and the baby. And we were both way too young to be married."

"Does he keep in touch with your daughter?"

Emma drained her glass in one swallow. "Hell no. He hasn't talked to her since before she started school. Some years he sends a Christmas gift, but he hasn't done that in two or three years."

"That's it? Not even birthday cards?"

"He doesn't even know when her birthday is."

"No child support?"

"Him? Shit, that'll be the day. I talked to a lawyer once, but he said there wasn't much I could do. He lives in North Carolina. I could get an order up here, but then I'd have to hire a lawyer down in North Carolina to try to enforce it. You can bet your ass that as soon as I did that, he'd move someplace else. I don't have the money to hire lawyers to chase him around."

"That's really awful," I said. "You'd think he would have some interest in his own daughter."

Emma looked at her empty glass. I emptied the pitcher to refill it. She seemed to be thinking as she took a sip. "Me and Molly get along fine. My mom and stepdad live not far outside town. They help a lot. It's easier now that she's old enough to stay at home by herself when I'm working, at least if I'm not working too late.

I checked my watch. It was after ten. "Should we go?"

"Don't worry. I'm on my own tonight. She's staying with my parents. They do that pretty regular. Keep her Saturday night and take her to church with them in the morning."

A few minutes later we had finished the pizza and beer and were walking in the crisp autumn air back to my car. Despite

Emma's offer, I had driven to the movie. As we walked, she wrapped her arm around mine and pulled herself close.

"So, you want to stop by my place for a drink? We could see what develops."

I stopped in the middle of the sidewalk.

Emma tugged me forward. "Look," she said, "I'm disease free and on the pill. I'm not looking for a husband. I'm not even looking for a phone call next week. We could have a little fun, that's all."

Emma was straightforward, delivering her proposition with a smile and a wink. Here words seemed an odd blend of innocence and world-weariness.

It wasn't an unpleasant prospect. I had not been with anyone since Kate. I had not even thought about it. I didn't know how to say no without offending her. So, I didn't.

I drove back to Emma's bungalow with small rooms crowded and worn furniture. Everything was clean and neatly organized. Emma went into the kitchen and poured Canadian Club and Coke into two tall ice-filled glasses. I looked around the living room. A small television sat on a makeshift table constructed from stained pine lumber and painted concrete blocks. Framed photos of Emma's daughter filled a curio cabinet. One photo showed an older couple that I took to be Emma's parents, or her mom and stepdad. Emma appeared in only two of the photos, standing alongside her daughter.

A battered bookshelf stained a dull brown stood against one wall, filled with paperbacks, all with bent pages indicating they had been read. I saw Valley of the Dolls and The Love Machine, Jacqueline Suzanne's steamy books that everyone was reading a few years earlier. There was a copy of the insipid but wildly popular romance, Love Story. But there were other books, too: The Andromeda Strain, In Cold Blood, The Confessions of Nat Turner, The French Lieutenant's Woman, several novels by Kurt Vonnegut, Jr. and Hemingway's A Farewell to Arms. All showed signs of having been read.

"You like to read?" I said as she walked back into the room and handed me my drink.

"I've always liked to read," she said. "If I hadn't got knocked up, I would like to have been an English teacher." She gave a short laugh. "Of course, I stunk at grammar, so maybe that wasn't going to work anyway."

"There are some pretty serious books up there."

She wagged a finger playfully at me. "I told you, I'm not stupid." She took my hand and led me back to the kitchen where we sat at a butcher-block table. Emma moved her chair close and slid one leg between mine. "The kitchen is my favorite room," she said. "It's always where I'm most at home."

We kissed. My body reacted in a way it had not in a very long time. We were not finished with the drinks when we started grappling with each other's clothes. We stood and stepped out of the last of our clothes. Emma took my hand and started leading me back to the bedroom. I reached back and downed the last of my whiskey with a single swallow, then followed her.

Emma made love with an uninhibited joy. She took the top position and seemed to relish in showing her body to me. For her, sex seemed more fun than passion. She smiled, giggled and laughed until our lovemaking began to build toward an orgasm. She came in several waves, eyes closed, biting her lips, making no sounds other than her rapid breathing. I followed quickly, and we collapsed side by side, our bodies lightly touching.

We lay that way for several minutes, not talking. Emma sat up, not bothering to cover herself. She pulled a pack of cigarettes from a bedside table. "Want one?"

"No thanks," I said. "I quit."

"I should, I guess. But I always want a cigarette after sex." She lit up and took a deep drag. With a long slow breath, she blew a stream of smoke toward the ceiling.

I lay in the darkness, the smoke flowing over me. From nowhere, I felt tears. I threw my legs over the edge of the bed and sat up, my back to Emma. Images, a voice, a touch, all swirled unexpectedly through my head, all from a life that no longer belonged to me. Dampness rolled down my cheeks. I wiped my face and fought back a sob.

Emma's hand gently touched my back. "Are you okay?"

I nodded, but said nothing.

We stayed there like that, in the silence, for a long time. Guilt swept over me. My chest ached with betrayal even though my head reasoned that this was just the next step in moving on. My reasoned reality did not ease the pain.

"I want you to stay," Emma said softly, her hand still gently moving across my back. "But if you want to go . . ." She paused. "If you need to go, that's okay. I told you, this was for fun. No commitments."

Again, I just gave a simple nod. More minutes passed in silence, Emma's open hand slowly, lightly, gently traced circles across my back.

"First time for a while?"

I gave a short laugh. "It showed?"

She moved up behind me, kissed my neck then whispered with her mouth so close to my ear that I could feel her breath. "Oh, no, hon, not the way you meant it. You were wonderful. But right now, you got someone else in your thoughts."

There was a long silence. I finally said, "Sorry."

"You don't have to be sorry," she said. She again kissed me on my neck. "We can't help what our heart feels. The work of the heart is never done. You know who said that?

I shook my head.

"Mohammed Ali. The boxer."

I gave a half smile. "I know who he is."

"Is she the reason you left Chicago?"

I nodded, curling my lips into each other to fight back more tears.

"Lay back and see if you can get some sleep."

I did, turning my back toward Emma. She gently nudged me on to my stomach, then continued to move her hand tenderly in broad circles across my back. She softly began to hum pleasantly. With excruciating slowness, Emma's touch and her silky voice acted like a balm on my wounds. I drifted into sleep.

THIRTEEN – *Blind and Other Justice*

November 20, 1975, WASHINGTON, D.C. (WIRE SERVICES): Former California Governor Ronald Reagan today announced his candidacy for the Republican nomination for President, challenging incumbent President Gerald Ford.

Reagan's first campaign appearance in Miami, Fla. was interrupted when a young man flashed a realistic looking toy gun at Reagan. Michael L. Carvin, 20, was taken into custody by the Secret Service. The candidate was unharmed.

It was one of those early November nights when the chill and dampness in the air cut through to the bone. I took Emma to Amelia to see a new Robert Redford movie, Three Days of the Condor. I didn't care for the film, but Emma said she would enjoy watching Robert Redford read the telephone book for two hours.

We grabbed a pizza and a pitcher of beer after the movie, and she again invited me back to her place. I drove back with Emma's hand on my thigh. I pulled to a stop sign three blocks from Emma's bungalow and waited for an approaching car with only one headlight. Without signaling, the car, traveling not much more than a walking pace, started a very slow turn in an ever-widening arc. As the car crossed over into my lane, I tapped the horn. It didn't stop, and it didn't change course.

"What the hell," I shouted, and laid on a long continuous horn blast. Still there was no change in the car's direction or inevitable trajectory. Like watching real life in slow motion, the oncoming car crunched into the left front corner of my Impala. "Shit!"

"What's wrong with that guy?" Emma asked.

I grabbed for the door handle to get out, but Emma put a hand on my shoulder. "I'll run up to the house and call the police," she said, her voice calm. "You be careful. That guy's gotta be drunk or high on something."

I nodded, but I was fuming. As Emma disappeared into the darkness, I got out and walked toward the car that crashed into mine. It was an early 1960s puke green Pontiac Valiant with more rust showing than the original paint. I walked to the driver's side and tapped on the window.

"What the hell are you doing?"

Behind the wheel there was a small man with stringy unkempt brown hair, wearing a stained white tee shirt. He stared at me with glazed eyes and an open mouth, a trace of drool hanging down to his chin.

"My friend is calling the police. Wait until they get here. We'll get an accident report filled out."

The man still stared at me with unfocused eyes. His hand eased off the steering wheel and inched toward the gearshift. I sensed he would not stick around for the police. I walked behind the car to get the license plate number. As I did, the car backed up, not moving faster than a crawl. I memorized the plate number. Suddenly the car took off, black exhaust smoke belching from its tail pipe. The car swerved wildly around my car, wheels going onto the sidewalk. At the next intersection, the car turned and was gone.

I ran back to my car, fished my notebook and pen out of the glove box and wrote down the license number. Then I leaned against the car and waited for the police.

But the police weren't the first to arrive. A boy who looked about twelve ran up, eyes wide. "Did you see that crash?" he said, excitedly.

I rolled my eyes a bit. "I was in the car when that guy hit me."

The boy looked puzzled. He shook his head. "The guy you were talking to, he lost control going around that turn down there. Crashed into a couple of cars. I think he hit a house."

"You're shitting me?"

The boy shook his head. "I was right over there, walking home. Saw the whole thing. He took off real fast, smacked a couple of cars, then headed toward a house. I didn't actually see him hit the house, but that's what it looked like he was going to do." He took off running toward the commotion.

I stepped out of the car, unsure whether I should follow or wait for the police. As I stood there, Emma came trotting up.

"Must be a night for stupid drivers," she said. "There's a big crash up the street. Car went through someone's yard and took out their porch."

"I think it's the same guy," I said. "Some boy ran by and told me."

Clint Avery drove up in a town police car, lights flashing but without his siren. He pulled alongside and rolled down his window. "You have an accident?"

I nodded. "Guy hit me. Dinged my front end. He took off, and I think he crashed into a house up there." I pointed in the direction the boy had run.

"Yeah. We got a bunch of calls. Look, why don't you go on home and stop by the station and fill out a report tomorrow. I gotta see what's going on up there that's got everyone so excited."

Emma and I got in my banged up car and took a round-about path to her house in order to avoid the accident scene. I grabbed my Pentax camera from the back seat. "I'm going to walk down there and take a look. Want to come along?"

Emma gave an enthusiastic nod. "Sure. Wouldn't miss this."

By the time we walked three blocks back to the flashing lights, Gus Kopetsky was on the scene. So too was the town's dual purpose ambulance / hearse.

Clint guided a staggering driver of the car back to the ambulance. He leaned unsteadily on Clint for support. A crimson river poured across the driver's face from a gash across his nose. Clint handed the driver off to the ambulance crew and walked back toward me. As Clint got closer, I noticed a big grin spread across his face.

"I think Homer outdid himself this time." Clint said. "He got two cars, not counting yours, and knocked out the four by four posts holding up John and Harriett Budka's porch roof. Brought the whole thing right down."

Clint was now laughing.

"Anyone hurt?"

"Nah. I mean Homer got a bloody nose and may have banged up his knee, but he'll be okay when he sobers up. That nose will sting for a while, though."

"You know this guy?"

"Sure. Homer Shaw. Every few months he gets liquored up and gets his hands on the keys to his daddy's old Studebaker and takes off. Funny thing is he never gets so drunk that he grabs the keys to his daddy's new Caddy. It's always the junker. Anyway, that's what he did tonight. He's pretty drunk."

"He's done this before."

"Sure. Lots of times. Usually he ends up in a ditch or against a pole. He hasn't hit somebody's car in a couple of years."

"And people are okay with that?"

Clint shrugged. "Not exactly okay. But Homer's dad always pays everybody for the damages. He owns the furnace plant on the edge of town and one of the biggest farms in the county. Everybody always gets paid. Homer's a good guy. A little slow, but he doesn't mean any harm.

"Does he have insurance so I can file a claim?"

Clint laughed again. "Homer doesn't have insurance. He doesn't even have a license."

I could feel my mouth hanging open.

Clint gave me a nod, obviously entertained by my reaction. "Can't get one. He's legally blind."

For the second time that night I said, "You're shitting me?"

Emma broke out in laughter that built in waves to the point she was gasping for breath.

"What's so damned funny?" I said.

She spoke through halting breaths. "You got hit by a drunk. Who has no insurance. And he doesn't have insurance because he has no license. And he doesn't have a driver's license because he's blind." She snorted. "A fucking drunk blind man. God, you know how to pick 'em."

"I didn't pick him. And I don't think it's so damned funny. If he's blind, how does he drive?"

Clint unsuccessfully tried not to laugh. "He's not stone blind. But his vision is bad enough that he's legally blind. Even draws a blind pension from social security."

I kicked at the ground. "Shit. I can't believe this."

Clint suppressed his laughter, but still had a big smile across his face. "I cited him for drunk driving and driving without a license. You show up in traffic court next week and the judge will make him pay for the damages to your car. You want to take a couple of pictures for the paper before we tow the car off what's left of that porch?"

I nodded, pulled out my 35-millimeter Pentax and walked toward the Budka's house.

A week later I showed up in traffic court along with the Budkas, who owned the other two cars that were damaged. The judge called the case, nodded with familiarity at the name on the file. Homer, now wearing an ill-fitting brown suit and Coke-bottle thick glasses, walked in front of the table that served as the dais for the judge.

"Homer, if you want to stay out of jail, you got to pay for all the damage you caused. That includes Mr. and Mrs. Budka's cars and the cost of putting up a new porch. And you have to pay for Mr. Carlson's damage, too." The judge looked at some estimates that had been provided, did some math, and announced the totals that Homer would have to pay.

A tall distinguished looking man in his early 70s stood from his seat in the front row. He spoke to the judge in a slow deep baritone voice. "George, I'm good for whatever damage my son caused. Give me a day or two to transfer some money, and I'll write the checks."

The judge gave Homer's father a sympathetic smile. His tone was friendly. "Henry, you gotta either keep him away from the bottle or keep him away from your keys. If you don't, one of these days he's going to hurt somebody. That happens, and I'll have to send the boy to jail."

Henry nodded. "I'm doin' my best, George. I'm doin' my best."

Before the end of the week, someone dropped a check by the newspaper office. If was for $100 more than the amount of the repair bill for my car. Neatly printed on the check reference line was "for repairs and inconvenience."

#

A week after the court hearing, I was spending a lazy Saturday afternoon sitting in the light coming through my bedroom window, trying to finish a John LeCarre novel. My thoughts wandered and I gazed out the window. Three boys about eleven or twelve years old were throwing a football in the grassy area on the other side of the railroad tracks.

I hadn't thrown a football around in years. I put down my book, grabbed my jacket and headed outside.

"Mind if I throw the ball around with you?" I said. "Sure," came a chorus from all three. One of them tossed me the ball and took off running. I hit him in stride with a perfect spiral.

"Nice throw," said the boy standing closest to me. "You're the newspaper guy, aren't you?"

I recognized him as the boy who had come up to me the night Homer Shaw hit my car.

"That's me," I said. "You can call me Zach. What's your name?"

"Ritchie Kyle. That's Sammy Moore over there, and Billy Young is the one you threw the ball to."

I nodded, and caught the ball Billy threw back. I arched a long pass toward Sammy. It wasn't quite as pretty as the first one and flew over his outstretched arms.

"Your name sounds familiar," I said.

"My brother Davey is the star on the high school basketball team."

"Football your game?"

Ritchie hung his head and shook it. "I'm not good at anything. Davey's six feet seven and can jump like a nigger. I ain't even gonna be six feet tall."

"Wouldn't use that term as a regular habit. Lot of people take offense."

Richie shrugged. "Ain't nobody around here cares."

I threw the ball with the boys until my arm ached with fatigue.

"All I've got for today," I said, throwing my last pass. "Thanks for letting me throw the ball around with you."

I headed back to my apartment and my novel. I was still a few steps from my apartment door when I heard the single whelp of a siren. A Stratton police car pulled up to where the boys were still throwing the football. Gus Kopetsky got out of the car.

Gus yelled and the three boys walked up to him. Gus held out his hand and said something. Ritchie stepped forward and handed his football to the town marshal.

Gus turned so he was facing in my direction. I was about sixty yards away, but was certain he didn't see me. His booming voice carried across the distance. I made out most of the words.

"This is railroad property," Gus yelled. "You little bastards stay out of here. I catch you here again, I'll arrest all of you for trespassing. Now get your asses home."

The boys dropped their heads like scolded puppies. Sammy and Billy walked off. Ritchie stepped forward and held out his hand for the ball.

"What do you want?" Gus barked.

I thought Ritchie said, "My ball."

"Your ball?"

Gus moved faster than I imagined was possible. He pulled his 18-inch black flashlight out of his utility belt and swung it down hard on Ritchie's outstretched hands. I cringed at the sound of metal smacking flesh. Ritchie cried out.

"Cry, you little hillbilly bastard."

Gus tossed the ball onto the ground, pulled his service revolver from its holster and fired off two rounds into the ball.

The gunshots cracked through the afternoon silence. Gus laughed, got back in his car, and drove away. Ritchie looked over at remnants of his ball. With his head hanging, he walked off.

#

The next day was Sunday. I sat in the office typing up my weekly column. I wrote about Gus and the way he treated the three boys. Writing from anger was not a good practice. And I was pissed.

After I finished the column, I called up Roy Shoemaker at home. I read the column to him. He did not respond.

"Well?" I said.

"It's good writing," Roy said, his words slow and deliberate. In that instant, I knew the column was never going to see print.

"As a business decision, we can't run that. Not now."

"He's a bully," I said. "The town needs to know it."

"The town knows," Roy said.

My muscles tensed from the anger percolating inside me. “How do they know if we don’t tell them?”

"Community newspapers differ from daily papers," Roy said, his voice calm. “It's not just the number of times a week we publish. Our newspapers are where people read about their kids making the honor roll, or Aunt Bertha winning a blue ribbon for her pies. We don't want to walk into town and start picking fights with the town marshal. Barrett has a chunk of cash invested and they're in it for the long haul. You've only been there a couple of months. You're still an outsider. Hell, you'll always be an outsider. Down the road, there will be a story that makes the point you want to make. But this isn't the time. This isn't the one."

I didn't respond.

"You're a journalist. So am I. But this is a business, too."

"You write the checks," I said, and hung up without saying more. I picked up the typewritten pages from my desk and threw them in the trash. I grabbed my coat and headed for the VFW. I needed a beer. Maybe several.

#

A few days later I stopped by the high school to shoot a photo of the science fair winner. As I walked down a hallway, I saw Garrett Deiter.

"How are you doing after that vandalism episode?"

Dieter shrugged. "I put in some new security lights out at my house, but that's really for my wife. If these guys want to get my car, they'll find a way."

"You know the Kyle kids, don't you?"

Garrett grimaced. "A bad lot. All of them."

"I ran into Ritchie throwing a football the other day. He mentioned that his brother is a star player on the basketball team."

Garrett nodded. "I don't know Ritchie. He's not in high school, yet. But the dad's a drunk and the mom isn't much better."

"How good a ball player is Davey?"

"Damn good. He's got college scouts falling all over themselves. But if he's not careful, he's going to blow it. His grades are barely good enough to keep him on the team, and that's with teachers giving him a break. And he's flirted with getting kicked out of school."

"That bad?"

"Remember that episode just before my car got vandalized? The one where I suspended a couple of kids for fighting?"

I nodded.

"Davey Kyle was one of the boys."

"You think he was the one who tore up your car?"

"Him or his family. But the cops around here can't prove it. And the school board would fire me if I tried to expel him before the basketball season was over."

#

It was a week later when I saw Ritchie Kyle again. He was walking down Main Street as I came out of the drug store coffee shop. "Hey, Ritchie," I yelled out. The boy turned, his expression and posture showing a wariness. "Wait there a second." I dashed into my office and came back with a bag I was keeping until the next time I saw Ritchie.

"Here," I said, handing the bag to Ritchie.

He looked at me, his face screwed into obvious distrust. Hesitating at first, he took the bag and peered inside. Even after seeing what was inside, his expression did not change. He pulled out a new football.

"I saw what Gus did to your ball," I explained. "Maybe if I hadn't been throwing the ball with you, it wouldn't have happened."

Ritchie stood with his weight on the back of his feet, distrust painted across his face.

"It's okay," I said. "No strings. It's yours."

Ritchie rubbed his hands across the ball, getting the feel of the shiny leather. In a small voice, he said, "Thanks."

I nodded. "So, how's your hand where Gus hit you with that mag light?"

Ritchie looked down. "I been hit harder." He turned and continued down the street.

FOURTEEN – *Meeting the Folks*

June 1973

June 7, 1973: NEW YORK, NY (WIRE SERVICES): Leaving the field in the dust by 31-lengths, Secretariat ran into history Saturday, winning the Belmont Stakes and becoming horse racing's first Triple Crown winner in 25 years.

In winning, Secretariat ran the fastest 1 ½ mile horse race ever.

My parents want to meet you." Kate sat across from me sipping a brandy. We were at La Villa, a new Italian place on Pulaski Road, where we stuffed ourselves with eggplant parmigiana and mostaccioli.

"That sounds ominous," I said, smiling.

Kate laughed. "Not so much. They're not the intimidating type."

"When?"

Kate twisted the lemon strip that the waiter served alongside the demitasse. "A couple of weeks. I told you about our cabin on Green Lake, didn't I?"

I nodded.

"They invited us up for a cookout and some fishing."

"I've never gone fishing," I admitted with more than a bit of embarrassment.

Kate reached across the table and gently patted my cheek. "That's okay, baby," she said. "Momma will put the worm on the hook for you."

I rolled my eyes as the waiter brought the bill.

#

On a Saturday morning two weeks later, we were sipping gas station coffee and listening to WLS out of Chicago as we traveled north on Interstate 41. Two hours into the trip, someplace past Fond du Lac, Kate reached over and turned off the radio.

"We need to talk," she said. "I should have told you this sooner."

"You're pregnant? I said, smiling. But when she didn't smile back I wondered if she was.

"My folks are, well, conservative," Kate said, a hesitancy in her voice I did not recall hearing before.

"They still think Nixon's the one?"

"Not that type of conservative," she said with a nervous laugh. "Okay, maybe that type of conservative, but they're, uh, well . . . We need to sleep in separate rooms."

I laughed. "Seriously?"

"Yes, seriously. I got you a pair of pajamas"

"Pajamas? I haven't worn pajamas since I was eight years old."

Kate gave a mischievous smile. "They're purple with big yellow bananas. Kinda sexy."

"Bananas?"

"Banana pajama." She gave a laugh, then again turned serious. "Look, they know we're sleeping together. I mean, I didn't say, 'Hey mom, I'm fucking Zach.' But they don't have to be wizards to figure that out. It's just that they're, well, old fashioned like that."

"You mean they don't think people should have sex without getting married first."

"I don't want things to get off on the wrong foot," she said. "I want them to be comfortable with you. To like you."

"And if I'm schtooking their daughter . . ."

Kate punched me in the arm. It was hard enough to deliver a message.

"This is serious for me. You and your mom aren't on best terms, but what my parents think means a lot to me. I want them to like you and respect me."

I leaned toward Kate and kissed her cheek. "I'll be the perfect gentleman." After a pause, I added, "As long as I don't sleep with your dad."

#

Doris and Jim Billings were not what I expected. Rather than austere humorless zealots, wearing homespun clothing, they were cheerful and welcoming. Doris greeted me with a two-armed hug that seemed to last well over a minute. Jim gave me a firm handshake and a clap on my back, followed by a joke that nudged to the edge of off color.

Kate's parents owned a two-bedroom cabin at the edge of Green Lake, a deep fresh-water lake surrounded by densely wooded rolling hills. I did not spend much time in the water growing up, and except for wading in Lake Michigan, had never been in a lake. But Kate was immediately at home. As soon as she stepped onto the dock, she ran full speed and launched herself into the water, hitting with a prodigious cannon ball splash.

Kate was at ease, as if the lake water cleansed her soul of all concerns about stock portfolios and returns on investment. Everything was stripped away except for the endless summer of a twelve-year-old girl. The way she moved, the way she smiled, the way she gleamed like sunlight on sparkling water. I loved her so much I almost forgot to breathe.

We spent Saturday afternoon swimming in the frigid water off a small dock. My fingers turned to withered prunes and cold stung my feet, but still we stayed in the water. In late afternoon, Jim and Kate taught me to fish. We used worms and fished from the dock. I sucked up my manly resolve and baited my own hook, but only to avoid the humiliation of asking Kate. I stood there with my line dangling in the water, staring at a nearly motionless bobber, while Jim and Kate pulled in a half dozen nice sized bass. I finally hooked a fish, but when it pulled in, I found a fish about the size of my hand. A sunfish, Jim told me.

Kate pulled out her camera and took a photo of me and my first fish. We tossed it back, but Jim fried up the fish he and Kate had caught. We ate sitting around a weather-worn picnic table at the edge of the water.

After dinner, we sat around a fire on the shore, passing around a bottle of Southern Comfort, taking turns drinking directly from the bottle. I liked Doris and Jim more and more. Darkness came quick when the sun disappeared. The sky filled with more stars than I had ever seen. A little after ten, Jim doused the embers in the fire pit and stirred the ashes. We retreated inside the cabin. In Chicago, the night was just starting. Here, the temperature dropped with the sun and the sky filled with stars. It seemed so much later.

Kate assigned me the pullout couch in the living room. Dutifully I changed into the banana pajamas. The ridiculous clown suit image in my head reflected at me in the mirror. I couldn't help but laugh. Heading toward my couch-bed for the night, I passed Kate's room. The door was mostly closed, but light shined through a two-inch gap. I overheard Kate and her dad talking.

"I like him," Jim said. "Your mom does, too. I think you've got a good one."

There was a pause and I imagined Kate giving her dad a goodnight kiss. "I kinda like him, too," she said.

The next morning, we rose at sunrise and walked out to the dock, where we caught breakfast. Still the fish I caught were disappointingly small, only a bit bigger than my hand. Kate apparently caught the look on my face.

"Those are bluegill," she said. "That's about as big as they get. But they're great eating."

An hour later, as we ate our way through mounds of fried fish and Johnny cakes, I realized she was right. Whether it was the freshness of the fish, or the briskness of the morning air, or my pride in eating what I caught, or maybe just being with Kate. Whatever the reason, it was the best breakfast of my life.

Kate and I took another swim off the dock. When we returned, Jim said, "Next time you come up here, we'll get out the boat and go fishing for some of the big ones – walleye, muskies, lake trout. Guy caught a world record inland lake trout a few years ago right out there." He pointed toward the expanse of the lake. "He's got to have a big brother."

Kate gave my arm a squeeze. I took Jim's offer as another sign of acceptance.

After lunch, we started back to Chicago and the far different world that waited for both of us.

On the drive back, Kate slipped off her seat belt and slid up against me. I put my arm around her like a high school boy driving his best girl.

She kissed my cheek. "I had a wonderful time. Thanks for coming."

"I did too," I said, and turned in my seat enough to give her a quick kiss. "I really like your parents."

"They like you, too," she said. After a few minutes, she added, "I love you." It was the first time she had said the words.

She soon fell asleep, resting her head against my shoulder. I smiled until my face ached as the miles back to Chicago rolled by.

FIFTEEN – *More Than A Game*

December 3, 1975, WASHINGTON, D.C. (WIRE SERVICES): By a 213-203 vote, the House approved a $2.3 billion bailout loan for financially crippled New York City. Without federal assistance, America's largest city will go into default on December 11.

Ohio Congressman Delbert L. Latta, who opposed the bailout, said, "I don't think I have any moral obligation to the people of New York City whatsoever."

I never covered sports, not even for my high school newspaper. But Roy had made it clear that when a town has only 1,800 people and the high school gym seats 3,000, covering high school sports, particularly basketball, is a priority.

On a Friday night in late November, the entire town and then some turned out for the opening game of the high school basketball season. Expectations for the team were high. The coffeeshop crowd chattered about a conference championship and the school's first trip to the regional in a dozen years. The team returned all five starters and two key substitutes from last year's sectional runner up. Excitement centered on Davey Kyle, not only the team's best player, but in the collective minds of local fans, the best player in the state. Top level college coaches and scouts filled the front row for opening night.

When the game started, fans were not disappointed. Neither were the college scouts.

Standing six-feet seven inches, Kyle ran the court with a graceful stride that outdistanced everyone else on the court. Around the basket, his athletic ability was obvious even to the unskilled eye. He grabbed rebounds above the rim before other players even thought about jumping. He drove by defenders and elevated over them. His jump shot was artistry in motion, a smooth stroke of perfection. He played at a level far above anyone else on the court.

At the end of the third quarter, Stratton led rival Amelia High 61-47. I checked with the scorekeeper sitting next to me. Davey had 29 points and 12 rebounds. With a full quarter to play, no one in the arena doubted the end result.

Then it all went to hell.

Amelia scored three straight baskets and a free throw to cut the lead in half. Basil Rowe, a portly balding man who looked as if he had done nothing athletic in his life, coached Stratton. Red faced, he called a time out.

When play resumed, Davey grabbed the in-bound pass and drove the length of the court, knocking down three defenders like bowling pins. The referee blew the whistle and signaled charging. Amelia scored again. The next time down the court, while a teammate stood unguarded under the basket, Davey forced a shot while guarded by three players. On the return trip down the floor, Davey tried to block a shot. The referee called yet another foul. In frustration, Davey slammed the ball to the court. The referee added a technical foul.

When the parade ended, the score was tied.

Rowe, his face turning purple, called another time out. While the coach barked his anger at the players, Davey looked around the arena, oblivious to whatever his coach said. Rowe reached out with a fat stubby hand and grabbed Davey's arm.

The next move was so quick it barely registered with the eye. The punch landed hard on the coach's mouth driving him back and over the bench. An audible gasp swept through the crowd followed by a stunned silence. Everyone near the bench froze, mouths gaping open. Rowe lay flat on his back, blood streaming from his mouth. Davey stood over him, his hands still in fists, spewing a barrage of obscenities.

An assistant coach stepped between Davey and Rowe. Two players closed around Davey, trying to calm him, but with no effect.

Gus Kopetsky and Kenny Wyman stood at one end of the gym. They were nominally providing security, but in reality, their primary job was to keep people with street shoes from walking on the court for which they got to watch the game for free. When the commotion started, they seemed unable to respond. Garrett Deiter and the two referees reacted immediately. Garrett pushed his way toward the scene while the game referees ran across the court, one already signaling Davey's ejection from the game.

Garrett reached the bench, forcefully grabbing Davey's arm. The towering boy pulled his other arm back, ready to strike the principal. A referee lunged forward and snagged the upraised arm. Garrett stared at Davey, as the player showered him with profanity-laced epithets. Gus and Kenny finally arrived, both looking confused.

"Get him into the locker room," Garrett said, through clinched teeth. "Then get him out of here."

Each officer grabbed one of Davey's arms and pulled him toward the nearest exit. Davey gave a quick jerk to free himself, then walked out ahead of the cops. As he reached the exit, Davey turned and yelled back at Garrett. "You think your car was bad, man. You just wait. You just wait."

It took several minutes to calm the mayhem. When the game continued, the enthusiasm and excitement had vanished. With their coach holding a blood-stained towel to his swollen mouth, Stratton sleepwalked through the final minutes. Amelia won, 78-66.

Back at the office after the game, I wrote quickly, not sure whether the story was about basketball or the fight. Afterwards, I met Emma at the VFW. The fight was the talk of the bar, much to the frustration of a local four-piece country band desperately trying and failing to stay in tune. I was poor company. My side of our conversation was a series of monosyllabic grunts that I thought passed for words. My muscles were tight like I had been in a fight myself. But Emma remained patient with me. After a half dozen beers. I started to relax.

#

The following Monday morning, I sat in my usual place in the Perry Drugstore coffee shop. Talk among the locals centered on Davey Kyle's tirade. Opinions varied.

"Suspend the kid for a couple of games, just so we get him back before conference games start."

"They don't need to suspend him. We can't win if he doesn't play. Give him some detention."

"Make him run laps 'till he throws up. That worked when I played."

"Can't blame the boy for wanting to win. They ought to fire the damned coach. He let things get out of hand."

I was on my second cup of coffee when Gus walked in. His belly was pulled in and his chest puffed out like the cock of the walk. He was bursting with news, trying to hold it until he was the center of attention. But he couldn't wait. Before he reached the first table, he blurted it out.

"They kicked that Kyle boy out."

"Kicked him off the team?" It was Howard Gudgel, owner of the IGA at the end of Main Street.

"He's not only off from the team. He's expelled."

Conversation in the coffee shop stopped.

Gus gave a confirming nod. "Deiter met with the school board yesterday. He's gone."

"For good?"

"For good."

There was a long silence. Bill Olsen finally spoke. "Well there goes the whole goddamn season."

SIXTEEN – *You Can See It From Here*

December 10, 1975, WASHINGTON, D.C. (WIRE SERVICES): The United States Government filed suit today against Penn Central Railroad and four other bankrupt railroads, accusing them of selling company assets designated for Consolidated Rail Corporation.

Known as Conrail, the new for-profit government corporation will take over selected routes and assets of the bankrupt railroads to insure essential rail service throughout the Northeast and Midwest.

On my way to the first town board meeting in December, snowflakes danced through the beams of my headlights. It was the first snow of the season. I made a mental note to put a short paragraph on the front page. This was not news in Chicago, but it would be the talk of the drug store coffee shop. That made it news in Stratton.

The town board meetings were routine – so routine I wrote much of the story in advance, most of it based on the last town board story. I would add a sentence here or there reporting citizen complaints about barking dogs or unfixed pot holes, but the sameness was remarkable.

The board met in a small assembly room that took up the half of the town hall not used by the police. At the front of the room was a small raised platform with a dull table marred with decades of use. Four well-worn chairs were arranged around the scarred table, three for board members and one for Clerk-Treasurer Orville Vehorn.

The public gallery had eight rows of uncomfortable folding wooden seats, empty except for the occasional complaining citizen. "We salvaged them from the old movie theater," Orville bragged, with frugal pride. "Didn't pay a dime for 'em."

I still thought the town overpaid.

Vehorn was an odd little man right out of a Charles Dickens novel. He was short with an enormous round belly supported by spindly legs. He wore thick glasses resting on his narrow pointed nose. Whenever he was called upon to read something, he removed his glasses, pulled the paper within inches of his eyes, and contorted his entire face into a prune-like squint.

The Board members were Bill Olsen, the Christmas Shop owner, Hank Pemberton, owner of the town lumberyard, wood mill and grain elevator, and Sam Bauserman, a local insurance agent.

The meetings droned into predictable routine. There was a rash of stolen street signs that Gus Kopetsky attributed to Halloween pranksters. The board shared its indignation at the cost of a new fuel pump on one of the police cars, but approved the expenditure. Orville Vehorn gave a monotone reading of the city's monthly financial report that only he seemed to understand or care about.

I began thinking the few snowflakes in my headlight beams might be the lead story for this week's newspaper.

The meeting moved on to new business, and there was nothing listed on the agenda. Orville packed away his papers, and so I folded my notebook closed. At one end of the table, Hank Pemberton held up his hand. Between his fingers he held a letter.

"I got this in today's mail," he said, his face glum. He waited until everyone had turned their attention to him. I flipped my notebook back open.

"This is a letter from Congressman Bohannan's office." He put down his hand, then took a sheet of paper from the envelope. He read the letter out loud.

To: Mr. Henry Pemberton, President, Stratton Town Board:

Dear Mr. Pemberton:

As you know, in the past two years, several railroads serving the eastern and Midwestern sections of the United States have filed bankruptcy. The largest by far of those is the Penn Central

Railroad. This has threatened the very existence of rail service in this part of the country.

Congress has determined that continued rail service is vital to the national interest, including the national defense. Therefore, a Congressional Study Committee has been working with the United States Bankruptcy Court for the Southern District of New York to develop a workable plan that will preserve future railroad service. This has led to the inevitable conclusion that railroads burdened with unprofitable routes cannot survive.

A new publicly owned company is being formed to take over ownership and operation of rail routes that can operate profitably. Unprofitable routes will be abandoned.

Stratton is served by three railroad lines, all of which are operated by companies in bankruptcy. These lines serve small businesses in Stratton and the surrounding area, including the Stratton Grain Elevator, Pemberton Wood Mill, Foundation Home Furnaces and the Liberty Station Grain Elevator. It is becoming clear that the evolving plans will not include the three rail lines in Stratton.

I will continue to work for continued rail service for Stratton, but I do not think those efforts will be fruitful. Stratton and its businesses need to prepare for a future that will not include rail service.

Sincerely,

Congressman Robert V. Bohannan

Silence hung in the air like death.

Bill Olsen shook his head and then turned toward Hank Pemberton. "Geez Hank, what are you going to do? Can you do all your shipping by truck?"

"Hell, I don't know Bill," Hank said, his hand going to his forehead then sliding to the top of his head. "With fuel prices going sky high and the oil shortage, I have a hard time just getting the grain from the field to the elevator. It takes five trucks, maybe six, to move one rail car of grain. During harvest, we run up to fifty cars out of here a week. That would be 250 truckloads. I don't even think I can find that many trucks. Even if I could, how I do I make a profit?"

Glum settled over the room, but there wasn't much to say. Stratton, like hundreds of other small towns across the Midwest, was losing its rail service. A handful of bankers, lawyers and railroad executives in big offices were looking at spreadsheets, expense projections, cost per mile, and return on investment. They saw unprofitable lines. They did not see hundreds of small towns dependent on railroad service.

Without saying much of anything, the Town Board adjourned. There really wasn't much to say.

I tried to talk to Hank Pemberton, but he waived me off. I chased after Sam Bauserman and caught him as he was getting in his car.

"How big an impact will this have on the town?" I asked.

Sam gave me a shrug and a grim smile. "One time when I was a kid, my dad took the family camping out west. We were someplace in Texas, watching the sun set across the scrublands. My dad turned and said, 'This may not be the end of the world, but you can see it from here.' I guess that's what it feels like right now."

I went back to my office and wrote the lead story for the front page. "Town Faces Rail Closings." The first snowflakes didn't make the newspaper.

SEVENTEEN – *I Carry Your Heart*

September 1973

September 21, 1973, NATCHITOCHES, La. (WIRE SERVICES): Singer-songwriter Jim Croce was killed in a plane crash last night, along with the pilot and four members of Croce's band. The plane crashed on takeoff following a concert at nearby Northwestern State University.

All summer Kate and I talked of taking a vacation together. We tried to coordinate schedules and budgets, but only managed a couple of get-a-way weekends in Wisconsin at her parents' cabin. As Labor Day approached, the window for taking a real vacation was getting narrow. Kate's high-pressure season ramped up in October. After that, there was no chance of getting away until January.

So, on a lazy Sunday afternoon in early August, we took our calendars and a stack of travel brochures to a small bistro a few blocks from her apartment. We looked for a place neither of us had been, a place we explore together. Over plates of pasta and two bottles of chianti, we settled on a mid-September vacation in Key West.

I called up the travel editor at the Examiner. She connected me to a travel agent who was an expert on the Keys. Two days later, I rented a bungalow with a garden pool a half block off of Duval Street.

#

We headed to Key West and left the rest of the world behind. No phone calls. No paperwork. No projects hanging over our heads. No worries about what loomed back in the office.

It was just us.

Mornings we lounged in bed, making love in golden sunlight that filtered through slotted blinds. We lay naked, letting the overhead fan dry beads of sweat. We spent our days strolling the shops along the narrow streets or lounging by the bungalow pool. Sunset found us at Mallory Square, watching the sun melt into the Gulf as the sky transformed from a palette of orange, pink, blue, and purple into a rich indigo. Nights were spent bar-hopping, drinking fruity rum concoctions and listening to troubadours playing for drinks and tips

Our third day on the island, we chartered a small sailboat with a single crewman. We sailed several miles off shore to Sand Key.

We swam and snorkeled along the reef, watching colorful fish dart among staghorn, brain, boulder and star coral. I swam next to Kate, sometimes our bodies lightly touching. At times, I allowed myself to drift behind her, admiring her shape as she glided among the coral and waving sea grasses as if it was her natural habitat. Her body moved with an effortless grace that I admired but could never emulate. With a flash of her fins, she would dive. I stayed just below the surface, breathing through my snorkel tube, watching her move among the coral thirty feet below.

The next day we rented our own boat, one with a motor, and retraced our path to Sand Key. This time we left our suits in the boat and swam lazily in the warm sparkling Gulf waters. Afterward we pulled onto a small island to make love, our heads apparently filled with images of Burt Lancaster and Deborah Kerr. But the reality of clinging sand and painful bites from what locals called no-see-ums, quickly dampened our zeal.

"This isn't working," Kate said with a laugh. We dashed into the water, rinsing off the biting insects. On the way back to Key West, we cut the engine and made love as the boat bounced on the gentle swells.

The last day, we spent the afternoon at the bungalow pool, sipping gin and tonics. We swam and sat in reclining chairs, our fingers intertwined, listening to the afternoon trade wind blow through the banana trees. An hour before sunset, we dressed and walked to Mallory Square. We found a spot by ourselves along the edge of the pier and watched as the sun melted. The last rays were fading when I turned to Kate.

"Would you consider moving in? Living with me?" I asked.

She looked at me with her emerald eyes, her face bronze from a week in the sun. She kissed me softly, holding the kiss. "Yes, Zach. There's nothing I want more." She gave me a quick kiss on the cheek followed by a playful smile. "But how do I tell my parents?"

"You're twenty-six years old and an investment analyst making more money than me. You work on billion-dollar deals. You can decide things like this for yourself." I looked out toward where the sun had disappeared. "Besides, they know we're fucking."

Kate smacked me on the back of my head and laughed. "Okay," she said. "But you have to tell my dad."

We kissed for a long time. "I carry your heart in my heart," I said, quoting a favorite poem. I had never said it to anyone before.

#

On the plane we discussed practical issues of our decision. We talked about our leases, when they expired, the penalties for breach, parking, utilities, commuting distance, who would fix meals, do laundry, clean the toilet. From the details of our discussion, she had considered the topic. With only two months left on my lease, we decided that me moving in with her was the most practical. When her lease was up the following spring, we would look for a place together.

Who would clean the toilet was left undecided.

Two weeks later, I moved in. I rented a small truck and bought a case of beer. A couple of buddies from the newspaper helped me load and unload my modest belongings. Hurley Meyers, the newspaper photographer, supervised and drank my beer.

I placed my deodorant and toothbrush next to hers with a trace of disbelief playing in the back of my mind. In the first two years after college, I lived with two girls. Neither time was there any expectation of a long-term relationship. They lasted three or four months, before we mutually parted ways.

This was different. Kate was different. If I was honest with myself, I knew I was different.

The night I moved in we made love slowly as if there was no time limit. Neither of us could stop smiling. Afterward, we turned to each other. Silly grins were still planted on our faces. We stared at each other until we broke into uncontrollable laughter.

#

I left it to Kate to tell her parents about our new living arrangements. Six weeks after I moved in, on one of those rare weeknights when we were both home, the phone rang as we were finishing dinner. It was Kate's mother. As they talked, I saw Kate's body go rigid, her face go pale and her hands drum nervously against her hip. I wondered something happened to her father. I moved toward her, but she waved me away.

After she hung up, she turned to me. "My mom and dad are coming to Chicago this weekend to do some early Christmas shopping."

"Good," I said. "I like your parents. We can all go out for dinner."

Kate looked at me, clearly trying to collect her thoughts. She finally blurted out, "They don't know yet, Zach."

"Don't know what?"

She took deep breath. "I haven't told them we're living together. Not yet."

I was surprised. It didn't seem like much of an issue. "You should probably tell them before they get here."

"They expect to spend the night here," she said.

"It will be a little crowded. I guess they can take the bed. You take the couch, and I'll sleep on the floor."

"You don't understand. I . . ." There was a long pause. "I was raised a good upstanding Methodist. My parents, I don't know how they'll react to their little girl living with someone." There was another long pause. "I'm afraid I'm going to disappoint them terribly, and I hate doing that."

"You drink, you smoke, and you cuss like a sailor. You really believe that your parents think you're a virgin?" My words came out sharp, my irritation evident.

I saw the hurt on her face. "That's Chicago me. My parents know the Wisconsin me."

"You just need to be who you are, not try to be different for different people. I'm sure they'll still be proud of you."

"This living together isn't something in their frame of reference. For them, only 'those type of girls' had sex before marriage."

I shook my head. "They're not so naïve. You're grown up. You do grown-up things. You make grown up decisions. They have to live with that."

"I'm their only daughter," she said, a quiver in her voice. "I don't want them to think of me like some type of harlot. It's different for you. You're a man. But I care about my parents' opinion of me."

"What do you want me to do? Move out?" I realized I had raised my voice.

Kate turned her back to me, her arms crossed. I heard her crying. Never before had I seen her cry. I walked up and put my arms around her. She shrugged, trying to free herself from my embrace, but I continued to hold her.

"I'm sorry," I said, quietly. We stood there for a long moment. I added, "You handle it the way you want. If it would make it easier on you, I can crash for the weekend on the couch over at Hurley Meyers' place. I'm fine with it." I kissed her on the back of the neck. "I love you. I don't want you to be upset."

Kate turned and we kissed. She leaned her face against my chest and pulled me tight. We stood that way for a long time.

"I can be pretty self-centered at times," I whispered. "If I interfered in your relationship with your parents, you would never forgive me. I don't want that."

Later that evening, Kate pulled me next to her as she called her parents. She told them that I had moved in with her. They weren't surprised.

"It's not what we grew up with," I overheard her mother say. "But times have changed. We're still coming, but we'll just get a hotel room."

"Thanks for understanding, mom."

"Now you and Zach are going to get married, aren't you?"

"I love you," Kate said into the phone. She hung up leaving the question unanswered.

EIGHTEEN – Pigstickers and Hillbillies

December 23, 1975: NEW YORK, NY (WIRE SERVICES): Pete Rose, whose hard-nosed play led the Cincinnati Reds to the 1975 World Series championship, today was named Sports Illustrated's Sportsman of the Year.

In making the selection, the magazine wrote: "We honor Cincinnati's Pete Rose in whose person are combined so many of the qualities of excellence that merit his selection as Sportsman of the Year."

I didn't trust technology. I didn't even like my state-of-the-art IBM Selectric typewriter, preferring my old Underwood manual I carted around since high school.

The powers at Barrett Newspapers had a different view. They were converts at the shrine of newspaper technology. Every office in every Barrett-owned newspaper was equipped with IBM Selectric typewriters with a special typeface ball that allowed typed pages to be read by a computer. Optical character readers eliminated the need for typesetters. They were let go on the day the new computerized equipment became operational. Some had been with the company more than twenty years.

Gone too from Barrett's production facilities were traditional hot lead presses, mechanical behemoths that took a small army of printers and mechanics to keep running. In their place stood new offset presses. Less than a quarter of the size of traditional presses, they operated with a fraction of the number of employees, and consequently at a fraction of the expense.

The Barrett business model called for purchasing the latest equipment and centralizing production in a few locations. Presses ran on a 24/7 basis. From a business perspective, the strategy was brilliant. From the standpoint of putting out a fine-crafted product, it stunk.

The centralized location of the press and the coordination with other newspapers meant early deadlines. For a newspaper reporter used to hitting deadlines with the latest breaking news, it was frustrating. For a weekly, a breaking story that took place two hours after deadline would not be on the newsstand for nine days.

The centralized system also meant that the newspaper's editor did not review a proof copy before printing. Instead, the newspapers depended upon near minimum-wage proofreaders reviewing a dozen or more weekly newspapers and shoppers, none of which they had any personal connection to. Their only interest was a paycheck that barely exceeded minimum wage.

It was only a matter of time until the system would bite us in the ass.

#

As the football season wound down, Garrett Deiter sent me a note that included a magazine article about Tony Abbott, a Stratton High School graduate selected as a second team Small College All-American. Garrett included a photo of Abbott in his high school uniform. It merited the lead story on the sports page.

I made a few phone calls, getting a quote from the kid's mom and a comment from his high school football coach. I typed up the story and sent it off along with the photo slotted for the next issue.

When the newspaper arrived Wednesday afternoon, I gave it a quick read, making sure stories were in the right place. Because I wrote, edited and proofed everything except the columns by the three sisters, I seldom read the newspaper once in print. Shirley, though, read through the paper as soon as we received a copy. She vigilantly rooted out every misspelled name, misplaced comma and typo, marking each with a red marker, then placing it in the center of my desk. But Shirley never read the sports page. So, it wasn't until Thursday night I learned of a problem. A big problem.

"Quite a story on that football player," Emma said as she came to my table to take my order that night.

I nodded, my mind focused on choosing between the fried chicken and the roast beef Manhattan special.

"Never seen a story before about how many asses somebody snagged."

I looked up, thinking I must have misheard her. If the dictionary contained a photographic definition of a shit-eating grin, Emma was wearing it.

"What did you say?

"That story about the Abbott kid. I mean, it's interesting. Never thought I'd see a story reporting on how many asses a kid grabbed in college."

My appetite slipped away. "What are you talking about?"

"Hon, that story is all that anyone is talking about. Don't you read your own newspaper?"

I jumped up from the table. "You have a copy?"

Emma patted my arm. "Sit down, hon, and relax. I'll find a copy and bring you a beer. You might need it."

Five minutes later I was reading the story on the back page in disbelief.

Anthony "Tony" Abbott, a 1972 graduate of Stratton High School, was selected to the 1975 Small College All-American Team by College Football Now. Abbot, a senior, played wide receiver at national small college champion Wittenberg College.

Last season, Abbot led the nation catching 41 asses. He holds The Wittenburg College career record, grabbing 83 asses in his four year college career.

"It's a remarkable accomplishment," said Stratton coach John Boles. "He's the best ass receiver we've ever had at Stratton."

I dropped the newspaper on the table. I couldn't decide whether to throw up or go to the bar and start drinking shots of straight bourbon.

Emma walked behind me, put her arm on my shoulder and leaned close to me. She gave me a small kiss, something she rarely did in the restaurant. "Look hon, people have been talking about this all day. They think it's funny. Tony's dad was in the bar earlier. He laughed so hard I thought he'd pee his pants."

I shook my head and drank my beer. And a second. And a third. I passed on the bourbon and headed home. All evening I kept picking up the paper and re-reading that story. I didn't find it funny.

The next morning, I called Roy Shoemaker. It took me three attempts before I reached him. I told him about the problem and how embarrassed I was to even show my face around town. Roy wasn't amused either.

By the end of the day, he tracked down the problem.

"Zach, I need you to take out that typing ball and clean it. There was a small stray mark on the typing ball. It might be dust or lint, or maybe a small blemish in the metal. I'm sending you a new typeball. You should get it Monday. This OCR stuff is so damned sensitive. Somehow the computer misread the text. It dropped some Ps when it scanned your story."

"The proofreaders should have caught it," I said. "Isn't that what you're paying those people for?"

"I know," said Roy, his voice full of resignation. He did not like this new system any better than me. "We're tracking down the responsible proof reader. We'll have a long talk with her."

#

But the college ass grabber wasn't the last production problem.

At the end of first semester, the high school held its Snow Prom. I took a photo of the Snow Prom queen, a lovely senior girl who wore an ice blue prom dress and a perfect smile. I slotted it for three columns under the banner on the front page. I marked the back of the print "Photo 1 p. 1 Snow Queen."

That same week, Miss Opal Zachary turned 100. She lived in the local nursing home, a dreary place that smelled of urine and disinfectant. Frail and confused, Opal did not comprehend why people gathered around her or why a decorated cake sat on the table in front of her. A nurse's aide told Opal that it was her birthday Opal responded with an uncomprehending gaze. I did my best to take a photo of her that showed some awareness, but was only marginally successful. I slotted the photo for page two, marking the back "Photo 2, p. 2 - 100th birthday."

Like every other week, layout sheets were used to tell production people where to place each photo. The reserved space was marked with an "X" and a description identical to the one written on the back of the photo. Getting a photo in the correct place required only matching up the descriptions.

I took Wednesday off that week. But when I saw the newspaper on Thursday, a day after it hit the newsstands, my mouth fell open. Opal Zachary's deep wrinkles and toothless grin stared back at me from the front page. The caption read "Gloria Tanner, Snow Prom Queen." Sure enough, on page two Gloria Tanner smiled brightly at me with a caption "Local resident turns 100."

#

But nothing matched what happened the last week in February.

Stratton wrapped up its basketball regular season on a Saturday night in an away game in Morton County. With the driving distance involved, it would be midnight or later before I got back to Stratton. It would be Sunday afternoon before I wrote the game story and processed the film. On Friday afternoon I sent in the sports page layout, marking the spot where the game story, box score and one photo would go. I marked the space for the photo, "Stratton game photo to come later."

On Sunday I wrote the story and developed the film. After reviewing the contact sheet, I picked out a photo to accompany the story. As usual, the company courier picked up the story and photo late Monday afternoon.

With the newspaper already put to bed and most town businesses closed on Wednesday afternoon, it was a good day for me to take off. It was nearly an hour's drive to the new mall in Merrillville. I shopped for some shirts, browsed the bookstore, and priced a new television. I caught a late afternoon movie by myself at the mall movie theater followed by dinner at a chain steakhouse. I got back to my apartment just after eight o'clock.

I was home about ten minutes when the phone rang. It was Gary Middleton, the teacher from my chess club. His voice sounded excited. "Zach, I know this is a stupid question, but have you seen this week's paper yet?"

"No. I've been gone all day."

"You need to get a copy and look at it. Sports page. I don't think it's what you intended."

"What is it?"

"Go get a copy. You have to see it to believe I'm not pulling your leg." Gary hung up.

A sense of dread sweeping through me, I grabbed my coat and keys.

I drove to Kopetsky's and bought a copy of the paper. I took it out to my car and turned on the dome light. I turned to the sports page and started reading through the stories. They looked fine. The stories were in the right place. No "P's" were omitted leaving embarrassing words. The correct photo was on the page.

Then I saw it. The caption.

"Shit!" I hit the steering wheel hard with my hand. "Shit!" Then "Shit! Shit! Shit! Shit!"

The photo showed a Stratton player grabbing a rebound. Under it was the caption.

"Hold for photo: Stratton Pigstickers vs. Bumblefuck Hillbillies."

I stared at it for a long moment trying to will the words to disappear.

What happened was obvious. Some smart ass in the paste up room put the remark on the page to hold the open space for a photo. During paste up, he failed to remove the placeholder caption and replace it with the correct caption.

Images swirled through my head. I saw people all around town picking up their mail and turning to the sports page to read about the season's last basketball game. Staring back at them would be the caption: "Stratton Pigstickers and Bumblefuck Hillbillies."

"Shit," I said again.

Every person in town would be offended. It crossed through my mind that I could go back to my apartment, pack up and sneak out of town before dawn. Before I had to face anyone.

"Shit."

I took several deep breaths in a futile effort to calm myself. With a ten-dollar bill in hand, I reentered the store and bought every issue of the Stratton Gazette sitting in the Kopetsky news rack. Karla, the obese late middle-aged clerk, looked at me with a peculiar grin. "Must be a picture of your kid in there."

"Something like that" I said with a forced smile.

I dashed back out and threw the copies in the trunk of my car. If they went in the trash, someone might retrieve them.

It could be worse, I told myself. The newspapers were delivered just before noon on Wednesday, and most stores in Stratton closed at noon. The IGA closed at six, so nothing more would be sold there tonight. If I got there when it opened at eight Thursday morning, I could buy whatever copies remained in the rack.

I came up with a plan to hit all the stores in town as they opened. The drug store at six when the coffee shop opened; IGA at eight; the hardware store at nine. I hoped I had enough cash. Thankfully the bank opened at eight if I needed more funds.

Subscribers accounted for most readers. They got their newspaper through the mail. A company van dropped off each week's papers at the Stratton Post Office on Wednesday afternoon. Local subscribers would receive their copy with the Thursday mail. I thought about following one of the local mail carriers and grabbing copies out of the mailbox, but I soon realized the folly of such a scheme. There was also something about tampering with the mails violating federal law.

Before I did anything else, I needed to call Roy. I reached him at home, interrupting his dinner.

"Shit," he said, as I explained the situation. It seemed to be a popular response. He added "goddamnit" for variety.

"How could this happen?" I said. "Isn't anybody looking at this before it goes to press?"

"I don't know what happened. When I find out, someone's going to lose their job. Maybe several someones."

Roy concurred about buying all the newsstand copies as soon as local stores opened. We came up with the outline of an apology for me to give when people called the office screaming about the obscenity in newsprint that invaded their homes. Perhaps even more worrisome was the reference to Stratton Pigstickers. It's one thing to slip with the F-word in the paper, and quite another to insult the entire readership.

"I'll call Ed Gordon as soon as we hang up," Roy said, referring to the associate publisher who had hired me. "We'll have to talk to Harrison Barrett, too. Call me at six tomorrow morning. We should have a plan to deal with this by then."

#

I was at the drug store coffee shop as soon as the waitress unlocked the door. I got a cup of coffee to go and picked up every copy of the Stratton Gazette from the news rack. The waitress looked at me, a quizzical expression painted on her face, but said nothing. She just took the money.

I got into the office a few minutes after six and called Roy.

He explained the plan decided upon by him, Ed Gordon and Harrison Barrett. "Buy every copy of the paper you can get your hands on," Roy said. "There's nothing to do about the copies in the mail. We are printing a corrected edition immediately. It will be on the newsstands and in the mail by this afternoon."

"I'll get on it," I said.

"Mr. Barrett drafted an apology that we'll put on page one with his byline. It will be on the corrected edition. The statement blames a production error. It also points out that you had nothing to do with the mistake. It includes an apology to you."

"Thanks," I said. "That will make it easier for me to walk down the street."

"I know. We're also requesting people who received the copies by mail to return them to us. If they do, we'll extend their subscriptions for three months for free."

"That should soothe some of those offended, but what happened?"

"I don't know yet. But as soon as the production staff is in, I'm going to find out who was working. Whoever put this in and the proof-reader are gone."

Roy gave me a script to use for irate phone calls. I hung up and waited for the onslaught.

I talked with Shirley as soon as she came in. I explained the situation without using the precise language, wondering if she would want a quarter in the cuss jar for each copy of the newspaper.

"I'll answer calls the rest of the week," I said. "You don't have to deal with this. If I'm out, take a name and number and tell them I will personally return their call before the end of the day."

But the angry calls never happened.

Gary Middleton, Gus Kopetsky and Bill Olsen called and gave me a hard time. I laughed off their efforts at humor, even though each one was like a drill hitting a raw nerve. Garrett Deiter called and let me know that the teachers were having a difficult time because students were passing around copies of the paper during class. He laughed. "Someone even posted a copy on the teachers' lounge bulletin board.

#

A week later the brouhaha simmered down. No one had mentioned anything about the Bumblefuck Hillbillies and Stratton Pigstickers for several days.

The following Thursday, the next edition was on news racks and in the hands of subscribers. The fiasco seemed to fade like the proverbial day-old newspaper and fish. That evening, on my way home, I stopped in Kopetsky's Convenience Store to pick up a frozen pizza and a six pack. Karla waited at the counter. She rang up my purchase, then asked, "Sure you don't want one of the new shirts?"

I looked at her, sure that my puzzlement showed. "What shirts?"

"Behind you on the table."

I turned. On a makeshift card table, in two stacks a foot high each, were bright yellow tee shirts. Silk screened across the chest in large black block letters were the words: "STRATTON PIGSTICKERS."

"Gus wanted to order a bunch that said Bumblefuck Hillbillies, but we talked him out of it. If you want one, you better get it now. That's our second order. First batch sold out same day we got them in. All the kids at the high school are wearing them."

I shook my head and walked back to pick up another six pack.

NINETEEN – *Fire in the Night*

January 20, 1976, LONDON, ENGLAND (INTERNATIONAL WIRE SERVICES): England's House of Commons today voted down a bill to outlaw caning of students at British schools.

Conservative Party MP Patrick Cormack referred to the effort as "specious do-gooding nonsense."

A wailing siren woke me from a sound sleep. As I tried to drag myself to consciousness, my first thoughts were of duck and cover drills in my grade school and the air raid sirens my hometown would blare on Tuesday mornings, preparing for a sneak attack by the Ruskies. But as I woke, I realized it was the Stratton Volunteer Fire Department siren.

Emma stirred next to me. "Damned siren," she said sleepily. "Wish they'd find a better way to signal the volunteers."

Emma was sleeping over after we spent a Friday evening enjoying my homemade meatballs and spaghetti, drinking beer and watching old movies on my new twenty-one-inch RCA color television. She showed up wearing a STRATTON PIGSTICKERS tee shirt and a shit-eating grin, neither of which came off until we went to bed.

I checked the clock. It was nearly 3 a.m. I was considering whether I really needed to get up to chase the fire truck when my phone rang. I walked into the living room without bothering to cover up.

"Carlson," I said.

"Zach, this is Jimmy over at the fire department. Thought you'd want to know, we just got called for a house fire. You know Garrett Deiter don't you?"

"Sure."

"Well it's his house. We gotta roll, but thought you might want to know."

I hung up the phone, flipped on the light and started getting dressed.

"What's up?" Emma asked, her voice still full of sleep.

"High School principal's house is on fire. You go ahead and stay. I'll be back in a couple of hours and fix breakfast."

Emma didn't respond. She rolled over and pulled the covers around her. I grabbed my camera bag and keys, turned off the light and took off.

#

The road was in total darkness, but the fire was easy to spot. Flames were visible for at least two miles. When I arrived, flames were still shooting through holes burned in the roof. It was obvious there was no saving the house.

Stratton's two fire trucks were on the scene, along with three pumper trucks from neighboring rural fire departments, several police cars and an ambulance. The firefighters were emptying their tankers in an effort to keep the fire from spreading to the detached garage and the propane tank that supplied heating fuel for the house.

I pulled my car haphazardly along the road, grabbed my camera and ran to the scene, snapping photos as I ran. I went through a full twenty-four shot roll of Tri-X 400 black and white film, guessing at my exposure settings and hoping for one or two useable shots.

I was standing in the front yard reloading when I saw Garrett Deiter walk from behind one of the fire trucks. Following behind was a woman and three kids ranging from about 4 to 12. They were all in nightclothes. I took a few more photos as the firemen seemed to get control of the blaze.

I snapped one last shot, then let my camera dangle from the strap around my neck. I walked to where Garrett stood by himself watching the flames slowly ebb into hot spots and glowing embers.

"You okay, Garrett?" I asked. "Your family okay?"

Garrett gazed at me, recognition slow to come in his dark faraway eyes. He nodded. "Yeah. Peggy and the kids are fine. Even the dog ran out with us." He shook his head and a small odd smile flashed on his face. "Don't think the gold fish made it, though. Lizzie will be upset by that."

I looked back at the house, then again turned to Garrett. "I have to cover this as a story. That's my job. But if there's anything I can do, if you guys need anything, just let me know."

Garrett nodded. "I appreciate that. I think we'll be okay. We've got insurance."

“You got a place to stay?”

“Peggy's parents live up in LaPorte. The firemen saved the garage and our cars. As soon as we get things straightened out here, we'll drive up there. Peggy used the phone at the neighbors and already called them. She told them to expect company for a few days while we figure out what's going on."

We stood there in silence for several minutes, watching the firemen go about their work.

"Any idea what happened?" I asked.

Red flashing lights rhythmically played off Garrett’s face. The flashing crimson added an angry hue to his grim expression.

"Yeah, I know," he said.

With a tilt of his head, he signaled for me to follow him. We stepped over several fire hoses and around a fire truck, walking to the side of the garage. "I don't think you can put this in the paper, but this makes it pretty obvious." He nodded toward the side of the garage.

The lights from the emergency vehicles illuminated the garage just enough to make it possible to read the message. Sprayed across the wall in bright red paint were the words, "Fuck you Deiter."

I took two photos of the writing on the garage. I looked around the base of the garage to see if there was an empty spray paint can, but I didn't see one.

"You can't print that, can you?" Garrett asked.

"Not without blacking out part of it," I said. "But I’d rather take the photo and not use it, than not take it and later want it. Did you see anything?"

"No. We were all asleep. We're lucky we have our dog. He started barking and woke us up. If it had been five minutes later, I don't know that we would have gotten out."

Garrett's veneer of control faded. His eyes blinked, and I could see a quiver at the edge of his mouth. I thought he was going to begin crying, but he took a deep breath. He set his jaw again, and his composure returned. We walked back toward where his family and neighbors were gathered among hoses and fire equipment.

"You know who did it?" I asked.

"Sure, I know. It was that damned Kyle boy, the one I kicked off the basketball team – kicked out of school. It was him or his family. They did my car the last time, but the cops couldn't prove it. Now this. But the cops around here won't be able to prove this, either."

For a long moment we stood, listening only to the crackling of the flames, the whoosh of water through hoses, and the periodic shouting of directions from whoever was in charge of the firefighters.

"What are you going to do?" I finally asked.

"Don't know," he said. Garrett looked out toward the ruins of his house, then back toward where his family was huddled. He kicked once at the dirt, then walked off to join his family.

#

I spent Monday morning developing and printing photos from the Deiter fire and writing a story for the front page. Just before noon, the phone rang. Shirley answered and a few seconds later was at my doorway. "It's Gary Middleton. Says he's a friend of yours."

It was the first time Gary had called me during school hours. I grabbed the handset and punched the blinking button on the phone.

"Hey Gary, what's up?"

Gary didn't bother with a greeting. "Garrett Deiter just resigned."

"What?"

"Yeah. I guess he came into the school before anyone was here, took all of his personal stuff out of his office. He left a note for the superintendent. From what I hear, it just said, "I resign effective immediately."

"How do you know this?"

"It's all over the school. They sent all the students to the gym an hour ago, and got the teachers together in the auditorium. Bill Simmons, the assistant principal, told us. He said Garrett was already gone and would not be returning. Garrett also left a note asking that none of the teachers try to contact him."

I scrambled to find a piece of paper and a pen and scribbled some notes.

"I gotta go, Zach," Gary said. "But I thought you should know."

"Thanks for the call." I hung up the phone and sat back in my chair, stunned.

That afternoon, I confirmed my information with the school superintendent. He also told me that Bill Simmons would now be acting principal. I asked about how to contact Garrett, but the superintendent said he didn't know. He was a bad liar, but I decided not to push the issue.

I spent forty minutes looking through old issues of the Gazette before I found the article when Garrett was hired as principal four years earlier. The article had a reference to his wife including her maiden name of Brodner. I called information and got the seven listed numbers for Brodners in the LaPorte phone book. After only two calls, I found a relative who gave me the phone number of her parents.

A man answered the phone. It wasn't Garrett, and I assumed was Peggy's father. When I asked for Garrett, he put the phone down without comment. After more than five minutes, the receiver at the other end was picked up.

"Yes." The voice was sharp, but I recognized it immediately.

"Garrett, this is Zach Carlson," I said. Then added, "With the newspaper."

"How did you get this number?"

"I'm a reporter," I said. "It's what I do."

"What do you want?" the voice was still terse.

"Two things, I guess. As a friend, I just want you to know how sad I was to hear that you resigned."

"Appreciate your concern," he said, but his voice was not any softer.

"As a reporter, I have to ask why you resigned."

"Isn't it obvious?"

"Maybe. But did you have anything you wanted to say. For the record."

"No," he said. But after a short silence, he continued. His voice was taut and filled with anger. "I've had enough. I'm not going to put my family in jeopardy. It's not just the animals who did this. It's the so-called good people who don't do anything while shit like this happens. My family could have been killed. The cops in that town don't have the brains or the balls to stand up to a bunch of hillbilly hoodlums. I'm not going to put my family through this anymore. I'm done." The phone went dead.

#

Deadline was approaching. I debated with myself how to handle Garrett's statement. I was certain he was talking from anger. I wasn't sure that he expected his words to end up in the newspaper. But outrage contained an element that the story needed.

In Chicago there was always a degree of anonymity to the stories I wrote. The subjects were just names, not people that I knew. After the story was written, I never saw them again. Other than an occasional irate phone call that I would listen to for a moment, then hang up, I never again talked to people I wrote about.

It was different writing articles in a small town. I knew these people, at least some of them. If I wrote a story about someone, it was likely that I would run into them during the next week walking down the street, picking up something at the IGA, buying gas or eating at Shelby's Place.

Courageous and principled journalism is much easier in an impersonal void. But stories in the Gazette were different. Journalism in a small town was more personal, more intimate. The decisions on what to write and what to leave out were not so easy.

I settled for a middle road that would likely please no one. I rewrote the opening paragraphs to the lead story.

> Stratton High School Principal Garrett Deiter resigned Monday following a suspicious fire that destroyed his home Saturday night. Damage was estimated at more than $50,000.
>
> Assistant principal William Simmons has been named as interim principal to complete the school year.
>
> According to Deiter, he resigned due to concerns for his family's safety. "I'm not going to put my family through this anymore," he said.

A spray-painted sign left on Deiter's garage points to the fire being set by someone with a grudge against the former principal. The State Fire Marshal has been called in to investigate.

#

Two weeks later, I was talking with Gus Kopetsky while I picked up the weekly police runs. “Any more information on the Deiter fire,” I said.

"It was arson," he said. "State fire marshal hasn’t released his report yet, but the investigator said there wasn’t any question. It was started with an accelerant. Probably gasoline. Somebody poured it all around the house then set it off. Lucky they all got out."

"Any suspects?"

"Sure," Gus said. "Everybody knows that Kyle kid done it. The one that got kicked off the basketball team. But can't prove it. His mom, dad, that little brother of his, they all said, 'Yep, he wuz home with us watchin' Lawrence Welk, or some such shit. They're lying out their asses, but we can't prove it."

"Isn't there some evidence at the fire?"

"Hell no. Nothing but ashes." Gus spit onto the trash can next to his desk then wiped his mouth with the back of his hand. "Nothing we can do."

TWENTY – *The Girl Upstairs*

January 9, 1976, SUTHERLAND, NEB. (WIRE SERVICES): Jury selection began today in the murder-rape trial of Erwin Charles Simants, a local 29-year-old unemployed alcoholic. If convicted, he faces death in the electric chair.

Simants is charged with shooting deaths of six members of the Kellie family, and raping Marie Kellie, 67, and her 6-year-old granddaughter before killing them.

The case drew national attention when journalism organizations appealed the trial judge's order gagging the press from reporting on the case. The U.S. Supreme Court overturned the gag order in a unanimous decision.

The last Chess Club meeting of the year was scheduled for the second weekend in December. After an unseasonably warm weekend with near-record temperatures, an early winter chill had returned. Libby and Gary Middleton invited Emma and me to dinner before the rest of the group arrived. Even though Emma was working, I accepted the offer of a home-cooked meal.

I arrived a little before six. Libby met me at the door.

"Zach, I'm so sorry for the smell. I'm not sure what it is or where it's coming from, but I can't seem to do anything about it."

I was fighting a cold and only noticed a hint of the odor as I walked up to the house. But now, with Libby holding the door open, the pungent scent was unavoidable. It became stronger as we walked into the living room.

"We were gone last weekend," Libby said. "When we got back Sunday evening, the house stank. It keeps getting worse."

"Did you call Orville?"

Libby shook her head in disgust. "I called a half dozen times. He keeps saying he'll come around when he has time, but he doesn't."

We stepped further into the house. The odor in the dining room became overpowering.

Gary walked in from the kitchen wearing a tee shirt, jeans and a sour expression on his face. "Smells like a dead turd," he said, holding out his hand for me to shake.

Libby gave him a small jab in the ribs. "I called everybody and cancelled the chess club. I thought we could go to dinner at Shelby's Place. Emma's working tonight, right? Maybe she can sit down with us for a while."

"Where's it coming from?" I asked, ignoring Libby's question.

"Can't tell," Gary said. "I thought some animal might have died in the crawl space. At first, I thought it came from under the house, and I checked and it's not coming from there."

I took a deep sniff. The putrid pungency was unmistakable. I had smelled it before. Too many times before.

"Anybody live upstairs?"

"Yes. I think her name's Rene something," Libby said. "We've seen her a few times, but she's never said anything. Not the friendly type."

"How do you get to her place?"

"Stairs in back," Gary said. "She's got the entire top floor."

I walked outside and around to the stairs. The stairway was an add-on from when the owner converted the house into two apartments. A roof protected the stairs from snow and rain. I flipped on the light switch at the bottom of the stairs, illuminating a single naked bulb. The yellow light revealed unkept bare wooden steps leading to a landing cluttered with trash overflowing from a metal can.

I started up the stairs, the weather-worn steps giving slightly with my weight. Gary followed behind. The odor became stronger with each step.

"Oh my God," Gary said from behind me. "Who crawled up someone's butt and died."

I turned back toward him. The look on my face stopped him in mid laugh.

I reached the top of the stairs and looked around for a buzzer or a door knocker. Finding none, I knocked hard on the wooden door. "Hello? Anyone home?" No response. I breathed hard through my mouth, trying to minimize the stench. I heard nothing but air hissing through my teeth. I pounded again, this time with my fist. "Rene? Anyone?" Still no response. "My name is Zach. I'm coming in just to check on you."

I reached for the door knob. The door was not latched. I pushed it open. Before I took the first step, I knew what waited for me inside.

Behind me, Gary said, "I think I'll wait for you downstairs."

I turned and saw Gary, the color drained from his face. I nodded. "I'll be down in a minute," I said.

I pulled a handkerchief from my hip pocket, covered my mouth and nose, and entered the apartment, careful not to touch anything. A small lamp in the corner cast a dim tawny light and stark shadows across the room. As my eyes adjusted, I made out an array of shabby furniture and dirty dishes scattered around the room.

A palpable stench of putrefaction filled the apartment.

I followed the obvious path to the single bedroom located just off the living area. Amid disheveled blankets and sheets, a woman's body was sprawled face down on the bed. The jeans and gold sweat shirt she wore no longer fit her body, deformed by gasses of decay. Dried blood from a wound at the back of her head left a frozen black stream along the side of the mattress where it pooled into a sickly mass on the floor. I had seen too many bodies, too many gunshot victims, too many murder scenes, not to grasp what I saw in front of me.

I fought back the sickness rising from my stomach. Working the crime beat for a decade, I long ago developed an immunity to human carnage, to savage wounds and gore. Truth be told, even as a rookie the sight of bodies and death never bothered me. Intellectually, I understood that the victim was once a living person robbed by unspeakable violence of everything – their dreams, joys, sorrow – their life. But for me it was always another deadline to beat, another front-page story, another byline.

Not so now.

I stood looking over the body for a long moment, wondering what type of person this woman had been. Did she have parents who would grieve? Did she have a boyfriend someplace? Did she have plans for the rest of her life? What was her last day like? Did she have any idea she was living her last day? What happened in those last minutes? Was there a fight? Did she recognize her killer? Was she aware she was dying? Did she suffer? Or did she exist, and the next millisecond she did not?

I bit my lip and wiped away the wetness at the corner of my eye. The world was different for me.

I retraced my steps out of the apartment. Gary and Libby stood in the middle of the back yard, clutching each other. Once at the bottom of the stairs, I removed the handkerchief from my face and took several deep breaths. After the assault to my senses in the apartment, the outside air no longer seemed to have an odor.

"Call the police," I said.

Gary and Libby just stared at me.

"Call the police. She's been shot. She's dead."

#

Clint Avery was the first to arrive. He took about fifteen minutes to get to the scene. I met Clint at the street as he got out of his patrol car.

"Dead woman up there," I said. "She's been there for a while. Looks like she was shot in the back of the head."

Clint seemed confused. He started to make a call on the police radio, then he decided to check out the scene first.

I walked up with him, but stayed outside on the landing. Only a few seconds later, he came out almost running as he passed me, the color drained from his face. By the time I reached the bottom, Clint was throwing up into a trashcan by the back alley.

"Christ," was all he could say. Then he retched again. "Oh, Christ."

He walked back to his car, spitting the taste of vomit from his mouth. I heard him call Gus Kopetsky on the police radio.

"We've got a dead girl. It's in the upper floor of that house on Maple Street that Orville Vehorn rents out."

There was some garbled response on the radio I couldn't make out.

"Looked like she was shot in the back of the head."

There was another brief transmission, then Clint ended the call with "Ten-four."

He continued to sit in his car, his door open staring off into nothing. He was pale and even in the dropping temperatures, sweat streamed down his face. He did not move until Gus Kopetsky drove up ten minutes later.

Gus stopped his car in the middle of the street with lights flashing. He walked over to where Clint was still sitting. They exchanged a few words, then Gus headed upstairs. He returned a minute later.

By that time, the town's third patrol car pulled up, siren blaring and lights flashing. Kenny Wyman jumped out of his car, an actual smile on his face.

"Turn that damned siren off," Gus yelled. Kenny did what Gus ordered, then trotted up to Gus.

"Got a stiff?" he said, almost gleeful. "Somebody killed her?"

Gus turned away saying nothing. He walked back to his car and got on the radio. Kenny walked up, still with a goofy smile on his face.

"What are you doing here?"

"I found her."

"You lookin' to get a little?"

I looked at him, puzzled.

"She was a whore, man." Then he added, "That's what I heard around town."

"I was visiting my friends who live downstairs," I said.

"I gotta see this," Kenny said. He took the steps to the upstairs apartment two at a time. A minute later he was back, retching in the grass, unable to make it to the trash can in the alley.

I stood waiting to give my statement, for someone to mark off the area with crime scene tape, for state police investigators to arrive. But none of that happened.

A few minutes later, a late model Oldsmobile pulled up and Orville Vehorn climbed out. His face showed agitation. Gus met him, and they engaged in an animated conversation. I moved in that direction, hoping to overhear. Gus saw me and yelled toward Clint and pointed at me. "Keep him back."

After issuing his orders, Gus led Orville up the stairs to the death scene. They were inside for ten minutes, perhaps more, before they trudged back down the stairs.

Gus yelled over to Kenny. "Call up the Sheriff and the State Police. Let's get them over here."

I walked the six blocks back to my office and retrieved my camera. By the time I got back, two county sheriff's cars and a state police car were parked in front of the house blocking the street. The town hearse/ambulance was just pulling up.

I snapped photos showing the police cars surrounding the house. Orville came running over, his rotund body bouncing with each step on his spindly legs.

"Stop. Stop. You can't shoot those pictures."

I repositioned myself and took another shot.

"Stop it," Orville shouted again, trying to put his hand in front of my lens. "This is my house, and I'm ordering you not to take pictures."

I gave a false smile, trying to look sympathetic, but in truth I wanted to shove him out of the way. "I'm sorry, Orville, but this is news. This is the biggest news this town has had in fifty years. I'm going to cover it. That means taking photos."

"But you can't take pictures of my house. I won't let you."

I had gone from moderately annoyed to true anger, but I tried to keep it from my voice. "Orville, you can't stop me from taking pictures. You can keep me off your property, but I'm standing on the sidewalk. That's public property. And I can shoot anything I can see from public property." I paused for a moment. When Orville did not move, I added, "That's the law."

"We'll see," Orville said, stomping off toward the gathered police cars.

Orville scurried over to where Gus was talking with a state police officer. Visibly agitated, Orville talked with the officers, jabbing his finger in the hair, flailing with his hands, and finally pointing in my direction. Gus took several steps toward me, but the state police officer reached out and grabbed Gus by an arm. The detective talked to Gus for several minutes, then ambled toward me, leaving an irritated Gus behind.

"I'm Detective Virgil Amundsen," he said. The greeting was friendly, and not what I expected after observing Orville and Gus. We shook hands, and I introduced myself.

"You've got Orville and Gus in quite a tiff," he said.

I shrugged.

"Orville wants you arrested, and I think Gus would do it."

"For what?"

"Well, neither of them is quite sure," Virgil said with just a hint of a smile. "But they're certain you can't take pictures of somebody's house when they don't want you to."

"I have every right to take those photos." My anger flashed, seeping into my voice.

"Don't get upset. I told him that newspapers have more lawyers than Heinz has pickles. If he arrested you, the lawyers would have you out of jail before you could use the pisser. Then the newspaper would sue them and the town. That simmered them down a bit. But I told them I'd come over and talk to you."

"About what?"

The trooper smiled. "I'm not really sure. But they calmed down. That's all I wanted."

Amundson was experienced handling crime scenes and the press. It was obvious in his relaxed confident manner.

"You in charge of the investigation?"

"Sure as hell Gus can't handle this. Guess that leaves me."

"Gus tell you I found the body?"

"Yeah. From talking with Gus, you were visiting the couple that lives downstairs and were investigating the smell. You touch anything when you went inside?"

I shook my head. "I've been to too many crime scenes. Only thing I touched was the door knob when I pushed the door open. You have an ID on the victim?"

"Rene Swisher, age 24. She rented the upstairs from Orville."

I nodded. "I'm friends with the Middletons. They're the couple that rents the downstairs."

"They know the victim?"

"Just to see her. They're not friends. I don't think they ever had a real conversation."

Amundson scribbled in a small notebook. "She moved in five, six months ago. She's from out of town, but Orville couldn't tell me where. All he cared about is that she paid her rent on time and in cash."

“As the case develops, are you the person I need to stay in touch with?”

Virgil nodded. "For now." He handed me a card with his contact information. "Call me any time. I better get back to Gus before he tries to arrest somebody else."

#

I called Roy Shoemaker to see if we could get a short front-page story in the upcoming issue, but it was already printed. It would be more than a week before the story could be in the Gazette. By that time, news of the murder would cover the town like peanut butter on bread. Gossip and rumors some real, most imagined, would proliferate in such volume that, if printed, they would fill a month of newspapers.

I spent the next week checking for updates and trying to track down something about the victim. Detective Amundsen was cordial and professional when I called, but also guarded in the information he passed along. Before the newspaper went to bed the following week, I gave him one more call.

"No change. No arrests. No suspects. The investigation is continuing."

I suspected that those lines were right out of the detective training manual for dealing with the press.

My investigation into the background of the victim was no more fruitful. No one in Stratton seemed to know her. Perhaps it was more accurate that no one admitted knowing her. I followed up on Kenny Wyman's comment about the victim being a prostitute, but the reaction was that Kenny was shooting off his mouth and didn't know what he was talking about. As far as I could determine, Rene Swisher did not have a job or any connection to Stratton other than her apartment.

The autopsy confirmed cause of death as a single gunshot to the head. Rene's body was returned to her only living relative, an aunt in Kokomo. I checked with her hometown newspaper and found only a death notice. No obituary. No funeral.

#

The story on the murder ran on page one with a three-column photo of the house surrounded by police cars. Orville called me to complain, but given that his name did not appear in the story, it seemed his outrage had lost much of its steam. Otherwise, the story seemed like most other news stories. Read one day; discarded the next day with the trash. The articles on a local school girl winning the county spelling bee had more staying power.

For a small town that had not had a murder in more than forty years, the crime faded remarkably quickly from the collective consciousness. But the ripples of a stranger's death everyone preferred to forget would come back as a wave crashing over the town and everyone in it.

TWENTY-ONE – *Even If Santa Gets Shot*

December 1973

December 23, 1973, TEHERAN, IRAN (INTERNATIONAL WIRE SERVICES): OPEC sent shockwaves through Wall Street and every corner of the economy yesterday when it doubled the price of crude oil.

The increase will impact prices Americans pay for everything from transportation to food.

Kate's December work schedule was even worse than the year before. Between early November and Christmas, the only day she did not work at least fourteen hours was Thanksgiving. It was over turkey and dressing on our Thanksgiving Day trip to Wisconsin that Kate suggested to her parents that they put off celebrating Christmas until after the New Year.

Doris and Jim were much more worried about Kate's workload than getting together for the holidays.

"Honey, we're just worried sick about you," Doris said. "You work so much. It can't be good for you."

Jim said nothing, but the look in his eyes conveyed worry for his only daughter.

They offered to drive to Chicago on Christmas, but Kate discouraged them.

"If you come down, I will feel obligated to entertain you. What I'll really need is sleep and rest. I'll be much better after the New Year."

"Is that job worth it?" Doris asked.

Kate didn't give an immediate answer which surprised me. After a long silence, she took a deep breath and exhaled slowly. "I don't know. I thought this is what I wanted, but I'm not so sure now. Next spring I'll look around, see if there are some other options. But for now, this is what I have to do."

Driving back, I asked Kate what she wanted for Christmas. I half way expected her to say "a ring." But she didn't.

She put her hand on my thigh and gave me a gentle kiss on the cheek. Her voice was soft as velvet. "I want you to quit smoking, Zach."

I turned, trying to see her and keep an eye on the road. "Are you serious?"

"Yes. We found out this week that a secretary at the firm has lung cancer. They're giving her six months. She's in her late-40s. That's the second person in the firm with lung cancer in the past year. Smoking's not worth it. As soon as I'm through this crunch, I'm giving it up."

"You are serious, aren't you?"

Again, she kissed my cheek, her lips soft like the touch of a feather brushing against my skin.

"I've never been more serious. I couldn't stand you getting sick like that."

We drove for a long time in silence. "I'll think about it," I finally said.

#

On Christmas Day I woke up in Kate's apartment – our apartment – shortly after seven. It was her first Christmas Day away from her parents. Our first Christmas together.

I eased out of the bed, trying not to disturb Kate. I watched the sheets rise and fall with Kate's rhythmic breathing like gentle ocean swells on a calm sea. Her dark hair formed a tangled halo about her head.

Outside, street lights glowed dimly through fog and mist. I was glad we would not make the drive up to Wisconsin.

I slipped on a robe, walked into the living room and plugged in the small Christmas tree that sat on a table under our living room window. Earlier that month, Kate gave me the job of finding a tree and decorating for Christmas. I found a three-foot artificial tree and decorations on the discount rack at K-Mart. It resembled Charlie Brown's pathetic little tree, but Kate smiled at my effort.

In the silence, I made a pot of coffee and filled my favorite mug. With only the light coming from the dancing bulbs on the plastic tree, I made my way to the couch and picked up the novel I had been reading.

My hand reached for the switch for the floor lamp next to my chair, but I stopped. I pulled my hand back and let it rest on top of the unopened novel on my lap. There was a creak from old wood contracting some place in the building. Through the window, I could hear the wind swirling among the rows of apartment buildings. A barely perceptible hum played across the room as something mechanical kicked on and heated air moved through the ducts.

That was all.

There were no cars. No voices. No clatter of the city. I sat in the multicolored glow of flickering lights in the silence of Christmas morning, looking at our eight-dollar plastic tree with fifty cent strings of light, and feeling its warmth far more than the coffee I was sipping.

I had not celebrated Christmas in more than a dozen years. After my parents divorced, I never saw Dad at the holidays. After he died when I was in high school, I had no contact at all with his second wife.

As for Mom, even before she moved to Florida with her second husband, Christmas was only an obligation, a once-a-year gathering for dinner and nothing more. I would eat with mom and my stepdad, then leave as quickly as I could without making a scene.

My job at the newspaper made it easy to bypass Christmas. The newsroom ran on a skeleton staff, just enough to cover the inevitable Christmas tree fire or holiday gathering that ended in an argument and someone getting shot. I volunteered to work Christmas so that reporters and editors with families could get the day off.

But this year was different. I told my city editor Charlie Kelso to take me off the holiday work list. "I'm taking my phone off the hook," I told Charlie. "Don't try to reach me. Not even if Santa himself gets shot."

For the first time since childhood, I wanted to treasure this day. I wanted to watch Kate open the pile of gifts I bought for her, experience the joy and surprise on her face. We would share a bottle of wine, sit on our couch and hold each other.

I pulled myself from my thoughts and got up to refill my coffee mug. On the way, I took the phone off the hook. This Christmas was for just Kate and me.

Kate slept until after ten. When she awoke, I prepared her favorite brunch – lox and bagels with cream cheese and small dishes of caviar, eggs, capers and red onion. Afterward, we opened our gifts. I was so focused on Kate that I took little notice of the sweater, gloves and books I unwrapped.

"I hope you like them," she said. "I didn't have much time to shop. I'll do better next year."

I assured her that I loved the gifts.

Kate opened her presents with the glee of an eight-year-old. She delighted in trying on the clothes, the earrings and bracelet, and dabbing Chanel No. 5 behind her ears. She squealed with delight at her biggest present, a new state-of-the-art stereo system with an assortment of rock and blues albums.

We played every album without a break. When "At Last" by Etta James played, we got up and danced, our bodies entwined. In the middle of the afternoon, we went to see The Sting, a new movie with Paul Newman and Robert Redford.

After the movie, Kate napped while I fixed dinner. We ate late and shared a bottle of wine in the glow of our little Christmas tree, a Johnny Mathis Christmas album playing on the new stereo.

By the time the wine was gone, Kate was asleep in my arms. I guided her to bed where I curled my body against the curve of Kate's form, careful not to wake her. My mind drifted back over the day. I felt the warmth of Kate against me, and the warmth of loving her.

Never was I so much at peace.

TWENTY-TWO – *Sons and Daughters*

February 17, 1976, WASHINGTON, D.C. (WIRE SERVICES): The National Council of Churches today took the extraordinary step of urging broadcasters to start airing prime-time messages informing teens about contraception and the risks of venereal disease.

The Council's action was prompted by recent statistics showing a spike in rates of venereal disease, unplanned teen pregnancies and teenage abortions.

The Saturday after the murder story ran in the paper, the Middletons again invited Emma and me for dinner. Libby assured me that the sickening odor from the upstairs apartment no longer lingered. Emma had the night off, so we accepted. It was the first time we had done something with other people.

Emma was nervous, something I had never seen in her. During dinner, she patted her foot under the table. Between bites, she twirled her fork absentmindedly, and was silent for long periods as the conversation swirled around her.

At the restaurant, she was bold and outgoing. But here in an unfamiliar environment with people who had college degrees, she seemed stripped of her brash confidence and withdrew into herself.

As we ate, conversation turned to school, as it often did with Gary and Libby.

"I'm lost two more of the girls in my classes to pregnancy," Libby said. "They didn't come back after Christmas break."

"How many is that?" I asked.

"That's six girls this school year."

"I lost a girl off the swim team, too," Gary said.

I shook my head. "Doesn't anyone talk to these kids about the pill or condoms?"

"I talked with some of the other teachers," Libby said. "One teacher tried. Included birth control in health class a couple of years ago. She got fired. They made up some excuse about not adequately controlling her classroom, but everyone knew it was bullshit."

"It's a little better at Stratton, but not much," Gary said. "They teach some basic sex ed, but students have to bring in a signed consent form. Most parents won't sign."

"Wouldn't help," Emma said, speaking up in a strong voice as if she had shrugged off an invisible shell. "These kids aren't stupid. They understand what causes them to get pregnant."

"They don't understand the consequences," Libby shot back. "They don't comprehend what being a teenage mother will do to their lives."

"They understand," Emma said. "But when a boy has a hard on and his hands in your pants, that's not what you're thinking about."

"That's why you have to teach them about this. So they will think about getting in those situations."

Emma shook her head and lifted her gaze to the ceiling. After a few seconds she looked directly at Libby. "All of you teachers, you grew up someplace else. You headed off to college for four years, hiding out from the real world. When you graduate, you've got all these great ideas you can't wait to try. You end up coming to Stratton or someplace like it, telling everyone what they should be doing and how they should be doing it. But you don't know shit about what growing up here is really like."

Libby's mouth opened a bit. She stuttered, "I don't mean . . ."

"Don't mean to tell us how to live our lives?" Emma interrupted. "Sure you do. You come here for three or four years, and then you move on to a bigger school where you can make more money, and leave the rest of us behind. But you don't understand what growing up here is like."

I could see tears beginning to form in Emma's eyes, but she blinked them back.

"Look around," she continued. "Do you see a future for kids who live here? Anything except leaving? You're fifteen, sixteen, and someone says there's a bunch of kids getting together out at the Sanders' barn, and they got a keg. So, you go. Then some boy, maybe the captain of the football team, tells you you're pretty. For the first time in a long time, you feel good about yourself, like you're worth something. You drive out on those country roads and find some lane going back into a field, and the next thing you know, you got your pants off. Then you don't get your period, and your boyfriend takes off. And there you are."

"That's what happened to you?" Libby asked, quietly.

"That's what happens to all these girls."

#

We stayed at the Middletons' apartment for a while longer, eating dessert while Gary dragged out some of his 1950s 45s. The music lightened the mood a bit, but the shadow of the dinner confrontation hung over us.

We excused ourselves early, and I took Emma home.

"Sorry if I made a scene," Emma said as I drove the short distance to her house. "I didn't mean to ruin your evening."

"You didn't ruin anything. You spoke from your heart. I don't think people do that enough. They come into this town like Gary and Libby – and like me. We need to hear what you said."

She gave me a smile and a kiss on the cheek. "Thanks."

When we got back to her house, Emma stopped me at the door. "I'm not in a good mood for company tonight," she said. "Is it okay if we just say goodnight?"

Driving back to my apartment, I thought about the dinner conversation. There was a story about this town and its teenagers that needed to be told. I wasn't sure how I would get inside the world of the local teens in order to tell it.

#

The following week, I started looking into teen pregnancies in the area, but I didn't get very far. The school refused to release any information on how many girls left school due to pregnancy. The county health department was equally obtuse. The clerk told me that such information was confidential and refused to provide me with any information or statistics.

A couple of weeks later, I covered a Friday night away basketball game at Glenwood High School. Danny Pemberton, the son of the town board member and owner of the grain elevator and lumber yard, had taken over as the team's best player after Davey Kyle was expelled. He was a solid player, but there were no college scouts or coaches in the stands. Danny scored sixteen points, grabbed six rebounds. Stratton won by five.

It was about 11:30 when I finished writing the game story. I gave Emma a quick phone call. She and Molly were staying up late watching creepy movies together. Emma invited me to join them, but I passed. "I think I'm going to grab a beer at the VFW and head home," I said. "It's been a long day."

On the way to the VFW, I passed the Dairy Point. The drive-in was closed for the season, but despite early February cold, there were eight cars parked around the restaurant as if waiting for the coming warm weather and carhop service.

Teens gathered around the cars in small groups of threes and fours. Some sat on hoods of fenders, others stood around smoking. I pulled in.

All eyes followed my car, but no one moved. I noticed one kid holding a hat upside down like a bowl.

I put my car in park and got out, leaving the engine running.

"Hey, how you doing? I'm Zach Carlson, editor of the newspaper."

"So?" The response came from a big kid leaning against his car. "What do you want?"

"Nothing. I was working late finishing a story on the basketball game, and was driving by. Saw everybody gathered here."

The big kid pulled a cigarette pack out of his coat pocket, took a cigarette out using his teeth and lit it. "What's that got to do with us?"

I looked at the cigarette. The kid threw the pack at me. "Help yourself."

I held the pack, rolling the familiar shape between my fingers and taking in the faint scent of tobacco. I tossed it back. "I quit," I said.

"You gonna preach to me about how I shouldn't smoke?" he said, replacing the pack inside his jacket.

I shook my head. "No. I'm not preaching to anyone. I'd still be smoking if I hadn't promised someone I would quit."

The kid looked back at me puzzled, but didn't say anything.

A small figure got out from the back seat of a late model dark blue Chevrolet Chevelle, the one with a 407 cubic inch engine and an air scoop on the hood. It was Richie Kyle. "Hey Zach," he said.

"What are you doing here?" I said, surprised to see Ritchie with these older teens.

"My brother," he said, jerking his head back at the Chevelle. I could make out Davey Kyle's tall lean figure sitting behind the wheel of the car. He was staring hard at me, his face fixed in a scowl.

"Davey wanted me to ask if you're here because of him?"

"No, nothing to do with him. I didn't even know he was here."

Ritchie nodded and ran back to his brother's car.

"So, what are you doing?" Again, it was the big kid who offered me a cigarette.

"I grew up in Chicago. I was curious about what someone your age does for fun in this town." I scanned around looking at the deserted town with only a single traffic light flashing red. "There don't seem to be a lot of options."

"Oooooh, a Chicago man. Well, Chicago Man, we mostly do this. Sit around, drinking beer, talking about what we're gonna do when we get outta this shit hole. In fact, getting ready to make a beer run now. Wanna come?"

"Where do you get your beer," I said, ignoring the invitation.

"There's a liquor store over in Amelia that doesn't look too close at IDs."

I glanced at my watch. "Don't the liquor stores close at midnight? It's past 11:30 now.

The kid laughed. He checked his watch. "Twenty-two miles." With that, he threw down his cigarette butt, grabbed the hat another boy was holding, and emptied the money in to his hand. He got behind the wheel of an older model fire red Pontiac GTO. "I got five minutes to spare," he said. The engine roared to life. With wheels squealing, he took off into the darkness.

#

Two weeks later, after a movie and pizza, Emma and I ended up at my apartment. Shortly before midnight, with Walter Bradshaw undoubtedly sitting in the quiet of his living room directly below us, we made soundless love. As Emma began to climax, she grabbed for a pillow to cover her mouth, but I tossed it away. She bit into my shoulder as she came, but she didn't make any noise. We collapsed into breathless laughter.

Minutes later, as we lay side by side, the police scanner crackled calling Stratton police. Kenny Wyman answered the call. "Stratton Unit 3. Whatcha got?"

"Kenny, we got a bad accident out on Route 144 at the curve just south of Little Deer Creek. I'm calling Stratton and Denham for ambulances. I've already got a sheriff's deputy rolling and I've called the state police, but you're closest. Can you get out there and put up some flares and help with traffic?"

"I'm rolling."

I jumped out of bed and grabbed my jeans. "This sounds bad. I need to check this out."

"I'll come, too," Emma said. "I know where that is."

As I was tying my sneakers, I heard the radio call to the state police. "Denham ambulance is already on the scene. Got one fatal for sure. Maybe two."

I looked over to Emma and the color seemed to disappear from her face. "Why don't you stay here. I'm sure I can find this place."

"No," she said firmly. "I'll go. But I'll stay in the car when we get there."

I grabbed my camera bag and we left.

#

I drove out Highway 144. About three miles south of town I saw the array of flashing lights ahead. I slowed behind the first police car and pulled to the side of the road. I left the car running.

"I'll probably be a little while," I said to Emma. "Turn on the radio and see if you can find something to listen to." I grabbed a notepad and pen out of my glovebox and my Pentax out of the camera bag in the back seat.

Kenny Wyman was standing in the middle of the road talking with Arnold Donaldson, the funeral home director who drove the hearse that doubled as the town ambulance. Donaldson was smoking a cigarette. They both looked up as I approached.

"What's going on?" I said.

Even in the dark, with emergency lights flashing off his face, Kenny Wyman looked stunned. "Bad wreck. Hit a tree." That was all he said.

Arnold was hardened from a lifetime of dealing with death. He took a last drag on his cigarette, threw it on the pavement and mashed it with his toe. "One dead. You can walk up and look if you want, but it's pretty ugly. Car slid off the edge of the pavement trying to make the curve. Looks like the driver overcorrected, swung back across the road and hit that big tree." Arnold pointed toward where several spotlights were blazing. "He must have been going like a bat out of hell."

"Got a name?"

Kenny stood silent looking like he wanted to be someplace, anyplace else.

Arnold answered. "Not yet. State police is handling the investigation. They retrieved the wallet so you can ask them."

"Anybody else in the car?"

"A girl. She was thrown out. Hurt pretty bad, but she's still alive. Ambulance from Dunham has her on the way to the hospital in Amelia."

"What type of car was it?" I asked, afraid that I knew the answer.

It was Kenny who finally spoke. "Red Pontiac GTO."

I thought of asking Arnold for a cigarette to take away the sour taste rising in my mouth. But I didn't.

After 45 minutes at the scene, I had all the particulars and returned to the car. Music was playing softly on the radio. Emma was asleep, stretched across the bench seat in my Impala. I carefully eased her up and slid in to my seat.

Emma stirred. "Done?"

"Yes"

"Anybody killed."

"Yes. A teenager. And a girl is hurt pretty bad."

"That's so sad," she said through a yawn.

"It is," I said. There was nothing else to say.

#

The story on the car crash was the lead story on page one. After thinking for a long time, I decided to include my encounter with the victim collecting money for a high-speed beer run to Amelia.

Phone calls inundated the office for two days after the newspaper hit the stands. The calls complained that I shouldn't be writing ill of the dead, particularly someone only seventeen years old.

"You think his momma ain't feeling bad enough already," one of the nameless callers said. "You got to rub her nose in it like that, you son of a bitch."

I slammed the phone down and walked to Shirley's desk. I pulled two dollars from my wallet and threw it in the swear jar. "Take the damn phone off the hook. We're not answering any more calls today."

"You understand it's not the accident, or even that boy dying, that's got them upset," Shirley said. "They don't want someone pulling back the curtain on what their sons and daughters do every weekend. It's nothing they don't know. They just don't want to see it staring back at them in black and white."

TWENTY-THREE – *Let's Have a Parade*

March 12, 1976, WHITESBURG, KY (WIRE SERVICES): Eleven mine rescuers, including 3 Bureau of Mines employees, were killed last night in a second explosion at the Scotia Mine in this small eastern Kentucky town. Fifteen minors died in an initial explosion two days ago, bringing the total killed to 26.

As winter ended, it became increasingly clear that railroad service to Stratton soon would be terminated and the tracks abandoned. A sense of gloom and inevitability settled over the three members of the town board as they met the first week in March. The impact seemed most onerous on town board president Hank Pemberton, whose grain elevator and sawmill operations largely depended upon rail service.

The board approved routine expenditures and discussed a citizen's complaints about potholes from an early spring thaw. Hank Pemberton looked down at his agenda. "Any new business?"

When Bill Olsen started to speak, Orville groaned and buried his head deeper into the ledger sitting on the table in front of him.

"The Bicentennial is coming up," Bill said.

"We know," Orville mumble without raising his head. "It's been in all the papers. Even Zach's."

"We should do something," Bill said.

"We are," Sam Bauserman said, showing no more excitement than Orville. "The fire department is spending extra money on fireworks this year."

"We can't just sit around here wallowing in our misery because the railroads are shutting down," Bill said emphatically. "A bicentennial only comes around once in a lifetime. Once in several lifetimes. We should really do something like this town has never seen."

"What do you have in mind?" Hank said, showing no more enthusiasm than the others.

"A damned big blow out party," Bill said. If nothing else, his energy caught everyone's attention. "Let's pull out all the stops. I have a friend up in Valparaiso who owns a hot air balloon. His ballooning group wants to do something on the Fourth, but nobody has asked them. He says we're a perfect location. No tall buildings. No big electric transmission lines. He could get twenty, maybe thirty hot air balloons here for the Fourth."

Orville lifted his head. "There's no money in the budget for something like that."

Bill slammed the flat of his hand on the table. The crack reverberated around the room like a gunshot. "We don't have to pay them. It won't cost the town a damn dime."

That got some attention.

"They just show up and fly their balloons because we ask them?" Sam said.

"All we have to do is provide a place, and that big field and parking lot next to the high school would be perfect."

Now there was interest around the table in what Bill was saying.

"They fly just after sunrise and at sunset," Bill continued. "Imagine the sky filled with hot air balloons at dawn on the Fourth, then again at dusk before the fireworks."

"You sure this won't cost us anything?" Hank said.

Bill shook his head. "Not a damn dime."

There was a pause.

"That might be worth doing," Hank said. "I've seen a couple of those balloons before. They're impressive. Can't imagine what twenty of them would look like. Even if we just got four or five, that would be entertaining. We could publicize it all around. Get some people in town."

"Exactly," Bill said. "And we should have a parade."

"Holy Jesus," said Orville. "You sound like Mickey Rooney. Let's have a goddamn parade, and put on a show while we're at it."

There were several laughs around the table, but Sam and Hank were seeing potential in Bill's idea.

"The school band practices during the summer," Bill said, pushing forward. "They could march in a parade. I'm sure the vets from the VFW would march. Henry Kunstler has those antique cars of his. He'd love to put them in a parade."

"We got the Boy Scout and Girl Scout troops over at the Methodist Church," Sam said. "I can talk to the scoutmasters and get them to march in a parade. Anybody know if any of the other towns around here are doing anything?"

"I already checked," Bill said. "The Fourth is a Sunday. Most towns are having fireworks Saturday night. But nobody is doing anything else. No parades. No hog roasts. We might even get interest from groups in those towns to come over here and be in the parade."

Enthusiasm often feeds off itself. Maybe it was a wave of patriotism for the Bicentennial. Maybe it had been so long since there had been anything exciting in Stratton. But over the next forty minutes the board came up with ideas for a parade, a dramatic reading of the declaration of independence, a hog roast and church ice cream socials.

Even Gus contributed from his perch in the back of the room. He suggested that the town's police cars and volunteer fire department trucks could lead the parade with their lights and sirens.

"What if there's an emergency," Hank asked? "What if there's a wreck or some moron sets a house on fire with a Roman candle? You just pull out of the parade?"

"No problem," Gus said, his thumb sliding into his utility belt. "The Sheriff can cover police calls, and we'll get one of the neighboring volunteer fire departments to cover any fire calls. They've done that before."

Bill was assigned the hot air balloon event and coordinating with the fire department about expanding the fireworks display. Hank took responsibility for the parade. Sam took charge of organizing a hog roast, contacting the churches and scout troops, and trying to get a local band that played '50s music to play on Main Street after the parade.

As the plans grew bigger and bolder, I became increasingly dubious of the town's ability to bring its dreams to reality. But what the heck. "I'll make sure you get plenty of publicity in the newspaper," I chimed in.

It wasn't my place to rain on their parade.

As the meeting was winding down, Bill Olsen took the floor again. "One more thing. We need a theme for this celebration." There was a pause. Bill seemed to puff up his chest. "I think we'd really draw people if we made this a Christmas Fourth of July."

"Oh, Holy Jesus," Orville said, and again dropped his head into his papers.

A crumpled ball of paper flew across the table from Hank Pemberton and hit Bill squarely in the forehead.

"No," Hank said, his voice decisive. He hit the gavel, and the meeting ended.

TWENTY-FOUR – *Secret Lives*

March 31, 1976, TRENTON, N.J. (WIRE SERVICES): The parents of Karen Anne Quinlan today won the right to disconnect the comatose Miss Quinlan from the machines that have been keeping her alive since a drug overdose last year.

In a 7-0 decision, the New Jersey Supreme Court ruled that the family's right to privacy superseded any other interest. The family's lawyer issued a statement saying that the family will make the decision when to disconnect Miss Quinlan in private.

Shirley Wilmes was never late, never sick, never took a day off, not even for vacation. She typed 100 words a minute without error, efficiently managed classified ads, and handled phone calls and customers with a detached politeness, rarely friendly but never rude. Her hourly pay barely exceeded minimum wage. She qualified for much higher paying jobs, but none existed in Stratton. She would have to move to a city to find them.

Her father was dead. She lived with her mother who was on Social Security, and her eleven-year-old son name Mark, whom I had never met. It didn't take much insight to conclude she struggled to make ends meet.

She was reclusive. I had never seen her at Shelby's Place, and only once had I seen her at the town's grocery.

She didn't swear. She didn't smoke. She didn't drink. She looked with thinly disguised disdain upon those who did. The only activity she ever mentioned was her church, which she attended on Wednesday night and twice on Sunday.

That was the extent of my knowledge.

One particularly slow day, I invited Shirley to lunch. She gave me a curt, "No thank you," not looking up from her work. I tried several more times, but the answer was the same. The final time I asked, her response was more pointed.

"First, I won't go where they serve alcohol, and every place in town except the Dairy Point serves alcohol."

"You don't have to drink, and I won't order anything to drink."

"I don't approve of alcohol and I won't support a place that does. Second, it wouldn't be appropriate for me to go to lunch with my unmarried boss," she said.

"I'm not trying to pick you up," I said, trying to keep a straight face. "It's just lunch. Besides, I'm sort of seeing someone."

Shirley gave a disapproving scowl. "I know," she said. "The whole town knows you've been, well, to be direct, spending nights over at Emma Musgrave's house."

I rolled my eyes. "Damn," I said, speaking only to myself.

"It's a small town," Shirley said, holding up the cuss jar. My pay in advance was long ago exhausted. I fished a dollar from my pocket and stuffed it in the jar.

"People see things and they talk," Shirley said. "There are no secrets here."

#

Sitting at Emma's one night sharing a bottle of wine, I brought up my curiosity about Shirley.

"I see her around town occasionally," Emma said. "But not often. She never comes in the restaurant."

"You serve beer."

"Really? Because we serve beer?"

I nodded.

Emma took a sip of her wine. "I bet there is someone who can tell you Shirley's story."

"Who?"

"One of your writers. Esther Bickel."

"I wouldn't exactly call her one of *my* writers," I said.

"Maybe she can't write, but the woman knows everything about everybody in town. You should ask her."

A few days later, I invited Esther Bickel to lunch at Shelby's Place. I set up the meeting on the pretext of seeking her opinion about how I was doing with the newspaper.

"Everybody likes that you didn't change the visiting news," she said, forking up a large bite of the chicken and dumplings daily special. "That's people's favorite part of the paper."

I nodded. Of course, it was.

"Those feature stories you do on local residents are really good. And the pictures. People think you take fantastic pictures."

I kept my expression serious and took notes. The notes would go in the trash as soon as I returned to the office, but I wanted to give Esther an impression of her importance.

As we finished our meal, I turned the topic to Shirley. I tried to make it as casual as possible.

"Shirley does a nice job typing up your columns," I said. "Her office skills are so much better than I expected in a small town."

"She went to business school in Chicago and worked in one of those big downtown office buildings for several years." To my surprise, Esther pulled a pack of cigarettes from her purse and lit one. "Where are my manners" Would you like one?"

I shook my head. "I quit. But you go ahead."

"I allow myself one after lunch, and one after dinner," she said.

"About Shirley?" I prompted her.

"Well, after she graduated from high school, she moved to Chicago for business school. Worked up there for several years before she came back home."

"Did she come back because her dad died?"

"Oh no. This was before Ray died." Esther took a long drag on the cigarette then stubbed it out. She looked around the room as if checking to see if anyone was eavesdropping on our conversation. Satisfied, she leaned forward, speaking in a conspiratorial voice just above a whisper. "You know about the boy, don't you?"

I sipped my coffee. "She has a son named Mark. But I've never met him."

"You probably won't," Esther said. "She keeps a tight leash on the boy. Too tight if you ask me."

Emma came up and asked us about dessert. It was peanut butter pie day. I couldn't resist. Esther ordered the apple pie with a scoop of vanilla ice cream.

As Emma walked away, Esther got a big smile on her face. "I heard you and that gal are seeing each other."

"We go to dinner and a movie occasionally."

Esther gave a knowing grin. "More than dinner going on, from what I hear."

I felt color rising in my face. Emma saved me from further discussion when she brought the pie. I dug in, hoping to avoid any more discussion of my personal life.

"You were talking about Shirley's son," I prodded.

Esther leaned forward again. "I was good friends with her aunt, Zelda Tinker, ever since grade school. Zelda's dead now. Just keeled over while canning beans. Only sixty-three. Such a shame. Been gone almost four years now."

Esther spoke in the same meandering style she wrote. I stayed patient, hoping she would get back to Shirley and her son.

"Anyway, Zelda talked to me about it a lot back when it happened. But I never put a word of it in my column. Not one."

I nodded as I chewed my pie. Esther's discretion surprised me. Perhaps I misjudged her status as the town gossip.

"She was just a normal teenager back then. Went to school dances. Had a couple of boyfriends. That type of stuff. Like most kids she wanted to get out of here as soon as she graduated. She took off for business school up in Chicago. Learning typing, shorthand, filing, secretary stuff."

Esther pulled out another cigarette. “I'll just have one more with lunch. I'm sure it won't hurt.” She lit up and took a long deep drag unlikely for a casual smoker. I kept quiet and waited for her to begin again.

"Her mom, Lula, she was so proud of Shirley when she finished business school. Shirley got a job in some office in downtown Chicago. Lula always bragged about how well Shirley was doing up in the big city. Shirley talked to Lula three or four times a week. It went on like that for three or four years. Everything seemed fine. Then Lula stopped hearing from her. Not a word. Lula was worried to death."

Emma stopped by the table, refilled our coffee cups and took away the empty dessert dishes. She left the check with me. After Emma was beyond earshot, Esther continued.

"Then one day Zelda gets this call from Shirley. That's her aunt, mind you. She didn't call her mom, but instead called Zelda. Shirley spilled the beans. She got involved with some guy from work. She ended up pregnant. Shirley never said who the father was, but it may have been her boss. He was married. Of course, he promised Shirley he would get divorced and marry her, but that never happened."

Esther stubbed out her cigarette. By now the lunch crowd was gone. We were the only customers left.

"There she was alone in Chicago with a new baby and a shattered heart. She wanted to come home, but was so ashamed, she wouldn't even call her mom. That's why she called Zelda. She asked Zelda if Lula and Ray – Ray's her dad — would let her come home."

"Obviously they said yes."

Esther shook her head. "It didn't happen that way. Lula wanted her to come home, but Ray said absolutely not. He called her a harlot and a . . ." Esther lowered her voice to a whisper, even in the empty restaurant. "A whore."

"You're kidding? He said that to his own daughter?"

"That's not all. He said he wouldn't have a B-word child under his roof. You said you haven't seen Mark, didn't you?"

"No, I've not met him."

"Well, he's, uh, different."

"Is he retarded or something?"

"Would be easier if he was," Esther said. She leaned forward. "When you see him, it's pretty clear his daddy wasn't white." Esther paused so I could absorb her disclosure. Then she continued. "He's not really black, but you can tell his daddy wasn't white like me and you. Guess he could have been a Mexican or maybe a light skinned colored guy. Zelda said the daddy was just swarthy, maybe Greek like that actor Anthony Quinn. I think she made it up 'cause she knew the daddy was a colored man."

I didn't bother telling Esther that even though Anthony Quinn's most famous role was Zorba the Greek, he was actually Mexican. "Ray wanted nothing to do with the boy because the dad might not be white?"

"He couldn't stand the thought his daughter had done, you know, *that,* with someone who wasn't white. Anyway, Zelda told Shirley to come back with the baby. Ray wouldn't let her move back home, so Shirley moved in with Zelda. Ray forbid Lula from even visiting Shirley, but that didn't stop Lula from spending time with Shirley and the baby."

"I can't imagine what Shirley was going through."

Esther nodded. "Lula finally had enough. She told Ray that if he didn't let Shirley and the baby move in, she would leave him. And she meant it. So, Ray gave in. But he never spoke Shirley's name again. Never held the boy. Every time he saw Shirley, he called her a Jezebel and told her she would burn in hell."

"Did they ever make peace?"

"No," Esther said. "It went on like that for several years. Then one day when Ray was working on his car, the jack slipped and the car fell on him. Crushed him."

I cocked my head and gave a suspicious "Hmmm."

Esther gave a conspiratorial smile. "Lot of gossip got spread around. People said Lula had enough and knocked the jack out from under the car. But it was a rusted old jack on a gravel drive. Police ruled it an accident. Nobody was too busted up about it. Nobody except Ray that is."

Esther laughed at her own humor. So did I.

"Shirley got the job at the paper not long after she came back to town. She's been there ever since. All she does is work, look after her mom and take care of her boy. Of course, she goes to church three or four times a week."

"Thanks for your time," I said, putting money on the table to cover the bill and tip. "I think I understand Shirley a bit better."

#

In conversations, Shirley often referred to the pastor at her church and the lessons in his sermons. Pastor Joe, she called him. One morning at the drug store coffee shop, I asked if anyone knew anything about a Pastor Joe.

Sam Bauserman sat at the next table. "Yeah. Joe Mullins. Church of the Consecrated Blood, or something like that. Real holy roller. From the hills down in Tennessee, I think. Some place down south. There are all sorts of stories floating around town about that church. Real backwoods primitive stuff. Women can't cut their hair. They speak in tongues. I even heard stories about snake handling, but I don't know if it is true. Why you asking?"

"His name came up in a conversation. Just curious."

#

Shirley attended church every Wednesday night. If I really wanted to learn more about her, the best way would be to attend her church.

The church stood in an unadorned whitewashed wood building without a steeple. It was located about three miles outside of Stratton on a small parcel surrounded on three sides by fields filled with soy bean stubble from the last growing season. A hand-painted wood sign identified the building as Church of the Consecrated Blood of the Lamb Our Savior Jesus Christ.

About a dozen cars were scattered haphazardly on threadbare grass adjacent to a gravel drive. I spotted Shirley's rusted Ford Fairlane among the cars. I heard voices from inside the church. I parked close to the road and got out. My plan was to slip in the back door and quietly observe without letting Shirley see me.

As I approached the building, I overheard rhythmic preaching from inside. I stood there for several minutes, hearing the preaching build into a crescendo sounding more like hollering than preaching. Cries of "Praise Jesus," and "Thank you Jesus" resonated after each sentence. For someone who grew up with a religious experience limited to going to a nearby Methodist Church on Easter and Christmas Eve, the cacophony from inside the church was beyond my frame of reference.

The shouting dissolved into something resembling words, but making no sense. Realization dawned that the preacher was speaking in tongues, the mystic language of fundamentalist faith. It was fascinating and disconcerting.

I stood there for long minutes, not moving. I was a voyeur, a peeper, in many ways no different than a pervert standing outside someone's window listening to private moans and shouts of passions to satisfy a libertine curiosity.

I walked back to my car and drove away as quietly as possible. When I got back home, I took a scalding shower trying to wash away the shame that consumed me. There wasn't enough hot water to do the job.

TWENTY-FIVE – *Drifting Apart*

April 1974

April 15, 1974, SAN FRANCISCO, CAL. (WIRE SERVICES): Kidnapped newspaper heiress Patricia Hearst has been identified as a participant in today's armed robbery of a San Francisco bank. Two bystanders are hospitalized after being shot during the robbery.

The bank heist was conducted by members of the Symbionese Liberation Army (SLA), the radical political group which kidnapped Miss Hearst earlier this year. The FBI strongly suggested that Miss Hearst was participating in the robbery against her will.

Sometimes people just drift away from each other. I don't know why it happens. The excitement of a new relationship gives way to the dullness of routine. With time, those little annoyances that at first seem endearing wear like water dripping on stone. Perhaps it is in the very nature of relationships and life.

For whatever reason, it happened to Kate and me. Eighteen months after we started dating and six months since we started living together, our relationship slid into the familiar: Friday night dinners, Saturday night sex, Sunday afternoon movies. Brutal work schedules and pressures from both of our jobs edged into our personal lives. Unexpected touches and suggestive kisses too often were replaced with an occasional sharp look or snapped response.

Even after Kate's end of the year work crush, her workload did not ease. She was sent to Seattle in late January where she spent three weeks working 14-hour days digging through the books of an auto parts retailer looking for investments to go national. A week after she returned, she flew off to Atlanta with one of Beinart and Telesky's senior executives. An expected two-day trip to negotiate the bank's investment in a heavy construction equipment manufacturer turned into two weeks. When I picked Kate up at O'Hare Airport, she was exhausted, turning down my invitation to dinner at Fanny's, her favorite Italian restaurant, choosing a quart of vanilla ice cream and fourteen hours of sleep.

My workload was not much lighter than Kate's. The skyrocketing murder rate left me with a heavy volume of stories, reporting the first story of the crime, then tracking developments until an arrest or the public interest moved to the next murder. Sometimes I felt like a scavenger surviving on the late-night carrion of drug deals gone bad, domestic passions turned violent and gang turf fights.

With Kate out of town, I spent more time in the downtown bars not far from the newspaper. Wild Turkey on the rocks washed down the latest double homicides. I wasn't alone. Examiner photographer Hurley Meyers was my regular drinking buddy. So were a half dozen other crime reporters from the city's other daily newspapers.

Editorial writers drank martini lunches at posh upscale restaurants. The political reporters got their information and manhattans at after-work hangouts in the Loop. But the crime beat reporters who worked in the dark recesses of the city, drank whiskey shots while chain-smoking cigarettes in dimly lit after-hours bars. We drank as hard as our stories, downing as many doubles as we could between the wrapping the final murder of the night and last call.

I was drinking and smoking too much. I knew it. But I did it anyway.

#

Shortly after St. Patrick's Day, Kate was gut-punched.

It wasn't an actual punch. That would have been better.

I was getting ready to leave the apartment to cover what reporters termed Chicago's Friday Night Knife and Gun Club. Kate walked in shortly before four o'clock. She had never been home that early from work.

Kate threw her coat on the couch. It slid off on to the floor, but she didn't bother stopping to pick it up. Without a greeting, she walked into the kitchen where she poured herself a full glass of Cabernet. She sat at the kitchen table and drank half the glass in one swallow.

My coat already in hand, I walked into the kitchen and I started to give her a kiss. She turned her head and pulled away. "Not now." Her jaw was firmly set, her voice sharp as a razor.

"What's up, babe?"

She finished her glass of wine with one more swallow and refilled the glass to the brim. "Those bastards."

"Which ones?"

"All of 'em. Every fucking one of them. The whole goddamn place."

"Beinart and Telesky?"

She took another long drink. "Who do you think?" I had never heard Kate filled with such venom.

What happened?"

"They fucked me over."

I put my coat over a chair and sat down. "Tell me about it."

"Barry Landersman," she said, spitting out the words. "That fucking Barry Landersman. He called me in to his office this afternoon. I thought he wanted to talk about that deal in Atlanta. But no. He wanted to talk about my career."

I listened. Kate continued to talk. And drink.

"He told me how he opposed hiring a girl to be an analyst, but I was doing a fantastic job. He really appreciated my work."

"That sounds great. What's the problem?"

"Then he tells me they are going to give me a raise. Six fucking percent."

"Is that bad?" I said.

"Do you read that newspaper you work for? That's the rate of inflation. Do you have any idea how much money they've made off me the last six months?" She again drained the wine glass and refilled it with the remaining contents of the bottle.

"But that's not even the reason I'm angry. Barry told me the firm has concerns. Women shouldn't travel so much. He actually said that. Said clients hit on women, and it's an invitation to trouble. So, they are reassigning me to the analytics desk. I'll be working strictly in the office. No more travel."

"That's a problem? You don't like all that travel."

"That's not the point, damn it. The analytics desk is a dead end. There's no way I can develop my own client base sitting in a fucking cubicle in Chicago. This means I will never be anything but a glorified number cruncher for them."

Kate stood up and began pacing around the room as if her anger could not be contained by sitting.

"To make the point even clearer, they promoted Gabe Mortensen to be my boss. He's a fucking buffoon. That little shit can't even understand half the stuff I do. It's beyond him. But he's going to be my supervisor. The only thing he has over me is that he pisses standing up."

She fought back tears and grabbed at her wine glass, nearly knocking it over before she got it in her grip.

"I'll call Charlie and tell him he needs to get somebody to cover for me tonight."

Kate slammed the glass down. I was surprised it didn't break. "No, goddamn it! I'm not your little girlie who has to have her man take care of her because she didn't get a promotion. I don't want you here. Go to work!"

I hesitated, but slipped on my coat and headed toward the door. "If you need me, you can call the office. They can reach me."

"I don't need you here!" She grabbed her wine glass and a fresh wine bottle and stomped off to the bedroom.

#

I finished my last story shortly after 2 a.m. and grabbed a quick drink with Hurley at a late night joint a block from the newspaper. I vented about how Kate had come home. He offered to buy a second round, but I felt I should check on her.

I got home about 3:30 a.m. Kate was in bed, still wearing the clothes she wore home from work. An empty wine bottle sat next to a half-full glass on her nightstand. Kate breathed deep, the rhythm punctuated by occasional gentle snores. I got undressed and slid next to her.

When I awoke at about noon, Kate was gone. I found a handwritten note next to the coffee maker. "Gone to my parents. Back Sunday."

I pounded my fist on the counter. I understood that Kate was upset about her job, but that was no excuse for taking off without talking it over with me.

I had plans. After breakfast, Kate and I would catch the new photography exhibit at the Chicago Art Museum, do some window shopping on Michigan Avenue, and grab a pizza and beer at Gino's. But I wasn't going to the museum by myself.

I decided to catch a matinee and checked through the movie listings. As I headed for the door, the phone rang. I picked up the phone on the second ring. It was Kate.

After rudimentary greeting, there was an uncomfortable silence.

"Are you okay?" I asked.

"I needed to see my parents and have some time to myself." Her voice was thin, lacking her normal self-assurance.

"That was a shitty thing you did, taking off without telling me. I thought we'd spend today together."

"I'm sorry, Zach, but I needed to get away."

"From me?"

"From everything. I'll be back tomorrow."

"You expect me to be here?" I regretted the words before they were out of my mouth.

A long silence followed. I heard a small sound as if Kate was fighting tears.

"I hope so," she said and hung up.

I slammed my fist against the wall, scraping skin from my knuckles. "Damn it!" I shouted, the dead receiver still in my hand.

Kate wasn't the only one dealing with deadlines, stress and lack of sleep. While she was gone for week-long trips to Seattle and Atlanta, I had been working long hours covering the city's skyrocketing murder rate. I planned a weekend for the two of us, hoping we could reconnect.

Now it wasn't.

My reaction was selfish. I knew it. Kate needed comforting words from me, and all I had given her was anger and threats. Three times I reached for the phone to call her back and apologize. But I didn't.

I headed to a neighborhood bar instead of the movie. I called up Hurley Meyers, who besides being the city's best news photographer was one of its most knowledgeable baseball fans. He met me at the bar just as an afternoon White Sox road game started on television.

"Where's Kate?" Hurley asked as he sat down and ordered a round of Old Style beers. "If I had a woman like that, I'd be spending time with her and not some broken down old photographer like me."

"She's up at her parents this weekend," I said, not explaining anything further.

We drank Old Style and smoked Lucky unfiltered, keeping a pace of about one beer and two cigarettes each inning. One of the great things about baseball is the ability to have a long conversation and not miss anything of importance. We lamented how bad the Cubs were and that the White Sox were worse. Hurley talked about how good some Negro League players were, and how black players had changed the major leagues.

"I go all the way back to seeing Babe Ruth and Josh Gibson play," Hurley said. "Ted Williams was a better hitter than any of them. But Willie Mays was the best that ever played the game. Sad to see him go out the way he did."

We kicked around our impressions of reporters and photographers on other papers, some outstanding, others unskilled hacks. Editors and the public didn't seem to notice the difference. We compared stories about the most gruesome crimes we had covered, some true and others exaggerated.

"I heard you started with that old camera on your desk selling photos to the black newspapers in town," I said.

"Nee-gro papers," Hurley said, exaggerating the pronunciation. "Weren't any black-owned papers until about ten years ago. Before that, they were all Negro newspapers. 'Course most of the cops called 'em nigger rags. You know, like, 'Get that boy from that nigger rag out of here.'"

"Had to be tough."

"Lot tougher than now. I'd show up with my camera and some Irish Mick cop would tell me he wasn't going to have a nigger shooting pictures of dead white people. Most cops didn't care. It was white photographers who put the cops up to it. They didn't want some nigger intruding on their turf."

There was no bitterness in Hurley's voice. He spoke as someone reminiscing about the start of a career.

"But I kept at it. Get to the scene first, take my pictures, get out of there. I'd run around to The Defender, The Crusader, The Bee, all damn fine newspapers. Sometimes they bought my pictures. Sometimes not. But I got pretty good. Wasn't too long until they started competing for my photos."

"How'd you end up at the Examiner?"

"White papers noticed and let me know they were interested in buying some of my stuff. They paid more so I sold some of my photos to the Tribune, the Sun and the Examiner. In 1955, that whole thing with Emmett Till happened. I took some photos that got some recognition. Not the ones that appeared in Jet, but some others. They got picked up by AP and went national. Wasn't long after that that the Examiner called and offered me a full-time job. I took it. Been there ever since.

By the seventh inning stretch, empty bottles and crushed packs of Lucky Strikes cluttered our table.

"You ever consider doing anything else?" I asked, after ordering another round of beers.

"Never wanted to be anything but a news photographer," Hurley said. "But I do sometimes wonder what would have happened if I went to Vietnam when I had the chance."

"Vietnam?"

"Yeah. When things were heating up, AP approached me. They needed experienced photographers over there. Offered me a helluva lot of money. Who knows? I might have won a Pulitzer or two if I'd done that."

"Might have got your ass shot off."

The bartender brought two more long necks and set them on the table.

"You ever wish you had gone?" I asked.

"Nope, guess not. I was getting a little long in the tooth for globetrotting into war zones. Besides, if I went over there, I'd have missed the Democrat Convention in '68 and that whole Richard Speck thing. Got some damned good photos out of that." Hurley took a long drink. "You go to Vietnam? I mean, you're the right age."

“Never got my name pulled,” I said.

"Lucky you," Hurley said. "You could have got your ass shot off."

The game moved into extra innings. I bought a another pack of cigarettes from a vending machine, and we ordered more beer. Dick Allen hit a two-run homer in the top of the eleventh inning and the Tigers couldn't score.

"Sox win!" Harry Carey yelled from the television, his words slightly slurred.

"So, who drank more beer during this game?" I asked. “Us or Harry?" We both laughed.

We ended up ordering dinner at the bar, steaks with baked potato and salad. Not imaginative, but it was better than expected. As we worked on our steaks, Hurley turned the topic back to Kate.

"I've known you for a while Zach. Something's going on?"

"Things seem to be, I don't know . . ." A long silent moment passed before I continued. "Everything gets in the way. She works her ass off, traveling for weeks on end. Long nights even when she’s in town. It's hard enough with me working nights, but for the last few months, we've hardly seen each other. When we do, she's so tired that, well, it's not much fun."

"Sounds like bedroom problems."

I shook my head. "It’s not that. I mean, yeah, she's too tired for that, too. But she's on edge from her job. She doesn't have time to be herself. Latest thing is she got passed over for a promotion. Now she thinks they're treating her like some bimbo from the secretarial pool."

"And she's bringing that home?"

"Yeah, she is."

Hurley pushed his plate back and pulled out a new pack of cigarettes. "How about you?"

"What about me?"

"I've been doing this a long time. Too long, probably. I tried being married a couple of times. It didn't take. Looking back, they were really good women. Better than me."

Hurley took a cigarette from the pack and lit it. He took a long drag, blowing the smoke out in a continuous thin stream. Then he continued.

"Photographer, reporter, doesn't matter. This job does something to you. We make our living on blood and death. That's not normal." Hurley paused for a moment, then added. "The worst part of it is, we like it."

Hurley drained his bottle and signaled for two more.

"Just look at our conversation. Here we are in a bar, getting drunk, watching a ball game, and we're talking about murders — heads blown off, naked girls strangled in alleys, murder-suicides. That's not normal conversation, Zach. That's not what normal people talk about on their day off."

The beers came.

"You've seen how Kate's job is impacting her, but have you looked at how your job is changing you?"

Hurley waited. When I said nothing, he continued.

"I've only met Kate twice, but she seems like a great girl. Smart and pretty. Better than you deserve. But I'm just saying that if she's what you want, you gotta keep this job from changing you. And you gotta work at keeping her. Otherwise you'll end up like me, an old fart hanging on long after he should have retired because he has nothing to go home to."

#

Kate returned Sunday afternoon. I was waiting for her when she walked in, my hangover headache long gone by the time she walked in the door. I gave her a quick kiss, then followed her to our room while she unpacked her overnight bag.

"Good visit?" I asked.

"Yes," she said, but didn't expand her answer.

"Your parents doing okay?"

"They're concerned about me, but doing great. Dad's getting the boat ready for the next time you're up there." She paused, turning to face me. "I'm sorry I left without talking to you, Zach. I was . . . well, just so upset. I wasn't thinking straight."

I wrapped my arms around her and we kissed. It was long, and slow and tender.

"I'm sorry, too," I said. "Sorry for what you've been going through. Sorry that your bosses are a bunch of pricks. And I'm sorry that I can be a prick to you, too. You don't need that."

We held each other for a very long time.

I led Kate into the kitchen where I had the classified ads spread open. There were scattered ads circled with red marker.

Kate's lease was up at the end of April. When I moved in, our understanding was that we would stay in Kate's apartment until her lease was up and then look for a larger place. But with only weeks left, we had not started looking. We never talked about it, but each of us seemed hesitant to sign the one-year financial commitment required by a new lease.

Kate sat down with the ads facing her, and I then pulled a chair next to her.

"I did some thinking while you were gone," I said. "I thought a lot about us."

She looked into my eyes. I thought there was a hint of anxiety in them. Was it my imagination?

"I love you," I said, wanting to reassure her where the conversation was going. "I want to make sure this works between us. It won't always be easy. I know that. But this is what I want."

I waved my hand toward the paper. "So here are some apartments I think we should consider. Maybe we could see some of them sometime this week if you can fit it in to your schedule."

"If we sign a lease, you're stuck with me for at least a year. You still want to sign a lease with me?"

"I'm not sure I've ever wanted anything more."

Kate smiled. She leaned over and kissed me. "What if I'm no longer that fancy investment banker you met?

"You thinking about quitting?"

Kate shook her head. "Not immediately. When I left Saturday, I fully intended to walk into Barry's office Monday and give him my resignation. But I did some thinking. That's why I went up to mom and dad's. Just wanted to think things through by myself. I decided not to just walk out. But I will start looking. I don't like what this job is doing to me. To us."

She squeezed my hand.

"If you quit, or stay, or decide you want to go someplace and grow potatoes, you'll still be the woman I love. You're who I want to be with."

TWENTY-SIX – *What the Hell Was That?*

April 19, 1976, SAN FRANCISCO, CAL. (WIRE SERVICES): Newspaper heiress Patricia Hearst, 22, who was kidnapped in 1974 by the Symbionese Liberation Army, was convicted today of armed robbery by a federal court jury. She faces up to 35 years in prison.

The jury rejected the defense offered by famed lawyer F. Lee Baily that Miss Hearst was an innocent victim forced by her captors to participate in the robbery.

The final plan for railroad reorganization was signed into law in February. In April, the government-created Consolidated Rail Corporation, known as Conrail, began operation. The fate of nearly a century of railroads in Stratton was sealed.

At the Town Board meeting in April, Hank Pemberton had the job of reading the town's fate like so many ill-positioned tea leaves in a cup.

"We got the final word, and it's the worst news we could get," Hank said. "Both Penn Central lines will stop operating at the end of July. The Erie-Lackawanna line will stop at the end of August. By September, the railroads will be gone."

"I thought they said end of the year?" Sam Bauserman said.

"That's what the Congressman said in his letter, but I guess he was wrong."

"What are you going to do Hank?" Sam asked. "Can you even operate the elevator when harvest starts this fall?"

"I don't know yet. I'll try, but without the railroad, I'm not sure the elevator and sawmill can make it. Trucking is so damned expensive. Now with OPEC driving the fuel prices up and up, I don't see how I can do it."

"How many jobs you going to lose?" Bill Olsen asked.

"Haven't figured it out yet. I can probably keep the feed store and the lumber yard going just on local business. Not sure about anything else. I'll probably have to cut two-thirds of the jobs. That's if I can survive at all."

The room fell into a deep silence. It felt like a wake without the promise of resurrection.

#

The story about the rail line closings ran on the front page with a two-word headline: RAILS GONE.

Nothing else needed to be said.

The news spread long before the paper hit the local newsstands. It cast a pall over the entire town. For a week it seemed everyone on the streets shuffled along with heads down and shoulders hunched. The morning crowd at the drug store coffee shop sat hunkered over steaming cups of coffee, not speaking. In the grocery and post office, people who regularly approached me with some piddly tidbit of news about a nephew or cousin, kept their distance as if I carried the plague. Even the weather was gray, cold and somber, without a trace of spring.

The following Saturday the weather broke into a glorious warm spring day. Puffy clouds marched in formation across a crystal cobalt background. A few heads lifted. Quiet conversations buzzed at the coffee shop and among the lunchtime crowd at Shelby's place. In slow measures, life began the process of adjusting.

The one person mired in the pall was Hank Pemberton. A regular at the coffee shop, he often lingered while reading the newspaper and exchanging gossip. Now he ordered his coffee to go. Without making eye contact with anyone, he walked to the counter and ordered his coffee. Hank fidgeted with the tooth pick holder on the counter while the server poured the coffee. Once in hand, he quickly left, his head down, not making eye contact with anyone.

Even when the longtime regulars shouted greetings, Hank didn't respond. One day Howard Gudgel invited him to sit down for a few minutes. Hank shook his head and walked out.

After that, Hank didn't show up at all. Instead, one of his sons would come in. Sometimes it was Danny, the high school basketball team player who would soon graduate. Other times, it was his younger brother Josh.

"Those are good boys," Howard Gudgel said one day after Josh left with the coffee intended for his dad. "Shame what's going on with the railroad. That's gonna kill Hank's businesses. It might even kill Hank."

#

I was home by myself on the last Friday night in April. Emma picked up a late shift, so I stayed home with a frozen dinner and a six pack. A week earlier, I noticed a copy of Saul Bellow's Humboldt's Gift sitting on Emma's bookshelf. I picked it up and thumbed through the worn pages.

"Take that if you want," Emma said. "I liked it, but won't ever read it again."

The book spent most of the past year on best-seller lists and was on my list of books to read. So, I took the book.

With nothing better to do, I found myself in my apartment on a Friday evening, a longneck beer at my elbow, starting a 500-page novel. I was seventy pages into the novel, nursing a second beer, when I felt a low rumble. My beer bottle danced across the top of the side table. Pots and pans rattled in the kitchen. It lasted several seconds.

"What the hell?" I said out loud.

I experienced a small earthquake a few years back while on vacation in California. My first instinct was an earthquake. Midwest quakes were rare, and served only to rattle dishes and maybe a few nerves.

I didn't think much more about it and returned to my book. Several minutes later, an emergency siren approached then stopped not far from my apartment. I threw on my sneakers and walked outside. A police car blocked the street, its emergency lights flashing.

I walked to the police car. Clint Avery stood next to his cruiser, flashlight in hand.

"What's up?"

"Derailment," Clint said, directing his light across a grassy area toward the Erie tracks.

"Anybody hurt?"

"Not that I know of, but you better ask Gus. He's over there." Clint pointed toward emergency lights flashing on the other side of the tracks. "Gus tried to talk to the engineer, but he won't say anything until the railroad people get here. The crew is all accounted for. Outside of a few bumps and scratches, nobody is hurt. Gus told me to block the traffic and keep people away from this side of the tracks."

"Okay if I check it out?"

"Sure. Be my guest. Just watch your step. That train tore up the ground pretty good. Don't want you to twist an ankle or break a leg."

I walked into the pitch-black night. My eyes adjusted. In the darkness, I could make out the faint outline of a large object. I walked a few steps closer and saw the massive shape of an overturned locomotive. The engine gouged a six-foot deep trench, forcing dirt, rocks and grass into a surrounding barrier. Behind the first locomotive, two more were nestled into the furrow. As I walked forward, I saw a half-dozen boxcars, perhaps more, stacked in twisted piles of steel and wood.

"Holy shit," I said under my breath. Then I ran back to my apartment for my camera.

The railroad officials did not arrive at the scene until the next morning. With them came several state police cars and an array of specialized railroad equipment. While the officials kept their distance from me, one of the state police investigators told me it looked like vandalism.

"Probably some kids," he said. "There were railroad ties wedged into the track. Engineer saw a couple of kids running away from the tracks as he approached, but he didn't see the ties. At that point, it was too late, anyway. We're lucky they weren't carrying something toxic or that it didn't catch fire. There was a derailment down in the south part of the state last year that poisoned the groundwater for miles around. This could have been terrible."

"Any estimate on the damage?"

"Around a half million, according to the railroad boys."

"Any idea who the kids are?"

"Not yet," he said. "But kids can't keep their mouths shut. They end up telling friends. Someone overhears. Eventually word will get back to us. We'll find them."

I wasn't in the same league as Hurley Meyers as a news photographer, but I was proud of the photo. It ran on the front page showing three locomotives on their side amid a panorama of twisted metal. A state cop was standing on top of the lead locomotive surveying the scene. His small figure on the huge wrecked train engine gave perspective to the size of the crash.

#

Two weeks later I was getting coffee at the Perry Drug Store along with my morning dose of town gossip. Howard Gudgel approached me as I sipped my first cup of the day. He spoke quietly, something seldom done in the coffee shop.

"Suppose you heard they found the boy that wrecked that train?" Howard Gudgel said as I sat down.

"Who?"

"Hank Pemberton's youngest. What's his name? Josh, I think. The younger boy that comes in here for his dad's coffee sometimes."

"You're kidding?"

Ezra Brown, the elementary teacher who was a sometimes member of my chess club, spoke up from a nearby table. "From what I hear, the boy found out the railroads were shutting down and going to put his daddy out of business."

"Police arrest him?"

"No," Howard said. "They went over to Hank's house a couple of nights ago. Told him what they found out. Guess Hank called his son down, and he admitted it. They're going to charge him with delinquency, but ain't taking him to jail, or anything like that."

Howard took a sip of his coffee. "Everybody understands what's going on. Most of us would have liked to do that ourselves. Some of us consider the boy a goddamn hero."

I made phone calls to the police and prosecutor's office to get confirmation. But it was a juvenile matter so they wouldn't release the name. They only confirmed that juveniles were responsible for the incident, and it would be handled in juvenile court.

The law prohibited the police or courts from releasing a juvenile's name, but nothing prohibited me from printing what I knew – what the whole town knew. The fact that the paper was a weekly gave me several days to contemplate the situation before my deadline. In the end, I decided that all the information I had to identify Josh Pemberton was rumor. No one with firsthand knowledge – the police, the prosecutor or the courts – would confirm the name. And I didn't like the notion of identifying a juvenile.

So that was the way I wrote the story:

Police have charged a juvenile with delinquency in connection with the April 30 derailment of an Erie Lackawanna freight train. The incident caused an estimated half million dollars damage.

Citing state law, court and law enforcement officials are withholding the juvenile's name.

TWENTY-SEVEN – *Crossing the Line*

May 15, 1976, NEW YORK, NY (WIRE SERVICES): More than 1,500 marchers took part in the sixth annual National Marijuana Day Parade in New York City today.

Accompanied by rock bands, pervasive marijuana smoke and a contingent of police officers who watched, the marchers made their way up Fifth Avenue from Central Park to Washington Square Park. Asked why they were not making arrests, one officer stated, "We're not here to incite people. As long as they behave, we ignore it."

I learned about wild marijuana pickers while riding with Clint Avery in his patrol car on an unseasonably warm late afternoon in mid-May. We were cruising along the state highway on the west end of town when I saw Clint take an interest in an older red over white two-tone Ford Mustang in front of us.

"Well, what have we here?" Clint said.

I looked over at Clint, not sure what he was talking about. He pointed at the car in front. "You see anything unusual about the trunk of that car?"

I looked. "No."

"Look closer."

I did. "I guess there's some weeds or something hanging out of the trunk. But that's it."

Clint looked at me and smiled. "Plates are from Illinois. Looks like some teens in the car. Maybe college age. Maybe younger. And you got some weeds hanging out of the trunk. I'd say we got us some wild marijuana pickers."

I looked at him, not comprehending.

"Wild marijuana pickers," Clint repeated.

"What are you talking about?" I said.

"Back in World War II, the Army paid farmers around here to grow hemp. They planted hundreds of acres to use for rope, cords, canvas, all sorts of stuff. Well, the stuff went wild. Farmers around here have been trying to kill it off ever since. But the stuff still grows wild along ditches and fence lines around the county."

"Hemp? Is that marijuana?"

"Piss poor cousin, as I understand. It's got the same chemical, but you'd need to smoke a pound to get high. Every spring word spreads that you can drive down here and pick marijuana right off the roads. We get a lot of kids from around Chicago looking for free pot."

"You going to arrest them?"

"Naw," Clint said. He hit his lights and blipped his siren to pull the car over. "We used to, but county prosecutor said the stuff may not qualify as marijuana. He told us not to arrest them because he doesn't have the time or the staff to deal with it."

"So, what are you going to do?"

Clint called in the stop and the license number on the radio. "We hassle them a bit so all their friends don't show up next week, then we let them go."

Clint put on his hat and a stony glare and got out of the car. I stepped out too, and walked close enough to see and hear what was going on, but not close enough to interfere. Clint asked for IDs, and all four figures started reaching in pockets and purses. A minute later, Clint walked back. "They're scared shitless," he said as he passed me.

As Clint was calling in the driver's license numbers, another Stratton police car pulled behind us, its lights flashing. Gus Kopetsky got out. He was wearing his dark blue uniform. Like Clint, he pulled on his hat as he exited the car. He walked up to Clint's car and leaned on the open door.

"Got some pickers?" he asked.

Clint finished calling in the licenses. He turned to Gus. "Yeah. Four high school kids from Evanston."

"How much stuff they picked?"

"Not sure. Haven't opened the trunk yet."

"You wait for the report back on the license. I'll take care of this."

I was still standing by the front of the car. Gus walked by me saying nothing. There was a snarl on his face. As he approached the car, he hoisted his belt and unsnapped his holster.

"Shit," was all I could say.

Gus kept his hand on his still holstered gun and yelled into the car, his voice gravelly and menacing.

"Get your asses out of there. Keep your hands where I can see them. You make any wrong moves, and I'll be calling your mommies to tell them to pick up their dead kids. Understand?"

The four teens, two boys and two girls, got out, two of them having to climb out from the back seat in the two-door car. They all looked scared, their faces white. The two girls visibly trembled.

"Put your hands behind your neck. Lace your fingers. Then walk over here and line up along the white line."

When one girl was slow, he walked up and put his face about six inches from her. "You retarded or you just want to get shot? Put your hands behind your neck!"

She shook so much that her hands could barely find each other to comply with Gus' order. Tears streamed down her face as she joined the others lined up along the white line at the edge of the road.

Gus reached in the car and pulled the keys out of the ignition. He walked to the back of the car, never taking his eyes off the teens. He unlocked the trunk and let it pop open. Inside was a loose pile of green leaves and stems. They looked more like roadside weeds than a marijuana harvest.

"What have we here?" Gus turned and yelled back toward where Clint was still sitting in his car. "Looks like we got some big-time marijuana dealers," he said, pronouncing the "j."

Gus walked up to the driver, a tall lanky clean-cut boy, his face covered in acne. "Is that we got here? Are you a big-time marijuana dealer?"

The boy shook his head.

"I can't hear you, boy. What's that?"

"Uh, no. We aren't marijuana dealers."

"No what?"

The boy looked puzzled.

Without warning, Gus swung his hand up and hit the boy behind his ear with his open hand. The boy's head jerked, and he grabbed the side of his face.

"Put your hands back up. Now, what do you say?"

"No, sir," said the other boy, a shorter stockier kid with hair down to his shoulders.

Gus grunted. "You look like a girl with that long hair. Maybe we should cut that while you're here."

The long-haired boy tried to keep calm, but his resolve was failing.

"I want all of you up against the car," Gus barked. "Put your hands on the roof and spread your legs." The same girl hesitated. Gus walked up to her and again put his face inches from her's. "That means you too, sweetie. Get your ass over there."

After all four teens were in place, Gus began frisking the boys.

I walked over to where Clint sat.

"Clint, if he feels up those girls, you're going to have to arrest me. I won't stand by and let him do that."

Clint had not been paying attention, waiting for the call back on the license check. He glanced up toward Gus and immediately was out of the car.

"Hey chief," he yelled as Gus finished frisking the second boy. Gus turned and Clint waved him over.

"Don't move an inch," he said. Keeping his eyes on the frightened teens, Gus walked back to Clint.

"You can't pat down those girls," Clint said, keeping his voice soft.

"Why not?"

"You can't. You put hands on them and we're all going to be in trouble. Even if you arrest them, a woman has to do the search. And you're not going to arrest them. You put your hands on their boobs, and they'll tell their parents, and you'll get the whole damn town sued."

Gus made a grunting noise. "Give me their licenses."

Clint pulled them out of his shirt pocket and handed them to Gus.

He walked back, holding the licenses in his hand. "You two," he yelled at the boys. "Get your asses back there and empty that trunk. Throw that shit on the side of the road."

The boys, their eyes full of fear, complied. When the trunk was empty, Gus faced the four, holding up their licenses. "Now I don't want to screw with the paperwork on a bunch of little piss ants. So, here's what I'm gonna do. I'm gonna let you go. But I'm going to hold on to these drivers' licenses. And if you ever end up in my town again, I'm going to throw you in jail and charge you with dealing. That's real prison time. You understand?"

The four nodded.

"What?"

"Yes, sir," came the reluctant response from all four, their voices permeated with fear.

"Now get in your car and get your ass out of here." The four started getting in the car, but the driver turned back. "Sir, I need my license. What if I get stopped between here and home?"

Gus smirked and slipped the drivers licenses into his shirt pocket. "Well, boy, if I was you, I wouldn't want to have to explain that to some officer. Guess I'd just be real sure not to break any traffic laws on the way back home. Now get out of here before I change my mind."

The driver got back in the car. Slowly the car pulled away. He was driving no more than twenty miles per hour as he headed down the street.

Gus turned back toward where I was standing next to Clint. He broke into a loud belly laugh. "Those kids will have to change their drawers when they get home," he said. "They won't be back."

Clint didn't join in the laughter. Neither did I.

#

When I got back to the office, I called Lee Phillips, a Chicago Detective I knew. I had his home number and called him there. We chatted for a few minutes, catching up on events, then I got around to the purpose of my call.

"You ever hear of a retired Chicago cop named Gus Kopetsky?"

"No," Lee said. "Should I?"

"Could you do me a favor and find out what you can about him?"

"You working on a story?"

"Just background. I deal with him a lot, and I'd need to know who I'm dealing with."

"Off the record?"

"Not for attribution," I said.

"I thought you said you weren't working on a story."

"I'm not. But I can't promise something won't find its way into the paper."

It was about a week before I received a call back from Lee.

"Well, your friend Gus is quite a piece of work," Lee said. "He joined Chicago P.D. right after the war. He was a patrol cop for fourteen years. He got bad reviews including from his partners on the street. Never promoted. Then in the late 50s, he beat up some kid pretty good he stopped for shoplifting. Left the kid with brain damage. Problem was, it wasn't the right kid. Department got sued and had to pay."

"He get fired?"

"Oh hell no. Back then he could have killed the kid and wouldn't have got fired. But they transferred him off the street. Put him on administrative work. When he got his twenty in, he was forced out. Officially, he retired."

"When was that?"

"Sixty-seven, before the convention."

All time in the Chicago Police Department was measured as before or after the 1968 Democratic National Convention.

"Nobody had anything good to say about this guy. After he left the force, he hung around doing private security work for four or five years. Rent-a-cop stuff. Then his mother died and left him some money. Not long after that, he left the city. Nobody has heard anything since then."

"Thanks," I said. "That fills in some holes." I was ready to hang up when Lee added.

"We're still working. Nothing new, but we haven't given up."

"Thanks," I said again. Then hung up.

#

It was a few days later I saw Gus at the Town Board meeting. I waited until the meeting ended. "Hey Gus, can I speak to you a minute. In private?"

Gus cocked his head toward me, but said nothing. He turned, and I followed him to the police side of the municipal building.

Gus unlocked the building, turned on the lights and started a pot of coffee. He took a seat at his desk and leaned back, putting his feet on his desk. "What can I do for you, newsman?"

I took a seat in a metal folding chair across from Gus. I put my notebook in my shirt pocket.

"This is off the record, Gus. It's just between you and me."

Gus crossed his arms across his ample belly. He said nothing.

"I watched how you treated those kids Clint stopped. If Clint hadn't said something, you were going to paw those girls."

Gus snorted, took his feet off his desk and leaned toward me. "Since when are you an expert on police business?"

"I've been around cops ever since I started as a reporter. I've seen Chicago cops bash guys with flashlights and trip them when they have their hands cuffed behind their back. I'm not naive about what cops do. Generally, I let it slide because of the kind of people they deal with."

"Damn Skippy."

"But I know when a cop crosses the line. When he becomes a bully with a badge. And Gus, that's what you are."

Gus face went cold. His brow furrowed, and he glared. "You better be careful where you're stepping, boy."

"I still have friends on the Chicago P.D. They checked your background for me. I know about the kid you beat up. I know about all the complaints. I know you were pulled off the street. I know all of that."

Gus stood up and hooked his thumbs inside his belt. He towered above me, his effort at intimidation obvious. I remained seated, never lowering my eyes from his.

"You print any of that, and I'll sue your ass. You understand?"

"I'm doing this to give you a fair warning," I said.

"Warning? You threatening me?"

I kept my voice calm, but I could feel blood rushing in my head, my heart pounding.

"A notice, if you prefer. But I've seen the way you bully people. I saw you pound on a guy who you thought took a candy bar from your store. I saw you hit that Ritchie Kyle kid with your flashlight and shoot his football. You shot his football, for God's sake."

"He's a punk," Gus said. "His whole family is a bunch of trouble-making hillbillies. You don't keep them in their place, they'll be stealing the town blind."

"Look Gus . . ."

"That's Marshal to you, you little peckerwood."

"Okay, Marshal Kopetsky. I've not put any of this in the newspaper. I thought about it, but didn't. But now it's a little different. I've seen too much. If I witness anything like that again, it's going in the paper."

"You little fuck. Who do you think you are?"

"I'm the editor of the town newspaper, that's who I am. You can threaten to arrest me, or give me tickets or withhold information, whatever you want, but if you ever hit Richie Kyle again, or abuse a bunch of teenagers like you did the other day, I'll make sure all this goes on page one."

"You better watch your back, newsman. You better just watch your back."

I got up. Never quite turning my back, I walked out.

TWENTY-EIGHT – *Spilled Beer and Diamonds*

June 1974

June 5, 1974, CLEVELAND, OH (SPORTS WIRE SERVICE): Cleveland Indians' 10-cent beer promotion turned into an alcohol-fueled ninth inning riot last night, forcing the home-team Indians to forfeit the game.

Drunken projectile-throwing, knife-wielding fans flooded the field in the bottom of the ninth inning. Players from both teams charged from the dugout carrying baseball bats to protect the players on the field. Fearing for the safety of everyone, the umpires forfeited the game in favor of the visiting Texas Rangers.

Kate's schedule eased a bit by summer, although her frustration with her reassignment at her firm did not. The relaxed schedule made it easier to make plans for a special dinner and evening out.

I made reservations at the Berghoff, not the standup bar where we met over a spilled beer, but the adjoining classic German restaurant. Kate protested that the food was too heavy, but I insisted that my heart was set on sauerbraten. In truth, it was set on something else.

The sun had dropped below the skyline, but had not yet set when we entered the restaurant. A waiter in a classic white apron tied in front showed us to a booth along the back wall. Kate ordered a Beefeater's and tonic and I ordered the draft house dark beer. We held off ordering food while we talked. I drank the beer in long gulps while she sipped at her drink.

"Careful with that, cowboy," she said, nodding at my now mostly empty stein. "You keep going at that rate, and you won't make it through the evening."

I laughed a bit. It was a nervous laugh that I hoped she didn't notice.

As we talked about how her week had gone, my hand slipped into my jacket pocket. I found what I was feeling for. I reached for my beer stein, grasping it by the top. I loosened my fingers and felt the beer splash up against the palm of my hand. I eased my hand forward, pushing the mug until it tipped, hitting the table with a heavy thud. The last bit of beer in my mug spilled across the table toward Kate.

Kate gave a small shriek and slid her chair back.

"Remind you of anything," I said smiling.

There was a pause. Then her eyes fell to the table. She spotted it. Gleaming on the wet tablecloth among dissipating islands of beer foam was a ring. A full carat solitaire set in white gold.

Kate's mouth dropped open, then her hands went to cover her open mouth. Tears formed in her shimmering emerald eyes.

I picked up the ring from the white tablecloth and dried it with a single swipe of my napkin. I moved to Kate's side and dropped to one knee.

"Really," she managed to say through her hands.

"Really, Kate. I didn't think I would ever truly love anyone. Not the type of love that would consume me. But I love you more than I ever thought possible. My life only has meaning with you in it. Will you marry me?"

Kate nodded her head rapidly.

"I need to hear it."

"Yes. Oh my God, yes, yes, yes."

I leaned in. Kate threw her arms around me and we kissed for what seemed forever. Applause erupted from around the room.

Kate held her hand up in front of her face and stared at the ring. "Oh, my God," Kate said again.

As I had arranged several days earlier, the wait staff quickly surrounded the table. They replaced the wet tablecloth and brought a bottle of Moët & Chandon in a silver champagne bucket with four glasses. From the doorway leading to a second dining room, Jim and Doris Billings walked toward us.

"Well, I guess she said yes," Jim said, a smile across the entire width of his face.

Kate looked up and saw her parents. She jumped up and put both arms around her mother. Their embrace seemed to last for several minutes as tears poured from their eyes. Finally, Kate broke free from her mother and gave her dad a hug that was briefer but no less heartfelt. She turned back to me and pulled me tight against her.

"Happy?" I asked.

She nodded her head.

We sat down and the bottle of champagne was quickly consumed with congratulatory toasts. A second bottle was on its way before we ever ordered food.

The evening went better than I had even hoped. There were smiles, and laughs, and more tears. We took our time at dinner. Afterward, we headed to the lounge on the ninety-fifth floor of the John Hancock Building for dessert and drinks. We listened and danced to a small jazz combo with a sultry torch singer until shortly after one o'clock.

Kate's parents called it a night and caught a cab back to their hotel. Kate started to hail another cab, but I didn't want the evening to end yet.

"Let's walk," I said.

We strolled along Michigan Avenue, our fingers interlocked, our faces beaming. I kept stealing glances at the ring on Kate's finger. So did she. We walked south to the Chicago River where we stood on the bridge, staring into the roiling water moving below us on its way to Lake Michigan.

Kate turned and took both my hands. "I have some news, too. I was going to tell you at dinner, but I didn't want to take away from this night."

"Are you pregnant?"

Kate gave me a playful slap across the shoulder. "No, I'm not pregnant. I've got a new job."

"What? Where? When did this happen?"

"Just like a reporter," she said, smiling. "What. When. Where. Who. I interviewed yesterday, and they offered me the job on the spot. It's a great company and a great opportunity. I couldn't pass it up."

"Who is it?"

"Wemsley Lamott. It's an investment company out of Denver."

The smile on my face dropped. After several seconds of silence, I said, "Does this mean you . . . " I caught myself. "Uh, we are moving to Colorado?"

Again, she punched me in the shoulder. "No. They recently opened a new office in the Loop. They promised me that the workweek is never more than fifty hours, and most times much less. I'll have to go out to Denver about once a month, but most times I'll fly out in the morning, fly back that night."

I slid my hands under Kate's butt and lifted her high above me. I spun her around several times.

Kate laughed as I set her back down. The world didn't quit spinning when I stopped, the product of an evening of alcohol and dancing.

"Don't you want to know how much I'll make?"

"I don't care," I said. "I just want you out of that hell hole where you work. And I want you to be happy." I kissed Kate again. "I want us to be happy."

"Well I'm not out of there yet. Not until the middle of August. I told Wesley Lamott that I was working on a big project that closes in mid-August. They thought it spoke well of me that I wanted to finish that project. So, I'm going to see that project to the end, then take three weeks off. I start the new job the second week of September."

"That may be the best news of the night."

"If you could get a week or two off while I'm between jobs, we could go back down to Key West."

"I'd like that."

We started retracing our steps back up Michigan Avenue toward the Water Tower. We walked several blocks in silence.

"So, when do you want to get married?" I asked.

She put her arms around my neck, pulled me to her and gave me a long slow kiss. When our lips parted, she said, "How about when we're in Key West?"

"That's pretty short notice. I thought you brides needed at least six months to plan."

"I want something simple. Just us. Maybe my parents. On a beach. Maybe even out on Sand Key."

I pulled Kate back to me and kissed her, holding her tight against me. We stood as one among the glimmering lights and humming traffic of early morning Chicago.

"Key West over Labor Day," I said. "Sounds perfect."

TWENTY-NINE – *Deadly Secrets*

June 2, 1976, PHOENIX, AZ (WIRE SERVICES). Don Bolles, 47, an award-winning investigative reporter for the Arizona Republic, was critically injured when his car exploded outside the Clarendon House Hotel today. Police say a bomb was placed below the driver's floorboard.

Bolles was working on a story involving organized crime in Phoenix area businesses.

I was stunned at how quickly the murder of Rene Swisher faded from the community's collective conscience. As weeks turned into months, there seemed to be no concern about a murderer being loose in the town. As far as I could tell, people still left their doors unlocked and parked with keys in their car.

I checked every couple of weeks with Detective Virgil Amundsen on the status of the investigation. All I ever got was a standard, "No new developments."

After several months, I decided to see if he would meet with me to discuss the case and where the investigation stood. It seemed the leads had all played out. I suspected that unless something unexpected turned up, they would never solve the case.

We met in a small cafe in Amelia on a Saturday afternoon. Other than an elderly couple sitting at a window seat, the restaurant was deserted. After some brief preliminaries, I got to the point.

"This investigation has been going on for a while and all I keep hearing is no new developments. I want to get the straight story. Are there any leads? Do you have anything to go on at all, or is this going to be one of those cases that never gets solved?"

Virgil Amundsen pulled out a pack of unfiltered Lucky Strikes from his shirt pocket, tapped it on the table then pulled one out and put it in his mouth. He offered me one, but I held up my hand.

"That's my brand, but I quit," I said.

He nodded, then struck a match and lit the cigarette. As he took the first drag, he stirred at his coffee even though he was drinking it black. "Why you doing this? Zach?" he finally said. "Why do you keep asking about this case when everybody in town wants to forget it?"

The question surprised me. "I'm a reporter," I said. "This is what I'm supposed to do."

Virgil blew a stream of smoke toward the ceiling. "I checked you out with a buddy of mine in Chicago. He said you're a straight shooter. That true?"

"I like to think so. I keep my word."

Virgil signaled for the waitress for more coffee. As she came over and refilled our cups, he took out another Lucky and lit it from the one he was finishing. When the waitress had left, Virgil started again.

"For public consumption, we are continuing the investigation. The victim was a prostitute dealing drugs. We suspect a drug deal went bad. Could have been sex. Maybe both."

"So that's public now, and I can use it."

Virgil nodded.

"You have any suspects? Maybe a list of her customers?"

"For public consumption, we are investigating all angles."

"How about on background."

"Not for print, right?"

"Not until you tell me different," I said. "If I get the information from another source, it's fair game. But if I'm going to publish some new information on the case, I'll call you."

"You're not like most of the reporters around here." Virgil said. "They're a bunch of clowns who are lucky if they get the names spelled right."

"I've spelled names wrong," I said, attempting a self-deprecating smile. "Rarely, but it's happened."

Virgil took a final drag from his most recent Lucky and crushed it out on his saucer, then continued. "I've been told I can trust you, so I can live with that. In return, possibly you can help us. If you find out something that might be connected to the investigation, tell me before you go to print."

"I can't make a blanket promise like that. But if I get new information and it doesn't violate any promise to a source, I'll give you a heads up. That work?"

Virgil stirred his coffee, considering his response. He nodded. "That will work."

Virgil took out his pack of Luckies and lit another one. Again, he offered one to me.

"Thanks, but I made a promise," I said.

"This is strictly background," Virgil said. "My friend in Chicago said I could trust you, so I'm expecting you to live up to your word. There's a lot of shit going on around this case."

"Some of that shit involves Orville Vehorn and Gus Kopetsky?" I asked.

"Where did you get that?

"Just watching them at the murder scene. I found the body, so I called it in. When Gus got there, first person he called was Orville. He didn't call anybody else until he and Orville had a little private confab then went upstairs."

A concerned look crossed Virgil's face. "That's new information. Gus interviewed you. All he said was that you and your friends investigated a smell from the upstairs, and you found the body."

"That's true."

"Gus didn't tell us he and Vehorn went upstairs before we got there. How long were they up there?"

"Ten minutes. Not much more."

Virgil took a long drag on his cigarette. "That makes sense."

"So, what is going on?"

"This is not for publication. Not now."

"I told you, not unless I get it from somewhere else."

Virgil took a deep breath and leaned forward. "What we believe happened – and mind you we can't prove this right now – was that Rene Swisher gave freebies to every cop in Lancaster County to look the other way while she sold drugs. That includes the Stratton Police."

"Gus in on this? Orville? Who?"

"Vehorn rented his place to her a couple of months before the murder. Orville doesn't have the balls to be involved in anything other than taking a few bucks to look the other way, but he probably suspected something was up. The victim didn't have a lease and paid her rent in cash, neither of which is unusual around here. But someone like Orville renting to a girl that didn't have a job? That doesn't happen unless someone vouches for her or pays her rent. Kopetsky is involved somehow, but I don't have anything definite on him, either. He might have paid the girl's rent and Orville isn't telling us. Hell, the county sheriff might have been in on it. There's nothing we can put our hands on."

"Any physical evidence?"

"Someone wiped down the bedroom pretty good. There were only a few partial prints. That's probably what Gus and Orville were doing. But there were plenty of prints other places -- in the bathroom, on the refrigerator, the furniture, the doors."

"Any matches?"

"About half the cops in Lancaster County, including Stratton P.D."

"Gus?"

Virgil nodded. "Kenny Wyman, too."

"Clint?"

Virgil have a half laugh. "She wasn't Clint's type, if you understand what I'm saying."

I did. "Was it a police officer?" I asked.

The detective signaled for more coffee. When the cups were refilled, and the waitress gone, Virgil continued.

"I'd be shocked if a cop is good for the murder. A cop would have arranged the scene. Probably put some type of weapon near her to look like she was resisting arrest on a drug charge. Something like that. Besides, the perp shot her with a .22. Police officers don't use .22s. Forty-fives and thirty-eights are cop guns."

Virgil pulled out another cigarette and lit it. "No, I'm guessing it was one of her drug customers. Might be a john, but more likely drugs. There's more violence around drugs than sex."

"Get any other fingerprints that are useful?"

"There were a few non-cop prints we identified. Low level drug users in the system already. We talked to them but none seem good for it. There were prints from at least a half dozen other people we can't identify. They could have come from her customers or from the last tenant. The way the apartment looked, she hadn't cleaned the place since she moved in."

"Why are you telling me this?"

"Like I said, you're a lot more savvy than the guys with most of these local papers. We're pretty much at the end of our rope. The local cops aren't helping because they're scared about getting busted for getting a little on the side to let her peddle drugs. I really don't care about that." Virgil paused and sipped his coffee, apparently rethinking his comment.

"Well, not much," he finally said. "I'm not internal affairs or the morality police. My concern is finding who killed this girl. You've got your ear to the ground in Stratton. If you hear anything, I'd be grateful if you passed it along."

"I can't be an undercover snitch."

Virgil chain lit another Lucky off the cigarette he was finishing. I wondered how many cigarettes he smoked a day.

"I don't want you to go around playing Dick Tracy, Jr., or anything like that. If you come across something that seems important, pass it along."

I nodded. "If I can, I will."

#

I wrote a brief story on the status of the investigation for an inside page of the next week's paper. The article ran with a headline, "Police Have No New Leads In Stratton Murder"

Drug dealing and prostitution were likely the reason for the murder of Stratton resident Rene Swisher, but there are no new leads, according to Indiana State Police Detective Virgil Amundsen, who is heading the investigation.

Detective Amundsen states that the investigation is continuing. Anyone with information is encouraged to contact Detective Amundsen.

On Saturday morning after the story ran, I was in the office putting together a feature story on Mike Short. Mike was a member of my chess club and owned the local HVAC business. Mike's hobby was making wooden toys in his workshop at home. They were intricate throwback toys with fine crafted details and moving parts that appealed far more to adults than to children.

Just as I was finishing the story, I looked out my window and saw Ritchie Kyle walking back and forth in front of the office. I walked to the front door and opened it as Ritchie started walking away.

"Ritchie, did you want something?"

Ritchie turned part way, hesitated, then walked back.

"Can I talk with you for a minute?" There was an unease in Ritchie's manner.

"Sure," I said. "I've been cooped up all morning working on a story. Let's take a walk."

It was a warm June day. By mid-afternoon the temperature would top ninety. We walked at an easy pace.

"Have any trouble with Gus, uh, the town marshal, lately?"

"He ain't been giving me any trouble. Not lately, anyway."

"Getting any use out of that football?"

A trace of a smile crossed Ritchie's face. "Some. Thinking about trying out for the football team next year."

"What position?"

"Quarterback, of course."

I gave a short laugh. "Only position worth playing."

"That's what you played?"

"Yes, but not very well. I quit after riding the bench on my high school J-V team."

We walked for another block. Ritchie looked down as he walked. He said nothing, seeming to weigh something in his mind. I tried to nudge him into talking.

"How things going with your brother?"

"Davey's okay, I guess. Even with getting kicked out of school, there's still colleges that want him to play basketball. They can get him in a special summer school so he can get the credits he needs to play college ball."

"Really?"

Ritchie nodded his head. "That's what all the college coaches are telling him. He's going to play at a junior college in Tennessee. He plans to go pro in a year or two. Wouldn't that be something?"

I nodded. "It would. But playing in the pros is a long shot. I hope he gets an education while someone is willing to pay for it. That will last long after he can't play basketball."

We walked for a while longer, past the library and town hall. Sweat trickled down the center of my back.

"So, what did you want to talk about, Ritchie?"

"I thought you . . ." Ritchie stopped. He stood in the center of the sidewalk, his head down. After a long minute, he spoke, his voice so quiet I could barely hear him.

"If I tell you something, do you have to put it in the newspaper?"

"No. I don't put everything people tell me in the newspaper."

"It's just, well, this isn't something I can talk to my teachers about. Or anyone else. I just thought, well, you deal with the cops and stuff all the time, and you seem like an okay guy, so maybe you could tell me what I should do."

"Did you do something? Something that could get you in trouble?"

Ritchie eyes opened wide. "No. No. Not me. I didn't do anything."

"So, what is it?"

""If I tell you, do you have to tell anybody else? Do you have to tell them it was me who told you?"

"You have to tell me first. If you're in danger, I can't stay quiet. But I'll tell you what. I'll treat you as a confidential source. Do you understand what that is?"

"No."

"Sometimes reporters promise people not to tell where they got information. That's called a confidential source. I don't ever reveal the name of a confidential source."

Ritchie's face tightened into a quizzical look. "Are you saying you won't tell anybody my name, not even the cops?"

"That's right. However, if you tell me someone is threatening you, someone like Gus, we'll have to talk about how to handle it. But I won't put it in the paper. I won't use your name.

Ritchie nodded.

I directed Ritchie to a worn wooden bench in front of the library, surrounded by a pair of overhanging elm trees. The library closed at noon on Saturdays and the sidewalks surrounding the building were deserted.

"What's up?" I asked.

Ritchie looked around again, took a hard swallow, and then began to talk.

"You know Davey gets into all kinds of trouble."

"Everyone knows that."

"Well, he uses drugs. He sells them, too."

"What kind?"

"He sells pot and some pills. Some other stuff, too. He sells it mostly to high school kids."

"Even after he got kicked out?"

"He doesn't sell them right at the school. He meets kids down at the Dairy Point, or over in back of the hardware store, or some abandoned farm house."

"That's not a smart thing to do. Smoking pot is one thing, but dealing is another. If he's really that good at basketball, he'll throw it all away if he's caught selling drugs. Even the pros won't take drug dealers, no matter how good they are."

Ritchie nodded. "I told him it was stupid, but he told me to shut up. He said he can make more money selling drugs than kids in town make at their shit summer jobs."

"So why are you telling me?"

Ritchie looked down at his shoes. He spoke in almost a whisper.

"Sometimes Davey makes me go with him. I try not to, but he knocks me around until I do."

"You tell your parents?"

Ritchie looked up and fixed his eyes on mine.

"They don't give a shit about me. My dad's mostly drunk. So's my mom, for that matter."

"Is Davey still doing this? Still knocking you around?"

"Not so much, anymore. It's been a few months. I'm not sure he trusts me."

"Is that what you wanted to tell me?"

There was a long pause.

"There's something else."

I waited. Ritchie seemed to be searching for the right words.

"I saw that story you had in the paper on that woman that was killed."

I nodded. "Rene Swisher."

"Do you talk to the police about it?"

"I'm a reporter. That's what I do." I paused for a moment, choosing my tone as carefully as my words. "Do you know something about this?"

Ritchie again looked down, studying a spot on the sidewalk. He got up and paced back and forth in front of the bench. I wondered if I had pressed him too much. After several times walking past, he stopped directly in front of me.

"This is secret, right? You won't tell anybody I told you this."

"No. You're a confidential source."

"You promise?"

I nodded.

Ritchie turned away from me. When he turned back, there was a single tear sliding down his cheek.

"What is it?"

"I been to that house. The one where the woman was killed."

I tried to keep the shock from showing on my face. I was not sure I was succeeding.

"That's where Davey got his drugs."

I could feel my heart rate rise. "She was his supplier?"

Ritchie nodded.

"Did you go in the house?"

"I never went in," Ritchie said sharply. "Davey had me sit in the car. Sort of a lookout, I guess. He told me that if someone started toward the house, I was to honk the horn, wait a few seconds and honk again. If it was a cop I was supposed to make it long honks."

"How many times did you go to Rene's house?"

"Four, five times, I guess."

"And you were never in her apartment?"

Ritchie vigorously shook his head.

"Did you ever have to honk the horn?"

"Once. But it was just some guy. Not a cop."

"Ritchie, do you know anything about the murder?"

"I . . . I don't know. Davey knew her, and he's got a temper. A bad temper."

I nodded, recalling his explosion on the basketball court.

"And he's got a gun."

I was no longer sure I was breathing. "What type?"

"Not a rifle or a shotgun. A pistol, I guess. It's not very big. I saw him pull it on a guy a couple of weeks ago."

"What happened?"

"I guess the guy didn't pay for his drugs. Davey put the gun up against his head and said if he didn't have the money the next day,

Davey would do to him what he did to that whore. That's the word he used."

"Was he talking about Rene?"

Ritchie nodded.

We stood there on the library walkway, not saying anything. My first concern was for Ritchie's safety. I put my hand on Ritchie's shoulder.

"Okay," I said quietly. "Is that what you wanted to tell me?"

Ritchie nodded.

"Have you told anybody else?"

"No. Nobody."

"Don't," I said, emphatically. "Don't tell any of your friends, your teachers. No one. Understand?"

Again, Ritchie nodded.

We started walking back toward my office.

"You did the right thing telling me. I need some time to think, but I won't put anything in the newspaper."

"You promised."

"I did. I want you to be safe. If something happens, and you don't feel safe, you call me. Any time. You know where I live, don't you?"

"Sure. You live upstairs at Old Man Bradshaw's. And if you're not there, you're sleeping down at Emma Musgrave's."

"No secrets in this town," I said with a short laugh. I turned serious again. "Anything happens, anything at all, you call me or you come to my apartment. If I'm not there, go to Emma's. The most important thing is for you to stay safe while this all gets figured out."

Unexpectedly, Ritchie put both arms around me and held me tight. As quick as he grabbed me, he let go, turned and ran down the street.

#

I spent Saturday night with Emma. I had trouble sleeping, wondering if I should be back at my apartment in case Ritchie needed me. Emma fixed a late breakfast Sunday morning, but my mind was elsewhere.

"You seem like you're a thousand miles away," Emma said, as she put a plate with an omelet, bacon and hash browns in front of me.

"When I was working on a story, I learned something that may put someone in danger. I'm not sure how to handle it."

"Can I help, hon?"

"No," I said. It was a knee-jerk reaction. I never revealed information or betrayed confidences. But this situation was different. "Maybe there is something."

Emma sat, waiting patiently.

"I can't tell you everything, but I'm going to ask a big favor. Feel free to say no. I won't think any less of you."

Emma sat quietly, waiting me to formulate the words.

"Do you know Ritchie Kyle? Boy is about the age of your daughter."

Emma nodded. "He's the brother of that basketball player. The one everyone at the restaurant was talking about when he got kicked off the team."

"That's him. If he ever shows up here, looking for me, could you take him in and keep him here until you can contact me?"

"What's going on?"

"He could be in danger. He isn't now, but if something happens, I told him to find me. And, well, it seems everyone in town knows that if I'm not at home, I'm here."

Emma gave me a wink. "It is a small town."

"Yeah, I've found that out."

"If he shows up, do I need to do anything? Call the police?"

"Oh God, no. Gus Kopetsky is the last person I'd want you to call. Just keep him here and find me. I'll take it from there."

Emma leaned forward and kissed me on the cheek, then on the mouth. "You're a good man, Zach Carlson, no matter what anyone else says."

Shortly after noon, Emma dropped me off at my apartment on the way to pick up her daughter from her parents. I tried watching a baseball game on television, but I couldn't focus. After an hour, I gave up, and I walked to my office where I worked on a fluff article promoting the upcoming Fourth of July balloon event. Words came at an excruciatingly slow pace. My mind kept slipping back to Ritchie Kyle.

#

Early Monday morning I called Virgil Amundsen.

"I picked up a little information about the Rene Swisher murder."

"I'm listening."

"Some kid connected with Stratton High School is selling drugs in the area. Rene Swisher may have been his supplier."

"Got a name."

"No. No name."

"That's it? Some school kid was doing business with the victim? That's not much."

"I heard he has a gun."

There was a long pause. "What kind?"

"Handgun. A small one. I don't know the caliber."

"Where did you hear this?"

"Just overheard kids talking."

"You got names to go with those kids so I can talk to them?"

"No. Don't know who they were."

Again, there was a pause. "You're not telling me everything, Zach."

"I'm telling you what I can," I said.

THIRTY – *Sunday Morning Among the Tombstones*

June 9, 1976, NEW YORK, NY (WIRE SERVICES): Frustrated by the lack of women in elected office, a group of female activists have announced a Women's Campaign Fund to raise money in support of female candidates.

The group noted that there are only 17 women among the 435 members of the House of Representatives, and there are no women in the Senate.

The police scanner squawked, waking me from a fitful night of intermittent sleep and frightful nightmares. I bolted upright, checking the clock radio next to the scanner. It was shortly after 6:00 a.m. The now familiar female voice was a dispatcher at the Sheriff's Department who handled the overnight radio for the entire county. In my mind I pictured a handsome woman with stylish brown hair and a tailored uniform with an extra button undone to show a bit of cleavage. But it was all in my imagination. I never met her.

The dispatcher was calling for Gus. After several efforts, Gus responded, his voice groggy with sleep.

""Yeah, this is Kopetsky. What's so important you have to wake me up?"

"Marshal, we got a call from the caretaker out at Union Cemetery. That's the one on 300 South, about two miles outside Stratton."

"I know where it is."

"Caretaker lives in that little house across from the cemetery. He says there's a Stratton police car parked in the cemetery. It's just sitting there. Nobody in sight."

"What the hell? Which car is it?"

"He didn't have any more information."

"Have him go up and check it out and call us back."

"Sorry Chief, but he's pretty scared. Says he ain't going up there."

Gus grumbled, uttering some garbled profanity. "I'll call my boys on the radio and see what's up. I'll get back to you. Out."

A few seconds later, the radio channel for the Stratton police crackled.

"This is the Gus. Who's out there on duty?"

There was a long pause before there was a reply.

"Hey Chief, this is Clint. I'm not on duty, but I'm up. I'm in the car heading for breakfast."

"You're not up at Union Cemetery?"

"VFW's got a pancake breakfast going this morning. I'm on my way to get something to eat. What would I be doing up in the cemetery?"

"Where's Kenny?"

"No idea. He had the late shift last night."

I already was jumping into my clothes and grabbing my keys and my camera.

"Shit," Gus said.

"Hey Chief, watch your language over the radio. Don't need more trouble over that."

Gus made several calls over the radio for Kenny, but there was no response. By the last call, there was a frantic edge in his voice.

"I'm calling Kenny's house," Gus said over the radio to Clint. "You get headed to the cemetery. If I can't raise him, I'm calling the Sheriff and state police. You wait there at the caretaker's until everybody gets there."

Before Clint even said "10-4," I was on my way out the door.

I made a wrong turn on my way to the cemetery. By the time I arrived, Clint was there along with one sheriff's cruiser. The cars lined the gravel drive in front of an aging farmhouse that desperately needed a new coat of paint. Clint and the county deputy were standing with a small man, in his sixties, unshaven and wearing a pair of too-big overalls without a shirt underneath. I assumed he was the caretaker. I stayed in my car until I could tell more about what was going on.

Across the county road was the cemetery. Aging tombstones sprouted across the hillside like an unharvested crop. A single gravel path made its way through the graves. At the crest of the hill sat a single black and white police cruiser.

Gus pulled up a few minutes later, followed by a second sheriff's car, and a state police cruiser. Since our confrontation, Gus and I had not spoken. I kept my distance as Gus conferred with Clint, the deputies and state police trooper. When they broke up, I got out of the car and approached Clint.

"What's going on?" I said.

Clint shook his head. "Nobody knows. But that's Kenny's car. We've all got a really bad feeling about this."

"What are you going to do?"

"We're going to go up there and check it out. But we're going with our weapons ready and taking it slow. There's no good reason for Kenny's car to be here."

The shorter deputy drove the sheriff's car ahead of the other officer, making his way up a narrow gravel path between the headstones. Behind, the rest of the officers walked in a loose formation. Gus, Clint and the taller of the two deputies had their hands resting on the butt of their revolvers. The state police officer held a shotgun across his chest.

I walked behind, keeping my distance.

The sheriff's car stopped about ten feet behind the Stratton cruiser. There seemed no sign of life. The only sound was a light breeze rustling through a half dozen poplars scattered among the tombstones. There were no other sounds.

The state police officer signaled everyone to stay behind the car. Crouching, he moved up to the rear fender of Kenny's cruiser.

I had my camera up, watching through my viewfinder with one eye, the other eye open. I didn't know what to expect, but I was prepared to snap photos and dive for cover, if needed.

The officer squatted, then duck-walked with his back against the left rear side panel of the car. He took off his hat and placed it on the ground near the tire, then slowly raised himself enough to see in the window.

There was a silent moment. The state trooper raised his head and stood, the tension visibly released from his body. He let his shotgun drop to his side.

"Well I'll be goddamned," he said, a big grin breaking across his face. Then he started laughing. He waved the rest of the officers forward. "Put your guns down. You gotta get a look at this."

Hands all around dropped from weapons. Everyone stood upright, and walked forward, me included. As we did, I saw a head pop up from the back seat and look in our direction. It was Kenny Wyman. Next to him a second head popped up with tangled dishwater blonde hair.

Great belly laughs broke out among all the officers before I made it to the car. Gus doubled over and seemed to have trouble catching his breath. None of the officers were making any effort to open the car door.

"Hey Zach, get your ass up here with that camera," Gus said. It was his first words to me in several weeks. "I want a picture of this for the office."

I walked up and looked in. Kenny Wyman and a woman sat in the backseat of the cruiser. I recognized the woman. She was close to fifty, and to be polite, on the hefty side. It was Karla, the clerk at Kopetsky's convenience store who also acted as dispatcher for the Stratton police.

Both were naked.

Each of them held their hands trying to cover the most intimate parts of their body, but it wasn't working very well. Karla glowed crimson. From her demeanor, it looked more like anger than embarrassment.

"Anybody got some blankets?" the State Police officer asked. "I don't want to see any more of this than I have to."

The sheriff's deputy who had driven the car up the gravel drive walked to his trunk. "I got one," he shouted.

"One will do," Gus said. "Kenny can stand out here naked."

"May take more than one to cover Karla," the state trooper yelled out, barely understandable through his laughs.

I peered inside the car. Clothes lay haphazardly scattered across the front seat. I snapped a few photos, not expecting any would make the newspaper, but I was sure I would get requests for copies from every police agency in the area.

The deputy with the blanket opened the rear passenger seat door and held the blanket up as the woman got out.

"What are you looking at," Karla snapped, not aiming her comment at anyone in particular.

Karla wrapped herself in the one blanket that had been provided. The other sheriff's deputy held out her clothes he had retrieved from the front seat. She snapped them out of his hand. As she stomped away, the officer called out to her. When she turned, she saw him holding out an oversized pair of pink nylon panties by the tips of his fingers.

"You want these?"

Karla walked back, snatched the panties from his hand. "You just wish you could get in them," she said.

“I don’t think they’d stay up on me,” the deputy said, with a smirk.

Karla turned. “That’s not the only thing you couldn’t keep up,” she said. She turned sharply and headed toward some nearby bushes.

As Karla stormed off, Kenny stepped out of the car. No one handed him his clothes or anything else. He opened the front door to his cruiser, grabbed his uniform from the front seat, and began putting his clothes on.

"You better not put any of this in the paper." Kenny yelled at me from across the car. He was trying to muster as much dignity as he could while pulling up his pants.

I lifted my camera and snapped a photo of him for my response.

Kenny, his pants around his knees, lunged toward me. He tripped and fell hard against the cruiser.

"If he doesn't run this story," Gus shouted from a few feet away, "I'm going to take out an ad and put it in myself."

I walked back toward my car. Clint fell in step beside me.

"How’d they get locked in?" I asked Clint, who was still laughing.

"You ever ride in the back seat of a cop car?"

"Fortunately, no."

"We don't want prisoners opening the door and walking away," he said.

Suddenly I understood. "No door handles inside?"

Clint nodded. "And you got that cage between the front and back seats so prisoners can't grab the officer."

"So, when things got going between Kenny and Karla, they needed a little more room."

"Well, anybody with Karla would need a little more room," Clint laughed.

"They got in the back seat and couldn't get out?"

"That's what it looks like."

"What's Gus going to do with him?" I asked as we got to the cars.

"Who knows? Probably tell Kenny to stay away from his store and keep his hands off the merchandise."

"Think he'll get fired?"

"Gus ain't gonna fire him. Kenny is Orville's nephew. Can't fire the nephew of the guy that signs your checks. He may suspend him for a few days." Then Clint gave his aw-shucks smile I had seen so often. "After all, can't fuck with government property." Clint snorted at his own humor.

I realized that laughing at Kenny's expense would soon be the most popular pastime in Stratton. Every time Kenny ate in a restaurant, or bought something at the IGA, or showed up at the Mouse to handle a Saturday night drunk, he would hear the whispers and the snickers of the town's gossip mill. It would be far worse, and last far longer, than anything Gus could do to him.

#

I wasn't sure what to do with the story. It was a police run involving not only Stratton Police, but also Lancaster County Sheriff's deputies and a state police officer. Was it news or just titillating gossip? By the time the newspaper hit the stands at mid-week, gossip would have spread through the town like a flu epidemic. Everyone would look for the story.

But how to run a story in a family paper about a cop and the store clerk getting caught having sex in the back of a patrol car? It didn't seem to fit with Aunt Minnie's gallbladder operation and the winner of the school science fair.

I settled on a four-paragraph story slotted for page two.

> A missing Stratton Police Cruiser was found Sunday morning at Union Cemetery with the officer alive and unharmed, much to the relief of local law enforcement agencies.
>
> Stratton patrolman Kenny Wyman and a friend became trapped in the backseat of the cruiser sometime early Sunday morning. They were unable to extricate themselves.
>
> Clarence Easterday, caretaker of the cemetery, called police when he became concerned about the police vehicle being in the cemetery overnight. Officers from Stratton Police, Lancaster County Sheriff's Department and the State Police responded to his call and released Wyman and his friend from the patrol car.
>
> "We're happy Kenny is okay," Town Marshal Gus Kopetsky said. "That's the naked truth."

I re-read my story. One made-up quote would not destroy my career. It might even make me a celebrity in Stratton. I laughed to myself, then struck out the last paragraph.

I submitted a six-paragraph version to Roy for the wire services. It included the names of all involved and detailed the circumstances in which Kenny and Karla were found. Within a week, the story ran in nearly four hundred newspapers across the country.

THIRTY-ONE – *The Good Kid*

June 12, 1976, WEST POINT, NY (WIRE SERVICES): An additional 34 West Point cadets have been implicated in the cheating scandal that has rocked the United States Military Academy, bringing the total cadets involved to 164.

The black eye comes at a particularly bad time for the military academy as the first West Point class to include women reports on July 7.

By the second week in June, schools were out. Most of the community teenagers were working summer jobs. A few worked at the Dairy Point waiting cars and flipping burgers. Others were life guards at the lake near Liberty Station or at the new high school pool. The unfortunate ones signed up to detassel corn in August. They faced weeks in sweltering corn fields, pulling emerging tassels off stalks until their hands blistered.

Just before school let out, I wrote a story on teens and summer jobs. One teen I interviewed said she would rather spend a month in summer school than a day in the baking fields among six-foot corn stalks planted inches apart where no breeze penetrated.

"You get hot. There's no shade. Your hands get blistered. The leaves scratch up your skin, and the gnats and mosquitos are all around your face and in your ears and up your nose. It's awful."

There were several teens who worked for their parents in their small businesses and shops around town. Lindsey Wheeler worked for her mother as hostess at Shelby's Place, a position that didn't exist unless Lindsey was out of school. It was easy money. Her mom paid her a dollar more than anyone else and the waitresses were required to pony up twenty percent of their tips to Lindsey. Emma and the other waitresses resented it, but there was no option if they wanted to keep their job.

Phil Gudgel worked for his dad at stocking shelves and bagging groceries. He worked a full day and got paid the same as everyone else. But he had the perk of leaving early if he felt the urge to go fishing or if his buddies headed out to swim at the lake.

Danny Pemberton didn't seem to have any of those perks. Despite being the salutatorian of his senior class and a star basketball player, Danny carried the same workload as any other employee at Hank Pemberton's lumber yard. He toted bags of concrete, moved barrels of nails, loaded orders of lumber and landscaping materials, and drove the front-end loader and a forklift.

"I started when I was twelve," Danny told me. "I'm at work by seven and don't get off until five — sometimes later." With a laugh, he added, "Bad thing is that if I do something wrong, I get chewed out at work. Then I go home and get chewed out all over again. If it's bad enough, I hear about it the next morning at breakfast."

#

It was mid-morning, and I was at my desk working on an update article on the Bicentennial Parade. It was a fluff piece promoting the town's planned festival. From what some long-time residents told me, it might be the biggest event in Stratton since the end of World War II. I wasn't sure it would end up as grand as the plans, but it seemed no harm promoting small-town dreams with a few stories.

A police siren caught my attention and a Stratton police cruiser sped past my window. I had been at the Stratton Gazette nearly ten months. This was the first time a police car had raced past my office, siren blaring. A minute later, a siren wailed as the hearse/ambulance pulled out of the funeral home garage, three doors from my office.

I put the final words on a sentence, then walked to the front door. Shirley stood holding it open, looking down the street.

"What's going on?" I asked.

"Don't know. They stopped down there," she said pointing to the obvious. "That's between the hardware store and the lumberyard."

I went back to my desk and grabbed a notebook and my camera. I started toward the scene at a brisk jog.

A Stratton police car sat crossways, blocking Main Street. The red emergency light splashed against the businesses and growing crowd of spectators. Just past the police car, the ambulance backed to a stop.

Visible behind the emergency vehicles was the yellow frame of a forklift, its blades stacked with treated lumber. Kenny Wyman stood by his car, hands on hips, seeming lost as to what to do.

"Hey Kenny, what's going on." Since the story about his escapade in the cemetery, he had refused to speak to me.

Kenny turned toward me. His face was ashen. "No pictures," he said. "No pictures."

I didn't argue the point. Kenny's admonition would not stop me from taking photos.

I walked around the police car and took a few steps toward the ambulance. Arnold Donaldson, the funeral home owner and ambulance driver, knelt on the pavement. Groceries from a torn bag littered the pavement. I moved a little to my left and I saw a pair of legs sticking out from under the tines of the forklift. A thin river of blood flowed across the street toward a nearby storm drain.

Danny Pemberton sat in the seat of the forklift, his expression fixed, his eyes glazed. His hands rested on the controls.

"Shit," I said under my breath.

Another police car approach from behind me, its siren blaring. Gus Kopetsky pull his car next to Kenny's. He turned off the siren and stepped out. Gus walked past Kenny, saying nothing.

Arnold stood up and shook his head at Gus. "Better call the coroner," he said.

On the forklift, Danny put his ashen face into his hands and burst into sobs.

Another car came from the opposite direction. It wasn't an emergency vehicle. The car braked hard, leaving skid marks and tire smoke. Hank Pemberton jumped out of his car and ran to the scene. He took one look at the protruding legs and the pool of blood, then looked toward Arnold. Again, Arnold shook his head.

Hank, his face growing pale, looked toward his son. With long quick strides, he moved to the forklift and climbed to where his son still sat.

"I didn't mean to, Dad," Danny said through tears. "I didn't even see her."

Hank put his arm around Danny's shoulder. "It was an accident, son. It wasn't your fault."

After several minutes, Hank slipped down off the fork lift. "You come down here," he said to his son.

Danny eased down from the forklift, each movement carrying the weight of the world. Hank put an arm around Danny's shoulder and pulled him close. He said something in Danny's ear, then led him away. They walked past Hank's still running car, heading down the street toward the Pemberton home.

No one said anything to them. Behind me, Gus spoke into his radio, calling for the coroner.

Cleanup of the accident scene would be grizzly. The woman's legs were pinned under the front forks, her torso crushed under the forklift's oversize wheels.

I didn't want to watch.

I talked to some of the onlookers, trying to find a witness. Mable Brusker, the frumpy middle-aged woman who owned Mable's Notions Shop, told me that the victim was Ethel Sunduvol, a retired teacher in her late eighties.

"She walked off the sidewalk right in front of the fork lift," Mable said, her voice quavering. "I couldn't believe she did that, poor thing. Did you know her?"

I shook my head. "Never had the privilege."

"Ethel taught third grade to almost everyone in town. Didn't retire until she was in her seventies, and only then because she was almost deaf. Otherwise, she'd still be teaching. Her vision wasn't any too good, either. But she was stubborn. Still living on her own."

Mable pointed. "She lived down there a couple of blocks." Mable broke into tears. "Nothing poor Danny could do. He wasn't going any faster than you can walk. He didn't even know he hit her.

Dragged her for twenty or thirty feet before Mr. Heinzman came running out of the hardware store waving his hands for Danny to stop. Worst thing I ever seen."

#

Late that afternoon, about the time Shirley would leave for the day, I worked finishing up the story on the accident. Shirley surprised me when she walked in to my office.

"I heard the door bell and thought you had left," I said.

Shirley leaned over my desk. She spoke, her voice barely a whisper. "Mr. Pemberton is here. He wants to talk with you. Said it's personal. Do I bring him back, or do I tell him you're too busy?"

Never had Shirley volunteered to lie, or even stretch the truth for me. In an odd way, it was touching.

"Bring Hank back," I said.

"Do you want me to stay?"

I shook my head. "I'll be fine."

Shirley showed Hank to my office. A minute later the locked clicked as she left for the day.

Hank slumped into the chair across from my desk. His eyes were red and puffy. His mouth sagged.

"You doing okay?" I asked.

Hank waited for a long moment before speaking. When he did, he ignored my question.

"I need to ask a favor of you, Zach. Would you please not run that story about my boy hitting Mrs. Sunduvol."

"I can't do that, Hank." I tried to make my voice sympathetic, but also businesslike. There could be no misunderstanding. "Everybody in town knows about the accident. If I didn't run a story, they'd think I'm incompetent or covering up something. I can't let people think either one. It's my job to report events. If I don't do it, I'd get fired."

I expected Hank to become angry, but he didn't. He sat without moving or changing expression, but somehow sinking deeper into his despair.

"It's not for me," he said. "It's for Danny and his momma. I don't want them to see all that in black and white next week."

"I'm sorry, Hank. I do understand. You don't know how much I understand. But if I don't report the news as a favor to someone, I'm not much of a reporter, am I?"

"Is there any way you can keep Danny's name out? You didn't print Josh's name when he did that damn foolishness with the train."

"That was different. Josh was a minor. He's what? Twelve? Rumors circulated about Josh being involved, but juvenile records are confidential. The police, prosecutor, the courts, none of them made his name public. I don't print stories based on rumor."

"But Danny's just a boy."

"Danny is eighteen. The accident happened right on Main Street. I talked to witnesses who described what happened. I saw Danny sitting in the forklift. I can't ignore that. If it helps, everyone says there was nothing Danny could do. She walked out right in front of him."

Hank stood up, his head down and shoulders sagging. He didn't threaten to pull the town's legal advertisements or threaten to keep me out of Town Board meetings. "Well, I thought I'd ask," he said.

I followed him to unlock the door and let him out. "Look Hank," I said as he stepped out. "I will not sensationalize this. It was a terrible accident. An old woman who was deaf and couldn't see stepped out in front of a forklift. Nobody could have avoided it."

Hank looked back at me. "Yeah, but I sent my boy out on that forklift."

I watched Hank walk away, headed toward his lumberyard. I had never seen the weight of the world pressing so much on someone's shoulders.

THIRTY-TWO – *Ink and Blood*

August 1974

August 8, 1974, WASHINGTON, D.C. (WIRE SERVICES): President Richard M. Nixon announced tonight to a national television audience that he will resign effective at noon tomorrow. Brought down by the Watergate scandal, Nixon is the first president to resign in the nation's history.

Vice President Gerald R. Ford will be sworn in as the 38th President of the United States to complete Nixon's term.

August in Chicago can be oppressive beyond imagining. When a mid-90s heat wave settles over the city, only air-conditioned offices and stores provide any relief. The sun bakes buildings and highways like giant bricks heated for hours in ovens. When the sun sets, the millions of tons of concrete, steel, brick and pavement radiate their accumulated heat like so many furnaces turned on high. While suburbs cool into the upper 60s, downtown stayed above ninety until just before dawn.

And when the temperature rose, so did the violent crime rate.

Chicago was in the second week of a near-record heat wave. The city's murder rate exploded to more than three a day. In the ten days since the heat topped ninety, I had covered fourteen murders, not keeping up with the pace of killings

Cops worked double shifts trying to keep up. So did crime beat reporters. The stress of long hours, heat and fatigue showed on nearly everyone. But I didn't mind the extra hours. The bigger paychecks would help with the upcoming trip to Key West and the wedding.

Kate turned in her notice at Beinart and Telesky in June. She was finishing her last project, working late hours, but with the end in sight. She had just over one week to go.

Kate was much quicker to smile these days. Her step seemed a bit lighter. She, her mother and two of her friends had worked out the plans for a small sunset beach wedding in Key West with only her parents and a handful of friends present. At Kate's insistence, I invited my mother. She declined.

"It's such short notice," my mother said, turning down the invitation. "I'm always so busy that time of year." But she remained vague, not identifying any specific conflict on her schedule. "Besides, I really don't like Key West." Then she whispered into the phone like someone might listen in. "Too many drunks and homosexuals," she said.

Kate and I rented the same bungalow where we spent our first vacation together. After a week in Key West, we planned to rent a car and drive to the new Disney theme park near Orlando. Kate was giddy about seeing the new amusement park

"You're more excited about seeing Mickey Mouse than getting married," I said.

"Nobody ever wrote a song about you," she said. Then she added, "But you do have cute ears," and gave me a wink.

#

It was just after 1 a.m. on a Thursday, the start of the eleventh day of the heat wave. I was doing the final edits on a story on the spike in violence and the relationship to the heat. When the story was done, I was ready for a drink.

A call came in over the scanner. Charlie Kelso, the night editor on the city desk, yelled at me across the newsroom. His voice carried above the din of clacking typewriters and wire service Teletypes. "They found a body in a parking garage on LaSalle, near Adams. Can you take that one, Zach?"

I didn't pass on good stories. There was a newsroom legend around town about the old warhorse reporter who thought he had put in enough work, and sent a young reporter to chase down a scanner report about an intruder at the nursing dormitory at the University of Chicago campus.. It turned out to be the slaying of eight nursing students by Richard Speck, one of the most infamous crimes in the city's history. The young reporter got the story and a career. The old reporter saw his career tumble, ending up with a desk job at a small daily in the Florida panhandle.

I saw Hurley Meyers wandering around earlier. I tracked Hurley down at his desk just outside the darkroom. He looked up from examining a contact sheet with photos from a double homicide earlier that evening.

"Got time to go with me? Cops may have a body in a Loop garage."

"Probably a wino sleeping. But sure. Nothing special here." Hurley put down the contact sheet and grabbed his camera bag.

We took what Hurley called his work car, a dinged up blue 1968 Plymouth Fury with stained cloth seats. It was littered with discarded paper coffee cups and fast food wrappers. But under the hood was a 496 cubic inch V-8 hemi engine that Hurley said could blow away anything on the road, including cop cars.

The parking garage was located on the lower eight floors of a decade-old steel and glass office building. Black and white units with their lights flashing blocked the entrance. Hurley pulled up against a yellow-lined section of curb and threw a big card into the window that said, "Press."

We walked to where yellow crime scene tape was strung across the garage entrance. I didn't know the overweight uniform cop on duty, but Hurley did. That was another reason I took him with me as my photographer whenever possible.

"Hey, Sully, how's it going?" Hurley said, as Hurley loaded a fresh roll of Tri-X film in his Nikon.

"Hotter than hell," Sully said. "Hope they get this wrapped up soon. My balls are sweating off in this heat."

Hurley nodded in my direction. "This is Zach Carlson. He's our ace crime reporter."

Sully nodded. "Yeah, I've seen the name in the paper. You do good work."

"Thanks," I said, and shook Sully's hand. I noted the name P. Sullivan on the uniform nametag.

"What have you got?" Hurley asked.

Sully shrugged. "Don't know. They don't tell us shit. All I know is they got a dead body up on the sixth floor. Lee Phillips drew the case. He's up there now."

Sully let us walk under the tape and into the garage. Rather than risk being stopped by a less-friendly patrolman at an elevator, we took the stairs, figuring that the cops would be taking the elevator in the heat.

When we walked out of the stairwell on to the sixth floor, the crime scene was to our left in the southwest corner. A few yellow light bulbs in wire cages hung from the concrete roof beams, bathing the concrete in dim yellow light and shadows. I counted seven cars scattered around the parking garage floor.

I saw Lee Phillips, the detective who Sully said was in charge, standing several feet apart from a group of officers gathered at what I assumed was the crime scene. Lee was smoking a cigarette and apparently wanted to keep the smoke from contaminating any evidence. He took one last drag, then dropped it at his feet, crushing it with his toe.

I moved toward Lee while Hurley made his way to where the other officers were gathered.

"Got an extra cigarette?" I asked.

Lee turned. He pulled the pack from his shirt pocket and flipped it to me.

"Don't you ever buy your own, Carlson?"

"I won't be bumming them that much longer," I said, taking a cigarette out and tossing the pack back to Lee. "I promised Kate I'd quit as a wedding present to her."

"You getting married? Really. Congrats. When?"

"Couple of weeks. We're flying down to Key West." I lit up the cigarette and took a deep drag. "What have you got?"

"Young woman. Looks like a professional."

"Hooker?"

"No. I mean like someone who works in one of these office buildings. Business suit, what's left of it. Nice shoes thrown over there in the corner. We won't know until we get the lab results, but looks like she was raped, beaten and strangled. Right now we're waiting to get portable lights up here so the crime scene techs can do their work."

"That will panic a lot of secretaries downtown," I said.

Lee nodded. "It will after you guys have your way with the story."

"Any idea what happened?"

"I'm guessing she was working late. Some of these secretaries can't leave until the boss is done. We think someone followed her up here. When he was sure they were alone, he attacked her. There are ligature marks on her neck, but nothing around that we've found yet. We think the bastard may have used his own belt. That's all just an educated guess. We won't know anything for certain until we get the autopsy."

Lee walked toward where the body lay behind an array of police officers. I fell in to step behind him. I had only taken a few steps when I saw Hurley quick stepping toward me, his camera dangling from his neck and his hands held out, palms facing me. His head emphatically shook side to side.

"Stop, Zach. Stop."

I slowed, but kept moving forward. Hurley reached out, his hands landing on both of my shoulders.

"You can't go over there, Zach."

"What are you talking about," I said, and attempted to move around him.

Hurley moved with me, blocking my path.

"You can't."

Lee had now stopped and moved back toward me, his face going gray.

"You can't go over there," Hurley repeated.

My heart pounded in my throat. I tried to push past Hurley but now both he and Lee were holding me. I could see tears forming in Hurley's eyes.

"It's Kate," he said. "Oh my God, Zach, it's Kate."

My scream echoed through the garage.. The men gathered around the body turned toward me.

I turned to Lee, pleading without words for him to tell me that Hurley was wrong. To tell me that this was a mistake. But he didn't.

Lee leaned in close, his hand on my shoulder. He talked directly into my ear, his voice quiet but firm.

"Your Kate. Her name is Katherine Billings, isn't it?"

I nodded, tears streaming down my face.

"I'm so sorry, Zach. It's her."

The world spun around me. I screamed again. And again. And again.

I turned away from the scene, then reversed myself and rushed between the outstretched arms of Lee and Hurley. Two officers near the body grabbed at me, but I shouldered my way past them.

I saw Kate, her face gray and lifeless. Her once piercing emerald eyes were now glazed and dull, staring sightlessly upward. Her head was twisted at an unnatural angle, her exposed body contorted into a pretzel shape. A trickle of blood lay in a line from her nose across her lifeless lips.

I screamed her name. I tried to reach her, but now there were hands holding me. I could not pull loose. Somewhere I heard a voice. "We can't let you, sir. It's a crime scene."

I screamed Kate's name again and again, until my lungs could no longer force out air. The universe spun, my knees went out from under me, and I collapsed onto the concrete.

THIRTY-THREE – *Truth and Other Lies*

June 4, 1976, WASHINGTON, D.C. (WIRE SERVICES): Elizabeth Ray, 33, who rocked Congress with allegations that she was a mistress on the payroll of powerful Ohio Congressman Wayne Hayes, has now claimed she was ordered by another Congressman to have sex with a Senator to obtain his vote on a specific bill.

In the wake of the scandal, congressional secretaries have been seen wearing "I Can Type" buttons as they walk through the hallways of the three Congressional Office Buildings.

In May, facing nice weather and summer vacations, the chess club reduced its meetings to once a month until school started back in the fall. In June, I called Gary Middleton to confirm that the next meeting at his house.

The first few times when Gary didn't answer did not surprise me. Despite being teachers, neither had the summer off. Libby taught summer school and Gary supervised the high school pool, including swim lessons and community open swim. But when a dozen calls went unanswered, I became more concerned. I stopped by the Middletons' house on the night scheduled for chess, but no one was home.

#

On Wednesdays, the high school pool opened at six o'clock for community swim. I called Emma and asked if she wanted to go swimming, but she had to work. I drove to the school, not bothering to take my trunks. I wanted to talk with Gary.

The pool was crowded with splashing and screaming youngsters, their yelps echoing off the walls. A few parents lazily ambled through the shallow end of the pool. One dad showed off on the diving board. In the four-row aluminum bleachers, several parents sat chatting. A few sported swimsuits, but most wore street clothes.

I looked around and didn't see Gary. I walked along the deck to his office, which had a large glass window that looked out over the pool. The office was empty, and Gary's desk was bare.

Staci Simmons strolled along the pool deck. She wore a neon orange one-piece swim suit with "Lifeguard" in bold black letters down each side. I recognized her from covering high school swim meets. I walked over to her.

"Mr. Middleton around?" I asked, reverting to the common school formality I now used in the schools.

She turned with a look of surprise that morphed into a smirking grin. "Mr. Middleton isn't here. He got fired."

I stood speechless.

"I'm surprised you didn't hear already since you're the newspaper guy, and all," she said, seeming to enjoy the shock.

"What happened?"

"Well, I don't think I'm supposed to talk about it." She looked around conspiratorially, then turned back to me. "But if you don't use my name in the paper, I guess I can tell you."

She wagged her finger at me to stand closer. When I stepped next to her, she spoke with her voice slightly above a whisper.

"He's a perv." She backed up and nodded to emphasize the point. "He used to wait until most of the girls left, then he'd walk into the shower wearing nothing but that little Speedo of his. He'd watch us getting dressed. Mostly he watched Darla Minnix. She was on the swim team, only she wasn't as fast as me. Her boobs are too big, I guess."

"That doesn't sound like Gary to me."

"You weren't there, were you?"

"When did all this come up?"

"Well, he did it all school year, but I caught him in the act two weeks ago. Darla and I are working as summer lifeguards. Darla finished her shift and headed back to the locker room to get dressed. I walked back to go pee. I saw Mr. Middleton grab Darla. He put his hands on her butt. He pulled her against him and kissed her right on the mouth. She tried to pull away, but he wouldn't let her. All he had on were those skimpy Speedo trunks he wears." She leaned up against my ear and whispered, "He had a boner. I mean, you could just see it sticking out there."

Again, she nodded for emphasis.

"Then he pulled down one of the straps of her swimsuit so her boob hung out. He put his whole hand on it. I mean, right on it. I yelled at him. That's when he stopped. He turned, saw me, and ran out the door."

"Did you call the police?"

Staci rolled her eyes. "That old police chief is probably a bigger perv than Mr. Middleton. He drools and sticks his tongue out every time I walk by."

I had a lot of problems with the way Gus behaved, but I had never seen him do anything like that. But then, I wasn't a teenage girl.

"I drove Darla to Mr. Kuertser house. He's Maggie Kuertser's dad. She's the really cute cheerleader with curly blonde hair. Mr. Kuertser's on the school board. We talked to him. The school board had a special meeting, and they fired Mr. Middleton."

"When did this happen?"

"They fired him last week."

One of the teenage boys in the pool yelled at Darla. She turned her head and stuck out her tongue at him, but not in an entirely innocent way.

"I gotta go," she said. "You can write a story about that perv. Just don't use my name."

I left the school and drove to the Middleton's. One of their cars was in the drive. I knocked on the door harder and more urgently than I intended. After a minute, I knocked again.

The door opened a few inches. Libby pressed her face against the small opening. Her eyes were red and puffy.

"Oh, hi Zach. I'm sorry, but I don't feel well right now."

"Libby, is it true Gary got fired."

I saw anger flash across Libby's face. Rage clung to her voice like boiled sugar.

"Where did you hear that?"

"Can I come in and talk?"

She looked at me for several seconds.

"As a reporter or as a friend?"

I stood dumbfounded, at a loss as to how to respond. The Middletons were friends, but I was a reporter. After an uncomfortable silence, I said, "Both, I guess. I need to understand what's going on."

Libby studied me for a long moment. She slowly opened the door wider.

"Oh, come on in," she said, more with resignation than hospitality.

She led me in to the kitchen where we sat at the same table where we had shared so many meals over the past ten months. She topped off a glass of white wine sitting on the table and offered some to me.

"Just a little," I said.

She poured and handed a half-full glass to me. She kept the full one for herself.

"To better times," she said, then took a long drink. I took a sip.

"What's going on, Libby?"

"Where did you get your information?"

Staci had asked me to keep her name out of the paper, but I did not promise to keep her name secret from others.

"Staci Simmons."

"That little twat," Libby spat out the words. "She and that bitch Darla Minnix are behind this whole thing."

"What's going on?"

Libby took another long drink, almost emptying her glass. She refilled it to the brim.

"Let's start with the facts. Gary wasn't fired. They asked him to take some time off while they looked into what that little bitch said. They made a point of telling Gary that he wasn't being suspended. It was voluntary. And he's still getting paid."

She took another drink. She seemed to be relaxing a bit.

"Staci said she caught Gary in the locker room doing something, uh, inappropriate."

"It's all horseshit," Libby said. "Did Staci tell you that Gary kicked both her and Darla off the swim team last season? The school doesn't pay a custodian to stay late and clean up after swim meets, so Gary has to do it. Gary walked into the boys locker room to pick up. I mean, it was the boys locker room. He found Darla and Staci having a three way on a locker room bench with Bobby Czapinsik.

Libby shook her head, and gave an artificial laugh. "Shit, when I was in high school, I didn't even know there was such a thing as a three-way. But there they were going at it. Bobby was on the locker room bench, and one of 'em was going down on him while the other one was sitting on his face. Gary kicked all three off the team even though Darla and Bobby had qualified for sectionals. He called up their parents that night and told them exactly what their little darlings were doing."

"These accusations against Gary, it's all revenge?"

Libby nodded. She walked to a cabinet and pulled out another bottle of wine, this one red, and opened it. After filling her glass to the brim, she offered some to me. I had barely touched my half full glass. I shook my head.

"If he kicked them off the team, how did they end up working as lifeguards this summer?"

"A little while before school ended, they came up to Gary, all sweet and sorry, and apologized. They told him they wanted to get back on the team next year. Gary thought they were sincere. He was short on qualified lifeguards for the summer. So, he told them they could work as lifeguards all summer. If they showed up on time, worked hard, and stayed out of trouble, he would let them back on the team. But they'd be on probation."

"And you think it was all a scheme to get back at Gary."

"Goddamn right it was," Libby said, slapping her palm hard on the table for emphasis. "They're just a couple of little cunts."

Libby realized what she had said and looked down. Her voice was softer now.

"I'm sorry. I don't use that word. But that's what they are."

"How'd the school react?"

"They went to Kuertser. His daughter hangs out with Darla and Staci. Hell, she may even have been in on it. Kuertser called up the superintendent demanding Gary be fired that night. Kuertser threatened to call the police and get Gary arrested for child molesting."

Libby stared past me as if she was replaying events in her mind. Finally, she continued. "I'll hand it to the superintendent. I don't agree with him on much, but he put the brakes on this. He knows the type of girls they are and that Gary kicked them off the swim team. He called a special school board meeting. It was those girls' word against Gary's, and Gary denied everything. None of the board members bought in to the story, except Keurtser. But he carries a lot of weight."

"Did anyone investigate?"

"The principal called in some students and asked about rumors floating around the school. He tried to find out if Staci or Darla bragged to other students about setting up Gary. He even asked the summer school teachers to report anything they overheard in the hallways, but nobody talked about it."

"Gary denies any of this happened?"

"Of course," Libby said, taking another long drink from her wine glass. "You know Gary. Does he seem like the type of guy who would go around playing grab ass and kissy face with a couple of 16-year-olds?

I had covered too many child molesting cases involving teachers, scout leaders and church pastors. Public personas never foreclosed private proclivities. But Libby was dealing with enough. I would not pile my experiences on top of her burdens.

"No," I said. "He doesn't."

We sat there in silence for several minutes.

"What happens now?"

Libby shook her head, biting her lower lip to hold back tears. I waited. She took a smaller sip from the wine glass. When she spoke, I could tell her words were not quite as crisp. The alcohol was having its effect.

"The superintendent suggested it might be better if Gary got a job someplace else. Of course, I'd have to find a job, too. He's given Gary several leads on jobs. That's where we've been most of the last week. Interviewing. That's where Gary is today."

"Can he get a job with all this hanging over him?"

"The superintendent said there is nothing in Gary's record about this. They are giving him a sterling recommendation. It might be a challenge for both of us to find jobs close together, but what choice do we have?"

I reached out my hand and put it on top of Libby's. "So, how are the two of you doing?"

Libby shrugged. Her lower lip quivered, but she bit it.

"I'll be okay." After a pause, she added, "We'll be okay."

The next day I went through my weekly routine of laying out the newspaper and writing my weekly column, this one promoting the town's upcoming Bicentennial events. But Gary's situation was never far from my mind. The newsman in me knew I had enough for a front-page story: "Local Teacher Accused of Molesting Student."

In Chicago, I would not have hesitated. I would have spent the day tracking down every member of the school board and school administration for their comments. I would have camped out to get an interview with Darla Minnix and with Gary.

If Roy became aware of the situation, he wouldn't take three seconds to demand the story be written for page one.

But it didn't feel right.

Once the story hit print, it would never die. Gary's career would be ruined. Even if Gary found a job at another school, inevitably someone would talk to someone who had seen the story. They wouldn't care that the whole event may have been the product of vengeful girls seeking retribution for being caught having sex in school. If indeed they were vengeful girls. If indeed they were not victims of a nice guy who let his sexual desires get out of hand even if only for a moment.

Every time I thought of calling the superintendent for a comment, I saw Libby's face, her teeth biting on her lower lip to keep from bursting into tears. Was she so upset because of baseless accusations against her husband? Or was she upset because someplace in her deepest fears, she suspected there was more truth in the accusations than she would ever admit? Or was she grieving over lost trust she knew could never be fully restored?

I had spent too many evenings with Gary playing chess to be his public prosecutor and executioner. Maybe I would get fired if Roy ever found out, but I couldn't do it.

The story never ran.

A week later, Libby called me at the office. "Just thought I would tell you that Gary got a job in Ramsford. That's a small town in Ohio. They recently added a pool, and Gary's going to be the swim coach. I got a job there, too, teaching junior high English."

"I guess maybe that's for the best. When are you leaving?"

"In about half an hour. We rented a truck. We're packing up the last of the stuff."

"I hate that you're leaving, but I understand. Wish we could have gotten together one more time."

"You come over and visit us when we get settled. Bring Emma. I like her."

"Drive safe."

We hung up. I knew I would never make a trip to Ramsford. I would never see the Middletons again.

THIRTY-FOUR – *Heroes Among Us*

July 2, 1976, HANOI, VIETNAM (INTERNATIONAL WIRE SERVICES): North and South Vietnam were officially united as one nation today, becoming the Socialist Republic of Vietnam. The declaration ends more than 25 years of war dating back to the French colonial era.

More than 55,000 American soldiers died during the Vietnam War.

Bill Olsen walked into Perry Drugs coffee shop about three weeks before the Bicentennial celebration. Since Bill had been the genesis of the idea of a parade, I asked him how the planning was going. I expected some enthusiasm might have worn off as reality closed in. But I was wrong.

"You won't believe it," Bill said, his grin spreading from ear to ear. "The hot air balloons are all set. And everybody we've talked to has jumped at the idea of being in the parade. Now we're getting calls from all around from groups wanting to be in the parade. We've got three high school bands so far. Two horse units, and maybe a third one. The hog roast and church ice cream socials are set. Even the penny pinchers over at the bank chipped in a nice chunk of money to upgrade the fireworks show."

"I'm amazed," I said.

"So am I," Bill said. "Now if we can get Alvin over there to be our grand Marshal, we'll be set."

"Alvin Perry?" I said. Alvin was the shy diminutive owner of the drugstore and coffee shop. He generally stayed behind his pharmacy counter, offering a thin smile but few words to his customers.

"You don't know about Alvin?"

I shook my head.

"He's a war hero. He never talks about it, but he won the Medal of Honor."

"You're shitting me?"

"No. Ask anyone. I'm surprised you didn't know."

"But he . . ."

"Doesn't seem like the hero type? No, but he's the real deal. We want him at the front of the parade."

In the ten months I had been in Stratton, I wasn't sure I had exchanged more than twenty words with Alvin. He never came out to the coffee shop to talk town news and gossip.

With a cup of coffee in my hand, I walked to the back of the store. Alvin was sitting at his desk behind the pharmacy counter working on paperwork.

"Alvin." I waited for a minute for him to look up. "We've met a couple of times. I'm Zach Carlson with the newspaper."

"I know who you are," he said pleasantly. "What can I do for you?"

"I'd like to talk."

Alvin waved me through the door to the pharmacy, which I was surprised to find wasn't locked. He motioned for me to sit on a metal folding chair opposite him.

"I understand you won the Congressional Medal of Honor."

Alvin sighed deeply, like someone publicly revealed he was a bedwetter.

"Suppose Bill Olsen told you." He spoke with a thin, high-pitched voice.

I nodded.

"Let's be clear. I didn't win anything. They gave me the medal, but you don't win it. Most of the men who got that award died."

"Sorry. Poor choice of words. But with the Bicentennial coming up, I'd like to do a story about it."

Alvin shook his head one time. "Nobody wants to read about that."

"Sure they do. People love to read about heroes, and particularly when it's one of their own."

Again, Alvin shook his head. As he moved his head, his black framed bottle-thick glasses slid down his nose. He pushed them up with a practiced motion.

"It was a long time ago," he said. "I don't think people would want to hear all that again."

I took a long drink of coffee. It was clear he would take convincing.

"There's a lot of crap going on in this country. Country almost tore itself apart over Vietnam. Race riots. People burning the flag. Watergate. Everybody getting shot like it was open season on the country's leaders – JFK, Bobby, Martin Luther King, even George Wallace. Hell, two people tried to shoot President Ford last fall. Gerald Ford! What's he ever done to anybody? Seems like the country's breaking apart. Going to hell."

"Yep," Alvin said sadly. "Does seem that way."

"Young people need a hero or two. Someone like you."

Alvin held his hands together, rolling his thumbs over each other.

"I'm not a hero. They gave me the medal, but the heroes are buried over in Europe and all over the Pacific. The heroes didn't come back."

I let his words settle between us. "Maybe it's their story that you tell. That's what people, these kids, need to hear."

Alvin continued rolling his thumbs, staring down at his feet. When he looked up, there seemed to be a look of resignation on his face. "Store closes at six. Come in before I lock up."

#

I wasn't sure Alvin would be in the drug store when I showed up at five minutes before six. I feared he would change his mind. But he was there.

The store clerk left and Alvin locked the door after her. We walked back to the coffee shop. He brewed a fresh pot of coffee and poured cups for each of us. We sat at one of the Formica-topped tables.

"You want anything to eat?" he said. "I can probably find a doughnut or two still fresh enough to eat."

"Coffee's fine."

Alvin still wore his white pharmacy coat with his name stitched on the left breast. His stringy thick hair was slicked straight back from his haggard face. He seemed reluctant but not nervous.

I pulled out my notebook and placed it on the table in front of me where he could observe what I was writing. In my experience, some people felt more comfortable if they saw my notes as I wrote them, a type of double check on accuracy. I started the interview by asking Alvin about growing up.

"I grew up right here in Stratton. It was during the depression, of course. My dad was an insurance man. The crash really hit him hard. But he kept the business going, mostly on hopes of better times ahead. He worked second, sometimes third jobs to keep food on the table. He delivered coal in the winter, hauled trash and picked tomatoes in the summer. Anything that paid."

"Tough times."

Alvin nodded. "Soon as I was old enough, I was working, too. My dad knew lots of people. He was respected. Made it easier when I started looking for work. A few farmers around here liked me. They gave me any work when they had money and something needed done – digging fence post holes, pulling stumps, baling hay, anything at all. But dad insisted I stay in school. I graduated in 1940. One of the farmers I worked for had a brother who was a plumber in Chicago. He hired me as an apprentice. If it hadn't been for the war, I'd probably have spent my life installing toilets and unplugging drains in Chicago."

I kept sipping at my coffee. I let Alvin tell his story at his own pace.

"When Pearl Harbor happened, it changed everything. I took a couple of weeks to get everything in order in Chicago and headed home to visit my parents for a while. After that, I hitch-hiked to South Bend and joined up."

Alvin took off his glasses and polished them on the end of his coat as if he was trying to sharpen his vision into the past. With a slow practiced movement, he slipped them back on, and continued.

"We were all so young, and full of piss and vinegar. All we wanted to do was get on a boat and go kill Japs. Teach 'em a lesson for Pearl Harbor, and get back home. So goddamn stupid. We didn't know shit. But I guess everybody going off to war is like that. Otherwise, nobody would go."

Alvin refreshed our cups from the coffee pot.

"What service did you join?"

"Marines. Is there anything else? Semper Fi."

He apparently noticed the surprise on my face.

"Hey, I wasn't always this weak old man who's nothing but skin and bones. All that farm work, I was pretty strong. Not big, but strong."

"Where did you serve?"

"Oh, all over the Pacific. I shipped out August 14, 1942. Didn't step foot on the good ol' USA until November 22, 1945. Thanksgiving Day, if you can believe it. Never was so thankful. I always celebrated Thanksgiving on November 22 no matter the actual date. That is until Kennedy got shot. November 22 didn't seem so special after that. Now I celebrate it on the same day as everybody else."

Alvin bit his lip at his memories. I could not tell if he was reliving his homecoming or the Kennedy assassination.

"In those three years, I saw things that no man should see. I did things no man should do."

Alvin took a sip of his coffee and stared out across the vacant store. He wiped his hand through his straggly gray hair as if trying to free himself from his memories.

We sat in the silence for a very long time.

"So how did you earn the Medal of Honor?" I finally asked.

"I'm not sure I earned it, but this is what happened. It was June 1944. We had just invaded Saipan. Back here, I guess the papers were full of D-Day and the invasion of Europe. But we was doing our job and dying out there in the Pacific. Just nobody noticed much."

Alvin again took off his glasses and polished them.

"You ever been in the South Pacific?" Alvin asked.

"No. Never been there."

"It's the hottest most miserable goddamn place on earth. Forget all those fancy pictures of palm trees and sand. It's so hot and humid, it's like you're getting steamed alive. It's filled with all types of insects and diseases you ain't never heard of. Your canteen is so hot it's almost like drinking boiled water. And you never know when some Jap is going to start shooting at you. You can't even take a decent shit 'cause you'll get your head blowed off wiping your ass."

Alvin got up and again refilled the coffee cups. When he resumed telling his story, his face glazed over. He seemed to be transported back to the horror of the South Pacific.

"Saipan was as bad as any of them islands. Everybody knows about Iwo Jima 'cause those guys raised that flag there. But Saipan was just as bad. It was a big rock with a mountain in the middle. Like all them islands. The Japs dug in for months before we got there, building tunnels and booby traps. We had to root them out tunnel by tunnel, cave by cave."

"We'd been fighting foot by foot for two weeks. I was a grunt, part of a forward platoon. We dug in among some rocks, taking turns grabbing a few minutes sleep and keeping watch. Shortly before dawn, the Japs hit us. That's what they did, mostly. Hide in the day; attack us at night."

"I can't tell you how many there was. Twenty? Thirty? More? Who knows? There was eighteen of us. They got inside our lines. We was too close to use our rifles except as clubs. It was all hand-to-hand. Brutal stuff."

"We fought em' off. Killed a dozen of them, but they killed five of us. We had another seven guys hurt real bad. Only four of us were in any kind of shape to fight. The radio was gone, so we couldn't call for reinforcements or medics."

Alvin paused. He seemed to be replaying a scene in his head. Perhaps the carnage of death scattered around him, the sounds of the wounded, or something else so terrible that he would never share.

I thought about asking about injured Japanese soldiers that may have been left behind. It seemed unlikely that the Japanese were all killed in the fight. But I stopped myself. Men in combat did desperate and sometimes despicable acts. It was war. If something else happened, I didn't want Alvin to tell me.

After a short moment, Alvin continued. "We worked patching up the wounded, trying to stop 'em from bleeding out. The Japs used the attack as cover to move a couple of machine guns in place behind some rocks. Guess that was their plan all along. Those guns had a view of the valley from there."

"I was cut up some, but I was in about the best shape of any of us. With them machine guns overlooking us, I didn't see that we had much choice. If we stayed there, those seven guys would die, and the rest of us were sitting ducks. Either the guns would take us out when we tried to move, or the Japs would eventually figure that we didn't have enough men to fight off an attack. I decided I'd rather die taking out Japs than crawled up behind some rock.

"I grabbed an extra gun and as much ammo and grenades as I could strap on, and told the other three guys to give me ten minutes to move into position, then start taking pot shots at the machine gun emplacements. I figured that would at least draw their attention for a few minutes.

"I slid out around a couple of rocks and made my way up and to the left. When the guys started peppering them with gunfire, I ran at the closest machine gun nest. Three Japs opened fire. I don't know how they missed, but they did. I got off a shot and took one of them out. I used my bayonet on the second. I hit the third guy in the face with the butt of my gun. Finished him off with a couple of rounds in his chest."

Alvin stopped telling the story. He stared off across the silent store. Seeing his fixed gaze, I imagined he was recalling the moment he killed those men at close range. After a long moment, he picked up his cup. Only when he brought it to his lips did he realize it was empty. He put the cup down, not bothering to refill it.

"I was carrying some white phosphorus grenades on my belt. They're nasty weapons. They kill more by burning than by explosion or shrapnel. I crawled along on my belly toward the other nest, using some rocks as cover. When I got close enough, I tossed a couple of them at that second machine gun and dove for cover. The grenades exploded. I felt the heat and them Japs screamed like I never heard before. I smelled their flesh burning. But I didn't have time to dwell on it. I got up and ran full bore into the smoke. I guess it covered me, 'cause I ran right into the second gun emplacement. I had a gun in both hands and shot two Japs before they turned their gun toward me. There were three of four others in there, but I guess they thought it was a full assault, and they took off. I shot two of them. Threw more grenades in their direction. I grabbed that machine gun and as many belts of ammo as I could carry, and high-tailed it back to our camp."

For the first time in our conversation, a small smile flicked at the corner of Alvin's mouth.

"I remember yelling at the guys 'I'm a Marine! Don't shoot! I'm a Marine dammit!' I wasn't as concerned about the Japs shooting me as I was my own guys. I didn't want to be killed by somebody thinking I was a Jap."

Alvin got up and walked behind the coffee shop counter.

"No more for me," I said. Alvin grabbed the coffee pot, refilled his own cup and returned to the table.

"Where was I? Oh yeah. Anyway, as I was running, the Japs started firing at me. I used to say God was looking out for me that day, but I don't do that anymore. I think about all them other boys that died over there. If you say I wasn't shot because God was looking out for me that would mean God wasn't looking after them. I can't believe that. I can't believe God was picking and choosing, looking out for me and not them. No, it was plain damn luck that the Japs missed me. I did get a ding on my calf and a couple of holes in my shirt. Ripped some skin. Guess it was enough for a purple heart, but really it wasn't nothing.

"We had to get the wounded out of there. Hell, we had to get all of us out of there. I stayed behind with the machine gun and as many grenades as I could find. I laid down covering fire as the other three guys carried out the wounded. They took out three, then came back for another three. I kept covering them with that Jap machine gun. When everybody had escaped except me and the last wounded man, I grabbed him and slung him over my shoulders. I took off with guns in both hands, firing blindly backwards and running like hell.

"I tried to carry the wounded man so he wasn't exposed as I ran. I got hit a couple of times, but I kept going. Wasn't no choice. We got down to where another bigger platoon was dug in. They had a radio. They called for reinforcements and evac teams for the injured.

"I didn't really notice at the time, but the last man I carried out was a captain who had come up to reconnoiter the front lines. Guess he's the one that nominated me for the medal."

"How bad were you hurt?"

"Not too bad. Got sent back behind the lines to the field hospital and bandaged up. They'd have sent me back to the front lines in a week or two. But a few days after they bandaged me up, I was sitting in the shade of a puny palm tree eating my first hot meal since we landed on that damn island, and some Jap come running out of the brush. Before I reacted, he ran his bayonet into me. One of the soldiers nearby shot him while he still had the bayonet in me. If I'd been out in the field, I would have died. But one of the docs from the field hospital ran out and got the bleeding stopped. A day or two later, they shipped me out to Guam, then on to Hawaii. I spent over a year in and out of Navy hospitals. I finally got released to return to duty the day we dropped the bomb."

Alvin sat back and took a deep breath. "I haven't talked about that in twenty years," he said.

I sat speechless and exhausted. It was one thing to hear the story, but quite another to sit in front of a man who had experienced it. I got up and moved behind the counter where I filled a glass with tap water and emptied it with a single gulp.

I walked back and took my seat opposite Alvin.

"Thanks for sharing this. I can understand why you don't like talking about it."

Alvin nodded, but did not say anything.

"So how did you end up with this drug store?"

Alvin seemed to be visibly relieved we were no longer talking about combat.

"That's the one good thing that came out of the whole mess. When I was in the hospital, I took a lot of drugs for infections and pain. I got to know the pharmacists pretty well. They encouraged me to go to pharmacy school. Told me it paid pretty good, and I wouldn't have to break my back like a plumber. So, when I got out of the service, I used the GI bill to get my pharmacy degree from Purdue. Old man Pemberton — that's Hank's grandfather — ran a general store out of this building. He hired me to open a pharmacy in the back part of the store. When he retired, he sold the whole store to me."

I closed my notebook and again thanked Alvin for his story. I walked to the door with Alvin. As he unlocked it, I thought of one more question.

"So where is your medal?"

Alvin slipped his hand on the back of his neck, rubbing it in thought. "Home someplace, I guess." he said.

"You don't know?"

"It's there someplace, but I'd have to hunt for it."

"When was the last time you looked at it?"

"Well, I saw the case when we moved into our house. That was 1956, if I remember right."

"Just the case? When did you last look at the medal?"

"Guess that was 1946, the day they gave it to me."

#

I ran the story on Alvin on the front page. My weekly column focused on the value of heroes and why we need them. Roy called me up to congratulate me.

"One helluva story. I bet you get an award for this one," he said.

But there was no photo of Alvin or his Medal of Honor. Alvin thought it would be pretentious.

THIRTY-FIVE – When It All Becomes Tears

April 1975

April 30, 1975, SAIGON, SOUTH VIETNAM (INTERNATIONAL WIRE SERVICES): In a frantic desperate crush of humanity, the final 1,000 Americans in South Vietnam were evacuated by helicopter from the U.S. Embassy, ending the United States 20-year involvement in that country.

More than 800 Vietnamese employed by the US and promised safe transport were left behind, according to sources.

After Kate's funeral, I was lost. I could not face our new apartment. The management was more understanding than I expected. They let me out of the lease with two months' rent.

I couldn't face the office, either. Charlie told me to take as much time as I needed. There wasn't that much time in the world. I put all of my belongings in storage and headed to my mother's house in Sarasota. I didn't know what else to do.

In Sarasota, I kept my distance and avoided my mother and her husband as often as possible. I avoided everyone.

I tried going to the beach to be alone with my emotions, but the sand irritated and the sun burned, but not deep enough to take away the emptiness, the hurt, the sense that nothing mattered. I tried aimless walking, but I was too tired from lack of sleep. I tried reading, but found myself re-reading the same page over and over, comprehending nothing.

Most afternoons were spent in beachfront bars getting drunk despite losing my taste for alcohol. I drank myself into oblivion, but the numbness I sought did not come.

I gave up smoking. I promised Kate and I would keep my promise. No matter how far I fell, no matter how the craving reached for me, I would not break my promise.

The one thing I could not do was cry. I had not cried since that night in the LaSalle Street garage.

Kate's parents reached out to me several times, calling me at my mother's house, even sending me a letter. I made excuses not to talk to them. I appreciated their concern and shared their anguish. But I couldn't talk to them. I couldn't talk to anyone.

Lee Phillips, the Chicago detective handling the case, called me once a week to update me on the investigation. There were no significant leads, but they would keep working the case. I impassively listened to Lee, his words barely registering. I didn't ask questions. When he would finish, I hung up without comment.

After four weeks in Florida, I returned to Chicago. I found a drab one-bedroom apartment a block from my old apartment, the one where I lived when I first met Kate.

On my first day back in the newsroom, Charlie called me into his office as soon as I walked in the door. He welcomed me back, then gave me the news about my reassignment.

"I've moved you off crime beat, Zach. I want you to cover the courts."

I protested, but Charlie told me the change was already made and Matt Clemens was handling my old crime beat.

"You take your time. If you need to take a few days off, let me know. I talked with the personnel department and have it covered for you."

"Thanks Charlie. But that's not needed. I'm ready to be back."

Charlie smiled, came around his desk and put his hand on my shoulder.

"You take your time."

Everyone walked on eggshells around me. No banter about recent murders. No jokes about the latest body found in pieces. No jokes at all. Charlie no longer shouted across the newsroom for someone to take the latest "slice and dice" on the west side. Instead, he made the blood and guts assignments in hand-scribbled notes dropped on reporters' desks.

It was not the same place. I wasn't the same person.

#

Two weeks after I got back to Chicago, I called Kate's parents and apologized for not taking their calls when I was in Florida. I gave them my new address and phone number and promised to stay in touch.

I knew I wouldn't.

I wasn't proud of distancing myself from Doris and Jim. They were wonderful people. Kind. Considerate. Loving. And they were heartbroken. I sensed that by staying in touch with me, they hoped to keep something about Kate alive through me. But every time I talked to Doris and Jim, I heard Kate in their voice, their accent, and the words they used, even the way they breathed.

I couldn't handle that.

I tried to stay out of the newsroom as much as possible. I arrived to get my assignments, then spent the day checking court files and sitting in trials. After court, I would sit at some small bar or coffee shop putting my notes together and outlining my story for the day, returning to the newsroom only long enough to type up twenty inches of copy. Then I was gone.

Most of my evenings were spent in a couple of local bars, nursing two or three beers for hours and mindlessly watching the television above the bar. I politely but firmly fended off friends who wanted to take me to dinner. I didn't want company.

Sometime after eleven o'clock I would make my way back to my apartment, turn on the television to keep my mind distracted, and fall into a fitful sleep, interrupted hourly by recurring dreams of Kate that dissolved into horrific nightmares. When I awoke, I found the nightmares were never as bad as my reality.

At seven, my alarm would blare. I would get up and do it all again.

Over Christmas, I again visited my mom and her husband in Florida. I left the house early on Christmas morning, long before anyone else was awake. I walked, mile after mile, hour after hour.

Near the water, I found a bench and sat, watching the waves until my eyes could no longer focus, and I stared at nothing.

Near sunset, I ended up at a convenience store open on Christmas Day. I used a pay phone and called my mother. I passed along the address that the clerk gave me. Forty minutes later, my stepfather picked me up.

I returned to Chicago and began my routine again. Lee Phillips, the detective in charge of Kate's case, continued to call, although his calls were less frequent.

"We don't have any new leads, Zach, but we're not giving up. We're still working the case."

I thanked him for the call and hung up. I still didn't want to ask questions. I wanted it all to go away. But it never would.

In late April, I sat at my desk writing a story on a jury verdict in the second-degree murder trial of Maryann Hayden, a battered wife. Her drunken brute of a husband worked in a steel mill during the day and got drunk and beat his wife at night.

One night, she had enough. She waited until he was asleep. With blood still on her face from where he had again broken her nose, she took a .38 from the bedside table and emptied the gun into his head. She reloaded and fired three more shots to make sure.

The lawyer gave an impassioned argument that the jury should acquit the woman based on self -defense. I talked with several jurors afterward. They had empathy for the woman and her situation, but thought the judge's instructions required them to convict. None of the jurors liked it.

Rather than just writing a who, what, when story, I wrote about Maryann Hayden. I wrote about all she had gone through: the beatings, the hospital visits, the disinterested police who responded when neighbors called about the screams from her house. I wrote how the jury believed her. Despite their sympathies, the law gave them no choice.

The next part of the story was about her children who had witnessed years of abuse of their mother. Now they were condemned to the city's inept child services system.

I slipped a new page into the typewriter and stared at it. No words came. I looked at my notes and my outline. The article was in my head, but when I tried to type, my fingers would not move, as if the connection between my brain and my fingers had been severed. I could not type a sentence. A word. A letter.

From deep inside me, the tears form. A single tear trickled down my cheek. Then a second. Then it became a flood. For the first time since the night Kate died, I cried.

The tears flowed like a great sea unleashed. My sobs went across the newsroom and everyone stopped and looked. But I didn't care. All I cared about was Kate. How sweet and smart and funny she was. The child-like joy she took in jumping into a cold lake or catching a fish. How she smiled and laughed. The scent of her skin, her hair. Her touch. The sweat on her body after making love. How I would never see her, never hear her voice, never touch her again. How much I loved her. And those awful last moments that no amount of alcohol or pills could wash from my brain.

Long minutes I sobbed. I wasn't aware that Charlie was standing behind me until his hand came to rest on my shoulder.

"I can't do this anymore," I said through my sobs.

The next day, I told Charlie that I was leaving the Examiner. Leaving Chicago. "I'm not sure what I will do, but I can't stay here."

Charlie didn't argue. He offered to help in any way possible, holding my resignation letter in case I changed my mind. A month later he gave me Ed Gordon's name and phone number.

"Ed's a good friend. He works for Barrett Newspapers. The corporate offices are out in Naperville. They have a bunch of community papers. He's looking for a couple of people. It may not be what you're looking for, but I thought I'd pass it along."

THIRTY-SIX – *Shadow of the Unicorn*

July 3, 1976, PINE RIDGE INDIAN RESERVATION, S.D. (WIRE SERVICES): As the nation decks out in its finest red, white and blue to celebrate the Bicentennial, there are a few places where the celebration will go largely unnoticed.

"The Bicentennial celebrates independence," said Oglala Tribal leader Hotah Little Bear. "We had our independence before the white man came."

It was peanut butter pie day at Shelby's Place. Like Roy before me, I was addicted. As usual, Emma was waiting on me. The evening dinner crowd had mostly left by the time she brought me a slice of the pie and sat down across from me.

"We sold out at lunch, but I saved a slice for you."

She watched with obvious pleasure as I devoured the pie.

There was a familiarity now between us that accompanies a relationship. But even in the most private of moments, I remained detached. I was aware of it. I was sure Emma felt it, too.

"You're working all day Sunday on that Bicentennial thing, but do you have any plans Saturday?"

I took the last bite of pie, thinking through my schedule. "Lutheran Church is having a pancake breakfast. I agreed to stop by and take a few photos, but I'll be done by nine."

"So, how would you like to go on a picnic over at Little Turtle State Park? I'm taking my daughter and one of her friends. I thought you could come along and keep me company."

In the months we had been dating, I had only met Emma's daughter on three or four occasions, and then only for brief moments. To me, it seemed I was being asked to something more than a casual picnic. It seemed more like being asked home to meet her parents. I still lived with ghosts of my prior life. I wasn't ready for that.

Emma was fun to be with. She was much smarter than most people gave her credit. She was well read and enjoyed good movies. And she was fun in bed, always smiling and laughing and bringing lightness to sex unlike anyone I had ever been with.

Turning down the invitation would hurt Emma deeply. I didn't want to do that.

"What time?"

"I thought we'd leave about ten. It's about an hour drive."

"What do I need to bring?"

"Just your cute self and your swim trunks," she said. "I'm an old pro at picnics. I'll bring everything else."

#

Saturday morning, I showed up at Emma's house before ten. The temperature was already in the mid-80s and thick humidity portended afternoon thunderstorms.

When I arrived, Emma's daughter, Molly, and another girl sat on the front porch sharing whispers and giggles. They were not quite teens, rail thin with a hint of the bodies they would soon develop into young women. Both wore shorts over one-piece swim suits and flip flops. Molly was the taller of the two girls, with Emma's pink complexion and wavy blonde hair that hung past her shoulders.

"Hi Zach," Molly said, standing up. "This is my friend, Jan."

The other girl, not as tall, with dark features and long straight raven hair, gave me a small wave.

"You run the newspaper," Jan said. "That's sort of cool."

"I don't know how cool it is, but that's what I do."

"So, you sleeping with Molly's mom?"

I'm not sure, but I think my mouth fell open.

Molly smacked Jan on the shoulder and the girls broke out into uncontrollable giggles. I suspected I had been the subject of a dare.

Emma saved me from concocting an answer when she walked out of the door, picnic basket in hand.

"What are you girls doing?" Emma said, eyeing them suspiciously.

The girls laughed again and took off running. Emma gave me a quick kiss on my lips. I took the basket from her.

"What were those two up to?" she asked.

"Being kids," I said.

I got into Emma's 1967 Ford Galaxy station wagon. Emma got behind the wheel, and the girls climbed in back. The car was dingy white with rust spots on the doors and along the undercarriage.

It did not have air conditioning, so we rode along with the windows rolled down. Emma turned the radio to a Top-40 AM station out of Chicago, the volume cranked all the way up to compensate for the wind noise. In the back seat, the girls sang along with the tunes.

Emma and I didn't speak much. The wind noise was too loud to carry on much of a conversation. I sat back and watched the mid-summer fields and stands of trees pass by at 60 miles per hour. As Emma promised, the drive took less than an hour.

Little Turtle State Park was a stretch of forest-covered rocky terrain around Little Turtle River, a small waterway that in mid-summer seemed more of a creek than a river. There were a few hiking trails, primitive camping, and a man-made lake big enough for swimming and canoes. Undoubtedly the park existed because the land was unsuitable for farming.

The parking lot near the lake was already three-quarters full with those celebrating the Fourth of July weekend. Emma parked in the back row, closer to the picnic grounds.

As soon as the doors opened, the girls were dashing toward the beach area on the lake. "Stay out of trouble," Emma yelled after them, then laughed.

As the girls skipped off toward the beach, towels draped over their shoulders. Emma lowered the tailgate of the station wagon.

"Want to help?" Emma said, nodding toward the picnic basket.

I grabbed the basket and a big plastic cooler out of the back of the station wagon. Emma grabbed a bag and a tablecloth. I followed her up a short path to a well-kept wooded picnic area. Ten weather-battered picnic tables were scattered around. Emma selected one in the shade of an overhanging maple tree.

"This will work," she said.

We spread the tablecloth, holding it in place with the woven basket at one end and the cooler at the other. Emma retrieved a blanket from the car. I helped her spread it in a patch of grass where the sun filtered through the trees.

Emma pulled off her yellow shorts and unbuttoned the white cotton shirt she was wearing, revealing a bright pink bikini. "You approve?" she said, twirling around.

I gave a playful whistle. "Very nice," I said.

Emma carried a few more pounds than the bikini was probably meant to hold. She had a small roll above where her belly slid into her bikini bottom, but it was not enough to be unattractive. With Emma, it even seemed to add to her sexiness, her allure.

Emma lacked any self-consciousness about her weight or her body. When we spent the night together, she never grabbed for something to cover herself when she got out of bed. She never tried to hide the faint stretch marks left by childbirth or the scar on her thigh from a bike accident when she was young. She never talked about being on a diet or needing to lose a few pounds. I had never known anyone who seemed more content in her own body, more comfortable in her own skin.

Emma pulled a bottle of sun lotion from her bag. She collapsed onto the blanket.

"Want to put lotion on me?"

I took my shirt off and sat on the blanket next to Emma. She handed me the bottle, then turned over and unsnapped her top. I massaged in the lotion. When I finished with her back and legs, she refastened the top and rolled over. I dribbled the lotion on to her stomach and the front of her legs, then massaged it in.

I applied my own sunscreen, leaving only my back. Emma rubbed in the lotion, using broad firm strokes along my back and shoulder muscles, reminding me of our first night together when she calmed me with her gentle touch.

Emma and I lay next to each other, our feet touching gently, absorbing the heat of the sun. After several minutes, Emma said. "The girls will want to swim for a while before lunch. Let's give them a half hour or so, then I'll go get them."

A gentle breeze blew over us, taking away the intensity of the sun. Above us, the broad maple leaves fluttered. A few insects buzzed around. I lazily swatted at them a time or two, but with no effect. In the distance, we could hear the muffled sounds coming up from the beach.

Emma took my hand. As we lay there, the heat radiated through my body. I dozed off.

I woke up with a cool spray of water dancing across my skin. Through half-opened eyes, I saw the girls leaning over the blanket, their heads, throwing spray from their wet hair. Emma stirred and the girls giggled.

"Mom, when we gonna eat. We're hungry."

Emma had made a lunch of tomato and cucumber sandwiches. She said the recipe came from Good Housekeeping. She also made potato salad, coleslaw and homemade oatmeal cookies. We washed it down with plastic glasses of homemade lemonade poured from a Tupperware pitcher that Emma had packed in the cooler.

The girls had lots of questions about working at a newspaper. They were particularly interested in my years in Chicago. It wasn't something I wanted to talk about, but I didn't want to be rude.

"How many murders did you write about?" Jan asked.

"Usually two or three a week," I said. "But I wrote about other stuff too."

"That many?" Molly said with disbelief.

"There were more. The ones I wrote about had something that made them newsworthy."

"Like what? What made them newsworthy?"

"Different things." I said, not expanding.

"What was the worst one?" Molly asked.

My memories flashed to that night in the parking garage on LaSalle Street. The moment of realization. The image of Kate's lifeless body that came every night in my sleep. I sensed the color draining from my face.

"That's enough," I heard Emma say. "It's his day off, so don't pester him."

I turned toward her. Concern registered on her face. Without taking her gaze from me, she continued talking to the girls.

"Why don't you girls go over to the beach? We'll clean up here and join you."

The girls grabbed their towels and headed off. Emma yelled after them "You just ate. No getting in the water for thirty minutes."

When the girls were beyond earshot, Emma turned to me.

"You okay?"

I nodded.

"When she asked you that question about the worst murder, you disappeared someplace else."

"I'm fine," I said, pouring myself more lemonade.

I helped fold up the tablecloth and pack all our supplies back into the basket. We carried everything back to the car.

"Maybe I shouldn't have invited you," Emma said when we got to the car. "I didn't mean to push you into something."

"No. I'm glad you did. I've had fun. And I needed this. I'm not used to pre-teen girls – or kids at all, for that matter."

When everything was loaded, Emma took my hand, and we sat on the tailgate of the station wagon.

"When Molly asked about the worst crime you ever reported, you went someplace else in your mind. That place has something to do with you being here, doesn't it? I mean, here in Stratton and not in Chicago."

I looked out across the picnic ground off toward the lake. We sat there for several silent minutes. Finally, I nodded. "You're pretty perceptive. Or was I that obvious."

"You want to tell me about it."

My gaze lowered to my hands that lay interlaced on my lap. Sitting there on the tailgate of a battered Ford station wagon, the sun baking down, a gentle breeze blowing, amid sounds of beach frolicking and buzzing insects, I talked about Kate for the first time since the murder. When I started, the words streamed out — meeting her, falling in love, planning to get married. Then I told Emma about the night almost two years before when my life came crashing down.

I spoke looking straight ahead, talking more to myself than to Emma. It wasn't until I was done that I realized tears were streaming down my face and Emma's arm was wrapped around me.

We sat there listening to the rustle of the summer breeze through the pines that surrounded us, saying nothing.

Long minutes passed. Emma said, "Thank you. I understand more now." She got to her feet. "We better get down to the beach and make sure the girls aren't getting in trouble.

We walked holding hands down the path to the beach, me carrying a blanket and Emma carrying two beach towels. The sand burned against bare feet. We found a spot separated from families with small children and groups of flirting teenagers.

Emma tracked down Molly and Jan while I spread out the blanket. I rolled my towel into a makeshift pillow and lay down. A few minutes later, Emma joined me.

"I told them where we are. They're having a great time in the water. You want to get in?"

"In a few minutes," I said.

We lay there quietly, the sun baking out the tension of our lives.

"I'm always looking for unicorns," Emma said, breaking the silence.

"What?" I wasn't sure I heard correctly.

"Unicorns," she repeated. "Those one-horned horses."

"I know what a unicorn is." With a smile I added, "You understand they aren't real?"

"Sure they're real," she said. Her voice was more serious than I expected. "My mom had a hard time when I was little. I'm glad she found Carl. That's my stepdad. But my real dad was a bastard. He ran out on us when I was about two years old. Just up and left." Emma shifted, raising up, bracing her elbow into the blanket and resting the side of her face on her hand.

"My grandparents helped a lot. I spent lots of time with them. I spent every summer with them until Grandpa Joe died. That was when I was twelve, about Molly's age."

"I wasn't close to my grandparents," I said. "My mom's parents died when I was young. I don't remember them at all. And after my mom and dad split, my mom didn't let me visit his parents."

"I'm sorry you missed that. I don't know what my life would have been like without them. They lived in a little farmhouse out by Liberty Station. They had a few milk cows, and chickens, and a vegetable garden."

"What's this got to do with unicorns?"

"I was about three years old. Grandpa Joe came into the house. He was holding his finger to his lips for me to be quiet and signaling for me to follow him. We walked real quiet out past the chicken coop to his workshop. Then he leaned down and whispered, 'Be real quiet and look around the corner there. Up against the barn, if you look close and don't scare him away, you'll see the shadow of a unicorn.' So, I peeked around the corner of the shed, and sure enough, against the white wall of the barn was a shadow. And it was a unicorn."

I started to laugh but recognized that Emma was not telling the story because she thought it was funny.

"Grandpa Joe leaned up against my ear and whispered, 'You can never see a unicorn. They're too magnificent, too magical. But if you're quiet and move real slow, you can sometimes catch a glimpse of their shadow.'"

"After that, whenever I went to stay with them, I always asked Grandpa Joe if we could hunt for the Unicorn's shadow. We would walk quietly, him holding my hand. We'd search all over. Most times, we couldn't find anything, but every occasionally, we'd see one."

"I started sneaking out by myself to catch a glimpse of the shadow. And a couple of times I did. I stood there, not moving, not saying anything. Sometimes I'd stand there for what seemed like hours. I thought if I was super quiet, I might actually see the unicorn. But I never did."

Emma sat up, pulling her knees up and clasping her hands together across her shins. She looked out across the water as if in gazing into the sparkling water, she could glimpse images of her past.

"One summer not long after I started school, I asked Grandpa Joe if we could go search for the unicorn's shadow. He said sure. So we walked out to our spot at the corner of the work shed. I peeked around, and there it was. I remember saying 'Oh grandpa Joe, it's still there,' and he said 'It will always be there for you, child.' I remember that like it was yesterday."

A small tear rolled down Emma's cheek.

"Then I saw another shadow. It looked like a person coming up behind the unicorn. A big hand reached out, and I screamed. I yelled for the unicorn to run. But it was too late. The hand grabbed the unicorn by the neck and suddenly it was gone. Just the person's shadow remained."

Emma turned and, for the first time since she started telling the story, looked directly at me.

"My Grandma came around the corner. She was holding a hoe and a mop in her hand. I can never forget the look of disgust she had when she walked around that corner. She walked to Grandpa and handed him the tools. 'For gosh sakes, Joe,' she said. 'Quit filling that child's head with nonsense. She's old enough not to believe in unicorns, Santa Claus and such nonsense.' Then she turned to me. Her voice wasn't any more kind. She said, 'It was just a shadow from a hoe and a mop, and a few bushes. Your Grandpa made it look like it was a unicorn. But there ain't any such thing.'"

Emma wiped her fingers across her eyes. "I ran to my room. I wouldn't come out. Wouldn't eat. Wouldn't talk to either of them. They finally called my mom, and she came and got me."

"That had to break your heart."

"It did." She paused, letting her eyes drift upward toward the summer sky. "But you know what? When I went back to their house, I'd still sneak out looking for the unicorn's shadow. I knew what I saw was more than hoes and mops." A smile formed across her face and she gave a small wink. "You know, there were times when I'm sure I saw that unicorn's shadow."

We sat in silence for several minutes, the noise and commotion of the beach all around us. It was Emma who finally spoke.

"That may be my problem. I'm always looking for that shadow of something that's not there. And sometimes I even think I see it." She gave me a tender kiss.

"I think that's what it is with you, Zach Carlson. I understood you weren't in this for the long haul. I told myself that right up front. And the more I was with you, the more I knew there was part of your life you weren't sharing. Why would a big city boy like you find himself in the middle of no place, in this little backwoods town."

"Emma, I . . ."

"That's okay Zach. Neither of us ever talked about love, or forever. It was a port in a storm. For both of us. I was company for you. Maybe a life line back to feeling something again. For me, you were a break from these local morons that constantly tried to get in my pants for a couple of nights. I knew someday you'd head back to Chicago, or someplace else where the buildings were taller, the streets crowded, the pace faster. Back to the life you were meant to have."

I protested, but Emma put her fingers across my lips. "Even if you asked me along when it's time for you to go, I probably won't. It's not that you're not tempting. You're the best guy I've been with in a long time. Maybe ever. But I'm not a Chicago girl. I'm a Stratton girl. I wouldn't feel any more at home in Chicago than you do here."

Emma's eyes glistened. "But I can't help looking for unicorns," she said.

Emma jumped up and ran into the water. I lay there for a long time thinking about Emma, trying to sort through the emotions swirling inside me. Here was Emma looking for shadows of things that didn't exist, and me, hiding out from things that were too real.

I got up and waded into the coolness of the water until my feet could not touch the bottom, then lifted my legs and let the cool silence of the water surround me. I floated with only my nose and mouth above the surface. The muffled sound of playing children danced over me. I stayed there for a long time, moving only enough to keep my face above water.

The drive back was quiet. We kept the radio off. The girls, exhausted from a day in the water, slept in the back seat, their heads resting against each other. Halfway back home, an afternoon thunderstorm broke loose. When the rain became so hard that it was difficult to see the road, Emma pulled into a roadside gas station. She scooted across the seat and lay her head on my shoulder as the rain drummed its rhythm against the metal roof.

"Thanks for listening to my silly story," she said.

"It wasn't silly," I said. "And thanks for sharing."

"Molly is spending the night at her grandparents. Would you like to come over?"

I was silent, thinking about the emotional drain of the day.

"I'd like company," she said.

I nodded.

We spent the night together. Our lovemaking was different. Gentle. Tender. Quiet. It was like we were saying goodbye.

I guess we were.

THIRTY-SEVEN – *Here Comes the Parade*

July 4, 1976, WASHINGTON, D.C. (WIRE SERVICES): Under perfect skies, more than half a million Americans crowded onto the streets of the Nation's capital to watch the National Bicentennial Parade followed by a spectacular fireworks display.

President Gerald Ford missed the celebrations. He was playing golf in Maryland.

Stratton's Bicentennial Fourth of July was planned as one of the biggest days in the history of the town. I still had doubts, but no matter how it turned out, I was going to be there to cover every event.

I woke before dawn when Emma's clock radio alarm went off. I stretched into the warmth of Emma's body and hated having to leave her.

"Morning, sleepyhead," she said in my ear.

"Sorry that I had to set the alarm so early. But those balloons take off not long after sunrise. I want to make sure I get some pictures."

Emma gave me a playful squeeze "I'm more fun than some old balloons."

I kissed her forehead. "Yeah, but what would I do for pictures in the paper?"

Emma jumped up, her feet straddling my shoulders, her hands thrown up. "How about this?" she said, throwing her head back with an exuberant laugh.

I took a quick shower while Emma cooked bacon and eggs. As I dressed, she said, "I talked to my parents. I'm going to meet up with them and we're going to see the balloons, too."

“I'll look for you,” I said. I took a cup of coffee in a Styrofoam cup with me and headed out the door.

The sky displayed a hint of pink in the east when I arrived at the high school. Bill Olsen promised thirty balloons. I expected that if we got four or five, it would be a success. I was afraid there might not be any. But by the time I pulled into the school parking lot, there were already a dozen deflated hot air balloons spread out across the forty-acre grass field waiting to be inflated.

I parked and looked for the coffee and doughnuts, which Bill had promised would be available. A candy-striped tent displayed a sign identifying itself as the United Methodist Church, and offering "Breakfast, Coffee, Homemade Pies." I made my way across the parking lot. As I did, more and more pickup trucks and vans pulled in, trailing hot air balloon gondolas.

By the time the first actual rays of the sun crested the horizon, I counted thirty-four balloons spread across the grassy tract. I had to admit, it was impressive. The first blast of propane broke the early morning quiet. It was quickly followed by another, then another. Soon a cacophony of propane burners rose from across the expanse of the field.

Standing with a cup of coffee and a doughnut, I watched in amazement as the parking lot began to fill with spectators. Cars lined up in both directions, trying to find places to park at the elementary school and on nearby neighborhood streets.

Bill Olsen and his wife Claudia walked up, looking for coffee. Bill was beaming. I took a photo of Bill and Claudia with the rising field of balloons in the background.

"Damn, I think you pulled this off, Bill."

For once, Bill was speechless.

"Nobody thought he could do this," Claudia said. She put her arm around Bill's waist and gave her husband a squeeze. "But he did. By God, he did."

After finishing my coffee, I rushed around the field, taking photos of the inflating balloons. The pilots grabbed eager bystanders to hold ropes as the balloons rose to ninety, perhaps a hundred feet tall. The balloons formed a palette of bright blues, reds, white, orange and green, like so many giants awakening from slumber.

I took photos of townspeople looking up, their mouths hanging open in awe. Shirley and her son stood at the edge of the field. A few feet away, Emma and Molly were standing next to an elderly couple I took for Emma's mom and stepdad. I waved and Emma gave me a smile and waved back. So did Molly.

The sky was cloudless. Thirty minutes after sunrise, the balloons were all nearly inflated. They seemed like out-of-place behemoths deposited by some aliens among the flatlands.

I felt a tap on my shoulder. I turned to see a petite athletic woman with short dark hair, wearing a light jacket and aviator sunglasses.

"Guy over there said you're the town newspaper editor."

"Guilty."

"I'm Suzanne Channing," she said, holding out her hand.

Her grip was firm as we shook hands. "Zach Carlson. I'm editor of the Stratton Gazette."

She gave me a broad smile. "So, soldier, you and your camera want to take a ride?"

"On one of those?" I said, pointing to the balloons.

"Yep. I have that one over there with the insurance company logo on it."

"Sure," I said, before I even had given it a thought.

"Here's the way I do things," she explained. "You can take as many photos as you want. All I ask in return is that you run at least one photo of my balloon in the paper and send me a copy. That helps me keep my advertising deal, which in turn helps pay for my hobby. That work for you?"

"Absolutely," I said. "Is it possible for you take more than one person?"

"I can take four passengers unless one of them is a lard ass."

"No lard asses. I'll be right back."

I jogged over to Emma. "Pretty impressive, isn't it?" I said.

Emma had a big smile across her face. "I never expected anything like this. I thought they'd have two or three. But wow!"

"How would you and Molly like to take a ride?"

"Really?"

I heard Molly squeal. "Say yes, mom!"

Emma looked dubious. "You sure? Is it safe?"

"Only one way to find out," I said with a smile.

Again, I heard Molly. "Say yes, mom! Say yes!"

"Okay," Emma finally said, a touch of reluctance still in her voice.

"Can Jan go, too?" Molly asked.

"If her parents say yes, and if she's ready to go right now."

Molly disappeared and returned in less than a minute with Jan in tow. "Her parents said yes."

"Can your parents follow us and give us a ride back?" I asked Emma.

"I'm sure they can."

A few minutes later, Emma, Molly, Jan, and me stood in the gondola with Suzanne Channing at the controls. We stood in a tight group, everyone holding hands. With a signal, the men holding the ropes released the balloon. The burner above our ears roared as the flame heated the air and the balloon slowly lifted. The two girls squealed.

Molly and Jan tensed and they grabbed each other. Emma squeezed my hand hard, but her face wore an ear-to-ear grin. After a few seconds, I gently pulled my hand loose to start taking photos. I shot photos nearly as fast as I could focus, check the light meter, and snap the shutter. I worked for the first fifteen minutes of the flight, shooting the better part of two 36-shot rolls of film.

"That should be enough," I said. I let the camera dangle from my neck, put my arm around Emma, and enjoyed the beauty of the farmland and forests passing below us. We floated a few feet above the tree line, then with an unexpected burst of the burner, the balloon climbed several hundred feet. Suzanne let the balloon settle only thirty feet above a field of cows. Molly and Jan started mooing. The girls broke into belly laughs when one of cows looked upward and bellowed in response. Even Emma and Suzanne broke into their best moos. The cows seemed to trail along behind the balloon as we crossed the field above them. With a burst of the burner, we climbed over a tree line and back into the sky.

We floated for nearly an hour before setting down at the edge of a soybean field. I helped lift Jan, Molly and Emma out of the gondola. The girls gave me big hugs and thanked the pilot. Emma kissed me.

"Thank you so much for thinking of us."

I got the pilot's card for forwarding the photo I would run in the newspaper. Arm in arm, we walked to the nearby road where Emma's parents were waiting in their car.

I got back in time to shoot a few photos of the community church service as it wrapped up. The closing prayer thanked the Lord for a perfect Fourth of July, echoed by a chorus of "Amens."

The parade was scheduled to kick off at noon, but by eleven o'clock, the sidewalks were already lined with people in chairs claiming the best spots. Originally the parade route was planned for the half-mile length of Main Street. But the route was expanded to accommodate the number of participants and the growing expectations for the size of the crowd. The parade started at the high school and finished down Main Street, a route covering nearly two miles.

I positioned myself on Main Street near the newspaper office, my camera bag filled with a dozen rolls of film. Shortly after noon, the faint sound of sirens drifted over Main Street, followed by the boom of base drums and oddly the chime of a xylophone. Twenty minutes later, the town's police cars with Gus in front, turned the corner on to Main Street, followed by the high school band.

Behind the band came a large sign carried by two Boy Scouts. The sign proclaimed Grand Marshal. Behind the sign were a dozen boy scouts carrying American flags. Behind them, Alvin Perry sat on the back of a late model white Cadillac Eldorado convertible. He wore his dress Marine uniform, which if anything, fit a little loosely.

Around his neck he wore the Congressional Medal of Honor.

All along the parade route, people stopped applauding and stood. Alvin had a trace of a smile. His back erect and shoulders back, he waved or nodded at friends who called out his name. Some in the crowd wearing service hats saluted. So too did some of the children. Alvin returned each with a crisp salute of his own.

Behind him, flanked by Boy Scouts and Girl Scouts carrying flags, walked VFW members. I recognized several from the local lodge, but it was obvious that VFW had gotten the word to veterans from the entire area. At the front riding in cars were veterans of WWI, now pushing eighty years old. Behind them came the WWII vets followed by a much smaller group that served in Korea. They marched, though not always in step. All wore service or VFW caps. A smattering had on full uniforms. Others wore their service jackets although few could actually button them.

At the back, in two loosely formed rows, walked a dozen or more younger men. Vietnam vets. Their hair was long, hanging to their shoulders or beyond. Several wore unkempt beards. They made no attempt to march. They wore jeans. Most wore olive tee shirts or battered fatigues. Their eyes did not carry the pride of the other marchers.

Theirs had been a different war. A different homecoming. But they were cheered with all the others.

The parade rolled by for nearly an hour. Antique cars, horse units, antique farm equipment, three more high school bands, make-shift floats, dance academies, scouts, civic and church groups, even a troupe of clowns.

By the end of the parade, I wondered if I had enough film on hand to get me through the rest of the day.

After the parade passed, pedestrians took over the street. An oldies band started playing on a vacant lot next to the hardware store. Across the street, people lined up at the hog roast put on by the Lions Club. Others made their way toward the nearby churches that were hosting ice cream socials.

I walked around, truly understanding, perhaps for the first time, how much of an outsider I was. I was a reporter covering a feel-good news event. But for these people, this was their community, their lives. The town was struggling. Businesses were on the verge of closing. A murder had shattered the sense of isolation and safety from violence in big cities. The railroad was leaving. But for one day, everything was forgotten.

After making the rounds of the church socials, I headed back to my office where I spent the rest of the afternoon developing film and reviewing contact sheets for candidates to print for the paper. It was early evening by the time I got all the film developed. I headed back to the high school for the evening balloon event and the fireworks.

The balloons lifted off for a second time an hour before sunset. A good portion of the town's population, as well as that from nearby communities, was at the high school football stadium waiting for fireworks. Half an hour before the fireworks started, the grandstands were full and people ringed the field on the quarter-mile cinder track. Emma sat with her daughter and parents sharing a large bag of popcorn. Shirley and her son found seats near the top of the grandstand.

The snow cone trailer was doing a brisk business. I patiently stood in line and ordered five. I took two to Emma and Molly, then walked up the stands to where Shirley was sitting. I held out the snow cones.

"Oh, no thank you," Shirley said, almost recoiling from the icy balls.

I smiled and kept holding them out. "I can only eat one before it melts. If you don't take them, they're going to waste. Doesn't the Good Book say 'waste not, want not?"

"That's not from the Bible," Shirley said.

"Okay, but still you don't want this to go to waste."

Shirley looked at her son whose eyes begged for the snow cone. Very deliberately she nodded. I handed one to each of them. As she took the first bite, the slightest smile crossed Shirley's face.

I took photos of the fireworks. Compared to the fireworks of my youth, the display was rather humdrum. With each explosion, the crowd erupted in "oooohs" and "ahhhhhs." One aerial bomb was knocked over and exploded at ground level, nearly covering the entire football field in a glorious red ball that for an instant seemed it would consume the entire crowd. After a momentary shock, the crowd erupted in cheers.

There was a grand finale of smoke, color and thundering booms. Then it was over.

The crowd made its way out of the football stadium, chattering about the day's events. I saw nothing but smiles. I caught a glimpse of Hank Pemberton and his entire family. Even with all the events hanging over them, they were walking arm in arm, huge smiles across their faces.

Bill and Claudia Olsen remained standing on the top row of the grandstand after everyone had filed out. Even from a distance, I could see his eyes glistening.

#

The next day, I scrambled to get the photos developed and printed, and the page layout completed. I was running nearly a full page of photos on both the front and back page, plus four inside pages of nothing but photos.

While I planned to put as many photos in the newspaper as possible, it still could hold only a fraction of the photos I took. I decided to print as many photos as I could and tape them to the newspaper's plate-glass windows facing Main Street. It took me most of the day, and nearly all the photographic paper in the newspaper's stock, but I ended up with seventy-four eight by ten black and white photos taped to the two windows fronting Main Street.

The one disappointment was the fireworks photos. The black and white images didn't seem to capture the excitement that capped off a day bigger than anyone in Stratton could remember.

Looking at a few of the photos spread across the darkroom table, an idea came to me from my college photography class. I sandwiched eight negatives together. When printed, the result was an array of aerial bombs far more spectacular than any single photo.

I cropped the photo and ran it across the full six columns of the front page. Was it journalism? Maybe not. But I thought the people of Stratton deserved something that looked like what they would remember, not what my camera recorded.

THIRTY-EIGHT – *Little Fish, Big Fish*

July 27, 1976, BENTONVILLE, ARK. (FINANCIAL WIRE SERVICES): Sam Walton, 58, has resumed the positions of chairman and C.E.O. of Walmart Stores Inc., a 138-store general retailer in the South.

Two years ago, Walton stepped down from day-to-day operation of the chain. He began the company in 1962 with a single store in Bentonville, Ark. Walton plans to expand the business beyond its current regional base.

It was the last week in July. I was walking to the office when I saw the large box truck parked outside Olsen's Christmas Shop. Two men in gray coverall uniforms were wheeling out stacks of boxes on dollies.

I crossed the street and walked into the Shop. I had not been inside since I did the story the previous fall. Apparently, few people had.

Bill Olsen was standing behind the counter, studying papers on the clipboard.

"Hey Bill, what's up?"

The answer was apparent from the empty shelves and brown boxes stamped "FRAGILE" and strewn across the floor.

Bill nodded a greeting. "Just give me a minute, Zach," he said, and returned to his paperwork

After a few minutes, the two movers excused their way past me and loaded more boxes on their dollies. Bill watched stoically. When all the boxes were loaded, Bill scratched his initials across the papers, then put the clipboard on the counter.

"Closing up," Bill said, a forced smile across his face.

"I'm sorry it didn't work out."

"Some things don't."

"Not enough business?"

Bill laughed. "That's one way of putting it. We had a good run last Christmas, but after that it dried up. Some months we only made three or four sales, none of them very big. We got a little business out of the Fourth of July, but that was it."

"Where's all the stuff going?"

Bill grinned. This time it did not seem forced. "Remember me talking about those year-around Christmas shops in Frankenmuth? One of those guys called me up and asked if I wanted to get rid of any extra summer inventory. I suspect he heard we weren't doing well and was calling to see if we were ready to throw in the towel. And I was."

"So, you were able to sell your inventory?"

"Every Christmas light, ornament and string of garland," Bill said. "Got a decent price, too. If he tried to gyp me on what stuff was worth, I would have kept the shop open for the tax write-off. But he made a fair offer. We will come out okay."

"That's some good news, I guess."

"We still got the pizza and chicken place, and that's going good. Going to miss that trip we were going to take to Germany this fall, though."

I wished Bill well and turned to leave. As I got to the door, Bill yelled after me. "Hey Zach, what do you think of a handmade toy store? Nobody's done that yet."

I smiled and kept walking

#

Tuesdays were always low-key days for me. But even if I took the day off, I usually stopped at the Perry Drug Store for my morning cup of coffee. If one wasn't too choosy, the coffee was drinkable, and I learned the latest news from the early-morning gossip among the patrons.

I sat at a Formica top table on one of the wobbly steel-legged chairs as I did nearly every morning. I could never figure whether it was the wooden floor or the table legs that were uneven.

Conversation about the Bicentennial celebration faded over the weeks since the event. Still, the topic came up. People seemed not able to believe the town had put the whole thing together.

Bill Olsen came in shortly after I arrived and took some gentle kidding about his Christmas Shop closing. Everyone knew Bill opened the shop largely as a tax write off for travel, so he wasn't losing his livelihood. That seemed to make it fair game without being cruel.

I was ready to leave when Howard Gudgel, owner of the IGA, walked in for his usual morning coffee and doughnuts. "Know what I heard last night after church?" he said, as he settled into one of the wobbly chairs. "I heard Home Value Drugs bought that lot out on the highway near Kopetsky's place. They're gonna put in a drug store out there. Start construction next week. Supposed to open by the end of the year."

The coffeeshop went quiet except for spoons rattling in coffee cups and the scrape of chairs shifting on the tile floor. Sam Bauserman broke the uncomfortable silence. "Jesus, Howard, have a little decency."

I turned to Bill Olsen, sitting at the next table from me. "What's this Home Value Drugs?"

Bill shook his head and stared down into his coffee. "It's the biggest drug store chain in the state. There's no way Alvin can compete with them."

"I'm just telling the truth," Howard said, indifferent to the looks he was receiving. "That's the biggest store coming to town in years. They got more stuff and sell it cheaper. I don't see how Alvin can fight that. They opened a store in Amelia last year and three months later the local drug store shut down."

A shuffling came from the back of the store. I turned and saw Alvin Perry in his pharmacist apron, standing with his arms crossed. His face was stone. He pivoted and disappeared into the back of the store.

"For God's sake, Howard," Sam said.

No one else said anything.

That afternoon I stopped back in the drug store for an cup of coffee. It was an excuse to talk with Alvin.

In more than a decade of newspaper work, Alvin was the only real hero I had written about. His kind of bravery was beyond uncommon. He returned from war to live an ordinary life. A quiet life. An unremarkable life. His medal could have been his ticket, opening doors at every turn. He would never have had to buy a drink or a meal. But that wasn't who he was.

With a cup of coffee in my hand, I found Alvin in his office. He was alone.

"You got a minute?"

There was a brief silence before Alvin said, "Take a seat."

I sat across from him at his simple desk. Behind him was a metal bookcase filled with product binders and boxes of sample prescription drugs. He closed the three-ring binder he was reviewing.

"No more stories about me," he said.

I gave him a small forced smile. "Not this time," I said. "But we sold out of that issue with your story on the front page."

"Don't you always do that?"

"Not even close. Only three issues we sold out of since I've been here are the one that had your story on the front page, the Bicentennial parade issue and . . ." I gave a little shrug. "That Pigstickers and Hillbillies issue. But I bought about half of those."

Alvin gave a small laugh. "I almost forgot about that one. Still see kids walk in here wearing that Stratton Pigstickers shirt Gus was selling."

"I wish I could forget about it."

"What can I do for you? You doing a story on that new Home Value Drug Store coming to town?"

I shook my head. "No. I mean if the store comes to town, I guess I'll have to do a story about it. But they haven't announced it yet."

Alvin stared up toward the ceiling. "They will," he said with a voice of certainty. "I knew it would happen. I hoped it would be another four or five years before they got around to Stratton, but guess not."

"You expected this?"

"Sure. Once they went in to Amelia, it was a matter of time."

"I don't understand them coming here. The town is so small, and you're so connected with people here. Hell, you're a goddamn war hero. People aren't going to like strangers coming in and trying to drive you out of business."

"You don't know much about retail, do you Zach? Not much about small towns, either. Home Value will be the shiny new penny. Everybody goes for the shiny new penny."

Alvin placed his arms on his desk and leaned forward. "If that was all, they might wander back after few months. But it's not. Their store will have four or five times as much merchandise as I can stock. And it will be cheaper. A lot cheaper."

"That's what happened in Amelia. I talked with Ralph Hagen. He owned the drug store in Amelia. He tried to keep the doors open, but he couldn't. Heck, they can sell stuff cheaper than I can buy it."

"Think they'll try to buy you out?"

"They don't have to. Their business plan for the past ten years or more is to go from small town to small town, opening new stores and driving local pharmacies out of business."

"Will they hire you? I mean, if you decide to close up this place?"

"Ralph tried that in Amelia. They wouldn't even take his application. They want young people just out of school. The pharmacist is a drug dispenser for them. Nothing more. The store manager runs the place. Seems back-asswards to me that the pharmacist at a drug store has to answer to some snotty-nosed clerk, but that's the way it is with them.

"Are you doing okay?"

"You mean am I going to put a gun in my mouth? No. I figure if I could get through Saipan, I can find some way to survive this. Not sure how, but I'll think of something. Always have, haven't I?"

THIRTY-NINE – *Nothing Changes*

July 27, 1976, CHICAGO, ILL (WIRE SERVICES): A toy designer walked into his place of employment and opened fire with a handgun today, killing 3 co-workers and injuring 2 others before taking his own life.

The killer was identified as Al Keller, 33. Police are at a loss for a motive.

I was sitting at my desk when Lee Phillips called. He still called with his updates on the investigation into Kate's death, but for the last year they had only come once every couple of months. When I heard his voice, I expected the message to be the same.

But it wasn't.

"We're pretty sure we know who killed Kate," he said.

I dropped the receiver from my hand. I took a few seconds to gain my composure enough to pick it up.

"Tell me," I said.

"You want the whole story?"

"Yes."

"Two weeks ago, this guy went in to Grand Avenue Pawn trying to hock a diamond ring. Harry Cohen owns the place. He's a pretty straight-shooter for a pawnshop operator. Harry noticed the engraving inside the ring and remembered a bulletin we circulated after the murder. Harry told the guy he might be able to give him a lot of money, but his diamond expert was at lunch. Harry convinced the guy to leave the ring and come back in a couple of hours. Once the guy left, Harry called the cops."

"Was it Kate's engagement ring?" I could feel the quiver in my voice.

"It had the engraving you put inside the ring."

"Did you arrest him?"

"Yes, but not for the murder. He's just a small-time thief with a drug habit to feed. But when we started talking a murder wrap, he was quick to explain where he got it. He bought the ring on the street for his own girlfriend. But when he went to give it to her, she was in the sack with some other dude, so he took it to the pawn shop to sell."

"He bought it from a street huckster named Eddie Duckworth. He's called Smooth on the streets. One of those guys that sells knockoff Rolexes, rings, sunglasses, that kind of shit. Most of it is fake, but he hit the jackpot with this one and didn't even know."

I made notes on a scrap piece of paper, trying to keep the timeline straight as Lee talked.

"We pulled Smooth in. When we started talking accomplice to murder, his memory improved. He got the ring from a street thug named Dequan Ellis. A real bad ass. Ellis told Smooth he gave the ring to one of his women. When Dequan dumped her, he took the ring back."

"A gentleman," I said.

"Vice worked street connections and found the woman. Hell hath no fury. She recognized the ring. She remembered that Dequan gave it to her around Labor Day a couple of years ago. That made it not long after Kate was killed.

"So, this Dequan, he's the guy?"

"Pretty sure. His history, the ring, and his blood type matched blood spots we found at the scene. I don't think there's any question."

I said nothing. After a long silence, Lee continued. "Zach, this guy was a really bad dude. Just evil. He served six years at Joliet for rape. He was suspected in a half dozen more. Vice suspected him of several drug-related murders. Street snitches were scared to death of him, so they never had enough to charge him with anything after he got out."

"Have you got enough to charge him?"

"We can't." Lee paused for several seconds. "He's dead. Killed about four months ago. Pulled a knife on some guy in a southside bar. Well, you've heard the old story about bringing a knife to a gunfight? When Ellis left the bar, this guy was waiting in an alley with a .45. Walked up behind him, put the gun in the back of his head and pulled the trigger. Ellis was dead before he hit the ground." Lee paused, then quietly added, "It's over, Zach."

I tried to speak, but the words wouldn't come. After several attempts, I managed to get them out. "Thanks for all your work, Lee. I do appreciate it. But nothing has changed. Kate is still dead. The rest doesn't matter."

FORTY – *If It Bleeds*

August 28, 1976, WASHINGTON, D.C. (WIRE SERVICES): The FBI reported today that violent crime in rural areas and small towns is rising far more rapidly than in urban areas and big cities.

Across the nation, a murder occurs every 26 minutes, a rape every 5 minutes and a burglary every 10 seconds.

Even in the early morning hours, the August heat was oppressive. As I rode along with Clint Avery in his police cruiser, he kept the windows down, running the air conditioner on low.

"I like the fresh air," he explained. "And I like enjoy the night sounds. You'd be surprised how many things I stumble on through the sounds as I drive around."

After my confrontation with Gus, I kept my night rides with Clint to a minimum. I didn't want Clint suffering fallout from associating with me. But after Kenny was caught naked in the patrol car, the tension between Gus and me eased enough so that I thought it safe to once again ride with Clint.

We completed a swing through an east side housing addition and headed back downtown.

"You still seeing Emma?" Clint asked.

The question took me by surprise. We seldom talked about our personal lives.

"We're not really seeing each other right now. We're friendly, but I'm not, well, I'm not sleeping over right now."

"Too bad. You're not going to find anybody better than her in this town."

"No, I don't think so either."

We swung on to Main Street. The clock in the liquor store window said 2:05. Clint turned on the car's spotlight and shined it down the alleys and in the storefront windows as we moved down Main Street at barely more than walking speed.

A radio call disrupted the quiet. "Stratton 2, this is Dispatch. Come in."

Clint picked up the mic and keyed it to transmit. "This is Stratton 2. Whatcha got, Connie?"

"Stratton 2, we got a call about some car prowling around the high school. Neighbor saw it. It's around on the backside of the school, driving without lights. Looks like someone may be snooping around there."

"I'll check it out."

Clint turned toward me. "It's probably nothing. You want to ride along, or you want me to drop you at your apartment?"

"I'll ride along," I said.

There was no sense of urgency in Clint's response. The streets were deserted, and the school was only five minutes away. Clint did not bother with his lights or siren. When we got to the school, Clint turned off all the lights on the patrol car. Again, he keyed the mic. "Stratton 2. On scene at the high school. I'm going to check around back."

"Roger, Stratton 2. Gus picked up the call at home. He's standing by if you need assistance."

Clint eased the car along the side of the school and around the corner. Across the parking lot near the loading dock for school deliveries, there was the outline of a car, the silhouette of a figure moving against the backdrop of a security light. There was a small red glow against the building.

Suddenly the glow erupted into a bright yellow and red fireball.

"Holy shit!" I yelled.

Clint hit his spotlight. As he swung it around, it flashed across someone jumping into the driver's side door of a car. The car took off, tires squealing and smoking, trying to find traction. Clint flipped on his lights and siren and hit the accelerator. He whipped the car through a 180-degree turn and took off in pursuit.

As he accelerated, Clint grabbed the mic. He was breathing hard, his voice urgent.

"Dispatch, Stratton 2. We got a fire at the school. I'm in pursuit."

"Say again?"

"Someone set a fire at the back of the school. Get the fire department rolling before the whole damn school burns down. I'm in pursuit. Assistance needed."

We turned onto the highway and headed for downtown. The patrol car slid in a wide arc that cost us speed. The car we pursued was two blocks ahead and pulling away.

"Stratton FD alerted and on the way," the dispatcher said, her voice flat.

"I'm in high speed pursuit, heading east on Highway 144. Need assistance."

"I'll get the message to Gus, if he's not listening in. We've got two county mounties in your area. I'll get them rolling in your direction. Keep me advised of pursuit."

The patrol car bucked as we crossed one set of railroad tracks. I looked at the speedometer. It was registering near 80 mph. Ahead of us, the lead car braked heavily and made a left turn into a residential street. Clint followed less than ten seconds later.

"Dispatch. Got a look at the car as he turned under some streetlights. Looks like a '68 or '69 Chevelle. Dark. Black or navy. Not close enough to read the license. He turned north on Garvey Street, still in Stratton."

"Roger that, Stratton 2. Gus will be rolling in two or three minutes. County units on their way."

Ahead of us, the Chevelle made a sharp left. Two blocks later, the car turned left again, its tires squealing as they struggled for traction.

"You know how to work this thing?" Clint said, indicating the mic on the police radio.

"I can handle it."

Clint tossed the mic to me, then got both hands back on the wheel. "Tell dispatch every turn we make and every landmark we pass. Keep them informed of our location and direction of travel."

The car ahead made a series of turns through the residential streets, trying to shake Clint. But Clint kept him in sight. I relayed each turn over the radio.

"County units are about six miles out, heading your way as fast as they can."

The car pulled back onto Highway 144, only this time heading west. The car in front finally turned on its lights. I watched the speedometer climb past 100 as we headed out of town and into the blackness of rural Lancaster County.

"Where's Gus?" Clint asked.

"Stratton 2 to dispatch. Can you advise on location of assistance, particularly the Town Marshall?"

There was a short delay before a response. "Gus just pulled out. He's a mile or two behind you. County deputies are closing on your location."

About three miles out of town, the brake lights glowed bright on the car in front, then disappeared to the right. A few seconds later, Clint followed, the rear end swerving dangerously close to a ditch before catching traction. I caught sight of the road sign as it flashed by.

"Dispatch. Now headed north on County Road 800 West. Still in pursuit. Fuck!" I let out the obscenity as the patrol car went airborne over a culvert and hit hard on the springs.

"Say again," the dispatch voice came across the radio. "I didn't get that."

"Nothing." I said, my breath and words now coming quick with surges of adrenaline. "Still heading north on 800 West. High rate of speed."

Clint shouted at me. "Tell them to move to cut him off."

"Dispatch. Have county move to intercept."

"Already heading that way," the dispatcher said, her voice still amazingly calm.

The big engine on the police cruiser strained. The Chevelle skated back and forth across the washboard surface of the county road, its taillights drawing closer.

"He's having a hard time controlling that Chevelle. It's not made for roads like this. We're gaining."

I saw the taillights in front of us go flying into the air and bounce, then bounce again.

"Hang on," Clint yelled.

The patrol car launched over a railroad crossing at more than 90 miles per hour. I grabbed the strap on my seatbelt and pulled it tighter.

Another mile down the road, the Chevelle braked hard and made a sharp right. Clint followed, smoothly guiding the car through a power drift. We were now only fifty yards behind.

I keyed the mic. "Now east bound on County Road 350 South. Closing on suspect car. Where are your deputies?"

"They're moving to intercept with you. Less than ten minutes away if you keep headed north."

In the dark, trees, fields and telephone poles flashed by. The speedometer now touched 110 mph. We were gaining visibly. Fifty yards. Forty. Thirty.

Light flashed from the driver's side followed by a pop. Then a second flash followed by the distinctive sound of gunshots cracking over the straining engine.

"Shit, he's shooting at us," I yelled.

"Call it in," Clint yelled back at me.

"Stratton Unit 2. Shots fired. Shots fired. Vehicle is firing at us. Shit."

The voice came back, not as calm as before. "Stratton 2, did you say shots fired?"

We hit a big bump, and I almost lost the mic from my hand. I regained my grip.

"Yes, dammit!" I was shouting. "The car we're chasing is shooting at us."

I saw Clint's right hand drop from the wheel and go to his side. Driving with only one hand, he unsnapped his holster and pulled out his service revolver.

Another flash came from the car and a harsh sound of a bullet hitting metal.

"Keep down," Clint yelled.

I crouched as best I could, keeping my eyes barely above the dash so I could continue calling in our location. I looked over at Clint. His jaw was set and his eyes fixed. He switched the gun to his left hand. With his right hand on the wheel, Clint held his gun out of the window with his left and fired three shots in rapid succession.

The noise inside the car sounded like canon fire.

Ahead of us, the car swerved from one side of the road to the other and back. Clint backed off his speed, creating a bit more distance. The Chevelle was still swerving. The right-side tires dropped off the road, throwing up a cloud of gravel and dirt. As the driver tried to pull back on the roadway, the tires caught the pavement edge. In an instant, the vehicle was totally out of control. The Chevelle came back onto the road and slid in a full loop, leaving the pavement rear end first.

The car came to an abrupt stop, its rear wheels at the bottom of a four-foot-deep ditch. The nose of the car was elevated, the front wheels barely in contact with the ground.

Clint hit the brakes hard. His tires squealed as the cruiser came to a stop.

The Chevelle's headlights shined up in the air like searchlights. The flashing emergency lights from the police cruiser danced across the Chevelle.

Clint breathing hard and sweating, grabbed the mic from me. His hand was shaking. "This is Clint. The pursuit is over. I returned fire. The car crashed into a ditch here on . . ." Clint turned to me. "Where are we?"

I gave Clint the location, which he repeated to the dispatcher.

"Backup is almost there," came the reply over the radio. "Hang tight until assistance gets there. Do you need an ambulance?"

"I don't know," Clint said. "We're okay, but I haven't seen anyone move in the car. You better get one rolling, just in case. And send extra backup. Anyone you can get here."

Clint hung up the mic. He directed the patrol car's spotlight toward the wrecked car. With a trembling hand, he reached for the door handle. Clint stepped out of the car, his weapon drawn. He stayed behind the open car door and pointed the weapon, using the top of the car door to brace his aim.

The only sound was that of insects and a gentle breeze flowing through the adjacent corn field, and the whir of the rotating emergency light. The air smelled of a distant mint field. Above us, a canopy of stars stretched out from horizon to horizon accented with the sliver of a rising new moon. Loose gravel crunched under Clint's boots as he shifted his weight.

In the distance, the faint wail of a siren, then two, cut through the night silence.

"Throw your weapon out on the ground," Clint yelled, his voice booming through the silence. "Show your hands and step out of the car. Slow. No sudden movements."

There was no response. Clint repeated his demand, his voice even louder.

The sirens drew closer. I stepped out of the car and looked back in the direction we had come. I saw red lights approaching in the distance

"Hey Clint, here comes your back up. Maybe you should wait. They'll be here in a minute."

Clint glanced my way for an instant, his look sterner than I had ever seen it. As he turned back, I noticed that even braced, his gun was shaking.

I howl rose from the wrecked car. I wasn't sure it was even human. It was guttural, like the wail of an injured animal. It stopped for several seconds, then resumed, louder and more painful.

Clint looked toward me. Still holding his gun in front of him, he moved around his open door and slowly edged toward the wrecked Chevelle.

"Clint. Wait." But he was already halfway to the car.

Behind me a car slid to a stop, followed by a second. I turned to see Gus and a county sheriff's deputy exiting their cars, guns drawn. Behind them, a third police car was racing in our direction.

I reached inside Clint's car and grabbed my camera. I checked the shutter and exposure, then hit the button to charge the attached flash. Holding the camera in position for a quick shot, I edged toward where Clint approached the wrecked car.

Another wail came from the car. Now louder, it was clearly human. It was a cry of unspeakable pain.

Clint positioned himself at the edge of the ditch, then eased himself down the banking, leaning low against the side of the car. He stopped short of the driver's side door. I saw Clint's hand reach out for the door handle. He pulled sharply. The door creaked metal on metal, but didn't open. Clint, holding is gun out, jerked on the door handle again. This time the door swung open

"Get out," Clint shouted. "Keep your hands where I can see them and back out of the car."

Gus and the deputy rushed passed me. With guns drawn, they took up positions on either side of Clint.

Again, the cries came from inside the car. Clint leaned in closer. I could not see anyone move inside the car.

"Careful," Gus said.

The cries from inside the car were now continuous.

Clint yelled his order again. There was no response except the continual wailing of someone in pain.

Clint moved suddenly, sweeping around the edge of the door and reaching in with his left hand while keeping his gun hand held back. I saw him pull on something. A pair of jean-covered legs slid part way out of the car. Clint jerked again. He had someone by the belt. It was a big man, long and muscular. As his body emerged, it was clear that he was the one crying.

With one final heave, Clint pulled the man out. I expected him to fall, but he didn't. He landed on his feet, towering above the three officers with their guns drawn.

"Well I'll be damned," Gus said. "Davey Kyle."

The towering teenager stood hunched, sobs coming with each breath. In the stark light given off by the police cars, I could see blood. When he turned in my direction, I saw that his entire shirt was covered in blood. Blood also covered his arms and hands.

“Oh my God,” I said quietly to myself

Gus came up hard from behind, grabbed Davey's arms and roughly slapped them into handcuffs.

"Get an ambulance," Davey said, between his sobs. There was desperation in his voice. "Get a fucking ambulance. Hurry."

"Suck it up, you piss weed," Gus said.

Clint used his flashlight and examined the blood that covered Davey's shirt, arms and hands. "We got an ambulance on the way," Clint said. “Where are you hurt? You need to sit down?"

"Get a fucking ambulance," Davey repeated.

"It's coming," Clint said. "But where are you hurt?”

"It's not me!" Davey screamed. "It's Ritchie! You dumb son of a bitch. It's Ritchie."

I threw down my camera and ran past Clint and Gus. They swung out their arms to stop me, but I pushed past them. I grabbed the door and leaned in.

Slumped on the passenger's side seat, blood pouring from a gunshot to his head, was Ritchie Kyle. The windshield had a golf ball sized hole surrounded by blood spatter and brain tissue. In the rear window there was a small hole in the middle of a spider web of cracked glass.

In death, Ritchie’s body looked even smaller than in life.

For several seconds I was frozen. A hand on my shoulder tugged at me, but I couldn't move.

I knew I was screaming as someone pulled me away from the car. Incoherent thoughts swirled and nausea overcame me. I lunged to the side of the road, fell on my knees and threw up.

For endless minutes, I stayed on my knees hovering over my own vomit. I eventually became aware of Arnold Donaldson, the funeral director who also drove the ambulance. He was standing over me, his hand on my shoulder, calling my name. Slowly he helped me to my feet. "Come with me, Zach," he said. "You'll be fine."

I had no idea when the ambulance arrived. There were several more police cars at the scene now, including several from the state police. Davey Kyle was still there, handcuffed and sitting in the back of a state police cruiser. His sobbing was audible through the closed doors.

Clint was sitting in another state police cruiser. He was in the front passenger seat, staring aimlessly into the blackness. With Arnold still helping me, I walked to where he was seated.

"How you doing?" I asked.

Clint looked up blankly at me. "He was only twelve."

That was all he said.

#

"If it bleeds, it leads."

I knew the age-old newspaper mantra as well as my own name. It survived through generations of news rooms because it was true. Blood before scandal, before money, even before sex.

Stories of violence wrote themselves. Who was killed? Who did the killing? Where did it happen? When? How was it done? If you didn't know why, more often than not you made it up from the circumstances.

I had written the story a thousand times. Probably more. It wasn't Pulitzer Prize stuff. But it was the stuff of headlines. It sold papers. It paid the bills.

As I sat at my desk the following Monday, I could only stare out my window. I couldn't bring myself to start typing the story that I knew I had to write.

In front of me were my notes. I talked to the prosecutor earlier that morning. Davey Kyle was being held on arson and attempted murder for the shots he took at Clint. There was a gun on the floor of Davey's car. It had been recently fired and the only prints on it belonged to Davey Kyle. Police were searching the roadside, trying to find the bullets fired at Clint for ballistics testing.

The prosecutor was also going to charge Davey with the death of his brother, but the arson and attempted murder charges would keep him in jail until the other charges were worked out.

As I sat looking at the blank sheet of paper, Shirley appeared at my door with a cup of coffee from the drug store coffee shop. She had never before brought me coffee. "Thought you might need this," she said.

"Thank you." I took a drink, feeling the burn of the coffee all the way to my stomach. It was nearly eleven. I took one more sip of coffee. Willing my fingers to move, I began writing the opening paragraphs destined for the front page.

A high-speed police chase following an act of arson at Stratton High School ended in the police action shooting death of 12-year-old Richard Kyle, Stratton, early Sunday morning.

David Kyle, the victim's 18-year-old brother, is in jail charged with arson and attempted murder of Stratton police officer Clint Avery. Lancaster County Prosecutor Michael Alexander stated that the older Kyle is likely to face further charges when the investigation is complete.

David Kyle set fire at the high school, according to police. Officer Avery pursued Kyle on a chase that reached speeds in excess of 100 mph. Kyle fired several shots at Officer Avery, who returned fire in self-defense.

The younger Kyle was a passenger in his brother's car and was fatally struck by a bullet during the chase.

I worked through lunch, and finished the story by early afternoon.

"If it bleeds," I said out loud, as I slotted the story for page one with a banner headline.

Through the thin walls of my office, I heard the door open and someone walk in. I recognized the voice as Arnold Donaldson from the town's funeral home. I walked to the reception area. Arnold held a single typed page and a school photo in his hand. Without looking, I knew it was Ritchie Kyle's obituary.

"This is late for this week," Arnold said. "I hoped you could squeeze it in somehow. They're taking the boy back to Kentucky to bury. It seems like there should be something in the paper about him."

"I'll make sure it gets in," I said.

I rewrote the obituary Arnold had prepared. Instead of focusing on the vital statistics of date of birth, date of death, survivors left to mourn, I wrote about what I saw in Ritchie. How he was a boy of strength and courage. It would run on page one next to Ritchie's smiling seventh-grade school photo.

By four o'clock, everything for the week's paper was done. There was no town board meeting that evening, and even if there had been, I wouldn't have gone.

On the way out, I stopped by Shirley's desk. I took out my wallet and removed a five-dollar bill and slapped it on to her desk.

"That's for the swear jar," I said. "I'm going to get shit-faced drunk tonight."

Shirley looked at me with sad eyes. Quite unexpectedly she reached out and patted my hand that still covered the bill.

"Take care of yourself Zach," she said softly.

I nodded, and then walked out, headed for the VFW.

I woke late Tuesday morning. I wasn't sure of the time, but I saw the sun streaming through the apartment windows. My ears were ringing and my head throbbed with a hangover. My stomach was raw, and I suspected that I had vomited more than a few times during the night. I didn't remember though. In truth I didn't remember much at all from the prior evening except for drinking oceans of Wild Turkey chased with Old Style longnecks. I had no idea how I got home, or how I made my way up the stairs.

I got up still wearing my clothes from the day before. They smelled of beer and puke, but as bad as my mouth tasted, I could tell that I hadn't been smoking. Even drunk, I had kept my promise.

I forced myself to make a pot of coffee and ate two slices of dried toast and peanut butter with the coffee. I sat at the kitchen table staring off at nothing. The sun was streaming through the kitchen window, and I finally glanced at the kitchen clock. It was after eleven.

I got up with the intent of taking a shower, but I turned back to my bedroom. I stripped off all my clothes and climbed back into bed and pulled the covers over me.

I hoped that sleep would come. But it didn't. Images spun through my head no matter how hard I tried to drive them out. The fire. The chase. The gunshots. Tossing a football with Ritchie. Walking with him while he talked of his brother. The crooked-tooth grin. The wild sandy hair. The blood. His lifeless body. Then I saw Kate. The garage. The blood. Her body twisted and gray.

The tears started, rolling slowly down my cheeks. I could not shut off the horrifying thoughts and images that looped continuously through my brain. I broke into sobs that soon shook my entire body. I didn't try to stop. I buried my face in my pillow to absorb the wails that came from some place deep inside me.

I cried until my pillow was soaked. Until I didn't think I could cry any more. But I did.

Sometime that afternoon the phone rang. I rolled away from it, hoping that whoever was calling would just hang up.

But they didn't.

Finally, I slipped out of bed and grabbed the receiver. It was Shirley.

"I'm just checking. I hadn't heard from you."

"I'm okay," I said instinctively.

"Emma is worried about you, too. She called. I guess they called her from the VFW last night, and she came and got you. Took you home."

I nodded my thanks as if Shirley could see me over the phone. "I won't be in today," I said.

"You sure you're okay?"

"I will be," I said. "Thanks for calling. And thank Emma, too. I do appreciate it."

I hung up. I stood there next to the phone for several minutes, still naked. My thoughts cascaded over me like a torrent over a spillway. But this time I didn't go back to bed.

I walked into the bathroom, avoiding the mirror as I passed it. I turned the shower on full hot and stepped in. The burn of the water slowly seemed to wash away something inside me. I stayed there until the water ran cold.

#

The next morning, I skipped the coffee shop. I didn't want to face the avalanche of questions from the coffee shop regulars about what had happened Saturday night. They could read it in the paper.

The phone rang not long after I walked in. Shirley was in the restroom, so I picked up the call. Virgil Amundsen, the detective in charge of the Rene Swisher investigation, was on the other end.

"How you doing," he said. "That was a pretty rough deal with that Kyle kid."

"Yeah," I said, not really wanting to hear anything that reminded me of Ritchie.

"I read your obituary on the boy. You did a real nice job with that. He sounded like a good kid."

"He was."

"Well, his brother isn't," Virgil said. "That's why I'm calling. You gave us a head's up on Davey Kyle and Rene Swisher. We got Davey Kyle's gun that he had in the car and ran a ballistics check. Seems that was the same gun used to kill Rene Swisher. It's a match."

My brain wasn't processing the information.

"I'm sorry. A match for what?"

"A match for Rene Swisher's killing. Davey Kyle is going to be charged with her murder sometime today. Thought I'd let you know."

"Thanks," I said, and hung up.

#

A few days after the newspaper came out, I saw Clint Avery buying some groceries at the IGA. He wasn't in uniform.

"How are you doing, Clint?" I said. Clint looked up from trying to pick out a few unbruised tomatoes from a bin. He broke into a small shy smile.

"I'm fine. How about you? You were pretty friendly with that younger Kyle kid."

"I'm managing," I said. "Has to be pretty tough for you, even if you didn't have a choice."

Clint nodded. "Gus has me on administrative duty for a while," Clint said. "Basically, that means until some shrink hired by the State

FOP clears me, I'm off the streets. I'm helping the county as a dispatcher. But that's okay. I can use the break."

"Is that regular procedure?"

"The town doesn't have any regular procedure on officer shootings. As far as anyone knows, this is the first one. But Gus and the town board talked, and they decided to follow what the state police and the FOP suggested."

"If you need a friend to talk with, you can always call me."

"Thanks, but I'll be okay. I'm taking a couple of weeks off. Gonna go back home and get some fishing in. Get my mind off things. But I'll be fine." Clint and I shook hands. I started walking back to my office, not convinced that Clint was as fine as he said.

I spent most of the following week by myself. I avoided the coffee shop and Shelby's Place. I was only in the office long enough to do what was required. By Sunday night, I had made my decision. I called Roy Shoemaker at home.

"Hey Zach," Roy said, not showing any irritation at having his Sunday evening disturbed. "Congrats on the shooting story. AP picked it up and went national. Great reporting. Our little chain doesn't often break an eyewitness account of a police shooting."

I was quiet for several long seconds.

"Roy, I promised you two years in Stratton, but I'm going to break that promise. I'll give you a couple of weeks to find someone to replace me. A month if you absolutely need that much time. But that's it. I'm quitting."

The other end of the line was quiet. Finally, Roy responded. "You want to take some time to think about this? You've done a helluva job. I'd like you to stay."

"I don't need more time. And I'm not going to change my mind."

"Church socials and 4-H meetings get to you?" Roy said. "This shooting story get you back in the mood for real news?"

"No," I said, sharply. "I'm not going back to the crime beat. I'd rather sell papers at a newsstand."

Again, there was a long silence on the phone. "You've done an outstanding job," he said.

"I came down here to get away from things. By now, I'm sure you know about Kate."

"Your fiancé'? I had lunch with your old editor last week. He told me about it. Said police finally broke the case. "

"I wanted to bury myself away from everything. That's why I took the job here. And for a while I did. But life has a funny way of catching up to you. It's time to get back to my own life."

There was another silence.

"I got a kid over at our Kenner paper. I think he's ready to move up. I'll talk to him tomorrow."

"Thanks," I said, and hung up.

The next afternoon I got news that Roy's young protégé accepted the position as editor of the Stratton Gazette. He would be in town by the weekend. Roy asked if I could stay for a week to introduce him around. I agreed.

FORTY-ONE – *The Last Train*

September 17, 1976, PALMDALE, CAL. (WIRE SERVICES): Described as part airplane, part spacecraft and part boxcar, the United States newest space vehicle rolled onto public view today.

Named Enterprise after the fictional Star Trek spaceship, it is the first in a planned fleet of reusable space shuttles intended to ferry astronauts and equipment into space. Test flights begin next summer.

The last train to pass through Stratton was scheduled for 2:30 the following Thursday afternoon. Stratton's history was disappearing before the town's eyes. I wanted to be there with my camera to record it.

About half an hour before the train was scheduled, I walked from my office to a spot where the Erie tracks passed by the old water tower. It was about a hundred yards down from Walter Bradford's house where I still had my upstairs apartment, not far from where the derailment happened.

In my pocket was a hand-written notice I was vacating my apartment. I planned to slip it under Walter's door on my way back to the office.

I loaded a new roll of film and sat in the grass, letting the late August sun soak through me. I was about fifty feet from the tracks. I had another fifteen minutes, provided the train was on time.

I was surprised no one else was waiting for the last train. So, I lay back, feeling the late summer sun and a gentle breeze. I let my eyes close, knowing that the rumble and whistle of the approaching train would wake me.

A few minutes later I felt a tap on my shoulder. I turned to see Emma standing over me. She was wearing a blue sundress, a broad-rimmed white hat and over-sized sunglasses.

"Waiting for a train?" she said, with a big smile.

I nodded.

"Can I join you?"

"Sure," I said, patting the grass next to me.

She sat down. "Just wanted to see how you're doing," she said.

"I'm leaving."

"I know. Sam Bauserman told me at lunch a few days ago. Did you find what you were looking for?"

"Don't know," I said with a shrug. "Guess I'll find out."

"We really could have been something, Zach Carlson. We surely could have been."

"When I get settled in Chicago, maybe you can come up and see me. Bring Molly."

Emma gave a knowing smile. "Now we both know that's not going to happen. You got your world back there. That's what you're going to. And I'm not part of that world. We both know that." Emma closed her eyes for a second as if she was seeing something in her thoughts. "I think my grandma was probably right. I'm done chasing unicorn shadows. I think I'll just stick to the real world from here on out."

"That would be a shame," I said.

In the distance there was a whistle. The rails began to sing with the vibrations of the train approaching from around the bend to the north.

"Well, if you ever make it back to Stratton, make sure to look me up." She leaned over, kissed me on the mouth, then stood.

"Aren't you staying to see the train," I asked.

She gave me a wink. "I've seen trains before."

And she walked away, not looking back.

The train whistle sounded again, much closer. Four diesel locomotives appeared from around the bend, hauling a string of boxcars, car carriers and tanker cars.

I began snapping, trying to catch the train passing in front of the old water tower with STRATTON stenciled on it in faded paint. I snapped a dozen shots, then lowered my camera and just watched. The train rumbled by. I was going to count cars just for the record, but I lost interest after twenty.

As I followed the last cars of the train as they passed me, I saw a solitary lanky figure standing near the tracks maybe fifty yards away. It was Walter Bradford. He gave a short wave to the caboose. A hand extended from the window, waving in reply.

Then the train was gone.

Walter turned and kept watch until the train disappeared into the horizon. Shoulders slumped, Walter turned and walked toward home.

FORTY-TWO – *Starting Over*

September 23, 1976, CHICAGO, ILL. (WIRE SERVICES): Powerful six-term Chicago Mayor Richard Daley in sworn deposition testimony denied "to the best my recollection" ordering Chicago police to spy on his political opponents.

Mayor Daley also denied any knowledge of the "Red Squad" unit within the Chicago Police Department responsible for monitoring "subversive activities" in Chicago.

I introduced Tim Barker around town as the new editor. I gave him tips on dealing with Gus, the town board, and the benefits and hazards of the coffee shop rumor mill. As a going away present, I gave Shirley a clock radio to replace the one she complained about at home. It was impersonal and not expensive enough to make her feel embarrassed or uncomfortable.

Then I sat down and wrote my last column.

I sat looking at the blank paper sitting in my typewriter for a long time. I wanted to make sense of all I had experienced in my year in Stratton — the chess club, losing the trains, teen pregnancy, the Bicentennial celebration, and what happened in the early hours two weeks ago that took the life of Ritchie Kyle. I wanted to write something significant about the people: Gus, Clint, Alvin, Shirley, Walter, the Middletons, and most of all, Emma.

And I wanted to leave my mark.

After more than an hour without a single word written, I realized the hubris of my task. This was home to all those people. I had stopped in for a year. I was an outsider, an observer, an interloper. Ten years, twenty years from now, most of them would still live here. It is where they would celebrate holidays, anniversaries and weddings. It is where their babies and grandchildren would be born, and where most of them would die. It was where their lives happened.

A year from now, maybe months from now, everyone in town would forget me. They would remember a story or a photo, but that was all. They wouldn't remember me. Except Emma.

I was a scrivener who recorded their comings and goings for a year. Nothing more.

I picked up Tim Barker's resume and used it to compose a six-paragraph column introducing him to the town. He was the scrivener now. I didn't even type a farewell sentence.

That night, I gave Kate's parents a long overdue phone call. We talked for over an hour. I told them about Stratton and Jim told me about the near record walleye he caught this past summer. We laughed with memories of Kate. And cried too.

After I hung up, I called my mother in Florida. I told her I was going back to Chicago.

“You were a damn fool going to a small town like that,” she said. "About time you came to your senses."

I didn't explain. I just told her I wasn't sure about my job situation, but I would try to get down to Florida to see her over Christmas.

Then I called my old photographer Hurley Meyers. I asked if he still had a couch where I could crash for a week or two until I got on my feet.

“Sure,” he said. “Glad you're coming back. ‘It's about time. Newsroom ain't the same without you. You going to call up Charlie? He'd love to have you back."

"I don't know," I said. "Only thing I'm sure about is that I won't work the crime beat any more. I'll sell shoes before I do that."

"What do you want to do?"

I considered the question for a moment. "I want to write about the people left behind. All those murders I covered, I never once went back to see how the people left behind were doing. There are a lot of stories that I didn't cover. A lot of stories that need to be told."

"Could work," Hurley said.

"That's the real story we're missing," I said. "These people that have lost husbands, wives, fathers, mothers, sons, daughters. But they go on. They have this gaping hole in their heart, in their soul, that never totally heals. But one step at a time, one day at a time, they keep on going."

"Sounds like you found a passion for something. That always helps," Hurley said. "Talk to Charlie."

#

I didn't bother packing anything except my clothes, stereo and television, all of which fit into the backseat and trunk of my Impala. The volunteers at the Methodist Church Thrift Store came with a pickup truck and loaded everything else I owned from my apartment.

I saw Walter peeking around the curtains as the volunteers loaded everything. He didn't step outside or say anything. After the Methodist volunteers left, I knocked on his door. I wanted to say something, although I was unsure what. I didn't need to worry. Walter didn't answer the door.

Shortly after eleven, I pulled out. Passing the Gazette office, I saw Shirley hunched over her typewriter, no doubt typing up the weekly gossip columns for the new editor. I tapped my horn, but she didn't look up. At the end of Main Street, I took a right. I pointed my car toward Chicago, and Stratton faded from the rearview mirror.

ABOUT THE AUTHOR

Stephen Terrell is an attorney and writer. He is the author of two 5-star reader rated legal thrillers, STARS FALL and THE FIRST RULE. Stephen's short story "Visiting Hours" received the Manny Award for Short Fiction at the Midwest Writers Workshop. His short stories appear in Speed City Sisters in Crime anthologies THE FINE ART OF MURDER and HOMICIDE FOR THE HOLIDAYS, and will soon appear in MURDER 2020. In his professional capacity, he is an experienced speaker and author of numerous articles on a wide variety of legal subjects.

In his personal life, he enjoys cooking, photography and is an avid motorcyclist.

Contact the author at:

Email: hoosierlawyer@gmail.com

Twitter: @Stephen Terrell

Made in the USA
Coppell, TX
27 July 2021

59557768R00173